PASIPHAE

Also by William Smethurst

Bukhara Express
Sinai

With Julian Spilsbury

Night of the Bear

PASIPHAE

William Smethurst

HEADLINE
FEATURE

First published in 1997 by
HEADLINE BOOK PUBLISHING

A HEADLINE FEATURE hardback

10 9 8 7 6 5 4 3 2 1

British Library Cataloguing in Publication Data

Smethurst, William
Pasiphae
I. Title
823.9'14[F]

ISBN 0 7472 1316 X

Typeset by Avon Dataset Ltd, Bidford-on-Avon, Warks

Printed and bound in Great Britain by
Mackays of Chatham PLC, Chatham, Kent

HEADLINE BOOK PUBLISHING
A division of Hodder Headline PLC
338 Euston Road
London NW1 3BH

For Carolynne, again

1

The Satellite Ring

Pasiphae's last rocket fell away. She was floating free, now; high above the Atlantic, parting the currents of microscopic debris, turning gently in the plasma tides. Above her was the ionosphere, and beyond that was space. Her orbit of the Earth was geo-synchronous, so that she remained stationary in relation to the land masses beneath. Around her were the commercial satellites of Intelsat and Inmarsat, and the military surveillance satellites of a dozen nations. She took her place among them: in among a secret, Anglo-US three-craft Magnum constellation. She was *Pasiphae*, the smallest, and the most advanced, and the most secret of them all.

Conventional signals locked her into position. Slowly her long whisper antennae floated out behind her, a trawling net of gossamer-white metal of almost incalculable cost.

She was on station.

In Utah, a touch pad was gently pressed.

She was enabled, her quantum transceivers armed.

There was a flicker: an unseen, ghostly spasm, a stirring of charged electrons.

Suddenly she was listening to the world.

It was a year when the world's weather system was awry. In Bangladesh there was drought, famine, and a cholera epidemic. In Florida, floods swept crocodiles and moccasin snakes out of the swamps and into the suburban streets of Leisure City. From Australia there were reports of kangaroos trying to hop through the floods and toppling over, their tiny, pouched 'roos drowning it was feared. From sweltering, humid England, there were stories of zoo staff making fish ice lollies for their penguins and polar bears to suck.

Days and nights passed. The pictures flowed upwards into the thin cold atmosphere, into the transceivers, where they were processed and beamed down again. The rescue boats in Miami with their police marksmen and their snakebite serum. The kangaroos trying to water-ski without skis. The jolly penguins of East Sussex with their blood and mackerel ice lollies. In Bangladesh the cholera victims just sat quietly, for the most part, and died, and did not earn themselves much in the way of picture coverage.

The Earth was – as they so often said – a global village. A schoolboy in a remote Andalusian village could view satellite weather maps of the US Eastern Seaboard an hour after they had been taken. It was as easy for him as downloading photographs of topless models from a Minneapolis lingerie catalogue.

An evening in late July. England, then Ireland, had fallen into darkness. *Pasiphae* remained in sunshine for another four hours, then the Sun's orb met the rim of the Earth and was, in an instant, swallowed by it. Information flowed upwards. To *Pasiphae* it came in a form no other satellite would have recognised: quantum signals, tiny, sub-microscopic fishes gently scooped up in her whisper antennae. They could not be detected (it was confidently believed) by any other receiving equipment in the world.

There was heavy traffic tonight. From the US embassy in war-torn Liberia, from an agent monitoring the decommissioning of the Russian nuclear fleet at Murmansk, from Foreign Department negotiators in Tel Aviv. There were routine signals from the Red Sea flotilla, and, towards dawn, from a lone nuclear sub south of St Helena.

Something was wrong.

Tiny pulses came alive in *Pasiphae*'s memory circuits. Telemetry encoders began to flicker – lifesaver programs started running, measuring voltages and currents, checking temperatures, verifying the parameters.

No faults. No faults.

The status messages went back along the downlink, via the HAARP ionospheric heater over Alaska, to the receiving station in Utah.

Stillness.

Then the flow of data resumed.

2

But something had been wrong.

In the Pentagon, Washington DC, at 0100 hours, an operative was processing a signal from the CIA agent at Poljarnyi on the Kola Peninsula. The *Petersburg* had left Murmansk, headed out into the Barents Sea on its regular six-week patrol. As usual it had gone out on the surface, black water rushing from its great, ugly fin, with its turret – as high as a two-storey house – sending huge white walls of spray into the sun. It had been followed, all down the Kola River, by a flock of seagulls. The Russians could not have publicised its departure more blatantly, the Pentagon operative reflected, if they had escorted it from harbour with a band from 101 Rocket Regiment playing 'Oh Fatherland, My Fatherland'.

'Have you ever thought,' the operative mused, his eyes on his screen, 'that the only reason they keep up the patrols is because we are watching them? That they daren't stop because if they did, well, we'd know they couldn't even provision and fuel up one single goddamn long-range nuclear sub?'

The operative next to him grunted.

'That if we weren't watching they'd just not bother – they'd simply stay in Murmansk drinking vodka and frying gently on leaked radiation. I mean, we don't have to *know* there's a Russian sub with nuclear missiles on the floor off Long Island. We just have to be unsure.' He paused. 'But with spy satellites,' he went on, a dog with a bone, 'there's no way we're unsure.'

He was a thinker, a philosopher. He was a night-school student of quantum mechanics.

'By observing it happen, we're making it happen,' he said. 'What does that remind you of?'

The man next to him was silent, staring at his screen.

'Well,' said the philosopher, 'it reminds *me* of Schrödinger's Cat.'

He waited to be asked about Schrödinger's Cat.

The man next to him sighed. 'I thought for a minute there was some sort of a glitch on a signal I've just processed through *Pasiphae*.'

'Want me to look?'

'Yeah, OK.'

But neither operative could find anything irregular.

'What kind of glitch?'

'For a couple of milliseconds,' said the second operative, 'it seemed to be saying its security had been compromised.'

There was a pause.

'But I guess I was wrong.'

'Thank God, my friend, that you were wrong,' said the philosopher, awed at the prospect of a security breach in *Pasiphae*, forgetting all about Schrödinger's Cat.

Again, high over the Atlantic, a tiny spasm rippled along *Pasiphae*'s whisper antennae.

But if there were boarders prowling these saltless seas they no longer excited the security alarms. If there were pirates climbing aboard, they did so noiselessly. Unseen and undetected.

2

London, January 15, AD 1400

There was snow in Cheapside, swirling down over the housetops, settling on the half-frozen mud. It would be pitch dark an hour before vespers; they would be lucky to reach St Pancras the Wells that night, and then only if the girl was ready, and if he wasn't detained too long by Yevele, and if the snow didn't come thicker. '*Jesu miserere*,' he said loudly, and his page, bobbing along behind him, said, 'Aye, sir, indeed,' airing his Latin. *Jesus pity me*. It was what the old king had said (or so they claimed) as Alice ripped off his rings and left him to die, though Toke doubted if he had been able to say anything, not after his stroke; as usual it was the priest talking.

They were at the Jerusalem, under St Paul's. He glanced up at the spire with its great cross embedded with a stone from Christ's sepulchre, stuffed with the old, cold bones of the saints. He ordered Hanchache, his servant, to stay outside. Then he pushed his way into the common room of the inn, full at this time of the day of rabbit-catchers and their wives, second-hand-furniture traders forever selling bits and pieces to each other. He shook black-specked rain from his fur cape. His boy-servant, Flesshe, called boldly for Rhenish wine but he had no time to wait for wine. The girl was in an upstairs room, said Cissy the tavern maid, eyeing up Flesshe, who put his arm round her, pinched her bosom, and gave her a small piece of cheese that he must have been hoarding against such an encounter. Toke clattered up the stairs and opened the door at the top. There was one window, tiny, half shuttered to keep out the drifting sleet and snow. The girl was sitting on a stool in the near darkness. She was hugging a small hairy child to her bosom. 'Worts,' she said, her voice trembling with indignation and a sort of desperate courage. 'Worts a day old!'

It was what the peasants had cried, back in Jack Straw's day. It had been written down by Langland, that mournful, passionate

5

man. It had become a joke at the court of King Richard. Toke called for a lantern. There were times when he had been glad to eat worts a day old, cold and caked and gnawed by mice, and there would be times ahead, he thought grimly, when he would be glad of them again.

'You know who I am?'

She nodded.

'You have been told that I am to take you from London?'

Again she nodded, shivering despite the thick woollen cloak round her shoulders. It was a man's cloak, much too big for her, its hem thick with mud. They must have been in a great hurry, he thought, the people who left her here.

There was a smell of urine. The mayor of London had ordered a two-shilling fine for pissing out of the windows, and now travellers pissed against the wall.

The boy, Flesshe, came behind him with a lantern. The child in the girl's arms was more wizened and hairy than he had thought: it was a deeply evil-looking child that shot him a baleful look. The page let out a cry of marvel. It was a monkey.

Toke said: 'What belongings do you have?'

She looked at him with mock humour, rolling her eyes. He saw that she had shaved her hair at the front to give her forehead a high, fashionable look, and had dyed the rest of her hair with saffron, again after the fashion. She had attempted, with only partial success, to pluck her eyebrows.

The room was empty but for a stool and a straw pallet. Then he saw, in the corner, a leather travelling bag on the floor, and by it a high-pointed headdress, a court headdress. In the light of the lantern there was a glint of gold tissue, a flash of cut stone.

He took the lantern and looked inside the bag. The girl said, 'Is it much past tierce?'

'Tierce?' said the boy. 'Why, it's almost noon,'

'Ah me,' said the girl, strangely.

A woollen kirtle. A gown, sanguine, a surcoat of blue stuff trimmed with fur, both thin material, unsuitable for travelling. A number of handkerchiefs. Yes, she was a child of the court, she had sat at King Richard's knee in his bad, mad days; played at knights, dragons and damsels with his child-bride Isabelle. Amazingly – two books. He held

6

one to the lantern. It was *The Knight of La Tour Landry*.

He swore softly. How many holy clerks, how many monks in rows, scribbling with red, chapped hands from tierce to vespers through the short winter days, had toiled to copy by the dozen, by the score, this salacious French nonsense? The second book was *The Householder of Paris*. Advice to a wife of fifteen on entering the marital state. Lessons on submitting her will to her husband's will, her body to his just chastisement. Lascivious, sensual – the talk of London town, its scandalous nature only thinly disguised by chapters of advice on how to get rid of grease spots and manage the servants.

What kind of age, sweet Lord, were they living in?

'You can read?'

She stared at him, surprised rather than affronted.

His page was asking her what her monkey liked to eat. 'I tell you what he does *not* like to eat,' she replied heatedly.

'Yes, we know,' said Toke. 'Worts a day old.'

'Is it very long to noon?' she asked.

He put the books carefully back into the bag. Any books, even these books, were to be treated with reverence.

There were footsteps on the stairs. It was Hanchache, looking terrified. Hanchache should never have left Staffordshire. He should never have left the womb.

'There's trouble in Gracechurch Street,' he stuttered. 'Men rolling barrels filled with stones. Rolling them down to the bridge. The hue and cry's out.'

Toke turned to the girl. 'We must go. I want us out of London in daylight, and I still have a visit to make.'

Yevele's workshop was behind St Paul's, leased from the dean and chapter. He worked in stone but his business supplied everything from Flanders tiles to plaster of Paris, and it was five years since he'd taken over from Brampton as the king's glazier. He was busy, now, working on a pane of white glass, applying a border to a window commissioned for the royal bathroom at King's Langley. He held it up, and the grey January light shone palely through the blue and yellow flowers, through the royal coat of arms.

Toke thought for a brief moment of kings, and of bathrooms with hot water that ran through copper pipes.

Yevele said, softly, 'They say he's dead.'
'Dick did not know.'
'You have seen him?'
'I have been to his house.'
'Ah well,' said Yevele. 'Dick would not want to know.'

It was two years since Dick Whittington had turned against his master. 'The people of London are not fighting men,' he had said, when King Richard demanded an army to lead against the Irish. But he had been ready enough to provide soldiers for the usurper Harry of Lancaster: twenty thousand men at marvellously high rates of pay.

'Dead,' said Yevele, 'somewhere in the north.'

Never again to soak his thin limbs in steaming water, while he watched the sunlight strike through his panes of coloured glass. King Richard was dead in a Norman cell, somewhere in the north where glass had never been heard of. Starved, said the tale – running this day through Cheapside and the murky waters of the Walbrook, seeping through cracks in merchants' doors and tavern windows – starved to death, not murdered, for none, it was said, had dared raise his hand to murder an anointed king!

Which was bullshit, as they knew in every tavern from the White Rose to the Tabard. They'd murdered Richard's grandfather well enough – first with pillows over his face then with a red-hot poker up his arse (which he'd enjoyed by all accounts).

It was the fifteenth day of January. Richard had been dead, said Yevele, since the tenth. The plot to restore him had been futile, the attempt to kill King Henry on the Feast of the Epiphany had been pointless. 'The noble lords died,' sighed Yevele, an appreciator of irony, 'in trying to restore a dead man to his throne.'

That morning King Henry had ridden back into London. The heads of the executed rebels had been carried behind him in sacks, although some of them, including Sir Thomas Blount's, had been carried on poles. It had been strange, Toke told Yevele, to see that familiar face waving over the crowd, looking down with so sardonic a grin for its friends.

They both turned to the girl, who was sitting with her monkey, hunched over the brazier of coals.

Yevele said: 'His sister?'

Toke nodded.

'Does she know?'

Toke shrugged his shoulders faintly.

They would be busy in the Tower, he thought, salting the heads before raising them over the gates of London Bridge.

'What of her other kin?' said Yevele.

'Her father died at Radcott Bridge. Her uncle, Hugo, was hanged a week ago at Cirencester.'

Yevele sighed. He built in stone, but he was not, he often said, stony by nature. He had wept for poor Richard in the Tower – poor sad Richard who had begged that he be not dragged to Parliament 'in horrible fashion', but had sent the Archbishop of York instead. *Gratanter, ut apparuit, et hilari vultu* – his crown surrendered with a cheerful countenance, said the chronicles. Somebody might believe it. Yevele remembered how only a year ago Richard had sat in his great hall at Westminster for the Christmas revels, in the great hall that Yevele built. Now a new king sat on Richard's throne. But would King Henry be a commissioner of art? Would King Henry accept the windows of decorated glass ordered by his predecessor? Did Henry Bolingbroke ever place his limbs, naked, in a bath?

The girl said, suddenly: 'Why do we not go? Why do we not go from here? I was told . . . I was told . . .'

'I have work to do. I have business.' He said the words coldly.

She looked puzzled, uncomprehending. Her eyes fell, and she turned back to the fire.

Alabaster was his business. Snow-white English alabaster with a smooth fine grain, the most delicate carving in England.

Toke was a rich man, thought Yevele. He had his fingers in the Italian trade, he had a quarter of a ship, the *Matthew* trading out of Bristol, and shares, they said, in a Genoan bark. He had bought himself estates in Staffordshire from some impoverished knight. He had more credit with the Flemish bankers than many a strutting lord.

'Her mother is retired to Ely,' said Toke, 'and I am to take her to a nunnery.'

A last commission, and this one without payment. 'Take my daughter to Dore,' the lady had said, half demented (her son's head was parted and separated from its body, and she cared only to bring them, somehow, back together again). She had not asked him to

9

swear an oath. He was a mere franklin, not a knight.

The girl sat with her monkey, shivering still, though she was seated by a brazier of sea coals. Her face was dirty, her saffron-streaked hair in rats' tails. The monkey peeped out from her arms with a mournful, worried face. It had a coat of squirrel fur trimmed with silver braid.

'I might give five shillings,' said Yevele, 'for the monkey.'

'The monkey,' said Toke heavily, 'is for the nuns.'

'It's a long journey. It might well die.'

Yevele was probing; he did not know where the nunnery was.

'So might we all die,' Toke said. 'If you will take in the consignment I will owe you great obligation.'

She was staring at them drearily. Did she know about her brother's death? Did she know that his salted head was this day being placed on London Bridge? Toke saw in his mind's eye those wide-staring eyes, he saw them being covered with merciful snow. He had made tombs for the Blounts, he had decorated the great hall at Lysle with panels of alabaster, the smoothest and whitest in all England.

The monkey suddenly let out a sharp cry.

The girl said, desperately, 'Pray, is it yet noon?'

The boy said: 'They are hungry. She asks if it is yet noon because they are so hungry.'

She was swaying, but tried to straighten herself, to shoot him a look of defiance. How old was she? Thirteen? Fourteen? When had she last eaten? When had she enjoyed her mess of beans a day old?

'There is a cookshop,' said the boy, wheedling, 'a cookshop that sells a roast hen for a groat.'

Toke sent the boy for food. He did his business with Yevele: arrangements to receive the shipment borne down the Great North Road at such terrible cost (for wagons lumbered at so slow a rate, and even though they were packed with straw the wastage was terrible). The price that the Italians would have to pay was agreed. The Italian merchants would cry 'Shame, shame!' in anger, but they would pay. There was no alabaster in the world like that of England.

The boy came back. He had three hot thrushes in a barley-loaf basket. Toke gave the girl two of them and told her to eat quickly. He ate the other himself, but when the monkey cried he gave it some meat from his fingers. The boy Flesshe stood with a look of saintliness on his face. He was always hungry, although he had eaten at eleven o' the clock, the usual time for merchants to have their dinner.

Yevele said: 'There are desperate men in the Savoy, in the old ruins. There are robbers on every highway. Sir Robert de Rideware was spotted near Highbury not a week ago.'

What a worrier Yevele was.

There was a banging outside. Hanchache, risking a beating, impatient to move. The girl took no notice; she gazed into the hot brazier, into the coals, her face flushed, her eyes closing. She had eaten, and like a small animal she would now sleep.

Toke said, 'Come. We must go.'

She stood up, obediently.

A flurry of snow came through the shutters. Yevele, thought Toke, ought to try glazing his own windows.

Outside Yevele said, 'Take care, my friend.'

It was already going dark. The air was acrid with the smoke from sea-coal fires. A thick mist lay over the Thames. A few torches flickered in the distance, from Cheapside.

Toke mounted his horse. Hanchache helped the girl to mount her pony. The boy Flesshe was also on a pony. Hanchache would run behind. He had long legs and liked to run.

Yevele, an old man, said anxiously, 'Take her to Westminster. Take her to the White Rose, it's within sanctuary.'

Yes, and every rogue in London lodged at the White Rose tavern. Men who would starve a king in a cell, thought Toke, would take no note of sanctuary.

They took the dirt track round St Paul's churchyard and turned west along Cheapside, past the merchants lighting their stalls, and the cookshops where boys as ever shouted, 'Lark pies and apple pies! Good geese and gammon!' They passed Hodgett the vintner whose cunning apprentice sang out 'Rhenish and claret give relish to a roast!' – a tripping phrase that bounced round Toke's head for a week.

At Newgate they turned south, taking the lane inside the wall to Ludgate. Lights glowed ahead of them in the vast Norman tower. This was where Chaucer had lodged, before the monks at Westminster had taken him into their care. Toke was a civilised man. He had read *Troilus and Criseyde* though he wished Chaucer had not written his *Canterbury Tales*. Stuff for the court – love and bawdy for the chattering French women – but it had been amazingly popular. Every group of pilgrims on the roads, these days, thought they had to tell stories to each other.

Aldgate. They clattered under the arch and across the bridge, watched by the nervous citizen guard. Twenty men summoned to do their civic duty – and they were all to be seen today, though in normal times it was a wonder if five turned out, the others risking a fine rather than leaving their firesides.

There were fewer houses west of the Fleet. They passed the Temple. The lawyers had returned – it was twenty years or more since Jack Straw had tried, with a fair degree of success, to kill every lawyer in London. Beyond the Temple Bar the road ran unpaved past the ruins of the Savoy, that had been John of Gaunt's great palace. Beyond the Savoy were grey, misty fields.

The road ran through them, into the countryside, towards the village at Charing.

Toke stopped. He looked back. Houses huddled against London wall, but the wall itself soared over them, black and invincible, pierced by its forty-foot-high towers – he could see three of them: Ludgate, Newgate, Aldersgate. The wall was two miles long, built by the Romans, maintained still in Roman fashion.

Darkness was falling. It was almost three o'clock in the afternoon, the hour of none. In a thousand monasteries up and down the land monks would be on their knees, even if many would be hazy on gin (to fight the plague), and stuffed on roast meats. It was the hour of none, and almost dark, and he was leaving London with a girl of perhaps fourteen, a monkey, a boy, and a servant whose bones chattered with terror when a cat mewled.

The girl, her head buried in the folds of her capuchin, said, 'We are taking the road to Westminster?'

Toke looked to the north. The Fleet River curved west as it left the wall. A track ran by it, disappearing into the marshes – the boggy wetlands that were used by cattle in the summer. It was not a road any man would choose to take at this hour, in this weather.

He looked back again at London. There was a flurry of snow. Like a curtain falling, it hid the wall.

Were men even now searching for the girl? Was her mother right to think that she was in danger?

'St Pancras the Wells,' he said.

They turned in the gloom, leaving the road to Charing and Westminster, heading north into the driving sleet, into the darkness.

3

The Satellite Ring

Twenty-two thousand miles beneath the satellite ring a cargo ship left a bubbling wake, white in the night, as she plied the New York to Cape Town sea route, five degrees north of Ascension Island. None of the satellites could see her, though several could pick up the *sweep, sweep, sweep* of her radar, and the Inmar commercial satellite had good reason to know her position, for one of her officers had spent an hour speaking to his wife in Melbourne, hearing about the terrible rainstorms sweeping through the southern hemisphere, the World Heritage aboriginal wall paintings destroyed by floods in Queensland, the plague of sodden mice seeking shelter in the towns and cities of New South Wales.

It was not information to interest *Pasiphae*, which was busy receiving quantum signals from a thousand authorised sources, and was listening in, illicitly and discreetly, to a thousand more: from the UN task commander's phone in Kurdistan, to the French War Minister's private line to her lover in Neuilly. It was processing the signals and sending them as pulses along its veins, back to its tiny, delicate transponders, where they were screened, filtered, and down-linked via the Alaskan HAARP to Utah, and from there to the Pentagon, to the Navy Department and to the CIA, and to the other agencies that subscribed to the *Pasiphae* programme.

There were intruders again . . .

Pressing gently at the logic gates. Clambering up the boarding nets. Insinuating themselves through the entry ports.

There was a query, a spasm – a millisecond's rejection by the microtubules that provided the scaffolding of the antennae's cells. Then – easily and without protest – *Pasiphae*'s whisper antennae took in and enfolded the unauthorised signals.

* * *

Even its designers did not know precisely how the net of whisper antennae worked; for nobody fully understood how the brain worked. Its memory circuits were a mystery to its creators; but then, the location of memory in the human brain was a mystery, so logic was maintained. When the antennae net received signals it did not expect – signals that did not have a destination – its logic told it that somehow it must find them a home; somehow it must pass them on, despite the disinfectant programs, despite the physiological barriers.

Occasionally during the long hours of the night a telemetry encoder was distressed, an anti-virus sensor flickered; but in Utah this was put down to cosmic storms on the highest of High Seas, to the sensitivity of *Pasiphae*'s quantum technology. To the enigma of the human brain on which it was based.

Only the Pentagon night-duty operative occasionally felt unease: felt that something was passing across his screen, there and yet not there, visible and yet invisible. A ghost of a signal – a thought – something that did not possess chemical substance or electrical energy.

He put it down, in the end, to the bizarre theories he was having to listen to, night after night, from his neighbour who was obsessed by Schrödinger's quantum theories. 'That cat is neither living nor dead until we look inside the box. Basically, cutting through the crap, nothing exists unless it is seen to exist. You understand that now, James?'

James looked at his screen and saw nothing.

He would not be the one to raise the alarm.

4

Dore, Herefordshire

For a split second an image flashed in her brain – a face almost against the retina of her mind's eye, so that she flinched – then it was gone. There was just a remembrance of sad, staring eyes, filled with anxiety.

Lizzie lay still, her own eyes closed, smelling wet dew on grass and canvas. Outside, she could hear Gareth asking somebody how many sausages they wanted. He was speaking in conversational tones, but his voice carried on the still, early morning air. 'Have you ever tried them dipped in maple syrup?' he asked roguishly. Another voice, female, said, 'Oh God, Gareth, that is gross.'

Close to the tent a sheep munched the grass. Next to her Sonia lay on her back and suddenly gave a huge snore.

Lizzie unzipped her sleeping bag, crawled over Sonia and un-Velcroed the tent's flap to peer out. Gareth was outside the mess tent, doing things to a gas camper stove. Next to him was Eloise, a good-natured girl with thin white legs, who sat on a canvas stool nursing a mug of coffee. Nobody else was up. The other tents, half a dozen of them, were like grey mushrooms that had sprouted in the night and died.

She crawled out and made her way across to the latrines that Gareth and the boys had dug. He was an old boy scout was Gareth, veteran of many a boyhood camp. She washed in a plastic bowl, dousing her face with the small amount of water they were allowed.

'Ah, Lizzie,' said Gareth when she went over and poured herself some coffee. 'Now you're a four-sausage girl if I'm not mistaken.'

He was mistaken. He was probably mistaken about many things, Lizzie thought. He would be mistaken in thinking they all wanted to sit round campfires singing 'The Quartermaster's Store'.

She took her coffee and went up the grass slope, along the path to the ramparts of the fort. They'd been at Dore now for three days, but the view from the summit still astonished and delighted her. The hill commanded the countryside for thirty miles or more: west towards Hay, east across the broad valley of the Wye, south-west as far as the long ridge of the Black Mountains. Men had lived, grazed their animals, built fortresses on this summit for twelve thousand years. Yesterday the group had examined a cave, on the western slope, just beneath the Iron Age ramparts, in which flint axes and animal bones from the Upper Palaeolithic period had been found.

Lizzie sat on the dry grass bank amid the daisies, and thought about the Old Stone Age. Suddenly her dream came back to her. In her mind's eye she saw the face, lean and brown, with its staring, anxious eyes.

Had she been dreaming, last night, about the Old Stone Age?

Perhaps that was it. Her dream had been full of worry, and the Old Stone Age had been a time of terrible worry, what with the Ice Age and everything. Perhaps in her dream she'd been here on this hilltop, watching the glistening blue cliff of ice appear on the northern horizon. She imagined voices saying 'We must go to the south!' and other, braver voices, urging, 'Stick it out, man, it'll be gone by next spring!'

Had the last Old Stone Age families of Dore trekked wearily away to the south, she wondered? Or had they huddled in the cave with their store of wild grain, berries and dried meat, listening to the crack of ice as it slithered over their heads?

There would have been a lot of worry there. A lot of stress.

Actually, of course, the dream was probably nothing to do with the hill fort. It was probably all to do with Malcolm, her lover. Her ex-lover. Her ex-middle-aged lover – though of course that wasn't the proper description either: he was still middle-aged, he just wasn't her lover any more.

Somebody was climbing the ramparts, towards where she sat. It was Andrew, a boy from Durham. He disappeared into the Iron Age middle ditch but she wasn't deceived. He would pop up in front of her at any moment, with a look of pretend surprise on his face, just as he had yesterday morning. She stood up, finishing her coffee, and walked slowly along the rampart away from him. After a bit she reached the gap made by the fort's western entrance and there he was, looking up.

He smiled modestly.

She turned back and sat down on the grass. A minute later he had climbed the rampart and was sitting next to her.

'Hi,' he said.

'Hi,' she replied, cool but resigned. Boys, boys, everywhere, as they had been ever since she was fourteen and had been given a bosom by God and a tight, canary-yellow knitted jumper by her insane mother.

He looked out, thoughtfully, over the valley towards the Black Mountains. He didn't say anything.

She said, after a minute, 'How long did the last Ice Age last?'

'About ten thousand years.'

'Yeah, right.'

She sighed a silent sigh for the last family of the Old Stone Age, huddled in their cave with their berries. Ten thousand years while their bones froze, and they waited for a spring that would never come. Well there you go, she thought. It didn't do to be an optimist.

He was still staring out over the valley.

'I think I'd have liked it here after the ice,' she said, mildly irritated that she was the one making the conversation. 'In the Warm Period when the wild horses came, and oak trees, and hazel and elm took root. When the little groups of families first came back up the valley. It must have been a clean new world. The berries must have tasted sweet.'

'Actually, they ate a lot of lemmings.'

'Lemmings?'

'So I believe.'

Lizzie imagined Middle Stone Age children, chasing after the wild horses, or perhaps setting little traps for the lemmings. The lemmings were a puzzle. In all England, were there any lemmings left? Or had they all swum out to sea and drowned?

Andrew said, 'There's a medieval chapel down there. Do you want to go and have a look?'

She stared down into the western valley, which was still in deep shadow.

'What for?'

'I don't know. It might be interesting.'

She already knew about the chapel. It was partially hidden in trees above the site of the lost medieval village of Dore. What she didn't know about was this Andrew.

Looking at it another way, of course, she knew everything about this Andrew. It was herself, as usual, that she wasn't too sure about.

'OK,' she said, after a moment.

They went down a path, through gorse and hawthorn and grass, then past a holly hedge, and into a wood. The air had lost its dawn crispness; it was already getting warm and humid under the trees. There was the sound of running water: a stream that trickled down the hillside from the hill fort, from the spring known as Vortipor's Well. After five minutes they emerged into a small glade. The chapel was before them, small and squat. It had an air of neglect, with tall, dry grass between its gravestones, although somebody, not very expertly, had mown the grass path to the porch.

A notice said that it was the church of St Michael and All Saints in the parish of Dore in the diocese of Hereford. Holy Communion (BCP) was celebrated on the first Sunday of every month at 9.30 a.m. A Victorian sign, painted on wood, said: REMOVE PATTENS BEFORE ENTERING.

'What on earth are pattens?' she said.

'I don't know.'

'You don't?'

He had struck her as a boy who knew everything.

She pushed open the thick oak door, the wood grey with age. Inside was a vase of white lilies on a small oak table. Beyond it were oak box pews and over them a wooden painted royal coat of arms from the time of George III. The walls were white-painted plaster or bare stone, the windows were of plain glass, except for the east window through which beams of dusty light – blue, mauve and blood-red – fell on the tomb of a knight who rested in the chancel.

'Actually I think they may be some kind of clog,' he said. 'They wore pattens in *Cranford*.'

Lizzie knelt in one of the pews. She could smell the scent of the lilies. She closed her eyes and said a prayer. 'Make me good, make me kind,' she said, as she always said. On the wall opposite, when she looked up, was a painted text: 'All flesh is as grass and all the glory of man as the flower of grass. The grass withereth, and the flower thereof falleth away.'

Yes, she thought, yes; the grass withered and the flower fell away. She sighed, wondering if there was any point in relationships, any relationships, when they all withered, they all fell away.

Andrew was watching her. She felt herself blush. She said, 'How old do you think the church is?'

'Fourteenth century, perhaps a bit earlier. The slipware tiles on the roof are late fourteenth century at a guess, or very early fifteenth century. They had kilns at Malvern in the fourteenth century. Those stairs that go nowhere are fourteenth century; they must have led to a rood loft.'

Ah, he did know everything. She studied him covertly. Fair-haired, not bad looking. Muscular legs (he was wearing shorts) with rather attractive little gold hairs on them. A joint archaeology and history graduate planning to do a law conversion because the law was a good solid profession – but he was not, she thought, as boring as that made him sound. She could picture him on the bridge of a destroyer, sea spray soaking his hair, a keen smile on his face as he took his ship in under the dangerous, enemy-held coast of France. It was really all a matter of opportunity: death by refrigeration in 10,000 BC, high adventure in 1940, and a law conversion in the twenty-first century.

'The Last Days of the World,' he said, reading a notice on the wall by the east window. 'The stained glass illustrates the text "All that lives shall then die" which marked the fourteenth day of the fifteen days during which the world would be destroyed. An English Allegory, also depicted at All Saints' Church in York.'

Lizzie looked up at the window. A medieval man and woman were lying dead under a coverlet covered in stars. A skeleton grinned down at them.

'Creepy,' she said.

She got up and wandered over to him. The knight, she found, wasn't a knight at all. Instead of chain mail, the figure was clothed in long red robes and a fifteenth-century merchant's hat. His head rested not on his loyal hound, but on a pillow of wool, from which escaped wisps of fleece.

'He's a franklin,' said Andrew.

'A what?'

21

'A franklin.'

'As in the tale of?'

'Yes. A medieval merchant – well, more a small landowner really. And look at this . . .'

He knelt down and ran his fingers lightly along a fresco under the plaster effigy. 'Alabaster. It's very rare at that period. He must have been a rich man.'

'Perhaps somebody thought a lot of him,' said Lizzie. 'Perhaps he had a very noble nature, and his widow – who was herself nobly born and had married him for true love – was heartbroken when he died. Perhaps his children cared for him very much.'

She also knelt. She ran her fingers along the cool creamy surface of the fresco, over the tiny effigies of saints interspersed with flowers.

Richard of Bordeaux has been starved to death somewhere in the north, said a voice in her head, *starved until the conduits of his body were contracted*.

It was her dream. It was a voice from her dream.

'So that's it, you're a romantic,' said Andrew. 'We wondered what you were thinking about.'

She had been in London. It had been the Feast of Epiphany. She had been in Cheapside and had watched a man put in the stocks for selling bad fish. She had seen a fire of straw flame up in the grey winter light. She had watched the rotten fish burned under the man's nose: the acrid smell had filled her nostrils.

Somebody had been telling her to *hurry, hurry* . . .

She was suddenly aware that Andrew's arm was pressed against hers. She moved away fractionally and said, 'Is there a booklet about the church, or anything?'

He cast an absent eye towards the table by the church door. 'Not that I can see.'

His arm was somehow touching hers again. She said, 'You don't think this is Dick Whittington?'

'What?'

'This tomb. You don't think it's Dick Whittington's tomb?'

'Why should it be?'

'I don't know. I had a dream last night.'

'About Dick Whittington?'

'Yes. At least I think so.'

'Did he have his cat with him?'

'No he didn't.'

'You're sure there wasn't a talking cat wearing boots and tights?'

'Don't be stupid.'

'Well, this isn't Dick Whittington anyway. This is a franklin.'

Light poured down on them from the east window. It filtered down through the parchment-yellow faces of the dead man and the dead woman, through the grinning skeleton and the coverlet of stars.

'Well I never,' she said, aware that his leg was now touching her leg, as he leaned forward to stroke the alabaster roses. 'A franklin's tomb.'

'OK,' shouted Bill Hastings, the dig leader, standing on one of the ramparts. 'We all know what we have to do. Venetia and Jacob have marked out the line of the trenches, which will bisect what was originally the main street of the Iron Age settlement. We should reach the mound in three weeks providing we stick at it, and don't keep buggering off to Hereford looking for ice-cream parlours and night-clubs.'

'Is he getting at me?' said Venetia Peel, cool and blonde and in Gareth's awed eyes highly sophisticated. She had a red BMW con-vertible with creamy leather seats parked in the farm under the western ramparts. Three times, already, she had wandered off on her own account.

'I expect so,' said Lizzie.

'A nightclub in Hereford. God, can you imagine?'

'We've come here to toil,' cried Bill Hastings, giving her a fierce glance, 'and toil is bloody well what we're going to do. Is that agreed?'

'I expect it's called Celebrities,' said Venetia. 'They always are, and it'll be full of BBC Radio Hereford disc jockeys, and mole catchers, and sixteen-year-old girls looking for safe sex. Shall we go in one night and have a look?'

'If you like,' said Lizzie, looking round, covertly, to see if Andrew had heard.

'Right then,' shouted Bill Hastings. 'Let's get started!'

They worked all day, cutting the turf from the trenches, wearing wide-brimmed hats against the sun, their arms coated with high-protection baby cream, watched by sheep and passing hikers. Occasionally Venetia – clearly not a girl to notice when people were aloof, or shy, or liked to keep to themselves – wandered over to Lizzie and said, bemused, 'Ice-cream parlours. I mean, where does he come from?'

In the evening they ate spaghetti, cooked by Badger and Jacob. 'Do you realise,' said Eloise, 'we are quite likely the first people to actually live here in the fort – working, eating and sleeping – since AD 74?'

Gareth said, 'I don't think that in AD 74 the Britons had tents, gas stoves, and their water brought up each morning by the National Trust.'

'Oh *you* . . .' said Sonia, punching his arm playfully.

'Now listen,' said Bill. 'I have warned everybody about water economy?'

A weary chorus, 'Yes, Bill . . .'

Tiger moths circled round the hurricane lamp. There was only the faintest breath of wind, little more than a slight movement of air across the ridge summit. They drank terrible red wine bought by Gareth, and Bill Hastings described the 1954 discovery of the barrow of Stone Age skulls under the western ramparts, the first indication that the post-Rome mound inside the summit camp might have had a religious significance.

Venetia, who was suffering from insect bites, said, 'It's creepy, creepy, creepy. I don't know why we don't move into a hotel. I mean, what is this stupid boy-scout stuff?'

Gareth looked troubled and unhappy.

'Stone Age man was obsessed with the dead,' said Bill Hastings. 'The barrow of skulls was his church.'

'Do you think they were cannibals?'

'Very likely.'

'Oh God,' said Eloise.

'It is probable that they ate their mothers and fathers in order to absorb their spirits, and, of course, to take advantage of a useful supply of protein. But it's the Iron Age that concerns us. Iron Age people who looked not to the past, but to the future. OK, they'd only got weighted sticks for digging, antler picks and the shoulder blades of deer for scraping out the ground. OK, they only had baskets slung over their backs to carry the soil. But they built forts like this one that have survived over two thousand years.'

'They didn't keep out Rome,' said Gareth. 'They didn't keep out the legions.'

'No,' said Bill Hastings. 'No, they didn't hold out against the legions. But some of them came back, once the legions had passed, and our job is to find out why. What caused the later rebuilding, the rebuilding post-Rome? Was it a religious shrine? Or did the Welsh make a last stand here, under a king like Vortipor perhaps, before they were driven back further into the mountains to the west?'

'Didn't Vortipor rape his daughter?' said Eloise.

'His willing daughter,' said Sonia, 'who was herself steeped in depravity.'

Lizzie saw that Andrew was watching her from the other side of the hurricane lamp.

'I thought Vortipor was a sort of King Arthur,' said Eloise.

'It is just so *hot*,' said Venetia Peel, thinking about air-conditioned hotel rooms and swimming pools.

It was gone midnight. Lizzie lay in her sleeping bag, in the tent with Sonia. Wherever her flesh touched the cotton, sweat broke out on her skin. Soon Sonia was snoring: gentle, coy little snores that stopped for a moment then started again. Lizzie closed her eyes.

The heat was terrible. The weather systems of the world were in turmoil, there had never been a year like it.

Twenty years of global warming, said the television pundits, coming all at once.

Sonia snored, then giggled.

Was she dreaming about Gareth?

Lizzie thought of an incident that had taken place in the early evening, just after they had finished on the dig. Sonia, standing on the ramparts, had called out, 'Catch me, catch me somebody!' and launched herself down the grassy slope. There had been a frozen moment. Neither Andrew nor Gareth had rushed to interpose themselves between the lower rampart and her substantial and fast-moving body.

'Wheee . . .' Sonia had cried, her voluminous shorts flapping, already halfway down to the bottom. Andrew, with palpable reluctance, had moved forward and held out his arms, but at the last moment the missile Sonia had changed direction, and it was Gareth who received the impact of her large, friendly bosom.

'Oouf!' he had said, laughing gallantly.

Lizzie, lying soaked in sweat, wondered what Sonia saw in him. What Sonia wanted such heartache for, because attachments always ended in tears, or in terrible guilt.

She was thinking about Malcolm again. Malcolm, her forty-year-old ex-lover. She had met him on a flotilla holiday in the Aegean. She had thought how refreshing it was not to have her breasts pawed in the first thirty seconds of a relationship. Back in England he had come to see her in Bristol, and they had made love through a long, rainy afternoon when she ought to have been attending a seminar on the Christian reconquest of Spain in the thirteenth century. From his marital home in Norwich he had e-mailed her long letters designed to show how youthful and yet sophisticated he was. 'Well, I've opened another bottle of Beaujolais – why does Beaujolais at three o'clock in the morning taste of cassis? – and I still haven't started marking Upper Sixth sociology and it's all your fault, Miss Draude . . .'

But it hadn't been her fault at all. She liked to be in bed by eleven every night with a mug of tea.

He was a boy, in the end, was Malcolm, like all the others. A sad, middle-aged boy – a footballer past his prime, not moving as fast as the young lads but with the same objective in mind.

Two weeks ago, in terrible tears, she had given him the push.

She wondered why she had to mull over the entrails, worry the guilty bones.

Would he go on a flotilla holiday again, this year? Would he go looking for another Lizzie?

She turned over, feeling the sweat break out afresh on her forehead. She felt dizzy, disorientated. She wondered if Badger had put dried magic mushrooms in the spaghetti – he had a supply, she'd seen him showing them to Jacob, she wondered if he could have been that stupid. A trip could last up to nine hours – how long was it since they'd eaten? Suddenly she could smell white lilies. She could smell their sweet, clinging perfume and see them, on the table by the font, in the coolness of the church. Who was it who put fresh white lilies in the church with the franklin's tomb?

Sonia snorted loudly and turned over, throwing out her arms, snuffling like a pig on the track of a truffle.

'Sonia? Sonia?'

The snoring stopped.

'Shall we go and sleep in the church?'

She said it without thinking, surprising herself.

Sonia muttered something.

'It would be lovely and cool.'

There was another little snore.

Lizzie got up quietly, picked up her sleeping bag and torch and went outside. It was fractionally less humid: there was the shadow of a breeze, a slight movement of the air. The sky was luminous, the grass still dry of dew. Some of the boys, she saw, were sleeping outside their tents, lying naked with their sleeping bags half un-zipped.

She saw Andrew lying asleep and stared down at him for a moment, at his bare, smooth chest, thinking that actually he looked rather sweet. Then she pulled her sleeping bag to her, and ran across the grass towards the ramparts. There was a red, winking light from the satellite station near Hereford; the lights of a car on the winding road to Hay-on-Wye. She turned along the ramparts, to the south-west. The long ridge of the Black Mountains was invisible; the valley beneath her, with its lost medieval village of Dore, was in deep blackness. She slipped down the track by the holly hedge, and into the dark under the trees. After a few moments she switched on her torch, and saw moths dancing over the trickling stream. Something went plop – a frog disturbed.

Then she was in the glade.

She stopped. What if the camp was suddenly moved during the night for some reason? A terrible storm, with everybody taken to Hereford in Land Rovers, nobody knowing that poor Lizzie had woken up in her church and was trying to find them on a Herefordshire hill?

Andrew, she thought, would notice she wasn't there. He would come looking for her, and find her running about, distraught in her rain-soaked pyjamas, and would carry her sobbing and grateful back to camp.

She wondered, fleetingly, as she turned the iron latch and pushed the heavy oak door so that it melted into the darkness of the church's interior, why she was having Andrew's fantasies for him.

It was cool, chilly almost. She shone her torch on the Georgian box pews, on the massive coat of arms of England. She walked softly up the aisle to the chancel. The east window was dark and solid, the skeleton and the dead couple invisible. She laid her sleeping bag down by the side of the franklin's tomb. She snuggled down into it, and turned off her torch, hoping that nobody on the Newbridge road would have seen the light.

Stillness. In a few moments a faint light shone in through the east window.

She breathed deeply but softly – the smell of old wood, of must, the smell of age. Images of the day floated behind her eyelids: the heat haze over the valley, the bent figures in their sunhats, the tap, tap, tapping of dental hammers, the quiet scraping of trowels. Bill Hastings was a good archaeologist, making a name for himself – it would be good on her CV to have done a dig with him. Eloise was silly but OK. Badger and Jacob were ghastly and immature, with their hunt for Pigsbum ale and Ratarse bitter. The awful Gareth – Venetia didn't believe that Gareth was for real, but what was Venetia doing here anyway? OK, it was a course requirement, but it was funny she hadn't found somewhere more exotic, in the south of France, perhaps . . .

But the south of France, she remembered, was a dry, barren furnace this year.

Andrew . . . what about Andrew?

Without knowing why, she put one hand out, against the smooth alabaster, the ribbon of frozen white flowers.

In her nostrils there came an odd smell. At first she thought it was the white lilies. Then she realised that it was blood.

Blood, mingled with the perfume of roses.

5

Utah

Midday in Utah. On the radio 'Wimoweh' gave way to Alan Jackson's 'A Lot About Livin' And A Little 'Bout Love'. The signal flashing on the duty officer's log was treble-A security, which was not surprising – few of *Pasiphae*'s signals were classified as less. It was from Tokyo Embassy to Naval Intelligence in Virginia, and Virginia was now on the line saying that the message was corrupted. 'It's like some other signal's trying to break in. Some signal from outside.'

'No conventional signal,' said John Koenig, the duty officer in Utah, 'can penetrate *Pasiphae*.'

'Maybe it's another *Pasiphae* signal, an authorised signal.'

John Koenig was a man with a conscience, a scrupulous, careful man, but this particular day he had his personal life to think about. He said, 'Stay on the line,' and again pressed the pad to activate the digital recording. There were soft noises, meaningless, and properly so. He watched the green lines on his screen.

'There's nothing . . .' his voice began – bored, mechanical – then it trailed away.

For a split second his brain had registered something round the edges of the signal, a brief fuzziness that came and went. He played it again, listening for a fractional change in the modulation. It was so faint, when it came, that he could have been imagining it – given the nature of *Pasiphae*'s quantum technology, he must have imagined it. The fault, if fault there was, was being detected intuitively.

He said, 'If I had the decode I might be able to help.'

'No way.'

The Navy didn't want him reading their signals. Why, the Navy didn't even know who John Koenig was, he thought, without resentment.

A voice on the radio: 'If the world had a front porch like we had back then, We'd still have our problems but we'd all still be friends.'

It was a nice song, a song with a heart-warming message.

29

'Jesus, did that guy rhyme then with friends?' said the man in Newport News, Virginia.

Koenig turned off the radio. There was no need to encourage the prejudices of East Coast sophisticates.

The signal flowed through the filters, twittering still like small chicks in a nest. Some of those sounds, he was being told, were cuckoo sounds.

The Navy man said, 'This is your problem, Utah. You can check out invasive elements without a decode. If we're being penetrated we want to know fast. Once I pass this fault signal up the line, which I do in fifteen seconds approximately, oh boy.'

A ten-billion-dollar state-of-the-art communications network, compromised. Not only the satellite – which itself cost more than the welfare budget of New York State – but the investment in the quantum computer at Berkeley, in the second-generation HAARP ionospheric heater in Alaska.

This could be crisis time. This could be mega.

'We'll come back to you,' said Koenig, thinking about his personal life.

'We'll be here,' said Newport News.

Koenig sat and listened again to the signal: three, four times, his eyes fixed on the screen. That faint blur – gone before his retina even established it. This quantum stuff was just so small – dear Lord, these were electrons he was trying to watch, *sub-electrons*, these were wave particles dancing before his eyes.

But there was something wrong. His instinct told his brain that there was something wrong, even as his intelligence told him that no way could he detect a fault visually. Or perhaps, he told his conscience, it was just him, going loopy. 'Too many hours, John boy,' he said to himself – for he was a man occasionally prone to self-pity – 'Too many hours with only Glen Campbell and the rhinestone cowboy for company.'

The thought reminded him that it was lunchtime, and that he had a date to keep. In Newport News the Navy would be halfway to bikini alert.

He moved quickly, for a man of his bulk, to get out of the building before, as he told himself, the shit hit the fan.

* * *

His custom was to lunch at the café at Bonanza, his usual order a BLT and a cherry-filled Danish pastry, washed down with toffee-flavoured coffee. But today – as on so many days recently – he swung out eastward across the desert, along the track towards Route 40. Soon a massive green brontosaurus shimmered in the haze ahead of him. As he got closer a single-storey prefabricated shack, the Dinosaur Diner, appeared nestling under its shadow. He drew up in the empty car park, and waved at a small anxious face that peered out through the window. Mary Lou, thin and bird-like and not, he reckoned, more than a couple of years over forty.

'Double portion crispy-grilled bacon,' she called out, as he went in through the door, 'with waffles 'n' syrup?'

He looked at her with affection. She wore jeans and a cowboy shirt, and an over-large chef's hat that made her look more beaky than she actually was. He'd been attracted to her last year, but then she'd gone off to Aspen for the winter, broadening her horizons, she said, learning something about life outside of Utah. Since she came back he'd taken to calling regularly, even though the Dinosaur Diner's regular lunchtime pie was not as good as the pie in Bonanza, and the Dinosaur Diner's coffee came without toffee flavouring.

He nodded his head.

'You coming this evening?'

Tuesday was Bluegrass Night. Mary Lou herself would be singing. Her hair would be in plaits and she'd be wearing a gingham check dress.

'I sure am,' he said, refusing to think of panics in the Pentagon, red alerts in Newport News. The bacon jumped and spat under the grill. She turned it with a practised flick of the wrist.

'If I can get here,' he said, having second thoughts, 'I'll get here.'

'You haven't missed yet. I guess you won't miss now.'

They were, he thought, *simpatico*.

She put bacon and waffles in front of him. He looked contentedly at the plate, reflecting that though Mary Lou was a sweet-natured, loving girl, and the best little country singer in Vernal County, the food of love was, at the end of the day, food. He said, 'Mary Lou, how about you and me getting married?'

It was not an impulsive move. He'd started thinking about it a year ago, before she went to Aspen. He was a slow mover for a man with two marriages in his past.

31

Mary Lou stood trembling for a while. Then she went to serve an air-conditioning salesman with a King Dinosaur Grill and fries. Then she said she'd like to think about it, because it was an awful big decision for a girl. Then, just in case he met some other girl on his five-mile drive back across the desert, she said 'Yes' and the salesman said 'Well well, this sure is a happy day', and gave them a leaflet for discount air-conditioning in their new home.

Koenig ate his lunch, promised he'd be there at eight p.m., drove back out to the station. He lived in a trailer park, and he supposed that that was where they'd stay, maybe getting themselves a bigger mobile home. There was talk of him being attached for a year to the Utah State University's new computer communications centre at Ogden. The trailer-park towns of northern Utah were not to everybody's taste, he thought, but they had their own bleak magic, particularly at sunset when the hills turned to orange.

There was a helicopter coming down inside the compound. The guys from Hill Air Force Base, from the Wendover desert station of the National Defence College: there hadn't been time, surely, for them to get here from Berkeley. They'd be looking for him, paging him in the staff restaurant (he never, ever ate in the staff restaurant) – administrators in suits running round like headless chickens as they tried to set up the disinfectant programs, let loose the sub-electronic hunters that would chase the virus – for what else could it be but a virus? – into the darkest, most hidden places in *Pasiphae*'s quantum system . . . find it, block its exits, then extract it, delicately, and examine it under the fiercest electronic microscope in the world.

He left his ancient Buick and crossed the compound. Another chopper could be heard – he could see it, a tiny silver shape against the buttes, a prehistoric dragonfly crossing the Green River. Yes, it was going to be a long job. But at least he'd seen it coming: he'd prepared himself, fortified the inner man.

'Jesus Christ, Koenig, will you get your fat ass into here?'

It was Sluder. Larry Sluder who had made his life hell for so many years before he was promoted to head *Pasiphae*'s project HQ at Berkeley.

He should have guessed.

He hurried a little, heaving his vast bulk into a sort of shuffling lope that he hoped might placate Sluder without sacrificing too much of his dignity.

32

6

Dore

Lizzie became aware of sunlight shining dustily through the east window.

She took her hand – chilled and bloodless – from the alabaster flowers of the franklin's tomb. She sat up and rubbed her fingers.

She had been back, again, in the Middle Ages. Not in London, this time. Not with Dick Whittington.

She had been riding a pony by a river, under trees dusted with frozen snow. Before her, on a horse, had been a man wearing a full-skirted black beaver coat. On his head had been a sugarloaf chaperon – the lower half pulled down over his shoulders as a cape, the upper half hanging down his back as a liripipe.

Behind her, on a second pony, had been a boy who wore a bright blue and yellow tunic, cloak, and capuchin. A man had walked behind them: cloth chausses on his long, thin legs, his feet encased in heavy felt.

The boy had played a flute.

The sun had struck down through the trees, through the sugar-spun snow. It had flashed on the clean, fast-flowing water of the Thames, and on the bright red berries of a bush overhanging the water.

The boy had said something in a low voice. It had made her laugh.

The man had turned and smiled, but it had been a cold smile and his eyes had been full of worry, full of danger, and Lizzie's heart had frozen, and the flute had died away.

It was gone. She rubbed her chilled fingers.

Then she looked up at the franklin's tomb.

At the cold, carved face above the red plaster robe: the sightless eyes staring into infinity.

'The Franklin of Dore?' said the assistant in Hereford library. 'Now there's a mystery for you. There's a puzzle.'

'I was hoping you could tell me his name,' said Lizzie. 'Tell me who he was.'

'Some students from Oxford, from the Medieval Society at Christ Church College, asked me the same question only last year, but it was no use. The manorial records of Newbridge were burned or stolen, you see, in the war with the Welsh.'

'The war with the Welsh?' said Lizzie. 'I must have missed that one.'

'Owain Glyn Dŵr's war. He came burning through the Marches with a scarlet flamingo feather in his helm.'

'Ah, right. That war.'

'It was a desperate business. The young Prince Harry did for him, of course, at Shrewsbury Fight. "On, on," he cried. "On, on you noble English." '

'Wasn't that at Harfleur?'

'There's nobody to say he didn't say it at Shrewsbury first.' She was having a joke. 'But anyway,' she went on, 'before Glyn Dŵr was defeated and slunk away to the mountains, he devastated the Marches. It was the usual story. Rape and pillage, pillage and rape.'

'And the burning of manorial records?'

'Yes, but what can you do with the Welsh? If it's not Owain Glyn Dŵr it's Hell's Angels from Abergavenny.'

She giggled. She was little and grey-haired and Welsh-like herself, sitting like a pixie behind the information desk. Lizzie said, 'So nothing at all is known about the franklin?'

'The children at Newbridge primary school did a project once. They discovered his name, I believe, and something about his background. I tried to find a copy for the students from Oxford, but it was done a long time ago, back in the late Sixties, and it was only a little pamphlet by all accounts.'

'You can't remember what it said?'

'In the late Sixties,' said the librarian, 'I was living in Seattle with a saxophonist, and had flowers in my hair.'

Of course, thought Lizzie, who felt she ought to have guessed.

'What I can tell you is that in the whole of England there are only four effigy tombs of franklins. They were only small landowners, you see, not much more than yeomen really, though they were said to be very pretentious, clambering sort of people, the sort that live in four-bedroom detached houses and vote Tory.'

'And you're sure the library doesn't have a copy of the pamphlet?'

'Not unless it's in one of the boxes in the storeroom. There's any amount we haven't classified and put on the computer. We're under-staffed. We close all day Monday, believe it or not, to save money. I told the students from Oxford, come back in another five hundred years and you never know, you might be lucky.'

'I don't suppose you could have a look for me?' asked Lizzie hopefully.

The librarian sighed and said, 'I don't know when,' and started to fill in a form. 'Address?' she said.

'The Iron Age fort of Montdore,' said Lizzie.

'Now that,' said the librarian, 'is what I call an address. Come back in a week or so, will you?'

Lizzie went to look for the others.

They went next door to the museum, looking at a picture of an auroch – the last wild ox, perhaps, in the world to be tamed – and of a ploughman who was forcing his iron blade into the ground, his shoulders arched, his muscles bulging, his fertile phallus massive and erect.

Sonia said: 'Imagine having sex with that.'

Gareth said: 'They were no great shakes.'

Bill Hastings – busy explaining Iron Age farming techniques to Badger and Jacob – turned and said, 'No great shakes? How do you know that, Gareth?'

'They only scratched away at the soil,' said Gareth, shaking his head in amusement. 'They had to plough all the land again at right angles before they broke it up enough for sowing.'

Bill Hastings looked at Lizzie and shook his head in disbelief, but she ignored him and looked at the sexually excited ploughman, the historical Asterix who had made such a momentous journey across the seas to Britain. IRON AGE B, said the notice, REFUGEES FROM THE MARNE BASIN, FLEEING THE PERSECUTIONS OF ROME.

'Annoying Iron Age A with their garlic and red wine,' said Bill Hastings, quietly in her ear, 'and by having bigger pricks than the natives.'

Oh oh, thought Lizzie, who had felt sure he was after Venetia Peel.

Jacob and Badger sidled away in search of strange beers or possibly cross-country railway timetables or computer magazines. Gareth and Sonia wandered off. Bill said, 'Do you reckon that that Gareth lad is for real?'

'You picked him.'

'There wasn't that much bloody choice.'

'No? I was led to believe that every archaeology postgraduate in England was begging to come on this dig. I was led to believe that I was one of the crème de la crème.'

'And so you are, poppet. Do you think Sonia fancies him?'

'Yes.'

'Well, bugger me, the world never ceases to amaze. Did you get what you wanted from the library?'

'No. But they're looking something up for me.'

'Fancy a coffee?'

Outside it was blindingly hot. The air smelled of melting asphalt. The trees in the cathedral close were dusty, their leaves grey. Tourists waiting to see the *mappa mundi* crouched in the shade, eating ice creams and panting like beasts of the veldt. Beer sales were booming, Lizzie had heard on the radio. Brewery shares were at an all-time high.

A red BMW convertible came round the corner, Venetia Peel at the wheel looking cucumber-cool in big sunglasses. She had volunteered to go to Sainsbury's and buy the grub. She had taken Andrew with her to help carry things. She saw them and waved in a languid manner. Bill said: 'Where's she off to now then?'

'A swim, I expect.'

'Well, bugger me.'

She watched Andrew being carried away in the red BMW and felt vaguely that something had been stolen from her. Something she might not have wanted, true, but theft was theft.

They went through the cathedral close and turned into a narrow medieval lane, and found a café with small tables outside. Eloise appeared, smiling a friendly smile and clutching a Marks and Spencer carrier bag. Bill said, in an irritated voice, 'Oh, are you having a coffee as well, Eloise?' which made her look puzzled and panicky.

Bastard, thought Lizzie, but without passion, for all men were bastards. Bill ordered three iced coffees. Perhaps feeling that he had been rude, he bought Eloise a small coconut cake and asked her about life in Surrey.

Lizzie sat with her back against a stone wall covered in trailing violet geraniums. The vast dark bulk of the cathedral towered over the little street. She drank her coffee, and listened to Eloise talk about her twenty-first birthday dance at Woking golf club, and all the smashing boys she'd danced with, although somehow they'd all got away, so here she was footloose and fancy-free, ha ha . . .

Bill said, 'Hey up, don't fall asleep.'

'Sorry,' said Lizzie, jerking her head back.

'And where did you get to last night then?'

'Last night?' she said, confused.

'I woke up and you were coming back to your tent, and I thought to myself that's funny but I didn't say anything.'

'That was very sensitive and discreet of you, Bill.'

'I'm known, love, for those very qualities.'

'It was so hot I slept in the church. You know the church, down in Dore valley? It was lovely and cool.'

'Happen tonight I'll come and join you.'

Oh, she thought, oh oh.

He was thickset with beefy thighs, a Yorkshire academic who said things like 'happen' and joshed heavily, and liked a bit of sexual innuendo. But he wasn't a fool, she thought, he wasn't a nerd like Gareth. He was looking at her carefully. 'Seriously, though,' he said, 'you shouldn't go down there on your own, not in the dark in your nightie. It's asking for trouble.'

'I had a very peculiar dream,' she said, ignoring his paternal concern.

'What sort of dream? I've heard girls have torrid lascivious dreams in hot weather.'

Eloise squeaked.

Lizzie said, 'Oh, for Christ's sake.'

'Well what, then?'

'If you must know I dreamed I was back in the Middle Ages. I was on a journey somewhere. I had a dream about the Middle Ages the night before as well. A dream about Dick Whittington.'

'What, thrice Lord Mayor of London Dick Whittington?'

It came back to her suddenly. He had been grieving for his friend, his dear friend Richard, lying dead in a cell somewhere in the north. 'But where in the north?' Whittington had asked, his eyes full of anguish, and she had shaken her head – which was strange, she reflected, because she knew perfectly well that Richard had died in Pomfret Castle.

Bill Hastings said, 'Oi, wake up. What was Dick Whittington doing in your dream then?'

'He was entering a cat food competition. Pussy likes to dine alfresco, on her Whiskas bought from Tesco. We ought to be getting back to the Land Rover,' she added, drinking up her coffee. 'We've come on this dig to work, remember?'

They were scraping through a stratum of blackened ash, the remains of buildings destroyed by fire – hoping to find fragments of broken pottery, carbonised grains of Iron Age wheat or barley.

Gareth, working next to her, said: 'Of course we can't expect much in the way of metal or bone. Not with acidic soil overlaying the red sandstone. I wonder if they took the acidic nature of the soil into account when they excavated in fifty-one?'

Sonia, who had been working on the topmost layer, said brightly, 'Yes, I wonder,' as if she actually did, then, abruptly: 'Hey, look at this.'

It was a pottery rosebud, almost like a mouth, filled with soil, half an inch long. They added it to their small tray of fragments.

'All right, you lot, let's call it a day,' called Bill Hastings, from further along the trench.

They stretched out under an awning and drank warm Coca-Cola while Venetia prepared supper. Gareth wanted to make a campfire, but nobody would let him because of the heat. Andrew sat by Lizzie, and she said politely, 'Did you have a nice morning shopping then?' and he said, 'Not really. I'm not happy in supermarkets. I worked at Safeway's for three summers on the trot.'

'What are you giving us for supper?'

'I'm not giving you anything. She bought it all. I was only the dogsbody.'

'Dogsbody, oh right.'

She turned and talked to Jacob about notable Wurzels concerts he had attended in Shepton Mallet.

Venetia called, 'Right, come and get it, you lot.'

She had bought Parma ham, smoked salmon, tiger prawns, cheeses, salad, and ciabatta rolls with unsalted butter. She had mixed a garlicky dressing. They ate, and everybody said, 'Jolly good, Venetia.' She said, 'Have some more wine, there's another two bottles of Chardonnay in the cold bag.'

Bill said, thoughtfully, 'That money I gave you.'

Venetia said, 'The grub allowance, yes?'

'I did say, I think, that it was supposed to buy food for three days?'

'I thought you just said grub allowance, actually. "Here's the grub allowance, pet," I think were your actual words.'

'The thing is, I don't see anything for tomorrow or the day after.'

'No, that's because there isn't anything.'

She took a mouthful of smoked salmon and prawns.

'Right, that's the last time Venetia does the shopping.'

'I'm so sorry,' said Venetia.

Darkness fell. Gareth lit the gas lamp. He said to Sonia, 'When we do the cooking we'll have a campfire.'

She said, 'Yes, Gareth.'

Bill said, 'OK, let's see what we found today.'

He opened a cardboard box and held something up in the light from the gas lamp. 'Well, come on, come on! What is it?'

Somebody said, 'It's a small pottery fragment.'

'Well yes, but. Anybody else? Come on, you found it, Sonia.'

A pause. Sonia said, 'It's a tit.'

Somebody sighed loudly. Sonia giggled in panic. 'Well that's what you told me it was – that's what you said when I gave it you.'

'It is indeed a tit,' said Bill. 'A pottery tit from a baby's feeding bottle. A small Roman baby drank from this. Several small Roman babies I wouldn't be surprised. Well, they didn't have plastic, did they, not in the first century AD? They couldn't munch on a Farley's rusk, either, for that matter.'

They went through the other finds. A small piece of blackened bone. A fragment of clay token bearing what might have been an ox-head motif. 'It's not enough to be certain,' said Bill, 'but clay objects with the Celtic ox-head sign were found in the mound at Croft

39

Ambrey. It's encouraging, that's all I'll say.'

'Is there any actual evidence,' said Jacob, 'that the ox head is the sign of the druids?'

'Is there any evidence,' said Venetia, 'that the druids ever even existed?'

'There's Pliny,' said Gareth. 'He called them "the Magi of the Gauls and Britons". And don't forget the bloodstained groves described in the account of Paulinus's attack on Anglesey in AD 60.'

'Thank you, Gareth,' said Venetia. They were only the second words she had spoken to him, the first having been, 'How do you do?'

'Or was it AD 61?' said Gareth. 'I wouldn't want to mislead you.'

Bill said, 'The druids existed all right. Before Rome and after Rome. They were the seers. They looked into the past, and into the future.'

There was a pause.

'I wonder what they saw?' said Eloise.

'Nothing good from their point of view.'

'Oh God,' sighed Venetia. 'It's just so hot . . .'

The sky was a vast bowl of indigo. The stars, as Lizzie lay on her back looking up, were drops of molten gold. She could hear Bill's voice . . . 'We're back to, what, 550 BC, about the time Danebury was being built in Wessex. The ramparts would have been a full metre higher than they are now but not to extensive . . .'

The stars were suddenly frosty. In her mind's eye came the picture of a small group of riders, and a man on foot, arriving at a monastery by the river. She could hear the bell tolling for vespers.

'Imagine this as a small plateau camp, just under two hectares . . .'

Lizzie sat up and said: 'Does anybody know anything about the franklin's tomb at the church of St Michael and All Saints?'

'Oh, Lizzie!' said Sonia, who was entwined in the darkness with Gareth.

Badger said, 'When you find a church called St Michael and All Saints it means it's an old church, an old foundation, renamed by the Saxons.'

Lizzie could see, on the far side of the gas hurricane lamp, Andrew looking curiously at her.

'I'm tired,' she said. 'I'm going to bed.'

*   *   *

It was gone midnight before Sonia's giggling goodnight kisses were over and she came creeping into the tent. Well, she'd got herself a bloke, she had reason to be content. She'd aimed herself on target, aware of her limitations, but also of her capabilities. Gareth was now trying to wear a roguish smirk as if he'd done the running, but nobody – not even Gareth – was deceived. Soon Sonia, a happy piglet, was gently snoring.

Lizzie lay listening to her heartbeat. She wondered if she was going to dream again about the Middle Ages. She wondered why the dreams kept coming back to her, during the day: why they had such a clarity – a reality – that made the actual world, the world of the dig, itself seem dreamlike.

She had caught Badger and Jacob – cornered them before supper, when they were guzzling from their little bottles of Ratarse ale. 'OK, which one of you's been putting magic mushrooms in the food? What was it, liberty caps?'

They denied it vigorously, but she wasn't convinced. Liberty caps were famously hallucinogenic – intensifying colours, sounds, emotions. 'Don't you dare do it ever again. Once the stuff's cooked it's a class A drug, remember.'

Badger had become quite angry and red in the face. Jacob had looked shocked.

One thing was for sure. There'd been no liberty caps in Venetia's tiger prawns or avocado mousse.

Perhaps that was why she was still lying awake. Why she wasn't dreaming.

Ah . . . there it was! A flute playing. Distantly. Sweetly.

Sonia gave a huge snore.

Shit!

She wanted to find out where they were journeying to – the man on the horse, the girl, and the page, and the man in rags.

She lay and listened for the boy's flute.

It was there, it was still there, but so far away.

She slithered out of her sleeping bag and crept out of the tent. Everyone was asleep. Soon she was hurrying down the path by the holly hedge. Under the trees the night was thick with insects and humidity. She didn't use her torch, not this time, she was safer in the dark and she knew her way, now, knew the lie of the land, the loom of the hedges; she was guided, too, by the sound of trickling water from Vortipor's Well. She felt her way down through the sticky warmth, into the small clearing.

She let herself into the church.

A faint, dim iridescence illuminated the vase of white lilies, and beyond them, the milky alabaster frieze below the franklin's tomb. The franklin himself was in darkness. The still, cool air smelled of ancient wood, of deathwatch beetle and must.

She lay down in her sleeping bag by the tomb. After a moment's hesitation she put out her hand to touch the cool alabaster flowers.

Immediately she could smell the blood, and the roses.

A moment of panic, then she breathed deeply.

'In a paternoster while,' whispered the page, ironically, 'we shall have our supper.'

7

Utah

It was evening, now, with long shadows falling from the Uinta Mountains. At the Dinosaur Diner the smell of charcoal-grilled meat and the sound of Mary Lou's siren voice enticed travellers to buy a barbecue supper, and maybe to stay overnight in the motel. Bluegrass Night was well under way. Each time a car drew into the car park Mary Lou looked out of the dusty window, hoping to see her fiancé's old Buick, not wanting to sing 'Stand By Your Man' before he was there to listen.

The sun went down, a blaze of apricot over the desert.

Mary Lou sang to her Bluegrass regulars: the sad, sentimental guys from the trailer park, the four old Indians from the Reservation, the lonely commercial travellers condemned to spend a night in northern Utah.

Koenig was grim and absorbed. He didn't notice when darkness fell beyond the grey-tinted windows of the transceiver room, a place with grey-carpeted walls that made them all think they were lunatics.

He sat hunched over his screen, refusing to believe that his options were exhausted.

He went and got himself a coffee from the machine.

Then he sat down and played the signal again.

He was watching a pattern of particles and relying on anti-virus software to throw up a warning if it found a stowaway. He was listening, over and over, to a pattern of sounds that he could not hope to understand, for no human voice could be conjured from these particles, these sub-electrons.

He was listening to sea surf in the quantum world, the way a blind man might listen to surf on the Pacific coast.

Other programme operatives sat along the two rows of screens. The building would normally have been empty but for a solitary duty technician. Tonight every terminal was manned, all treble-A *Pasi-phae* signals were being reviewed.

A young female technician, a kid from Chicago State, leaned back in her chair and said brightly: 'It may be I'm way out of line, but *Pasiphae*'s signal transmission system, with the axons insulated because of the impulse speed . . . you guys know what it reminds me of?'

Nobody replied.

'The positively charged ions? The use of the ionosphere to carry the electrical signals?'

She was new, still revelling in the wonder of it all.

'Well listen,' she said, 'you guys name for me a cell that contains potassium and sodium positive and chlorine negative.'

Silence. They were tired and aware that they were wasting their time.

A chopper landed outside, throwing up dust in the security lights. Maybe, thought Koenig, it was bringing sandwiches and French fries from Vernal or Fort Duchesne.

'OK,' said a technician flatly, 'tell us.'

A pause. She said, a touch hesitant now, 'Neurons?'

Silence, then another weary operative: 'Yeah, OK, *Pasiphae* receives and transmits like the human brain. What exactly are you saying?'

'Maybe it's picking things up somehow?'

'Jesus.'

'OK, but I guess there's a lot about the human brain that nobody understands.'

'Well that is perceptive. Yes sir, that is real perceptive.'

Koenig felt sorry for her.

Larry Sluder came striding in, a ball of fire. He'd spent the last eight hours on the phone, covering his back, protecting his ass, letting everybody know that he'd been at Caltech for over six months now, many a long mile from Utah. 'OK, has anybody found the source of infection?'

He didn't even like to use the word virus.

'Maybe it's the Navy?' – a technician, hopefully, wanting to go home. 'Maybe it was on the microwave link, maybe it's a virus in the equipment at their end.'

But they all knew it had come down, already corrupted, from *Pasiphae*. The quantum computer at Berkeley had found evidence nestling in the downlink transponder's log, an hour after the alert from Newport News.

The helicopter was from Pasadena. It brought Charles Pope, the English physicist who'd helped design *Pasiphae*'s quantum detector systems, the guy, next to Hollbecker, behind the whisper technology. Sluder brought him into the computer room, leading him straight down the thick blue-grey-carpeted corridor between the stations. 'I want you to meet John Koenig, our senior technician,' said Sluder loudly. 'Been at this game since, oh boy, since the first one-voice channel back in sixty, that right, John?'

He was talking about SCORE, the army's first low-altitude orbit device, and it hadn't been launched in 1960 but in '58, the year Bill Haley was crying 'See Ya Later Alligator', and Koenig was still at high school. How old for Christ's sake did Sluder think he was? But yes, it was true enough; he was an old hand. He'd been in the business before the girl from Chicago was even born. He'd been on the Telstar programme in '62 – at the launch party (some Brit instrumentalists called The Shadows) he'd got drunk, got laid, and soon after got married. They planned to have a little girl called Star ('Star Koenig, our very own little star that twinkles on earth,' said Virtue, his Tennessee wife) but the marriage had been childless.

'The one-voice channels? Really?'

It was Pope, the physicist. Middle-aged, polite but looking harassed.

'Yeah, really, really,' said Koenig, hostile, trying to imitate an English accent, though it was Sluder he was angry with. What sort of person-manager said 'Get your fat ass into here' to a guy who'd been in the game since '62, since the days when advanced telecommunications technology was no more than an aluminised plastic balloon floating sixteen hundred kilometres over Florida? To a man with his experience? Why, he'd become engaged to his second wife at the party for senior technical staff, *senior technical staff* on Intelsat I – two hundred and forty telephone circuits across the North Atlantic! They'd been right at the cutting edge, yes sir – 'bringing continents together' as Lyndon Johnson had said (making Koenig and his new wife Cindy feel it was all their doing). For Koenig, Intelsat I had been the peak. The high point. By the time of his second divorce, in 1989, Intelsat VI was carrying a hundred thousand conversations and it seemed technology, just like Koenig and the state of marriage, had nowhere left to go. But even then, in the corridors of Caltech, there had been talk of a small, secretive, Pentagon-funded communications technology unit, of a receiving station in Utah. Talk of *Pasiphae*. Technology, thought Koenig, would always find somewhere to go.

'So what do you think, John?'

It was the Englishman.

If he were honest, Koenig thought that a comms satellite ought to be just a platform in space, reflecting and relaying messages, encouraging understanding among nations, bringing continents together, possibly carrying Utah's bluegrass country music to the weary, hopeless, and morally bankrupt peoples of the world.

He said, 'It's something there, on the edge. It's not breaking up the signal, it's sort of attaching itself to it.'

'You know that?'

Sluder said, proudly, 'With this guy it's an instinct. I told you about this guy.'

There was the fuzziness that had registered sightlessly in his brain, a fuzziness he would have seen, truly seen, even with his eyes closed.

The Englishman was staring at his monitor, at the frozen green ribands of the quantum signal. He was thin, pallid-looking: he needed a good meal, he needed sustenance. Mary Lou – Koenig remembered Mary Lou, suddenly, with a stab in his heart – would have finished singing now, and would be serving up char-grilled Montana steaks and lemon chiffon pie with whipped cream. If this guy needed somewhere to stay the night he'd suggest the Dinosaur Diner: he might even take him there.

Sluder said, bright and energetic: 'Yeah, right. OK, John. There's something on the edge, and you're going to find it? By sun-up you reckon?'

It was a cue for Koenig to say, 'Sure will or my name ain't John Koenig.'

'Nope,' he said. 'No way.'

*   *   *

46

Pope had been in the British Airways club-class lounge at LA airport, his baggage already checked on to the aircraft, reading *The Times*, when the LAPD sergeant came in and said happily, 'Dr Pope? I got instructions to pull you off your flight even if it means driving out on the runway.'

Fifteen minutes later he was in an Air Force plane to Salt Lake City. When he should have been enjoying dinner over Kansas, a helicopter was carrying him up over the Wasatch ski slopes, then due east along the Strawberry River. 'Navy claim *Pasiphae*'s compromised' had been the brief message, relayed through the Pentagon's Intelligence and Security Command. He pondered it, disbelieving, as they crossed Starvation Lake and entered Indian country as darkness fell. The lights of small settlements appeared – Arcadia, Roosevelt – the small town of Vernal. Then, in a pool of inky blackness, he saw the illuminated H of the helipad at the receiving station. Beyond it – four or five miles beyond it – he was astonished to see what appeared to be a large brontosaurus, frozen and glowing green as it bounded across the desert night.

Sluder took him, now, to an office with a computer link to Pasadena. Pope no longer had the password, having checked off the program twenty-four hours previously: it took ten minutes to get himself re-accredited. He read that CIA diagnostic experts were sceptical: the disinfectant tools at their disposal were showing *no error no fault no infection*. He brought the coded Navy signal up on the screen and passed it through the anti-virus programs, through the quantum computer link via Berkeley.

Somebody brought in coffee and sandwiches.

An hour later one thing was clear. The signal had been read. Somewhere along the line, between its origination in Tokyo, its uplink to *Pasiphae*, its transmission to the HAARP ionospheric receiver over Alaska, and the ground station in Utah, it had been tampered with.

Somebody had opened it. Somebody had had a peek.

A quantum signal, a pattern of electrons, will *change its nature* once it has been read, once it has been observed. According to the quantum computer at Berkeley, the Navy signal had been observed.

But there was something more.

The observation had not – as Pope had hoped, sitting on the plane

47

to Salt Lake City, the chopper over the desert – been a freak occurrence, a harmless, one-in-a-million accident caused by a university physics department somewhere messing with particle waves and carelessly letting them loose into the atmosphere to read other people's private mail. There was, according to the Navy, an intrusion, a textual corruption.

Sluder came in with more coffee. He said, 'How are you doing?'

It was one a.m.

Pope said: 'In what way, exactly, was the signal changed?'

Sluder said: 'They don't want to tell us.'

'Ok, they don't want to tell us what was in the signal. I appreciate that, but the corruption, the alien element, how can that be a Navy secret?'

'When you say alien . . .' said Sluder, startled.

'Alien as opposed to known.'

Sluder looked relieved, then disappointed. He'd have been on coast-to-coast TV, he'd have been in the history books: Larry Sluder, the first man to receive a message from outer space, the first scientist on earth to be told: 'Greetings, Earthling'. But no, he thought, drinking his coffee, wondering how close he was to caffeine poisoning, some guy in Newport News would have got the credit. Perhaps that was why the Navy Department was being so secretive. Perhaps their signal from Tokyo said *Greetings from the Planet Og*.

He said, 'If an intruder's lurking in *Pasiphae* it's got to have a physical presence, right? A group of electrons, a cluster of particles? Maybe we just have to keep looking.'

Pope looked wearily at the screen. It was true that every action, every thought process, had to involve a chemical reaction of some kind: but they were still using four-dimensional, late twentieth century technology to try to solve problems in the quantum world which had twenty-six dimensions. He said, 'Maybe, in theory, I ought to be able to find an infection in a signal without reading it *en clair*, but it is not helpful, it does not make things easy.'

Sluder said: 'OK. I'll get on to the Navy.'

He went. Pope drank his coffee and ran a further series of tests on the coded signal. He was wasting his time. Outside, another helicopter came down; or perhaps it was the same helicopter, ferrying its way back and forth to Salt Lake City.

48

At three in the morning he went outside for a breath of air – air that hadn't been recycled dehumidified and filtered twenty times. There was a ridge of mountains to the east, a long black monster against the night. Desert stretched to the south. Somewhere, out there, was the Green River. This was Indian country – cowboy country. Huge open spaces, less than two million people in the whole state of Utah. Salt Lake City, with its streets wide enough for a horse and wagon to make a full circle.

He leaned against the compound wall. There was a pale, watery moon. He watched spindle grass blowing slowly across the desert. He'd spent three years commuting between Oxford and Berkeley, so that they had merged into one place: hi-tech laboratories, dreaming grey spires with orange trees. This, he thought, was the real West. He pictured wagon trains coming down the track by the Green River, down Desolation Canyon. He pictured the Indian scouts on their ponies, seen by wagon-train kids as dawn came over the high mesas, the children crying 'Momma, Momma!' as the Apache war drums started and the trail master cried 'Move 'em on! Move 'em on!'

It all came, he reflected, from a childhood in north London, watching *Wagon Train* on TV.

Sluder came out. He had with him a woman who had arrived on the helicopter. Her name was Martha Crawfurd, and she was with the National Security Agency. Pope guessed that she was in her late twenties. Sluder lit a cigarette. 'The HAARP,' he said, 'is suspect number one. We're still in unknown territory with that thing.'

HAARP was the High Frequency Active Aural Research Programme. From two sites in Alaska it bombarded the upper atmosphere with high-frequency radio beams, turning the ionosphere into a vast antenna of super-heated electrons. The HAARP not so much received as *folded into itself* the signals from *Pasiphae*, before shooting them down the high-frequency tube to the Alaskan ground stations.

Pope said, 'I doubt if it's anything to do with HAARP. The HAARP's a glorified energy conductor, its technology is actually very simple.'

'Yeah, well what else? C'mon, Charlie. There is no nation on Earth within five years of *Pasiphae*'s quantum technology, right?'

'I'm not in intelligence.'

49

'Oh come on, Charlie, *come on*.'

Sluder was acting strong; a man of energy even at three-thirty in the morning, out to impress the blonde from the NSA.

'No. Nobody's close.'

'Great Britain?'

'Great Britain?' said Pope. 'You've not noticed that I'm English, not noticed my being here, Larry?'

'You guys sell secrets, right?' Sluder insisted, winding him up to no apparent purpose. 'Pinkos? Cambridge homosexuals? Queers?'

Outside of California, Pope reminded himself, the American West was not a place with a pronounced liberal tradition.

Sluder turned to the woman for confirmation. She smiled faintly and shrugged, or maybe shivered. A cold night wind flowed down from the mountains. Overhead, a red light winked – a plane heading towards some airfield not marked on any map outside the Pentagon or the KGB's Frunzenskaja Embankment in Moscow.

This was no longer cowboy country, Pope told himself wryly. South, where the Green River ran down to the Colorado, there were more hi-tech military installations than cactus plants.

'All I'm saying is that England,' said Sluder, dogged, determined to involve the girl from the NSA, 'is not famously secure.'

She said, 'Larry, this is all published stuff. It's been in the magazines. Everybody knows about Aurora but they can't build a spy plane like it because they don't have the technology and they don't have the incentive. What would the Chinese want with a spy plane that costs half the Gross National Income? Why would they want to spend five billion dollars on a quantum communications network when they don't even have digital telephones?'

'Sweetheart, they just *want*. They don't need, they just *want*. Banana Republic presidents with personal jets bigger than Airforce One.'

'I can only tell you my instinct,' said Pope, 'but I don't believe that *Pasiphae* is being infiltrated by a foreign power.'

'Listen,' said Sluder, 'if somebody, anybody, is penetrating *Pasiphae* we are dead men. You understand me?'

Well, no. Not unless Sluder was saying his career might downsize itself, with a few billion dollars of research wiped out, but it was only money.

50

A programme operative came out. '*Deus ex machina*,' she said, exhausted.

But Pope knew there was no ghost in the machine.

The operative looked as though she ought to have been still at school. She said confidently, 'There's nothing we can get hold of. John Koenig's the only one still trying. Listen, you don't think the machine could have picked up something from, well, the brain of an operator? The guy at Newport News maybe? I know this sounds crazy,' she went on rapidly, not giving them the chance to say how crazy it was, 'but you think how neurons receive and transmit information, the way they have the capability of producing a nerve impulse, then, well, just think of *Pasiphae*'s system of transmitting electrical impulses—'

'Jesus,' said Sluder, laughing suddenly. 'A brainwave. She's had a brainwave, get it?'

'Well I'm sorry, it's just an idea—'

'A brainwave, kid, even in beta activity cannot transmit higher than fourteen hertz per second, while *Pasiphae* uses frequency bands around two thousand megahertz, you follow me, *megahertz*—'

'But if the guy's linked to the machine, the machine in front of him—'

'Leave the science to the scientists, OK, honey?'

She stood pale in the moonlight. She was only six months out of college.

'It's a theory,' said Pope. 'Thanks.'

Sluder said, 'Jesus, crank ideas from amateurs we do not need.'

'Listen, asshole,' the girl said, suddenly, 'I've got a first-class physics degree from Chicago State—'

'I don't care if you've got the fucking Newton Prize—'

'OK, OK, Larry, let's calm down,' said the girl from the NSA.

Pope went back inside. The air of urgency in the signal receiving room was dissipated. No other faults had been reported: *Pasiphae* signals were being downlinked from Alaska and were being passed to clients and were getting the OK from disinfectant and anti-intrusion programs. Newport News was quiet, or quiescent. Nobody in Washington was going ape. It was four a.m.

He got himself a coffee.

Infection from the brain of a computer technician . . . Dear God, if that was the answer . . .

The current scientific model wouldn't have it – *brainwaves are strictly located in the brain and communicate with other brainwaves only through the five senses* – but quantum mechanics was outside and beyond the current scientific model. Psychiatrists at Southampton University, he remembered, were carrying out experiments on extrasensory perception that turned Newtonian physics inside out. Penrose, at Oxford, believed there was quantum activity in microtubules, minute structures once thought of as simple scaffolding for brain cells.

The long, grey room was dark and almost empty. Only John Koenig was still at his station. His face looked grey-green in the reflection from his screen. His hand was on his pad but was not moving. Pope, who had forgotten Koenig's name, called out, awkwardly: 'You all right, then?'

Koenig did not reply. Pope went down the aisle towards him. 'I think maybe it's time you took a break . . .'

Koenig's eyes were staring at the screen. They were unblinking, and there was the wet glisten of tears on his cheeks.

On his pad, in the flickering light from the screen, was written: *Missile strike Wilcox.*

Also on the pad, written in a different, spider-like hand, were the words: CRIMEN LEFÆ MAJEFTATIS.

Sluder appeared in the far doorway.

'The chopper goes in five minutes. They're calling a conference at Berkeley at noon. Hey, don't tell me Koenig's come up with something. You found something, John? What did I tell you? This is our number one guy . . .'

Sweat poured through Koenig's glands, a pulse raced on his forehead. Pope swung him round, looked at his eyes. He passed his hand in front of Koenig's face.

'Lights,' he said.

Sluder said 'Shit', hurried to the wall and pressed a switch. Fluorescent lights plunged the outside world, smudgy grey in the dawn, back into blackness.

Sluder said, 'You think he's had a stroke?'

Koenig's pupils were pinpricks. The eye is a camera, thought Pope, with a retina instead of film. What image had Koenig's retina sent down his optic nerve?

He shook his head. He was being stupid – exhaustion fighting adrenalin: Koenig had seen nothing visually. The image, the information, whatever it was, had been passed intuitively.

'Hey John boy, John boy,' said Sluder, returning and peering into Koenig's pouchy face. 'You have any idea of this man's diet?' he asked, sadly. 'You any idea of the stuff this man eats? Two broken marriages, a broken-down trailer home next to an Indian Reservation and boy, comfort eating takes on a whole new meaning. There was no way this was not going to happen.'

'Is there a doctor on site?'

'Vernal. I'll tell the pilot.'

He turned and went. The agent from the NSA, Martha Crawfurd, came in, looked at Koenig for a shocked moment then quickly called up first aid on a screen. She said, 'Numbness of the face or limbs? Loss of speech or comprehension? Loss of vision?'

Pope said, 'All three.'

'It's either a blockage in blood flow or maybe he's suffering a haemorrhage of blood vessels in the brain. It says don't do anything except keep him warm and get him hospitalised fast.'

Two men from security came in with blankets. They carried Koenig out. Pope followed them, vaguely feeling that having found Koenig he had some sort of responsibility to see him safely hospitalised. Martha Crawfurd, now on the phone to Washington, waiting to be connected, watched through the tinted windows as they lifted his ungainly bulk into the helicopter. It rose in a flurry of red dust. Koenig's notes were in front of her.

Missile strike Wilcox.

CRIMEN LEFÆ MAJEFTATIS.

She tore the page quickly from the pad.

Then she tore up the pad itself.

She found Pope outside, watching the sun rise over the Colorado Mountains. She said, 'Where's Sluder?'

Pope shook his head.

'Listen.' She looked round, lowered her voice. 'He's not exactly – how do I put it – out of things from now on, but any theory you come up with you tell me, OK?'

'OK. You saw what he'd written on his pad?'

'Yes, and we're assuming Wilcox to be Wilcox Army Base in Arizona, near Fort Huachuca. You know what's at Wilcox?'

'No.'

'Nor should you. I'm running a check on Koenig but he's got to have full clearance to be working here. Nobody understands the second part of the message. *Crimen* is Latin, it's where the English word crime comes from. Perhaps it's nothing to do with the Navy signal.'

'*Crimen lesæ majestatis*,' said Pope, an Oxford man, 'is just an old-fashioned way of saying treason.'

8

Dore

She woke in the night – in the hour of lauds, in the deep darkness, the time of the monks' first morning praises. A bird had got in through an open window of the church and was batting against the panes, trying to escape. She lay in her sleeping bag wondering how she could help it, but before she could move her dream, her interrupted dream, dragged her back into its warm black folds. 'He that doth abjure the realm,' she murmured, her mottled, chilled hand coiling itself back round the alabaster flowers, 'he that doth abjure the realm must have upon him but his coat, his shirt, and his breeches, and his head shall be uncovered, and he must carry a cross in his hand . . .'

It was six o'clock when she opened her eyes again. The sun was bathing the franklin's tomb in hues of rose and deep purple. From outside there came the sound of pigeons, and the soft gurgle of water from the stream.

'A cross in his hand which is a token,' she whispered, 'that his life is saved by religion.'

She remembered it clearly.

She had been in a forest of scrub, soaked to the skin and freezing. She could feel, even now, the sodden cloak heavy on her shoulders, her pelisse clinging wet to her body, and her wrists and thighs raw from chafing. She had tried to give the monkey to the boy, but it had clung to her, screaming, and its claw-like nails had drawn a ribbon of blood across her neck. Under bare trees, crouched panting in dead bracken, had been an abjurer – thin, bony, starving – and his two stout keepers. The boy had asked the abjurer to describe his crime and the man – looking for alms – had replied, 'Ravishment, though she was content, and was indeed with child' – and he would have told his story (the page and the ragged servant were eager to listen), but the man on the horse would not stop – it was almost the hour of none, the weather was filthy, and there were high hills still between them and Oxford.

'They that abjure the realm so long as they be in the highway shall be in the King's Peace and be troubled by no man!' a keeper had cried. But cottagers had appeared through the drizzle and stoned the abjurer, all the same.

She remembered the bright blood that spilled over the wet bracken. She remembered the man on the horse shouting: 'Come, my lady!' – his sharp, anxious eyes always on the track behind them, as if fearing pursuit.

She stood up. She looked down at the effigy of the franklin.

She put her hand, softly, against his cheek; ran her fingers over his chipped, plaster eyes.

'Bill? Bill, can I go into Hereford?'

He turned round, ready to say no, she bloody well couldn't, but saw her thin, eager face; saw her awkwardness. Amazing himself, he said, 'You can go with Jacob and do the shopping.'

She smiled. 'Thanks, Bill.'

'But be back by dinnertime,' he said, making his eyes bulge, 'or else.'

He watched her run across to Jacob. She'd been and slept down in the church again, by herself, which was damned stupid: at least she said she'd slept in the church, and she certainly hadn't slept in the tent with daft Sonia, as daft Sonia had told everybody several times over their breakfast porridge.

He would have to do something about it, but he wasn't sure what.

They went to Sainsbury's and bought food, and ate a Sainsbury's cooked breakfast. She listened to Jacob denying – at length and with quiet indignation – that he had ever put magic mushrooms into anybody's spaghetti Bolognese. 'Did anybody act as if we'd put magic mushrooms in the spaghetti Bolognese?' he kept saying. 'Did anybody freak out?' She told him that she believed him. 'I'm sorry, Jacob,' she said humbly, and he looked surprised.

They drove into the city, past little shops with newspaper bill-boards saying 'New drought order shock' and handwritten notices saying that they'd run out of ice cream. Jacob went to W. H. Smith's to look at railway magazines, and she went to the museum and library. She spent an hour reading up on the deposition of King Richard II, and the reign of Henry IV, then went in search of Mrs Ifor-Williams, whom she found sitting behind her polished Victorian mahogany desk.

'Ah, now, my lovely,' said Mrs Ifor-Williams, 'here's a question. If, in 1940, you needed threepence to buy what a farthing would have bought you in 1279, what would you need now, to buy what threepence would have bought you in 1940?'

'I don't know,' said Lizzie, honestly.

'Well, let's say you could get a loaf of bread for threepence in 1940. How much is a loaf of bread today?'

'I have absolutely no idea.'

Mrs Ifor-Williams looked at Lizzie sadly. She said, 'You girls.'

'Nobody in the flat seems to eat toast for breakfast.' (On his visits Malcolm had said, youthfully, 'Breakfast? What on earth is breakfast? Christ, give me a fag . . .')

'Well, never mind. I only ask you because the murage grants of 1279 allowed the city of Hereford to impose a sales tax to pay for the upkeep of the town walls. One farthing, it was, on five shillings' worth of goods. That was the price they had to pay to keep drunk Welshmen from coming on motorbikes and being sick in the Rowe Ditch.'

'If you don't mind my saying so,' said Lizzie. 'Ifor-Williams is not a very English name.'

'Marry in haste,' said Mrs Ifor-Williams, 'repent at leisure.'

'You were wrong about Shrewsbury Fight. I've just been looking it up. Glyn Dŵr wasn't even there. It was Harry Hotspur who was killed. His body was chopped up and sent all over the kingdom, and his head stuck up on the Micklegate at York.'

'So die all traitors,' said Mrs Ifor-Williams.

'I wondered if you'd found the pamphlet, yet, about the Franklin of Dore?'

Mrs Ifor-Williams shook her head. 'I had a quick look yesterday, but it would take a month to go through all those boxes. I asked Mr Hewlett – he's a retired librarian – about it, but he couldn't remember anything. To be honest, he couldn't remember what day it was, although he said there was a little old lady in Hay who remembered a story told about the franklin, a story passed down by word of mouth through many generations.'

'Perhaps she could pass it to me. Do you have her name?'

'No, and anyway she'll be long dead.'

'Perhaps she told the story to her children or grandchildren, passed it to another generation?'

'They've all got television sets. They have no need to pass stories down. The old grandma says "Hist, hist to a tale of Owain of the Shining Helm" and the grandkiddies shout "Shut it, Grandma, we're watching *Home and Away*".'

'So all the old tales are dying,' said Lizzie. 'True tales, passed down through ten or more generations, just dying.'

'For the most part they're dead. Your best bet is Dr Emlyn Dyson-Jones of the Medieval History Society. He knows more about the old village of Dore than anybody. If you'll wait a moment I'll write down his telephone number.'

'I've been having dreams,' said Lizzie, suddenly, 'about the franklin.'

'Dreams,' said Mrs Ifor-Williams, writing down a number and passing it across the desk, 'are very mysterious things. There are things about dreams that few people understand.'

'There was an abjurer in it. But I'm not sure what abjurer is.'

'An abjurer was a criminal who repented, turned to God, and whose life was spared on condition that he left the king's realm.'

'This one was a rapist. Though he might have been a felon as well. He denied the rape, because, he said, the woman was pregnant.'

'It was for centuries the law of England,' said Mrs Ifor-Williams, 'that only a woman who consented to intercourse could conceive a child.'

'Dear God,' said Lizzie.

'Come back at four o'clock, when we've loaded the library van, and I'll help you look it up.'

'I can't. I've got to get back to the dig. We've got a ferocious team leader. I'm only here because Jacob and I are buying food, but we've promised to be back by lunchtime and I don't suppose he'll let me come back to Hereford for ages.'

'Well never mind,' said Mrs Ifor-Williams, looking at Lizzie interestedly. 'Perhaps you'll have had another dream by then. Be sure and come to me if you need help. Help of any kind,' she added, with slight emphasis.

'You're a very unusual librarian, Mrs Ifor-Williams, if you don't mind my saying so.'

'I'm just an old hippy,' said Mrs Ifor-Williams, 'who lost her way. How is the dig doing? Have you found the cannibal bones yet?'

'To be honest, we haven't found anything much.'

But that afternoon their luck changed.

First Sonia's trowel teased stones from the compacted earth and came across something black and flaking, about fifteen centimetres long. It was not something the British Museum would want to put on display, but it was still the undeniable remains of an Iron Age sword.

'It's unbelievable!' Sonia cried. 'First the Roman baby bottle and now this – and I only took over this section of the trench from Eloise two minutes ago. If you'd stayed here another two minutes you'd have been the one to find it, wouldn't you, Eloise?'

'Yes,' said Eloise, dumbly.

'I'm lucky, oh my God I'm lucky!'

'Well done, Sonia,' said everybody.

'I mean, for God's sake, Eloise worked on this section for three hours this morning and found nothing!'

'We work as a team, and we take joint credit,' said Bill Hastings, examining the fragment of sword. 'It doesn't make a fart's worth of difference whose trowel actually turns things up.'

Later, just before they stopped work, Lizzie's trowel encountered a curved shape. She took up a dental pick and gently scraped away the black soil. The curve revealed itself as the top of a pottery jar. She said, quietly, 'Look what I've found,' and Andrew came across and leaned over her shoulder, and watched as she teased away the compacted earth of two and a half thousand years.

'What level is it?' said Venetia, also peering over her shoulder.

'Iron Age A, around 700 BC,' said Lizzie, a constriction in her throat, for this was her first real find in four years as a student archaeologist: this was the first time her trowel had ever encountered anything other than pottery shards, carbonised sheep droppings, or bits of charred bone.

'Careful . . .' murmured Andrew.

What was revealed was four centimetres across. A pottery jug, perhaps – too early to tell. What if it proved to be Roman? That would foul things up, that would put Bill Hastings's calculations into chaos – a Roman jug a thousand years before its time. She scraped away, but gently, oh so gently, slowly revealing the curve of the side of the vessel.

'Is it decorated? I think it is . . . yes, look . . .'

'What's up?'

It was Sonia, from the other trench, her voice suspicious, her lucky-person's antennae on maximum alert.

'Nothing,' Andrew called back.

The mouth of the jug was revealed now, full of soil, hard and compacted. The side of the vessel was ten, fifteen centimetres long. Would it prove to be whole, entire? Lizzie delicately scraped at it with the dental tool, Venetia brushed away the soil with a soft paint-brush. The smooth, hard pot surface gave way to soil. It was not whole, not entire. The Second Law of Thermodynamics was in operation: disorder increases with time. In his search for perfect artefacts, the archaeologist was challenging one of the basic physical laws of the universe. She felt a stab of disappointment.

Andrew said, 'Just because it's broken doesn't mean the pieces aren't all here. And whatever it contained might still be here.'

Venetia said, 'I'll get a torch.'

'No,' said Bill Hastings, who had joined them. 'No, leave it. It's going to be too risky to mess about by torchlight.'

That night she lay down to sleep in the open, with the others. She lay, for perhaps an hour, in a half-world, then drifted to sleep. She dreamed not of the franklin, but of Celtic tokens: of early La Tène bronze brooches; of priceless gold necklaces hastily buried as the entrance to the fort was breached by the Roman legions: of the king's druids digging a pit to the sound of Celtic slingstones rattling on the shields of the legionaries: of the Celtic queen, perhaps, urging them to hurry – of spades hacking down through the strata, of hands reaching down to lay the treasure in its pot container.

She surfaced, briefly, in the hour before dawn, then slipped back into a sleep that was dreamless.

* * *

'It is,' said Bill, 'very nice, very nice indeed.'

The mouth and side of the jug were sharp and black in the morning light. 'Handmade, crumbly even when it first came out of the kiln. Scrape a bit further . . . can you see the pattern? Can you make it out?'

Lizzie scraped gently. Ten minutes later she was able to lift it: the complete mouth, still full of earth, the rounded side, part of the base.

There was no glint of gold, no sign of treasure.

There was a pattern on the clay, running round the rim.

Ducks.

Ducks swimming. The Willow Pattern of the Iron Age – to be found in every Celtic lord's hall from Iona to Brittany, but most often found in the midlands of Britain. 'What pattern on thy pots, my liege?' asked the trembling, eager artist, hoping for something new, something different, but the king always replied: 'Oh, the ducks, the ducks.'

Bill said, 'Early Iron Age, which confirms what we expect from that level. It's a pity there isn't more of it, but it's a very useful find.'

Lizzie looked at it sadly.

'Bill?' she asked.

'What?'

'Can I go to Hereford again?'

'Oh bloody hell, no . . .'

'Well I want to go,' said Venetia, firmly. 'It just isn't on, working through the middle of the day. It makes me feel sick, positively sick, and anyway there's things I have to get.'

'What things?'

'Fucking tampons, right?'

'Bloody hell, bloody hell . . .' Bill muttered, shambling off as fast as he could, calling for coffee and shouting like a bear because somebody had eaten all the Kellogg's Frosties.

'The Church of St Michael and All Saints, yes, yes, of course, a truly lovely church, up on the hillside under Vortipor's Fort,' said Dr Emlyn Dyson-Jones, on his knees, scrabbling through a box file, producing a leaflet. 'Here we are. The church with the franklin's tomb.'

'Do you have any idea who he was?'

'None at all, but I can tell you that there are only three other churches—'

'In all England with tomb effigies of franklins, yes. Mrs Ifor-Williams gave me your name. She thought you might be able to help me.'

'Ah, Mrs Ifor-Williams,' said Dr Dyson-Jones, a note of cold steel entering his voice.

'She was very helpful.'

'Oh yes indeed,' he said, 'I've known Mrs Ifor-Williams many a long year.'

He was a widower, retired. He lived in a gloomy, semi-detached Victorian villa. His study had once been his surgery, and still had cream walls, utilitarian shelves, and an institutional feel to it. He sat her down on a hard, black leather couch, and fussed round looking things up. Suddenly he cocked his ear like a terrier and darted to the window. Down the path, beyond the thick flowering-currant bushes and the strip of neat lawn, Venetia Peel sat in her red BMW convertible listening to her CD player.

'I'm sorry, I'll go and tell her to turn it off—'

'No, no, she'll damage her eardrums irreversibly, but no matter, she'll be in company with half her generation. You'll know all about Vortipor's Fort, nothing I can tell you about that, obviously.'

'We don't really believe that it ever was Vortipor's Fort, not really,' said Lizzie. 'As archaeologists we wouldn't put our seal of approval on a sign saying "Vortipor slept here".'

Dr Dyson-Jones was on his knees again, rootling along a low dusty shelf. 'There was a battle at the fort,' he said, 'in which King Vortipor, who was in all probability the real and only true King Arthur, defeated the bastard Saxons. King Vortipor was a Welshman and patriot, and if Mrs Ifor-Williams told you that old chestnut about his throne being stained top to bottom with murders and adulteries, or his having raped his daughter or having been the tyrant of the Demetae—'

'Surely it was Gildas who called him the tyrant of the Demetae?'

'His tomb calls him Vortipor the Protector, and you may see it still where it stands at Castelldwyran, and I have no interest in Saxon black propaganda but only amazement that it should still be being spread about, and disgust that folk like Mrs Ifor-Williams, who are employed in a public library, should have such little regard for the truth as to abuse their position of trust.'

'Yeah, right,' said Lizzie, a pilgrim on a quest who was suddenly in the middle of somebody else's war.

'Still, let us not stray into areas of controversy.' He stood up, holding a volume. 'The first mention we have of Dore is, of course, Domesday. "The Prior of St Mary's, Worcester, holds Dore. Guy de Ferester holds it of him. There are fourteen hides. There are four plough lands in demesne with eight serfs. In the time of King Edward it was worth eighty shillings" – and I think there's something from later. Yes, here we are. A manuscript of 1254, which details the services due for a villein on the manor of Dore. "Toll for each horse born to him, should it be sold within the manor, one penny and for an ox, and for a pig over a year old one penny, and of less age halfpenny, but it may not be a sucking pig." Goodness, but this is fascinating stuff!'

'Yes,' said Lizzie. 'But about the franklin in the church—'

'The villein could not sell pork from the Feast of St Peter in Chains to that of St Andrew without leave of the lord and, would you believe, he owed ale-making for the lord's cellar? This is what illuminates the past. What care we for kings in marble halls, what care we for dukes and princes? This is the stuff of history – the day-to-day life of a villein in a Herefordshire village – this is what makes history live and breathe!'

'But it's not getting me very far towards the franklin.'

'Patience is a virtue,' said Dr Dyson-Jones, who had been a widower for a decade, and was a lonely man. 'The next mention of Dore, after 1254, is the lay subsidy roll of 1332 which paints a picture for us from the years directly before the Black Death. We're a generation away from your franklin – two generations, maybe, because the first one was pretty well wiped out in mid-century.'

Outside, the music suddenly swelled. Venetia was getting bored, she wanted to be at her leisure centre.

'Here we are. The lay subsidy roll of 1332. Though it's a dangerous guide, because it is a tax return only, and cannot tell us about those who avoided paying tax or were too poor to be taxed. In 1332, you remember, the young Edward III had seized power from his mother Isabella and had hanged Mortimer – a sorry event for this part of the world, the Mortimers were ever Lords of the Marches – and had to raise money to beat the Scots and avenge Bannockburn.'

Lizzie wondered how she could escape.

'The total tax paid by the twenty-three taxpayers of the village of Dore was three pounds and tenpence, an average of two and seven per person taxed. Now, if we go to 1344 – closer and closer, you see, to your franklin, why, he could have been alive at the time – we find the system of collection changed . . .'

Lizzie stood up. 'I'm afraid I really have to—'

He waved her back down again. 'Villages were required to pay a certain amount – four pounds eleven shillings for Dore – and details of the levy were left to the villages themselves to decide. Now the fascinating thing about the 1344 assessment is that it was exactly the same fifty years later, after the Black Death, when the nuns of Dore were appealing, on behalf of the villagers, against the levy of four pounds eleven shillings on the grounds that there were not enough inhabitants to pay—'

Lizzie said, 'I'm sorry?'

'The Black Death by then had spread north from Bristol—'

'Did you say the nuns of Dore?'

'Indeed. There was a small community at Dore in the late fourteenth century, though nobody knows how, or why, it was established. It did not fall under the aegis of the bishop of Hereford, although he claimed pastoral jurisdiction; it was certainly gone by 1405, and the belief is that . . .'

Take her to Dore! Take her to the nuns at Dore!

Dr Dyson-Jones put out his hand and felt her arm.

'Sit down,' he said, abruptly. 'Slowly. Here, let me help you.'

He took her pulse. He took a stethoscope from a drawer of his desk and listened to her heartbeat. Then he left the room. She sat with her eyes closed. The sounds of heavy rock came from outside. The music cut suddenly and she opened her eyes in panic – but she was still in the room, in the old surgery.

A moment later Venetia was looking down at her anxiously.

'Are you all right? Oh, Lizzie, you look awful.'

'I think it was the heat.'

Dr Dyson-Jones came in bearing a tray with a paper doily, two cups of tea and a plate of biscuits. He looked cheerful: it was turning into an eventful, interesting day.

Lizzie said, 'I'm sorry.'

Venetia said, 'What happened?'

'I felt giddy, that's all.'

Dr Dyson-Jones said, 'Your skin was blue. You were as cold as ice. For a couple of seconds you seemed to be having a fit of some kind. Have you any history of epilepsy?'

'No.'

'Your family? Has anyone in your family suffered from fits?'

'Not that I know of. I'm sure it was just the heat. I haven't been eating very much. I haven't had anything all day.'

'Well, you must go and see your doctor and tell him what happened. If he wishes to speak to me, you must give him my number.'

9

Herefordshire

They took the Abergavenny road, then forked right to Vowchurch. Venetia drove quickly and skilfully. Next to her Lizzie sat back with her eyes closed, her fine, gold hair blowing about her face. She was a funny girl, Venetia thought, glancing at her: shy, according to Bill Hastings; snooty, according to Gareth and Sonia. Flitting off at night to commune with nature. Andrew was obviously crazy about her.

Lizzie's eyes opened. She said suddenly, 'Do we have to go straight back?'

'No, of course not. The longer we stay away the better. We probably won't escape again for a week.'

They bought a bottle of chilled Malvern water from the shop in Peterchurch, and drove to the old motte-and-bailey castle at Dore, and walked up the hillside a little way to sit in an orchard.

The heat beat down. The humidity. Cows were lying in the shade of a hedge, looking as though they would never move again. Venetia felt thunderbugs crawl across her scalp. 'How are you enjoying the dig?' she asked. 'I was going to the Andes, but it got called off, and my bloody professor said I had to go somewhere. I nearly packed it in the day after we arrived, when Gareth started playing "I spy", but I don't know, Bill's got something about him, hasn't he? Something a bit different? Anyway, I suppose you want to spill the beans and tell me all about the mysterious guys who're blackmailing you, and make you go down to the church at midnight to hand over the loot, even though you keep telling them you haven't got it.'

'What?'

'That's Gareth's theory. Eloise thinks you have assignations with a man.'

Lizzie drank from the water bottle. She said, 'I've been having dreams.' She paused, looking down the valley, at the grass knoll of the old Norman castle, the winding lane with its high hedgerows. 'Not ordinary dreams.'

She looked quickly at Venetia, then looked away. 'I seem to be, well, called to the church. Summoned.'

Venetia stared at her.

'I'm in the Middle Ages. There's a girl travelling with a franklin, travelling to a nunnery here at Dore. Today, Dr Dyson-Jones told me that there really was a nunnery here in the late fourteenth century.'

'Is that why you went into shock?'

Lizzie nodded.

Venetia lay back on the burnt grass. She looked up through the dappled leaves. The branches were full of small golden-yellow plums, ripe before their time.

'You might have read it somewhere,' she said. 'You're a history graduate.'

'I have never, ever read anything about medieval Dore. Do you believe in reincarnation? Do you think I could have been the girl – the girl with the franklin? Not that she liked him much. Reincarnation isn't exactly way out as a concept, is it? There's hundreds of millions of people who believe in it. I was talking to Eloise about it in the pub and she believes in it totally. There are a lot of false reincarnations, apparently. If somebody says: "I'm the reincarnation of a woman who lived in Thebes in the reign of Rameses II" you know she's fantasising because Thebes wasn't called Thebes then, it was called Waset, and the Egyptians never thought to call their kings by numbers. What do you think?'

Venetia sat up. She said, after a moment, 'I don't think you ought to sleep in the church again.'

'Why not? If I don't sleep there how will I ever find out what happened?'

'What happened?'

'To the franklin. To the franklin and the girl.'

There was a pause.

'Well?'

'I think,' said Venetia, carefully, 'that you were right the first time. When you said it was the heat.'

'Venetia, have you been listening at all? I dreamed the franklin was bringing a girl to the nunnery at Dore – and before that I dreamed

I was in London, in January 1400. Venetia, I can describe to you exactly what people were doing in London in January 1400, I can tell you what they were selling in the shops – there was a man put in the stocks in Cheapside for selling rotten fish, and the fish was burned under his nose.'

Venetia said, 'Maybe it's sex.'

'What?'

'Maybe you're dreaming about sex. The franklin and this girl – you said she doesn't like him much. Why did you say that? What does that have to do with anything? He fancies you but you don't fancy him, but even so you're in his power—'

'Oh, Christ, Venetia—'

'You're in his power and he's taking you somewhere. You don't like him, but you're drawn towards him, you can't resist him, you're just waiting to be taken by him, physically taken, if you understand me . . .'

She was thinking, thought Lizzie wearily, about herself and Bill Hastings.

'Venetia, I have just discovered that there really was a nunnery at Dore, at exactly the same time in history that I dreamed about it. That is mind-boggling.'

'I still think you could have read about it.'

'Where? Where?'

'Well I don't know, do I? A book about nunneries.'

'No way did I read the kind of stuff I'm dreaming!'

Venetia said, 'OK, OK, so you're reincarnated.'

Below them, beyond the knoll of the old castle, were four detached houses – built in the Seventies by the look of them, before the planning regulations tightened up. They had back gardens that were neat and trim, well equipped with patios and barbecue pits. A keen gardener lived in the end house. He kept coming out and looking at his rows of wilting brassicas, his poor, sad cabbage and cauliflower, and then he looked craftily at Venetia and Lizzie in the old fruit orchard: he wanted to water his vegetables, but thought they might be spies from the water company.

Venetia went on, 'But if it is reincarnation, does it work like that? I mean, does a soul, or whatever, hang about in limbo for five centuries before being allocated to another body?'

'There's some confusion, actually, on that point. Some hypnotists – you've heard of hypnotic regression? – say that the change from death to new conception is instantaneous, and happens within a close physical radius, so that the person, the personality, the soul or whatever, leaves the body and is immediately, or almost immediately, reborn in a baby nearby. Other hypnotists find that they can unearth half a dozen past lives in the people being hypnotised – their past lives can include incarnations in the Iron Age, then ancient Greece, all the way through to, I don't know, the American Civil War.'

'I suppose that's more logical. There are always more people being born than there are people dying. I don't see how there can ever be enough reincarnated souls to go round unless they plunder the past. I wonder when the last new baby was born that didn't have a second-hand soul?'

'You don't believe in it,' said Lizzie, 'do you?'

'No.'

'Why not?'

'Because,' said Venetia, after a moment's thought, 'it's a load of bollocks.'

'Well, what then? Give me an answer.'

Venetia stood up and picked a plum and bit into it, carefully holding it away from her Armani shirt.

'Well?' said Lizzie. 'Tell me how I knew that there was once a nunnery at Dore, and that it was here, where we are now, and these trees are the descendants, generation by generation, from trees that grew from plumstones that fell in the Middle Ages, and somewhere under this turf are masonry blocks and somewhere the bones of an African monkey.'

'A monkey?' Venetia paused, her mouth open, a dribble of plum juice dripping down her chin.

'The girl who was with the franklin had a monkey.'

'Listen, I think perhaps you ought to go to your doctor. It's what that Dyson-Jones bloke said – and to be honest if I suddenly thought I was Hiawatha or Tiger Lily I'd be in Harley Street in no time. And you must not sleep in that church again. OK?'

A pause. Lizzie said, flatly, 'So you reckon it's the heat.'

'Yes,' Venetia said firmly. 'It's the heat. Come with me, this afternoon, to the leisure centre. What you need is a swim, a cold shower, and a long cool drink in a bar with air-conditioning. And stay away from that church, all right?'

But Lizzie's face had become remote again; aloof, secret. 'We'd better go,' she said. 'We were supposed to be back an hour ago, and you know what Bill's like.'

Venetia sighed.

They went back down the track to her car.

They had all eaten supper. Sonia and Gareth, after lighting a fire that nobody wanted, went off to the pub. Jacob and Badger played cards. Venetia said, 'Who's coming for a walk? Come on, lazy lump,' and grabbed Andrew and pulled him, astonished and mildly protesting, away towards the ridge beyond the ramparts. Soon they could be seen, walking along Vortipor's ditch, silhouetted against the dark red sky, deep in earnest conversation.

Bill Hastings said, 'What's all that about? I thought he was yours.'

'Why on earth did you think that?' said Lizzie.

'I don't know. Somebody told me he was,' said Bill, thinking things. 'Well now, if he isn't yours . . .'

'I'm off men.'

'Nay, pet, don't say that.'

'Sorry,' she said, friendly but friendly from a million miles away: when Bill said 'pet' he was getting ready to be affectionate.

Venetia and Andrew came back. They sat and watched her. The sky turned to deep purple. They all rolled out their sleeping bags, settled for the night – it was only Sonia and Gareth, these days, who retired, modest and pleased with themselves, to a tent. A night bird, an owl, flew overhead. The embers of the fire died. Venetia said: 'Are you awake?' and Andrew said, 'Yes,' and Venetia said, 'Night, everybody.'

So Andrew was on guard.

Lizzie smiled, curled herself up and slept.

She was awake. Far above her in the sky a red light winked; some kind of aircraft silently crossing the heavens. Everything was still. What time was it? Midnight, perhaps later. The monks would be at their prayers, the night office would have commenced.

The flute – there it was again. Distant.

Without conscious decision she quietly unzipped her sleeping bag. She paused to look down on Andrew, who was dead to the world.

Ten minutes later she lay down in the church. She was eager, not apprehensive, as she slipped down into her sleeping bag, and put out an arm, and touched the white alabaster flowers. She lay, calm and unafraid, as the stench of blood and the perfume of roses, the smell of the High Middle Ages, filled her nostrils. It was easier now, much easier. She was slipping back before she even closed her eyes.

'Liquorice and cumin,' said the page, greedily, 'is best for a mazelin, for a true loving cup.'

10

The High Road

Ill news travelled fast along the road. Two of King Richard's followers had been executed by the mob at Thame, pulled from their horses, stabbed and kicked to death; their servants robbed and forced to flee half naked. The hue and cry was out, and not just the hue and cry, but the mob. *With King Richard and the true-hearted Commons!* they had shouted in the days of the Peasants' Revolt, but to each other – then and now – they whispered, *When Adam delved and Eve span, who was then a gentleman?*

A grey mist was falling. The bright sunshine of the morning was long gone. In its wake had come first a mizzle of sleet and then two hours of heavy, icy rain. The woods were silent, which did not mean that they were safe. He would have stuck fast to the high road to Oxford had it not been for the girl. Treason. *Crimen lefæ majeftatis* – to the majesty of government, to the peace of the land . . . ever since the Conqueror's day traitors had had their bowels cut out and burned before their living, seeing eyes, their flesh divided and made food for the birds of the air.

He turned and looked at the girl, at the lady Eleanor Blount. Did she know that her brother's flesh was fed to the birds of the air? That his salt-glazed eyes now looked down from London Bridge?

She was deep in conversation with Flesshe. They were talking about sweetmeats; about loving cups.

At Marlow, on the bridge, two friars, drunken St Johns, bawled insults at them and gibbered playfully at the monkey. As they climbed into the woods a group of knights, with their squires and packhorses, forced them off the road and terrified Hanchache, who thought that every knight who loomed up through the cold steaming mists was Sir Robert de Rideware, the famous highwayman. 'It's Sir Robert,' he cried hoarsely at every horse he saw, and every time he

73

did so the boy turned pale, and the girl looked interested and clutched her monkey.

Toke sat under the dripping trees as the knights passed, his shoulders hunched, his mood dark. There had once been an age of courtesy, he told himself bitterly, an age of manners. After Poitiers the Black Prince had waited on the French king at supper – and when they had entered London the French king, although his prisoner, had ridden before him on a white horse.

The age of manners had ended, thought Toke, in the days of his own youth. It had ended when the mob chopped off the heads of the Lord Chief Justice of England and the prior of St Edmund's, and stuck them together on a paling, their cold lips kissing. The merriest joke in all England!

No, he thought; no, it had died before then, before Jack Straw. It had died with the coming of the Black Plague – when men ceased to believe in the glory of God, and began to believe in his malice. When they sought to propitiate him with charms, and gave power to witches.

The knights had disappeared, down the hill, their packhorses, servants and dogs with them. Hanchache and the boy were staring at him. The girl was gazing into the trees, in a dream. Where was she? Back in Richard's court, listening to Chaucer recite verses in praise of ladies? Laughing and tittering while the child-queen made the old poet hop and skip in rhyme? Poor Chaucer. He never did get his knighthood, not for all his years as a page, his nimble word-skipping and his verbal posturing, not for going to fight the French or having married the sister of the old king's whore.

Well, he was dying now, they said. Taken in by the monks of Westminster; his tales of Canterbury scorned at court, though not in the country.

Rain dripped from the trees. Hanchache was shivering like a dog. Hanchache had no furs. His long legs were sheathed in thick mud.

'It must be near the hour of noon, sir,' said the boy, Flesshe.

Yes, and the mists were thicker.

He urged his horse forward and they followed him. The track took them up towards the long ridge of the Chilterns. Occasionally they emerged into a clearing and caught a glimpse, beneath them, of the swollen Thames. Toke rode ahead. Behind him Eleanor and the boy talked together in low voices. They had stopped discussing sweet-meats and were discussing the degree of drunkenness of the two friars.

'Oh, they were truly ape-drunk,' said the boy.

'Ape-drunk is to be sanguine. Oh page, how much must I teach you?'

'Well then they were mutton-drunk.'

'Mutton-drunk is to be phlegmatic – and do not say swine-drunk, for they were far from melancholy.'

'Well what then?' said Flesshe, intimidated by her learning.

'Why, they were *lion-drunk*.'

They emerged from the woods and he saw with relief the old, straight path across the high downs known as Grimm's Ditch.

He heard her laugh.

'Unicorns? Oh page . . .'

'Are there then no unicorns in England?' the boy asked – this his worldly London servant.

The girl replied, 'Not in this age.'

Toke turned in the saddle. 'On this journey, I will show you a unicorn,' he said.

The girl looked blank, as though he had not spoken.

He had aimed to reach the abbey at Great Missenden, but darkness found them in a village where the inn was a hovel and the travellers' bour dank and stinking. The girl walked into it and looked round her – thinking no doubt, thought Toke, of glazed windows and tapestried walls.

He ordered a brazier and asked what food could be prepared.

'Mutton?' offered the landlord, but in an evasive manner. Then his eyes lit up and gleamed with hospitality. 'A brace of January hedge-hog?' he suggested. 'Dug up from their slumbers with their fat still about them?'

Toke hesitated, his mouth starting to water.

There came a sound of retching from the inner bour.

Toke ordered mutton, even though it would be rancid, a mess of fat and gristle.

'Ah me,' cried Eleanor from her bour, where she was sitting in the darkness on a stool waiting for her brazier. 'Ah me.'

'What, my lady, did the French queen eat?' he called.

Silence.

The French ate frogs, said the boy. He had seen them do so.

It was the hour of vespers.

In the inner bour the girl was at her prayers.

Our father that art in the heavens, hallowed be thy name. Thy kingdom come to. Be thy will done in earth as in heaven.

Langland, Toke thought, as he sat steaming gently over the common fire, had ended up saying prayers for rich merchants: guiding their souls to heaven for a groat a day. He had been a poor man with a rich vision. He had seen the follies and corruptions of the age, and he had, in a way, become a part of them.

And forgive to us our debts as we forgive our debtors. And lead us not into temptation but deliver us from evil.

Toke said: 'Amen.'

Silence.

Did she know that her brother was dead?

Whittington, always a man for gossip, said Blount had been tortured by Sir Thomas Erpingham. 'Who else was in the plot? Who else was in the plot?' Blount had been asked, but he had said not a word as the nails were parted from his fingers, his limbs twisted on the rack. 'Now go and seek a master who will cure you,' Erpingham had mocked, as Blount was carried – for he could not walk – to his execution in Green Ditch.

Had she been told of this, before she was bundled away from the palace at Sonning, abandoned in a London inn?

Again he tried to reckon her age. Thirteen, fourteen perhaps. It was time she married. There had been talk of an alliance with the Mannys – the eldest boy was not more than eighteen. Now she would be a bride of Christ.

The landlord came creeping from the kitchen, holding the remains of a Jack o'Dover pie on a platter. Worts in a barley crust, and more than a day old by the look of it.

There was a minstrel, a hungry minstrel, who sat in the corner and watched while they ate. His bagpipes lay on the floor beside him. Eleanor said, her mouth full of food, 'Sing for us, minstrel, and you shall have a silver penny. Sing for us the Song of Roland.'

The minstrel looked at her, puzzled. She said, 'If you cannot sing of Roland, then sing of King Arthur.'

But the minstrel could sing of neither.

'Oh minstrel,' said Eleanor, 'I would never send you to rescue the Lionheart.'

The boy, standing behind Toke to serve him, said, 'Come, minstrel, what lays can you sing?'

But the minstrel could sing no lays.

'Then you shall not have your silver penny,' said Eleanor.

The minstrel coughed. He crept forward, closer to the common fire. He sang two verses of a song about a cuckold.

Flesshe said, 'That song was everywhere in London two years past.'

Eleanor said, 'Play your pipes.'

He played his bagpipes. It was a thin, despondent sound.

'That tune,' said the boy, 'was everywhere in London two years past.'

'Oh minstrel,' said the girl, sadly. She turned to Flesshe, who was taking a platter from the table, and whose fingers were seeking meat in the greasy gravy. 'Put not thy fingers in thy dish,' she said, 'neither in flesh, neither in fish.'

The boy gawped at her. He was the son of a vintner.

'Pick not thine ears nor thy nostrils. If thou do, men will say thou com'st of churls. Did nobody teach you that, my master?'

He shook his head.

She sighed and turned back to the minstrel. 'Can you tell us a story?'

He was half starved, but the world was half starved, and to eat he must tell a story.

She suddenly sang: 'Do come my minstrels . . .

> Jesters for to tell tales.
> Of romances that are of royals
> Of popes and cardinals
> And of love likings . . .

Tell me a tale of love likings, minstrel. Tell me a tale of true love.'

Toke ate his bread and watched her, and thought how forward she was.

'There were two merchants,' the minstrel said, 'who each boasted of having the most obedient wife in England. And they decided on a test to judge who was right.'

He stopped, fearful that they would have already heard it, two years since in London.

'And?' said the girl.

'And? Why, they went to the first merchant's house, and the merchant put a porridge pot on the floor and said to his wife, "Wife, jump in that pot," and she said "Why?" so he put up his fist and dealt her three mighty strokes.'

It was usual, when he said this, for there to be a roar of approval from the rabbit-catchers and the hedgers and the millers. It was sometimes known for his ale mug to be filled just on this line, on this line alone.

'And?' said the girl.

'And? Why, they went to the second merchant's house, and the second merchant ordered his wife to put salt on the table.'

He paused for effect. 'And she,' he said, gurgling with false laughter, 'mistook the French word *sel* for the olden-time word *syle*, which the world knows means to jump – and up she jumped on the table, breaking all the pots and scattering the food!'

The minstrel laughed and laughed.

'A man took his neighbour to a house,' he said, stopping his laughter abruptly, 'from which they could hear the sound of voices. And he said to the neighbour, "Neighbour, how many are a-talking in that house?" And the neighbour replied, "Twenty men, or, or – two women!" '

Again he roared.

The boy, Flesshe, bringing in the platter with more food on it, sniggered.

Oh for some rabbit-catchers, some tinkers and some ditchers!

Toke and the girl stared at him and ate their mutton. Pale, grey, its fat already congealing, mutton the minstrel would die for.

Would they give him his supper? Give him his supper, and then could he, the minstrel, give Toke in return a game of chess? His thin hands shaking, the minstrel poured his chessmen from his dirty yellow-and-scarlet bag, eagerly showing them his wooden board of painted squares.

It was what all the minstrels were at; it was the latest fad, the latest thing entirely.

The girl said sadly, 'Oh minstrel, why cannot you sing to me of King Arthur?'

Why? The minstrel had a dim childhood memory of the lay of King Arthur, but that had been before the second coming of the Black Death, before the minstrel in the castle had died and taken half the village with him. He stared at her, too tired and hungry to reply.

The girl said that she would play chess. 'A game,' she said, 'for your supper.'

It was an old-fashioned set: the vizier had not yet been replaced by the queen. The minstrel was light-headed with hunger and anyway a poor player, confused by the moves, still allowing his king to leap squares, though the girl told him over and over that it was no longer allowed.

'Your king is lost,' she said. Then she said, softly, 'As is my own.'

Toke looked at her carefully. She was, he thought, like the rest of them: the men had sworn they would die for Richard of Bordeaux.

Or perhaps, he reflected, she just liked the 'romance of royals'.

'Alas, minstrel,' she said, 'no supper.'

She turned to the boy. 'Will you play, my master?'

'Will you teach me?'

'Oh, oh,' she mocked. 'I must teach a London boy to play chess, must I?'

They played chess, and laughed, and the minstrel ate the remains of the Jack o'Dover pie and laughed with them.

The wood burned brightly in the fire.

Toke went outside and scanned the road. The dark, misty night was still; the countryside lay deep in January silence. 'Get her from London,' the Lady Blount had told him. 'Get her to safety.' But the country was thick with men who would murder for a morsel of bread. Danger, danger, he thought. Hanchache would guard the door this night with his thin, Italian knife.

11

Utah

'One of the anti-virus trips went off at around two o'clock,' said Martha Crawfurd. 'That would have been three a.m. in Western Europe, depending on the time zones. But there's nothing showing, no report of any corruption, so it could have been a false alarm. Those anti-virus trips are so delicate. It might even have been caused by freak weather conditions, something in the ionosphere over Alaska. You think that could be possible?'

'Yes, it's possible,' said Pope.

'The corruption in the Navy signal, and the things on Koenig's pad, are still all we've got.'

They climbed the last wooden steps and reached the observation platform. They were the only tourists around. The view was spectacular: the buttes and mesas of the Dinosaur National Monument, the quarry face etched with flying reptiles, brontosaurs and allosaurs; the river flowing south to Desolation Canyon.

'Further downriver, in Arizona,' said Martha, 'there's an extinct volcano that last erupted in 1066, at the time of William the Conqueror. I find that truly amazing. An eruption that covered half of Utah and Arizona in thick ash, and nobody in England knew a thing about it. And nobody here in Utah knew that England even existed.'

Not terribly many did now, Pope reflected.

She said: 'Well, there's your dinosaurs. Seemingly there was a colony of them, Mummy dinosaur, Daddy dinosaur, and two point four dinosaur children, sitting here in the canyon when they got caught by a flash flood.'

Pope leaned on the rail, smelling the pines. It was cool: temperatures that usually reached the nineties had barely reached 60 degrees fahrenheit for a month. Salt Lake City radio stations were full of stories of farmers in Bountiful and Fruit Heights facing bankruptcy; which just showed you, he thought, that wherever you happened to be, and whatever happened to be happening, there were always farmers complaining about the weather.

She said: 'OK. Let's look at this thing calmly. Let's consider how far we've progressed.'

She sat at a wooden picnic table and unwrapped a high-fibre Fruzel bar. She was a history graduate from the University of Southern California, he'd learned, with an MA in communications systems from Berkeley. She'd been with the NSA for two years, and had just spent some time in England, at GCHQ in Cheltenham, as security liaison officer on the Magnum project.

He said, 'What did the Army say about the note on Koenig's pad?'

'The Army went berserk. The outer perimeter of Wilcox base has been searched and secured ten kilometres in depth. Three hundred guys have been out there all day, and boy, were we popular. That base is now ringed with advanced seismic detectors and DIRID infra-red directional intrusion devices. Any rattlesnake that rattles, any terrorists thinking to pay a visit with a hand-held missile, they're all going to show up on the screens.'

'Army Intelligence?'

'The only explanation Intel can come up with is that it might have been something to do with a war-games scenario they held last fall. Do you believe that could be the case?'

'If Utah receiving station was used in the war-games exercise.'

'It was.'

'OK. Maybe.'

'OK. Maybe.' She sighed.

He watched a group of distant hot-air balloons floating upwards, like multicoloured smoke signals over the Green River and the Yampa.

'I know it's not easy,' she said. 'I know people like me are always looking for quick answers. I know you want to shut yourself away in Oxford for six months, going through the computations. I really do know, even if I can't understand, the complicated nature of the quantum mechanical processes involved. But this system is operational. It's got commercial and military contracts worth more than half a billion dollars a year, and we can't keep an infection under wraps for six days, let alone six months. The anti-virus trip that sounded an alarm this

82

morning – OK, it might have been a mistake, but maybe somebody's trying a different method of infiltration. Maybe they have succeeded. Can't you give me any idea of what's in your mind?'

He was gazing down the gorge, through the trees towards Desolation Canyon.

'Dr Pope?'

'I was just thinking,' he said, after a moment, 'of a wagon train coming down the shale bank to the Green River, looking for a place to cross.'

Outriders whooping as they urged their mounts into the foaming waters. Children and dogs running by the wagons. Then the keen eye of the trail scout, and the arm pointing to the smoke signals rising in the clear, distant air . . .

The pony riders on the butte. Navajo?

Apache!

She said, 'A Wild West movie freak, huh?'

'The thing is, it doesn't matter if you're starting your journey on a plane from Heathrow, or on a wagon train from Independence, Missouri. When you go into unknown territory – and the quantum mechanical process is something we use without understanding, something we know works but have not the foggiest idea why it works – then you are travelling into a land of unknown dangers.'

'I say that, do I? I say that to the Director of Intelligence and Security Command at the Pentagon? Be of good heart, for we are travelling into Comanche country with a Bible in one hand and a Winchester repeater in the other?'

'Uintah and Ouray,' he said. 'Not Comanche. Unless you were planning to head south, of course, into Comanche and Apache country, into the lands of Geronimo and Cochise. But say it, by all means. It's as useful as anything else you could say at this precise moment. Can I see the Navy signal?'

'In clear?'

'Larry Sluder said he was going to get permission.'

'It takes a US citizen of good repute a year to get clearance to view triple-A classified military documentation. You're not even a US citizen.'

'All right, so never mind the document itself. What about the corruption, the intrusion?'

83

She opened her bag, unzipped an inner compartment, took out a small buff envelope. She passed him a small slip of paper. He read:
A GOWNE OF SANGUINE OR OF BLEW.

'This was in the Navy signal?'

'All the way from Tokyo Embassy. You know what sanguine means? Well, in the late thirteenth century it meant something different, in those days it meant bright red. It goes with what Koenig had written on his pad, right? Late thirteenth century English. Now listen, and don't get angry – there's no way, is there, that this stuff might somehow be coming from you? Coming out of your brain?'

He looked at her.

'It's Sluder's theory. OK, he's an ape, but he's an ape with friends, and this is his theory, so . . .' She was embarrassed. She said, 'Oh shit . . . you're English, an Oxford don, you knew what *crimen* meant. You don't recall if any of this stuff was running through your mind, maybe, when you were working on the quantum software last fall? I know it sounds way out, but it's not just Sluder, it's something NSA physicists in Washington also came up with.'

'No, it's not way out. That girl, last night, the software technician?'

'Miss Pagetti.'

'Well, she pointed out the correlation between *Pasiphae*'s transmission technology and the working of the human brain. But it's a fairly desperate theory, and it doesn't account for "Missile strike Wilcox". And it doesn't account for why a moment's casual electrical activity in my brain, six months ago, should appear within a secure coded signal from Tokyo yesterday afternoon.'

She finished her Fruzel bar.

'I've a feeling,' she said, 'that this is not going to be easy.'

Pope said, 'I want to go and see Koenig.'

'He's still in coma.'

'I still want to see him.'

'OK, but listen, a computer comms technician from Utah would never have this stuff in his head.'

'He wrote it on the pad,' said Pope. 'He got it from somewhere.'

They drove back to the receiving station. The helicopter took them to Salt Lake City, and landed them at Hill Air Force Base. The doctors at the military hospital confirmed cerebrovascular accident

– a stroke. They'd injected radiopaque dyes into Koenig's neck and head and used a brain scan to isolate defects in the blood/brain barrier. The stroke, a neurologist said, had been caused by spontaneous intracranial haemorrhage – massive bleeding on the surface of the brain. Koenig was still in coma.

Pope sat looking at the brain-scan data. He said, 'Do you know why he haemorrhaged?'

'We suspect aneurysm rupture. You know what I'm talking about by aneurysms?'

'Only in the most general sense.'

The neurologist drew on a pad.

'Small portions of blood vessels,' she said, 'get themselves enlarged. If they are present in the brain they can burst, as they did in this case.'

'Do you know what could have triggered it?'

'Not at the moment.'

'Could it have been a sudden shock of some kind – a sudden, extreme mental stimulus?'

'Yes, it could have been.'

'When will he come out of his coma?'

'It's not possible to say.'

'But he will come out?'

'We're hopeful. One encouraging sign is that the muscles in his right arm have already shown signs of movement.'

'So other functions might follow?'

'Anything that moves in the first three months he ought to get back one hundred per cent.'

'Is he suffering brain damage?'

'Again, we can't tell as yet. We've tried various non-invasive techniques to find out what's going on in there. We've done at CAT scan and an MRI – magnetic resonance imaging to isolate the protons in his brain tissue – and we're doing a PET scan. PET meaning Positron Emission Tomography.'

'You're injecting compounds into his brain?' said Martha. 'That is not non-invasive.'

'In our terms it is non-invasive.'

Pope said, 'Can you tell me what you're hoping to achieve?'

'The compound is tagged by a radioactive isotope. The idea is that as the isotope decays, it sends out positrons, and they sort of collide in the brain and form photons that can be recorded on the PET scanner. Now what this gives us, OK, is information on the varying levels of glucose metabolism at various brain sites. Where the levels are normal, as they generally are, we can reasonably hope there has been no damage.'

Martha said, 'We're not medics. You're saying there's a chance he's going to make a good recovery?'

'All I can say is that the next few days are crucial.'

'Will you operate?'

'Not for two weeks, maybe not at all. After an aneurysm, if it is an aneurysm, red blood cells degenerate and there can be vascular spasms and further bleeding. Second time round, I have to tell you, is very often fatal.'

Pope said, doggedly, 'You have no idea, no idea at all, why it should have happened?'

'Why? Why? If I say hypertension I could be taking in anything from smoking to sitting hunched over a computer screen all day. I could be talking about a sales executive who has a mortgage on his Sundance house that's bigger than Mount Everest and who hasn't hit his sales quota in three months, but mostly I'm talking about exercise and diet. Have you any idea,' she said, awed, 'of this guy's cholesterol level? Have you any idea the amount of saturated fats this guy's been taking?'

Koenig's poisoner sat at his bedside, in the small room that looked out over Antelope Island. She was still wearing her cowboy check shirt and jeans. She looked small and lost and far from home.

Martha said: 'Excuse me, are you a relation of Mr Koenig?'

'I am his fiancée.'

She'd waited long years to say that of a guy. But what kind of girl, she thought, gets proposed to and then her guy collapses in a coma?

She stared down at Koenig. It was rarely that she had ever seen him with his mouth in repose. A tear rolled down her cheek, reminding Pope of the tears that had stained Koenig's jowly face as he stared at his computer screen. Had Koenig's tears been just a defensive mechanism of his eyes, the tear ducts reacting to the blank, unblinking staring at the screen? Or had they a mental cause, an emotional cause?

Martha said, 'You've known each other long?'

'A couple of years. I went to Colorado for a while.'

'You live near the station?'

'I've a room in Bonanza.'

A room she'd been looking forward to quitting.

Pope sat by Koenig's bed. He stared at the temperature chart. Mary Lou wondered if he was some kind of doctor. He was dressed scruffy, with a dirty shirt, and his hair needed a wash, but he looked clever.

Martha said, 'Dr Pope's connected with the work they do at the receiving station. I'm Martha Crawfurd from the National Security Agency.'

Mary Lou looked up at Pope. 'You reckon he's going to be OK?'

'I hope so,' said Pope, 'but I'm not that kind of doctor. I'm a physicist. Mr Koenig's been working on a programme I was involved in.'

'Right.'

She had no interest in her fiancé's work; she knew nothing about it, except that it paid well, and didn't always give him regular meal breaks.

It was dark outside. The sun had gone down over the Great Salt Lake, over the distant Cedar and Lakeside Mountains, over Skull Valley.

'Did you drive here, Mary Lou?' asked Martha.

She shook her head. She'd hitched a lift with a travelling salesman, a guy who'd stopped at the Dinosaur Diner – who'd been there, eating spare ribs, when she'd found out that her fiancé of twenty-four hours was hospitalised and in coma. It had been a four-hour drive, up over the Wasatch Mountains, the ski slopes and the Interstate highway, with the guy saying 'Jesus, I can't believe such terrible bad luck' every mile of the way. She didn't know, now, whether to get herself a room in Salt Lake City or try to get back home again. She didn't know how quickly the owner of the Dinosaur Diner's sympathy would turn to annoyance – he'd said 'You get to that hospital right now, Mary Lou!' but his voice had lacked conviction, he'd been echoing the warm, generous words of the travelling salesman. She didn't know what to do. She had a sister in Bountiful, living on a trailer park, but they hadn't met in years. 'Stand By Your Man' – she truly would, but she feared Koenig might come round and not remember they were even engaged. She feared his proposing marriage had somehow been a part of his illness. They'd only kissed the once, a peck, across the counter, John trying to reach over to embrace her, but impeded by his bulk. It was not, she thought, a great commitment.

She looked down at her fiancé.

'They reckon he ate badly,' she said bleakly.

Pope also stared at Koenig's motionless face, his closed eyelids, his mouth with saliva that bubbled slightly as he exhaled, the pouches of fat under his chin. He thought: *Yet each man kills the thing he loves.*

Which would let Sluder off the hook. Sluder believed that he was the guilty party, having induced Koenig's stroke by making him run across the station compound. But no one would ever accuse him of loving Koenig.

And anyway, Pope was convinced, now, that it was nothing to do with cholesterol, exercise, or diet.

Outside he said: 'The technician, the girl, Miss Pagetti, she was on the right lines. But it wasn't Koenig's brain affecting the machine, it was the other way round. Koenig got those words by direct information transfer between the computer and his subconscious. In my opinion he experienced something, saw something – a mind picture – that exploded the aneurysm.'

Martha stared at him.

'Something invaded his brain, his electrical system. That was what induced the stroke.'

'You know this?'

'Not in any way that can be proved; not, at least, until Koenig regains consciousness.'

'You do realise what you're saying?'

'Yes. I think we might have a bit of a problem.'

'A bit of a— bizarre, meaningless signals that invade the most secure communications network in the world and have the ability to use human brains directly as transceivers – that's a bit of a problem?'

'You don't understand me. Its implications are a lot more far-reaching and a lot more serious than that. Can you arrange to have somebody with Koenig all the time? Somebody who knows the questions to ask, the things to look for?'

She looked at him helplessly.

He said, 'You don't happen to live in Salt Lake City by any chance?'

'I live in Washington.'

'I need a shower and eight hours' sleep and a clean shirt.'

'You do, huh?'

Her security phone started to bleep gently. It was Utah receiving station. Another corrupt signal from *Pasiphae* had been identified.

'This time,' said Sluder, his voice metallic as it passed through the scrambler, 'it's really going to blow your head off.'

12

Department of Defense Training and Doctrine Command Staff College Arizona

China was about to invade Taiwan by sea and the only US military force within six hours of the Straits of Formosa was a guard flotilla comprising the cruiser *Michigan*, three destroyers, a minelayer, and a resource ship of Military Sealift Command. US 3rd Fleet was on exercise off Honolulu and 7th Fleet was in the Indian Ocean.

Should the guard flotilla commander pull his ships back out into the East China Sea – thus seeming to give tacit US approval to the invasion?

Or should he spread his ships in a line across the western approaches from the mainland, in the hope that the Red Chinese navy would not dare break through the symbolic cordon?

It was a knotty problem for the guard flotilla commander; for Pacific Command in Hawaii; for the president in the White House. For the moment they'd packed it in and gone to lunch, leaving their dilemmas and possible solutions scrawled over the blackboard. Those who came back early found a marine on the door. Their seminar room had been hijacked: like the US Pacific Fleet, they had been taken by surprise.

Inside, a voice said, 'OK, it's coming up now.'

The lights dimmed. Words appeared on the huge white screen.

> *My ryght good Lord, moft knyghtly gentyll Knyght*
> *On to yo' grace in my moft humbyll wyfe*
> *I m:e comand as it is dew and ryght*
> *Befechyng yow at leyfer to advyfe*
> *Upon thys byll and p'don myn empryfe*
> *Growndyd on foly for lak of provydence*
> *On to yo' Lordshep to wryght w' owght lycence.*

A pause.

Sluder said, 'What's it mean?'

Martha Crawfurd said, 'My right good Lord, most knightly gentle knight.'

Another pause.

Sluder said, 'It's some sort of romance?'

'Yeah, Sluder. The writer's a woman. She's addressing her most knightly gentle knight.'

'Girlish dreams,' said Sluder.

Another pause.

'What,' said Sluder, 'is that stuff about a humble wife?'

'Unto your grace in my most humble wise, *wise* – listen, she's saying she commends herself humbly to her lover, as is due and right, beseeching him when he's got some leisure to read her letter, and forgive her enterprise – her presumption, Sluder, which is caused by her foolishness – in writing to her lover without permission.'

In the safety of the dark seminar theatre a male voice muttered something, and another laughed.

Martha said, 'Yes boys, OK, those were indeed the days.'

Sluder said, 'The Navy's had it analysed by a guy at Harvard. The language is that of King Richard II of England, not the guy with the Lionheart, the one after. It's seemingly significant that desire rhymes with pleasure.'

Martha said, 'So far neither word appears.'

A voice, from a control room somewhere, said, 'The rest of the message is coming through from Berkeley now.'

> *For when I cownt and mak a rekŷg*
> *Betwyx my lyfe my dethe and my defyer*
> *My lyfe alas it ferveth of no thyng*
> *Sythe w' yo* p'tying depertyd my plefyer*
> *Wythyng you* p'fence fetyth me on fyer*
> *But then yo* abfence dothe my hert fo cold*
> *That for the peyne I no not wher to hold.*

Sluder stared at the screen. He said, 'According to the guy at Harvard, this is both beautiful and perfect. Anybody here recognise where it comes from?'

Silence. The lights came up.

Sluder looked at Pope, the Englishman. They all looked at Pope. 'Not too hot on Shakespeare, eh Charlie?' Sluder sounded sad.

A voice said, 'Alas poor Yorick.'

'Oh, for Christ's sake,' said Martha.

Sluder said, 'This stuff was found inside a signal from a US airbase in Turkey to Logistics Command in Ohio. It was not penned, in case you are wondering, by a homesick pilot trying to send love poems on the cheap. It's not identified by any computer retrieval system on the Net. It's not known to any academic in Harvard's department of English Literature, and their medieval literature guys are the best in the world. Let's break for thirty minutes and then talk this through.'

Outside, the President of the United States and his five-star admirals of Pacific Command were told that no, they could not have their seminar room back; it was the only secure room at the base and they'd just have to go and play their war games someplace else.

In the canteen Sluder said, 'OK, Charlie. We've a ten-billion-dollar communications network, and somebody's using it to send bits of pseudo-medieval poetry. You reckon we've got another Chatterton on our hands, but this time a computer-literate Chatterton with a degree in quantum physics?'

Pope spooned thousand island dressing over his salad and attacked his char-grilled burger.

'You know Chatterton?' Sluder continued. 'The guy who's famous for dying? The brilliant young poet who counterfeited romantic medieval verses when he was only fourteen years old, whose stuff was so good it influenced leaders of the Romantic Movement, Wordsworth and Shelley, and who killed himself when he was eighteen?'

Martha looked at him in amazement. 'You're into eighteenth-century English poets, Sluder? You're interested in the Romantics?'

'Something wrong with that?'

'Well, no . . .'

'You think I'm some kind of ignorant asshole?'

'Of course not.'

'Hey, Charlie, you don't think this is genuinely written by Thomas Chatterton? That he's kind of trying to talk to us? Unfinished business from the other side?'

Pope stared up from his burger.

Sluder laughed. 'OK, then, Charlie,' he said warmly. 'OK. You tell me what's going on.'

'I can't. Not yet.'

'You can't, not yet. No, no, early days. On the other hand there's a feeling,' he said, delicately, surgically, clasping his huge paws, 'that maybe you're a bit lost in all this. Nobody's saying it's your fault – if Professor Hollbecker hadn't died last fall the two of you maybe would have gotten a clear idea of the way forward by now.'

Martha said, 'Did the guys from Harvard tell you about Chatterton, Sluder?'

'Maybe you're just lost in all this,' Sluder said, ignoring her, 'or maybe you're not telling us openly and honestly what you think.'

From a nearby table a voice said, 'We should never have allowed the French to sell China the *Clemenceau*. Once you've got a carrier, you want to do something with it.'

'Listen,' said another voice, 'one anti-ship missile launched from under water and the *Clemenceau* is dead.'

Pope abandoned his burger. He sat in thought for a moment. 'OK,' he said. 'Let me tell you where I am so far. First, I'm fairly sure that Koenig's stroke occurred when his brain accepted quantum signals from *Pasiphae*.'

'Direct transmission from his computer? Jesus . . .'

'I realise that the implications are fairly mega.'

'Yes,' said Martha. 'I'm still, after several hours, trying to cope with the implications.'

'What I can't explain,' Pope went on, 'is why he alone should have been susceptible. It may be something to do with the time he spent chasing the infection – there's a lot of intuitive action takes place in those circumstances, and you told me yourself that he was your best and most experienced operative. Or it may be something to do with his individual brain frequencies.'

'But his brain accepted only corrupt material?' said Martha. 'You think his brain could only receive material introduced to *Pasiphae* from an alien source?'

Sluder said, 'It's that word again. I want to be totally clear that nobody is suggesting extraterrestrial—'

'No, Sluder, not that kind of alien.'

'Jesus, how many kinds of alien are there? Are you guys speaking some different language to me?'

'I suspect that Koenig's brain could only pick up the infections,' said Pope. 'I haven't seen the message *en clair* but you tell me that neither of the fragments on his pad form part of it. I'm trying to work out in my mind why that should be. I think it might be the key to the problem, but I can't get my head round it, not yet.'

He got up and went to the coffee dispenser. At a nearby table a voice said, 'You have to think of the effect on US naval prestige if the Red navy just ignores the cordon, if they just steam right through.'

Another said, 'US prestige? Oh boy, you have to think of the effect on prestige if they sink the entire guard flotilla and steam straight through.'

Sluder lit a cigarette. He opened his mouth to speak. Martha said, 'Just hear him out, OK?'

Sluder let out a long sigh.

Pope returned with three cartons of coffee.

'OK, Charlie, let's leave aside Koenig. Let's leave aside how it's happening, how the penetration is being achieved. What we need to know is where this stuff's coming from. What we need to know is who's doing it. I have my theories. ESC in Texas have their theories. Let's hear yours.'

'I can only tell you the way my mind's working, the direction it's taking me.'

Martha said, 'We understand that.'

'Yeah,' said Sluder. 'We are all seeking the truth here.'

'General received opinion is that every human thought somehow involves a chemical process. When you have an idea, that idea is stored away in order that it might be recalled at some later date – it becomes a memory and to be a memory it has to have a chemical existence, although no examination of the human brain has yet succeeded in finding precisely where or how memory is stored. OK?'

They both nodded.

'Well I want you to consider another possibility. You're probably aware of the theory that individual organisms might somehow be psychically connected across space – it's not new, it's not revolutionary. Hardy, the President of the Society for Psychical

Research in the late Sixties, said that if it could be proved then it would be a massive scientific breakthrough.'

Martha said, 'But it hasn't been proved.'

'No. It hasn't been proved, but even so there are scientists, now, who go one step further, arguing that physical, chemical and biological systems can not only connect over distance but can do it *without mass or energy of their own* by utilising morphogenetic fields.'

There was a pause.

'Organised fields,' Pope went on, 'that can somehow transcend both space and time.'

'Yes,' said Martha. 'I've heard the theories.'

Sluder smiled, the smile of a man not born yesterday. 'Oh Jesus,' he said, his head shaking slowly from side to side.

'In essence, it's been postulated that atoms and molecules impose different patterns – vibrating patterns – on the world line web of plasma space. Some physicists have speculated that there may be ways to recover imprints that have been left in the past. I'm suggesting *Pasiphae*'s new generation of sub-molecular detectors is already, now, doing just that.'

Sluder said, 'Let's get this right. You *genuinely* think that poem we saw in there was written by Thomas Chatterton? You *really* think he's still forging verses from beyond the grave?'

'No of course not.'

Sluder sighed, extravagantly, with relief.

'I'm saying that the verse picked up by *Pasiphae*'s whisper antennae was transmitted, as a thought, without mass or energy, in the early part of the fifteenth century.'

She saw him off from Phoenix. It was a direct British Airways flight to Heathrow. She bought him a cowboy hat in the airport shopping mall; a way of trying to be nice.

'Nobody's going to be cute about this,' she said, brightly. 'Your contribution's being taken real serious. Honest.'

He took the hat. He said, 'We none of us understand what is happening. Until we do, it is dangerous to let *Pasiphae* stay in commission.'

'I think people are beginning to realise that,' she said, awkwardly.

'They're shutting it down?'

'Well . . .'

She was a sunny, open Californian girl, a poor liar. Sluder had said to her: 'One thing we don't need right now is way-out English physicists playing fantasy games. Put the guy on a plane.' Now she said, 'It's a big move closing down a brand-new ten-billion-dollar network. And the intrusions seem weird rather than threatening.'

'Missile strike Wilcox.'

'There's a feeling it might just have been in Koenig's head. I told you about the war-games exercise he worked on.'

'No way.'

'Right.'

'You tell them, no way.'

'Right.'

'Jesus . . .'

'I'm sorry.'

'That girl at the receiving station in Utah, Miss . . .'

'Miss Pagetti.'

'She had the right idea about *Pasiphae* and the way neurons receive and transmit information. Can I liaise with her?'

'Sure. Why not?'

A pause.

He said, 'You'll be able to get back to Washington.'

'Yeah. My cat's probably forgotten I exist.'

'Your cat?'

'A tom. He's real wild and undisciplined. He's got an ugly nature through being a doorstep cat, always left to his own devices.'

'Still, it's nice,' said Pope, looking forlorn in the airport concourse, 'to have something to go home to.'

'I guess so.'

'Get the material to me in Oxford as soon as you can.'

'Yes, of course.'

She looked away. It had been a struggle to persuade Intelligence and Security Command to keep Pope inside the sanitised cordon.

He said, 'Well, cheerio, then.'

'Cheerio!'

The plane took off, westward over the desert, then circled back over Scottsdale. Pope looked down as the plane banked. Northwards was the Grand Canyon, and beyond it Utah and Salt Lake City. He wondered if John Koenig was all right, down there in the intensive care ward, with his fiancée at his bedside and an NSA agent guarding the door.

The last bulletin from the hospital said that he was showing no sign of regaining consciousness. Motor control was still not returning to limbs flexed rigid when the stroke occurred. It was hoped that a brain opiate, dynorphin, might prove effective.

He wondered if Koenig would remember the minutes that preceded his attack – or if he would find his memory of those last seconds erased by his own internal protection system. For surely, Pope thought, it had not been a love poem that had burst the blood vessels in his brain.

Four hours later, approaching the Eastern Seaboard and the Georgia coastline, working on his laptop, his figures finally posed a tentative solution. If his theory was correct and *Pasiphae* was picking up signals from the past that had originated in the human mind, then somehow there had to be a transponder, a late twentieth century transponder, linking them from the past to *Pasiphae*.

And the transponder had to be a living, existing, human brain.

Whose brain?

Did he – or she – know what was happening?

An hour out over the Atlantic, he finally slept.

13

Dore

A cry from the church, in the dead of night.

A young dog fox, faint almost to death with hunger, grubbing the soft earth by the stream for insects, stopped and listened.

A tawny owl hooted softly.

There was the distant drone of an aircraft.

Another cry came from the church – short, full of anguish.

The fox hesitated, for he had not eaten for two days, and had not the strength to catch even the slowest, most unworldly rabbit. Then he abandoned his hole and slunk away, up the hillside, into the undergrowth.

She was back at the palace at Sonning. The Plot to kill King Henry had failed, and the corridors were filled with the writhing smoke of torches, and the air was thick with panic. She could hear Richard's child-queen Isabelle shouting in French, and Young Manny – her very own young lord – crying '*Benedicite! Benedicite!*' (he was drunk on the Gascony wine they had stolen from Windsor Castle) 'Oh what has happened that the lord Henry of Lancaster so flees from my face?' But King Henry had fled only to London, as everyone knew, and had already raised the city militia. Her brother Thomas was urging her to hurry, and her mother was explaining that she was to go to Dore – and someone, a great lord, Kent or Despenser, was telling her that she must never, ever, even on pain of death, speak of the meeting with the auburn-haired Maudelyn, never tell anyone the names of those who had been in the London room when the plot was hatched.

Then, in the first light of dawn, with driving snow sheeting in from the west, and the bridge over the Thames lost, and King Henry's men not an hour away, with the last men-at-arms already mounted and desperate to be gone, Thomas had leaned down from his horse and taken her cold hands in his and said: 'I will come for you, sweet.'

His armour had been enamelled with the Blount arms, the gilt bright and glowing, freshly applied for the New Year tournament at Windsor.

'Go to Dore, sweet, and I will come for you.'

She woke sobbing, with tears in her eyes.

Would Thomas rescue her? She longed for the hours to pass. For it to be night again.

Bill Hastings came and crouched in the trench, and watched her scraping at the dry, black soil, and showed her a copy of the *Shropshire Star* which had a story about the dig – SEARCH FOR HEREFORDSHIRE'S LOST HEADHUNTERS with a picture of Sonia holding her bit of Iron Age sword – then he said, 'I'm not happy about you sleeping down there in the church. Not on your own.'

'I'm OK.'

'Oh come on!' he said, confidential and hearty. 'Going off every night wearing nothing but a little T-shirt. Nobody would be able to hear you if you were attacked. Nobody would be around to help you if you were raped.'

'I do not go anywhere wearing nothing but a little T-shirt and you are not,' she said, '*in loco parentis.*'

'And what's all this reincarnation stuff?'

'Just sod off, Bill, all right?'

He said nothing for a few moments. Her trowel scraped, scraped at the crumbling fabric of the past. Then he said, 'OK,' coldly, and went.

That night, when they were all down in the pub in Newbridge, Lizzie said, 'Eloise, you believe in reincarnation don't you?' and there was a sudden hush – eyes meeting, looks exchanged – and Bill Hastings said, in a forced, hearty manner, 'Don't tell me. You're really a Red Indian princess?'

'It's all tosh,' Venetia said firmly, 'and anyway we can't do anything about it so why worry.'

Eloise said, 'Well the fact is that yes, I do believe in it.'

'For Christ's sake, Eloise' – Venetia, annoyed.

'There's a woman whose children from a past life are still alive,' said Eloise. 'She goes and visits them in Ireland, I saw it on television.'

'You see a lot of things on television,' said Gareth, wisely.

'Yes, shut up, Eloise,' said Sonia, for they all knew that Lizzie had gone bonkers, and that nobody had to talk about ghosts or visions or the paranormal or she might really flip.

'No, actually, I won't shut up,' said Eloise, a girl with a passion. 'Look at the way they select a Dalai Lama. They offer the little baby a selection of the old Dalai Lama's walking sticks and the truly reincarnated Dalai Lama always chooses the humble stick of the previous lama. There are a lot of frauds, of course, especially in India. Some parents teach their children to claim they're the reincarnated souls of rich people who've passed away.'

'Imagine,' said Venetia, trying to make a joke of it, 'if your father died and three years later a ghastly kid from a housing estate called Darren came up to you saying "Help me, son, help me". What would you do?'

'I'd say "Bugger off you little monkey",' said Bill, with transparent honesty.

Badger said, 'My name's Darren.'

Eloise went as red as a beetroot.

'Don't be silly,' said Venetia. 'Your name's Badger.'

'I wasn't called Badger from birth,' he said. 'Nobody gets called Badger.'

'Baby Badger,' said Sonia, falling about.

Venetia said, unfazed, 'Whoever heard of a badger called Darren?'

Lizzie felt Andrew's eyes on her. But then, Andrew's eyes were always on her.

She said, 'I believe in reincarnation. I didn't used to, but I do now.'

She dreamed, that night, of a grey stone abbey in a world of grey water. It was raining – it had rained for three days, and for three days she had stared out of the window of her bour, or played draughts with Flesshe, or sung 'Come Hither Love To Me' while Flesshe played his flute. She had asked for parchment and ink, and been given them by an amazed monk. *Right honourable and most tender good Mother* she had written – tears in her eyes, though her mother had beaten her soundly and often – *I recommend me to you, beseeching you to have for me, as my trust is that I so have, your daily blessing. Pray write me at Dore. Pray send me word of Thomas.*

The monk was watching her from behind the grille, watching her quill move on the parchment. In England there was not one baron in ten who could write, not one lady in a hundred. She would have astonished him less (far less, all women who wore sanguine gowns were surely witches) had she flown out of the window.

I thank you of your good motherhood wrote Eleanor, her tears splashing on the parchment. *For your kindness, cheer, charge and costs, which God give me Grace hereafter to deserve. Pray tell me how Thomas does, and the young lord Manny.*

'I know you don't like people interfering' – this time it was Andrew – 'but I think you ought to talk to somebody about it, somebody other than Venetia, and let's face it I'm the one responsible for what happened.'

They had stopped work for the morning. Venetia had taken Bill to her swimming pool (they had started an affair, everyone had suddenly realised). Gareth was indulging his hobby of digging new latrines, together with a new arrival, Wolfgang from Hamburg. Badger and Jacob had headed off to find a famous real-ale pub near Leominster, and Sonia, a tired, pink little pig, was dropping off to sleep in her tent.

Lizzie had walked up to the highest ramparts, to sit gazing at the Black Mountains of the west, the blue-remembered hills of Shropshire to the north. Andrew had followed her. She had said, at one point, 'I want to be on my own, OK, Andrew?' but he hadn't taken any notice.

Now he was lying next to her on the grass.

'You are responsible?' she said, although she had been determined not to speak to him. 'In what way exactly are you responsible?'

'I took you to the church in the first place.'

'Nobody took me anywhere!'

'Now that,' he said, 'is your good nature trying to stop me feeling guilty.'

She looked out at the distant hills.

'Venetia says you have weird dreams.'

A pause.

'I can't pretend,' he said, 'to know a lot about dreams.'

'No, well, there we are then.'

'Except that spiny anteaters don't have them.'

'What?'

'Spiny anteaters are the only mammals in the world that don't have dreams. Babies, on the other hand, spend around ten hours a day dreaming.'

'Babies?' she said, astonished. 'What have babies got to dream about?'

'One theory is that their brains are being downloaded with software.'

'Dreams are software programs?'

'It makes sense when you think about it. Their brains can't load stuff until they're out of the womb and breathing, just as a new computer can't load software till it's up and running.'

'Yes, yes,' she said, interested despite herself, 'but what sort of software? Babies don't suddenly open their eyes and find they're equipped with Encarta 2000. They're not suddenly able to recite Shakespeare.'

'Just think of the thousands of things a baby has to know about in the first hours of its life. Eating, crying, shitting—'

'But who's sending the software?'

'How would I know?'

'You're crazy.'

'In that case there's two of us, so can I come and sleep in the church?'

'No.'

She started to get up but he put out his hand and stopped her.

'OK. I'm sorry,' he said. 'The franklin. What's he like?'

She thought for a moment. 'Not very happy.'

'And you really think you're his reincarnated soul?'

The franklin? No, she wasn't the franklin . . .

She was puzzled. She stared down the hillside, at the woods, the oak trees surrounding the church. She felt a sudden unease.

He said, 'You know you shouldn't sleep there alone.'

'Don't worry,' she said, suddenly. 'I'm not going to go down there again.'

Why had she said that? She had to go to the church again! She had to find out what happened . . .

They sat in silence. He opened a can of warm Coke. They shared it. He put his arm round her, but she moved it away.

She said, 'I'm going for a lie down.'

She left him. In the tent Sonia was snoring, happily. Lizzie lay down for a few minutes, then got up again.

She slipped away down the hill, and hitched a lift into Hereford.

'By the Statute of Lincoln,' said Mrs Ifor-Williams, leading her into a back room of the library, 'while an abjurer is in the church his keepers must not tarry in the churchyard, unless it is believed that the abjurer might escape, and the abjurer must not be compelled to leave the church, but must be given those things necessary for livelihood, and may leave the church unmolested to discharge nature.'

Several large, dusty tomes lay on a table. 'You know, I suppose, why abjuration was permitted?'

Lizzie shook her head. She sat at the small table. Mrs Ifor-Williams sat opposite her and opened a book of statutes. 'It was to cope with the extraordinary number of felons who had sought sanctuary. Hanging about, year after year, having to be fed and watered, drinking and dicing when honest folk were trying to say their prayers. So Edward II decreed that felons in sanctuary were to be allowed to leave the country, and as they travelled their sanctuary was to go with them. Dear me, there's a woman here, poor soul, "desirous to be delivered from her husband" who fled to a church and said she was a felon, and begged to be allowed to abjure. Goodness, if I'd known about this in my long years at Pontypridd I'd have broken the Co-op window, fled to the chapel, and demanded a flight to the Seychelles.'

Lizzie said: 'What happened?'

'The husband went into the church after her.'

'No, in Pontypridd.'

'Never you mind about Pontypridd. Taffy was a Welshman, Taffy was a thief. This poor woman in the fourteenth century wasn't a felon at all, she'd made it up just to escape the man who owned her, so there was no question of sanctuary and her husband was totally justified, would you believe, in beating her to a pulp. She ran out of the church, actually, and he ran out after her, out of the pages of history, never to be heard of again.'

'I'd have stabbed him to death,' said Lizzie.

'Now there's passion,' said Mrs Ifor-Williams, admiringly. 'Although not wise, for in those days a wife who killed her husband was guilty of treason.'

'What?'

'Not *crimen lesæ majestatis*, you understand, not treason as compassing the death of the king or deflowering his wife, but *petite treason*. The best thing a wife intent on murdering her hubby could do was to get a stranger to do the deed. That way, if she was found out, she got hanged instead of burned.'

'Men, men, what they've done to us!' said Lizzie, adding, because she wanted to hear about Pontypridd: 'I'm sure we all have a tale to tell.'

'This interest in sanctuary and abjuration,' said Mrs Ifor-Williams, not to be diverted. 'It's something different, is it, from your research into the story of the Franklin of Dore?'

'No,' said Lizzie, 'it's all part of it. It's just that I'm not getting any further forward. I still don't know anything about the franklin.'

Mrs Ifor-Williams looked at her across the small table. 'Dr Dyson-Jones couldn't help?'

'He told me there was a nunnery at Dore at the end of the four-teenth century. That was an amazing find because the franklin was taking a girl to a nunnery at Dore in the middle of January, 1400.'

'And how do you know that?'

Lizzie said, embarrassed, 'What I mean is, that's what I dreamed.'

There was silence for a moment. From the next room they could hear a party of young children chattering excitedly. They were attending a holiday museum project. Two of the museum staff were dressed up as ancient Britons, painted with woad. The children had been promised that they too would be painted with woad.

'I told you,' said Lizzie, 'that I had a dream?'

Mrs Ifor-William nodded.

'Actually, I think it's more than a dream. You see, I've been sleep-ing in the church and having these experiences and I've promised someone I won't go and sleep down there again' – she was gabbling, the words suddenly tumbling out – 'but if I don't sleep there, how will I know if the franklin ever reached Dore? How will I know if the girl with him was rescued?'

Mrs Ifor-Williams was staring at her across the little table, across the dusty chronicles of the past. Outside, the children were being told to be quiet please, and listen to Mr Ancient Briton.

'I wish I knew,' said Lizzie, 'what was happening to me.'

After a moment she started to cry.

Tears fell from eyes already red with crying for her brother Thomas, and for herself, Eleanor, lost and alone as she was, on a journey so full of peril.

14

Utah

'The tracker satellite that is now going up,' said Sluder, 'will pinpoint the source of any signal originating in Western Europe or the Eastern Seaboard of the US to an accuracy of less than five metres. It has infra-red detectors that can transmit at 1.2 gigabytes per second and that can – wait for this – scan for intruders 622 million times per second.'

He was watching the screen as he spoke. Hurricane Delilah had struck Miami but the McDonnel Douglas Delta 111 was tearing itself a hole through the swirling grey vortex, challenging the 120 mph winds and bringing, for a small moment of time, an unnatural calm in which leaves, flying planks, and uprooted palms fell like rocks to the ground.

The tracker satellite – a Space Technology Research Vehicle code-named Fox – was now being carried up through the storm clouds into the high atmosphere over the Atlantic.

In Washington, Martha Crawfurd said, 'There are those who don't believe it is possible to hack into *Pasiphae*.'

Sluder smiled. 'But somebody already has hacked into *Pasiphae*,' he said, almost crooning into the mouthpiece. 'Somebody has hacked into *Pasiphae* at least twice, and that does not include the messages scrawled down by John Koenig.'

'You're assuming it's all been done deliberately.'

'I guess that's because my name is Old Suspicious.'

'You ought not to rule out other possibilities. Accidental empathies may be being set up. Dr Pope is concerned about operatives working too long on decode and disinfectant programs.'

'Ah,' said Sluder. 'Dr Pope.'

'He's worried about them developing mental communication links with the *Pasiphae* transmission system.'

Pope was a pain. He'd got some computer model running in

Oxford. He was daily asking for CIA classified computer program runs, for copies of corrupted *Pasiphae* files, forever complaining that nobody listened to him.

'Yeah, yeah,' he said. 'You know Koenig's doing real well?'

'I know he's still in coma,' said Martha.

'It's not so deep. And listen, the operatives in Illinois are being monitored for stress on a daily basis.'

'You've seen the reports from Eagle?'

'We're checking out what happened in Eagle.'

'So are we. Bye, Larry. Good luck with your hacker.'

He was still sitting there, a spider in its web, watching disinfectant system reports scroll down the screen, when yet another call came through from Oxford. 'Shit,' he murmured, then heartily: 'Charlie! How are ya?'

'I hear there's trouble at the HAARP site.'

Sluder chuckled, his eyes bleak as they flicked across the monitors. 'You hear more than I hear.'

'The security guard and monitoring technician. I heard one of them turned violent, and the other guy called the police.'

'Well maybe,' said Sluder. 'How's Oxford? Been punting yet today?'

'It's six o'clock in the morning. What do you mean, maybe?'

'I believe they may have got in a fight.'

'Do we have an ESC report?'

Electronic Security Command, based in Texas, was responsible for US Army communications security.

'Nope.'

'NSA?'

'Not interested.'

'Martha Crawfurd isn't bothered?'

'Martha's feeling relaxed about this whole situation. How did you know about it, though, Charlie?' he asked, his voice silky.

'I asked to be told of anything unusual that occurred – in terms of behavioural patterns, mental state – to personnel working on *Pasiphae*.'

'Well, I think somebody overstepped their authority giving you that information, Charlie.'

'Oh for Christ's sake—'

'Two guys stuck in Alaska, north of a one-caribou town like Eagle with only each other to talk to and the TV not working because of electronic storms, and they can't sleep because there's twenty-two hours of daylight, and, depending on the humidity, Charlie, the woods are crawling, and I mean *crawling* either with spaced-out environment freaks singing Bob Dylan songs or insects that bite them to the bone the moment they put their heads out of the cabin door.'

He spoke from the heart. He'd spent two months at Eagle, setting up the HAARP site. 'Guys like that, they get in a fight,' he added sincerely. 'Two months in Eagle and anybody would get in a fight.'

There's never been a problem at the Fairbanks HAARP.'

Sluder decided he'd had enough of all this. 'It was a personality clash. The security officer has been replaced. End of story. So, how's the computer model doing?'

'The words used in the last fragment, the poem,' said Pope, 'they indicate a writer – I say writer although these are likely to be thought processes we are talking about – who lived in the West Midlands. This is the language of Langland rather than Chaucer.'

'Yeah, right,' said Sluder, pulling a map of the UK West Midlands up on screen. 'You're saying this nut might be living in' – peering at the screen now – 'Birmingham or maybe Sandwell? You think he may be in Hagley or Kidderminster?'

Pope, surprised: 'You know the West Midlands?'

'No more than most places, I guess.' Sluder said. 'I'm a global communicator. You reckon maybe this nut's in Worcester? Well don't worry, we've got the tracker satellite in position, and the next time he starts playing games we'll get a fix.'

The hacker, the computer freak, the 'Nut on the Net' – Sluder's favourite phrase – would be exposed. A finger from the sky would point downward, he told Pope, and the guy would be revealed.

'He'll think he's won the lottery.'

'We have that in mind,' said Sluder, wondering what Pope was on about.

'No amateur hacker can have infiltrated *Pasiphae*'s whisper antennae.'

'In theory, Charlie, I'm right with you. In theory we've got frequency-hopping transmissions it's impossible to detect. In theory

109

we've got encryption methods several light years ahead of the code-breakers but in practice, oh boy, have you noticed how in practice it's always sixteen-year-old boys from Wisconsin using hundred-dollar games machines that end up being caught inside the Pentagon's war computers?'

'*Pasiphae*'s signal detectors are sub-molecular—'

'I guess I know that, Charlie—'

'You can't pinpoint thoughts. You can't get a laser fix on emotions that had their birth five hundred years ago.'

'We'll see, OK?'

'You're hiring a trail scout to read Indian smoke signals,' said Pope down the line, 'when the Indians are all using mobile phones.'

'Well, Charlie,' Sluder sighed, wanting to get off the phone, 'I guess the old trail scouts knew a thing or two about Native Americans, whatever they were communicating with.'

Secretly, deep in his subconscious, he had a germ of a theory. It would not come as any great surprise to him, Larry Sluder, if Pope himself turned out to be the Nut on the Net. Pope was the only non-American with inside knowledge of *Pasiphae*'s quantum systems, the only non-American on the design team, the only guy west of the Rockies with any interest in medieval literature. No, it would not come as any great surprise if Fox (with its 1.2 gigabytes-per-second infra-red sensors, its 622-million-times-per-second laser sweeps) showed infiltrations beaming upwards from Oxford University, and Pope ended up trussed in a white jacket shouting 'But I'm the President of the United States, you fools!'

'Well, anyway,' said Pope, after a moment, 'I think you should get a report from the psychiatrists in Alaska, get somebody to go in and do an assessment.'

'I take note of that, Charlie. Thanks for your interest.'

'Have there been any more corruptions?'

Sluder said, 'Not a single one. Bye, Charlie,' and put the phone down. Through the smoky-grey plate glass he could see tumbleweed blowing over the desert; a dust storm somewhere to the south. He got up and went in search of Miss Pagetti.

'Tracker in position,' said a voice from behind him, from the NASA link. 'Systems enabled. Link to *Pasiphae* established.'

* * *

110

There was a minuscule spasm of energy high over the Atlantic: a ripple of electrons through the gauze of *Pasiphae*'s whisper antennae.

Twelve hours later a commercial signal from Frankfurt to a Wall Street broking house was found to be corrupted. Woken in his rented apartment in Vernal, Sluder drove in high excitement out to the receiving station. He found calls waiting from the Pentagon, from Electronic Security Command in Texas, and from Martha Crawfurd at the NSA in Washington. There was a fax from Eagle Alaska telling him things he did not want to know. There was a query from personnel about his demand that Miss Pagetti be transferred to non-operational duties. By five a.m. decontaminant experts at Army Communications Command in Illinois, the people who had deciphered the medieval poem, had found the parasite, had uncoiled it, and had extracted the words: *As for ye tomb I charge yow fe it yowr felffe, and when I fpeke wt yow I woll tell yow the cawfes why yt I defyr thys to be doon.*

'Tomb?' Sluder said, blankly, thinking for no reason of pharaohs, wondering if they were now into the ancient Egyptians.

The phone rang softly.

The tracker satellite, the Fox, had detected nothing. Its anti-intrusion systems were seemingly asleep. It was two million dollars of equipment, sitting over the Atlantic, and doing no good whatsoever.

15

Hereford

A spherical crystal hung over the door: wind chimes sounded softly
as she went inside. The room she was shown into was full of wild
flowers: big vases of creamy yarrow, wild geranium, campion and
ox-eyed daisies. French windows led out to a small, dry fountain
in a lawn the colour of brown copra. From upstairs came the
rhythmic chanting of a meditation class. From the next room a low
voice said, 'Remember that muscular relaxation induces mental
relaxation.'

She could hear waves on a seashore.

She looked at the mantelpiece, stuck over with cards advertising
psychotherapy, reflexology, Tibetan folkweave rugs and mystic music
festivals. A woman came in.

'Hello,' she said briskly. 'I'm Caroline.'

'Why is Herefordshire full of alternative lifestyle centres?' asked
Lizzie. 'And courses in Kadampa Buddhism?'

'Hippies,' said Caroline. 'Hippies old and sad, though sweetly so,
still living in the cottages they bought and never got round to
renovating, still listening to sitar music and smoking pot. Go into
any wood at dawn and you'll see miniskirted Mary Quants looking
for strange fungi. It's only when you get close you see that they're
getting on for fifty.'

'Mrs Ifor-Williams.'

'Now there, I have to say, is a woman who has lived.'

'Was he terrible to her?'

'Broke her heart.'

'But was it reasonable to expect the manager of the Co-op hardware department to wear flowers in his hair?'

'Reason? I don't know that we can be judged by reason. She loved
him. Why are you interested in hypnosis?'

'I believe that I have lived before.'

'There are,' said Caroline, 'perhaps five per cent of people who can remember their past lives.'

'Jesus,' Lizzie said in panic, 'I'm not remembering it, I'm living it.'

Caroline looked at her. 'Yes. Mrs Ifor-Williams said. You'd better sit down and tell me about it.'

She walked over to a side table. 'Mind your ears,' she said, pressing the button of a vegetable juice extractor. Several organic carrots and a turnip were abruptly changed in their molecular structure.

'They're dreams,' said Lizzie. 'At least they started as dreams. I'm in the Middle Ages, travelling with the franklin of St Michael and All Saints. Do you know about the franklin? Buried in the church at Dore?'

'I'm afraid not.'

The juice, when she had poured it, tasted sweet and earthy, and full of iron and vitamins.

'I'm a girl of fourteen called Eleanor Blount. I'm travelling across England in January 1400. I don't know it's 1400 from when I'm dreaming – regressing or whatever – but I've looked up the events. In my dream people have just heard of the death of King Richard, and apparently that was known in London on January the fifteenth. Everything was terribly muddled. There was a plot to kill Henry of Lancaster at the Epiphany tournament at Windsor. It failed because a prostitute who was sleeping with one of plotters was actually in love with one of Henry's soldiers, and she warned him. I was with Richard's queen, his child-queen Isabelle, at the palace of Sonning. It all happened to me. It all happened around me.'

'Have you looked up the Blounts? Was there an Eleanor Blount?'

'Not that I can find. There was Sir Thomas Blount. He was my brother. The thing is I knew I was going to a nunnery at Dore – and now I've discovered that a nunnery existed at Dore, at the beginning of the fifteenth century. Please don't tell me I've read it all in a book.'

'There was quite a famous case, back in 1906. A clergyman's daughter, given hypnotic regression, claimed to be in contact with a woman called Blanche Poynings, a friend of the Countess of Salisbury in the reign of Richard II. It was claimed that she was either communing with Blanche Poynings on a psychic level, or was possessed by the unquiet spirit of Blanche Poynings, or that she was the reincarnation of Blanche Poynings. The detail she gave was tremendous.'

'What happened?'

'It transpired that when she was a child she had somehow come across a book her mother was reading, called *Countess Maud*. She only remembered it much later. The basic facts were all there, all in the book. Her imagination had done the rest.'

'In the middle of the day, in Hereford,' said Lizzie, 'I turned blue. My skin turned blue. I felt the cold of a winter storm nearly six hundred years ago, and my skin turned to ice.'

'That could easily be explained by self-hypnosis. If a hypnotised person is told they are hungry they will feel hungry. If they're told a pen is red-hot, and are then touched with it, they will not only cry out with pain but a *physical blister* will appear on their skin. I can make it happen to you, if you like.'

'No thanks.'

They drank up their juice. Lizzie described her nights in the church.

'You remember things only at the moment of awakening?'

'Yes – but then, during the day, other bits come back to me. It's as if I'm suddenly sucked back into the past. And it's getting more frequent.'

'Do you still sleep in the church?'

'Yes. I promised someone I wouldn't, but I can't help it.'

'Why can't you help it?'

'I have to know what happened to Eleanor.'

'You find yourself called . . . summoned?'

'Well . . . sometimes I can hear a flute playing, far away in the distance.'

'Do you have a feeling of danger?'

'Danger? Goodness, at Epiphany in 1400 there was nothing but danger.'

'No . . . do you feel any kind of sinister presence? Can you sense any attempt to control you, to take over your mind?'

She saw the eyes of the franklin: cold, inquisitive.

'To take over your body?' said Caroline.

She thought of the franklin's bones, snuggling next to hers in the night. She shuddered, feeling her skin crawl, her heart beating fast.

'I don't know. Perhaps.'

Caroline stood and looked out of the French windows. Beyond the far houses was a tall radio mast hung with satellite dishes. Bees buzzed. If a bee landed on your head, Lizzie remembered – lying back in the chair and listening to the waves lapping a tropical shore – you had to be patient, for it would bring you luck.

'Sometimes I'm frightened,' she said. 'Sometimes I think about what I'm doing and break out in a cold sweat. But I must know what happened to Eleanor.'

'All right,' said Caroline, as brisk as a major-general. 'Let's try hypnotic regression. Let's have a rootle back and see what we find.'

'No,' she said, an hour later, 'no, it's no use.'

'I'm sorry.'

'You have to let go. You have to trust me.'

Lizzie sat hunched and miserable.

'I'm not concerned with your recent past, Lizzie.'

A voice from the floor above said, 'Next week at the same time. Remember you must blend cosmic energy, which is Rei, with the energy within you, which is Ki . . .'

'To reach into the past,' said Caroline, 'I have to go back through your childhood. You're not letting me go back at all. You are not letting me go back a year even.'

Lizzie said nothing.

'What's his name?'

'Malcolm.'

Not a name that did him any favours: he called himself Mick; the others in the Bristol flat called him Malc. One of the lads, Sam, used to throw his arms about and say 'Why does Beaujolais at dawn remind me of sun-drenched Ios and young girls with pouting breasts?' – they having found one of Malcolm's letters, which she had abandoned, with such criminal carelessness, in the toastless kitchen.

'And what,' said Caroline, 'happened to Malcolm?'

Lizzie said: 'He tried to commit suicide.'

'Because of you?'

'Yes.'

'If that's what he said, don't you believe it.'

'What?'

'Don't flatter yourself for even a second.'

'No,' said Lizzie, surprised. 'No, you're right. It was all nonsense.'

A middle-aged secondary-school teacher who wanted to be bold, bad, and dangerous to know. Drinking a bottle of whisky and being sick all over the carpet in the flat living room (mind you, would any of the lads even notice?) and then saying, 'I was trying to kill myself.'

It had actually, when you thought about it, been pathetic.

Lizzie's guilt flickered and was gone.

'It seems likely that you were fighting hypnosis because of Malcolm,' said Caroline. 'If you want to try again . . .'

'Thanks, but no. I didn't feel anything, you see. In the church – when I touch the tomb – I slide back so quickly, so easily. I don't think it's reincarnation. I think it may be a sort of possession, a benign possession if that's possible.'

Caroline looked doubtful. 'Is there anyone who can help you?'

'Oh, I've plenty of friends.'

'If you're thinking of exorcism,' said Caroline, penetrating her thoughts, 'it isn't something to go into lightly.'

Lizzie smiled. 'It's all right. You've already exorcised one ghost. I think that's more than enough for one day.' She reached for her bag, for her chequebook.

Caroline took the money: she was the wife of an SAS officer, her part-time income helped pay for two boys in expensive public schools, the army's allowance being so hopelessly behind the times.

Andrew was outside in his car, which was a small grey Morris Minor almost as old as the Old Stone Age. He looked at her warily as she approached.

'Did you follow me into Hereford?'

'No. The car just happened to stop here. It wanted a rest.'

She looked down at him. 'To put the blame on a little old car like this,' she said, 'is pathetic.'

'Do you want to go for a drive?'

'Why?'

'Because it would be nice.'

'Where to?'

'Well,' he said, 'I suppose the world is our oyster.'

She looked at the car. If it got to Tesco's, she thought, it would be doing well.

An hour later they were lying in a woodland clearing, three miles from the hill fort, and therefore just about safe, they hoped, from Gareth's extended latrine-digging activities. Through her closed eyelids, the oak leaves danced in the sun.

'It's always oak and holly, did you ever see so much?' she said. 'I mean, not just here, but all along the ridge, and down the hillside to Dore.'

'No running water,' said Andrew. 'If you're thinking about sacred enclosures.'

'Sacred enclosures?'

'The sort of places where druid priests came with nubile young maidens.'

No, she thought, that wasn't what I was thinking about; that was what you were thinking about.

She lay pondering on men, on maleness. On druid priests in animal skins and speckled bird headdresses. Cernunnos had been a warrior god, she reflected, a *hornèd* god, great and terrible to the women brought before him.

She said, without opening her eyes, 'There's running water by the church. And oak and holly. But I suppose its natural enough – Christians took over the pagan festivals, they'd have taken over the sacred sites. I hope you're right, Andrew, and this grove wasn't a sacred site – not with what you're doing. Would you do this in the middle of a church service, well would—'

His mouth was over hers, his hand over her shirt, over her breast. His touch was burning hot, sticky and sweaty. 'No,' she said, breaking her mouth away from his, opening her eyes.

His face was a few inches above her, his hand over her heartbeat. She said, 'No, Andrew.'

His eyes were brown and gold. They looked pretty determined.

He took his hand away. With a finger he traced a soft line along her mouth, down her throat, down over her shirt, then down her body.

She felt an overwhelming comfort.

'Oh God . . .'

It would be another exorcism.

118

The franklin lusted after Eleanor. She knew it, suddenly, clearly. Lust? Love?

Andrew was unbuttoning her shirt, slowly unzipping her jeans. Ah . . .

She closed her eyes, and watched the oak leaves dance.

Andrew woke sometime after midnight. Sonia and Gareth were in their tent, arguing in low voices: they were back from the pub – perhaps he was in revolt against her insatiable demands?

He turned his head to look at Lizzie, whose sleeping bag was, or should have been, next to his, she having refused to move into a tent with him ('I'm not having Bill going "Oi oi" and Sonia giggling, anyway I never said I would sleep with you, honestly, one shag on a hot afternoon and you think . . .') but the camp bed next to him was empty.

He looked round. All the others were there. Bill Hastings and Venetia Peel were, it seemed, in the same bag.

He got up and pulled on his trousers and shoes. He gathered up his sleeping bag, ran across the plateau, then jumped down the ramparts until he reached the path. It was dark in the wood, but he was guided, as Lizzie was always guided, by the sound of water trickling down from Vortipor's spring.

He reached the clearing. The church was black against the luminescent sky.

The trees were still. There was not a breath of air.

He hesitated at the church door. He didn't want to wake her, to frighten her. Yet if he crept silently in, and she woke anyway, she'd be terrified . . .

There was a faint creak as he opened the door. He slipped inside. Darkness. Silence.

Slowly, by the dim light of the east window, he was able to make out the boxed pews, the arch of the nave.

Under the east window, with its dreadful allegory of the death of all mankind, was the franklin's tomb.

It was some time before he made out the shape of a sleeping bag; the pale arm, the hand resting against the white alabaster frieze.

16

Radcott Bridge

Thin. Weasel-thin, as Chaucer would have said. Supple, riding her pony easily, mile after mile through a still, watchful land. Her gaze always somewhere over the horizon. Wool-gathering, as they said in Staffordshire. Daydreaming of knights in thrall to fair ladies, of the land of Fastnesse. Or did she think about *The Householder of Paris* (which she liked to read at nights, when she had said her prayers) with its account of how young French wives were taught – taught with the rod as often as not, he reflected, watching her lithe young body – the things a young French wife should know?

Oh, those lascivious monks, pale and fat, a-scribbling and a-copying! Void of conscience, sunk in sensuality!

The saffron dye was washed out of her brown hair. Her face was thin: high cheekbones like all the Blounts. Her eyes were large, her lips pale but full.

She was smiling, faintly. What was she thinking of?

He watched her, hour by hour, as they slowly rode along the Iknield. Under her man's cloak and her pelican (or *pelisse* as she liked to call it), and her surcotte with its low bosom and tight, belted waist, she wore her woollen pettycotte, and God only knew what beneath that. In the evening, in the guest room of whatever abbey they lodged in, she wore her sanguine gown, or her gown of blue.

Clothes for women had once been shaped for modesty. Now they were shaped to show their bodies. Eleanor's gowns had been given to her by Queen Isabelle, the daughter of France, which was the very home of sensuality. Blue for devotion, red for lust – it was the red velvet gown, close-fitting, powdered with gold fleurs de lys, that nightly brought misery and scourging for virtuous monks and sent unvirtuous monks scampering in search of their drabs.

Toke had travelled to Italy and grown fastidious, and would have been better pleased had she washed, but was there a nobleman's daughter in all England that washed?

They arrived at Wantage as the bell tolled for vespers, to the sound of the monks chanting out the hours. For the traveller this was an abbey of good repute, where a generous fire was provided and food was served on clean pewter plates. There was another guest: an Oxford lawyer prosecuting a Wantage yeoman who had beaten the oaks of his manorial lord to collect acorns for his pigs (which pigs, the lawyer said, did the more wickedly go unrung). After they had eaten, Toke and the lawyer and the abbot sat by the fire while Eleanor sat at the board still, eating apples and reading her book. The abbot would have liked to send her to her bour, to her cold and candleless cell, but he was a polite priest, and a hospitable host, and he knew that travellers in this day and age expected to be cosseted for their money. Should the monastery – he anxiously asked Toke now – provide forks at dinner, in the Genoese fashion? (Though it had been Gaveston, the painted boy-whore of King Edward II, who had invented the fork, they said, to eat his pears). Should they move with the times, and provide a wooden platter and drinking cup for each man who dined, instead of laying out a platter and cup to be shared between two guests, in the ancient, gentlemanly way?

Toke had shared his platter and cup with Eleanor, Flesshe waiting on them both. He said, 'The old ways, father.'

They drank their wine. The room was warm and snug: the rushes on the floor were fresh and mixed with dry meadow flowers, fragrant apple logs blazed on the fire. They talked of French pirates raiding Southampton, of rumours of a Welsh rising. Toke said that he had come south, round Oxford, because of talk of bloody riots.

'Flee, flee, the Welsh doggie and her whelps!' said the lawyer. It was the cry of the Oxford mob, he said, as they plucked Welsh scholars from their rooms and killed them.

But many of the Welsh had already slipped away, were gone back to their mountains.

'Beware of Wales, Christ Jesus must us keep,' said Eleanor, suddenly, showing that her ears had been pricking all this while, 'That it makes not our child's child to weep.'

The abbot looked as though he wanted to tell her to keep silent.

122

Wantage was a small, backward place, unused to ladies of the court. Eleanor laughed. 'Oh, this is terrible,' she said.

Silence.

Toke said, 'What is terrible?'

'Three ladies discover that the same knight has, you know, been making love to all three of them.'

She was reading *The Knight of La Tour Landry*. It was – thought Toke, seeking small mercies – marginally less scandalous then *The Householder of Paris*.

The abbot was looking at him reproachfully.

'If you wish to read,' Toke said, 'I can lend you the tales of Robyn Hode and the Earl of Chester.'

The abbot sighed. If she wished to read, which was unnatural anyway in a woman, she should read her psalter.

'What do you think the ladies did? They called him to give account of himself, and bade him sit on the ground by them, and he replied' – she adopted a high, falsetto voice – 'Since I am come and must sit, pray let me have some cushion or a stool, for I might, if I sat low, break some of my points!'

She snorted with laughter. 'Oh what an age we live in,' she said, 'when knights wear points to hold up their stockings, and love all the ladies.'

She bent back over her book.

The lawyer fell asleep.

The abbot said, quietly: 'They say the Lord Glyn Dŵr has raised a standard for King Richard.'

So, he was a Ricardian. Many Franciscans were loyal to Richard, which was strange, for Richard had scorned to have a Franciscan for his confessor.

'They say that Richard is escaped,' the abbot went on, 'and gathering a force at Radcott Bridge.'

They say, they say . . .

They were such dreamers, such plotters, these monks. They wove such webs; intricate gossamer webs, but without substance. London was for King Henry, for Lancaster, and the world knew that the man calling himself King Richard was a monk called Maudelyn.

The abbot leaned forward, his little eyes bright and inquisitive. 'The girl . . .' he whispered. 'She is kinswoman to Sir Thomas?'

Toke nodded. Yes, she was sister to Thomas Blount.

'In Oxford, more than thirty noblemen were killed,' said the abbot, his eyes flickering around, from Eleanor to Toke, to the lawyer, to the blazing logs in the chimney grate. 'Executed in the Green Ditch, their bodies quartered in the manner of beasts taken in the chase, for what is called high treason.'

'It is high treason,' said the lawyer, who had not been sleeping after all, 'when a man doth compass or imagine the death of our sovereign lord the king, or of our lady the queen his wife, or if a man doth deflower the king's wife, or doth deflower the king's eldest daughter being unmarried, or doth deflower the wife to the king's eldest son and heir . . .'

Eleanor was listening, though her head was in her book. She said, suddenly, 'Then is it high treason, sir, to imagine or wish the death of the king?'

'Why yes, it is high treason certainly for a man to think in his heart to cut off the king's life by violent death, for that compassing or imagining must come from a false and traitorous heart, even out of cruel, bloody and murdering minds.'

'Ah,' she said, smiling secretly, 'ah then, there are many traitors in London this night.' A moment later she added, 'In London and in other places.'

She thought her brother Thomas was alive.

She did not know that somewhere, as they came along the Iknield, they had crossed the place where his quartered remains had been carried in a sack to the Tower.

It was before dawn, the hour of prime.

Eleanor's clear voice: 'O Lord God Almighty who has brought us to this beginning of this day, so assist us by thy Grace that we may not fall this day into sin . . .'

She was on her knees in her cell. Her cloak was round her shoulders.

Toke drank from his cup of hot ale, and watched her through the grille. When he turned, the anxious abbot was waiting for his lodgings fee.

The snow was returning, the horses could smell it on the wind and were fretful. He would not risk Oxford and the ford at

Bablockhythe, said the monks, was unpassable. They would continue west towards Bristol, then north on the Ermine Way. At first the road was still the Iknield, and their mounts' hooves clattered in the darkness and sent sparks flying from the stones. It was a good road – better now than Watling Street or the Fosse, which had been smashed by the royal artillery trains as they trundled west to subdue the Welsh, or north to hammer the Scots.

Dawn brought a blood-red sun at their backs and word of plague in the villages ahead. They were at a place where a track led to the north, a high path over the downs, far older than any made by the Romans, a royal road of Berlinus and Arthur. Toke hesitated. It was a good road, but it would lead them to a place he would have avoided at all costs.

Eleanor and the boy were talking in low voices. They were always a-chatter. She was too familiar with him, calling him 'page' as though he were not the lad of a London vintner. 'When Henry of Lancaster was crowned at Westminster,' he heard her say, in a confidential whisper, as if passing a state secret, 'his head was found to be full of lice.'

Flesshe made an exclamation of disgust, though his own hair had been full of lice, Toke did not doubt, since the day that hair first grew on his pate.

'But Math,' the boy said, 'what of Math?'

'Oh Math!' she said, in a voice of despair.

The entire English nation, it seemed to a weary Toke, was fascinated by the conduct of Math, King Richard's loyal greyhound, that on the day of his master's abdication in Westminster Hall had padded across the floor to lie at the feet of Henry of Lancaster. For every minstrel who recorded King Richard's last words, when he was taken from the Tower on his final journey, as a loud, weeping lament that he had ever been born, there were two others who said he asked for Math, and wept because he was not there.

'We go north,' he said.

He could not risk the plague.

An hour later they climbed to a high point on the long ridgeway. Before them was an ancient fortress, its walls of sod and stone decayed, only the stumps of its huge gateposts remaining. Before they reached the ramparts they could smell woodsmoke and sizzling meat fat: scents whipped before their nostrils by the wind.

Flesshe said he was reminded of the cookshops outside St Paul's with their fatted songbirds turning on spits. He said he was reminded of Cissy in the Jerusalem.

Eleanor said, 'Cissy in the Jerusalem! Oh, Cissy in the Jerusalem!'

Flesshe looked suddenly sorry for himself.

'Who is this Cissy in the Jerusalem?'

Flesshe had tears in his eyes. He had never before in his life been further from St Paul's than Aldersgate. He was remembering things.

'Oh, Cissy in the Jerusalem,' said Eleanor.

Toke marvelled, and wondered if she would ever stop saying it.

Six men were sheltering in the lee of the castle. The fierce warmth of the fire scorched their faces, the keen cold wind froze their backs – but their eyes were merry enough, absorbed by their game of dice, or in watching scraps of smoke-blackened pig turn on the spit, their breakfast of *porc*. They were archers. Carefully propped against the rampart were their massive, curved bows, protected from the rain by stitched canvas. *Killer* said one, *Nut Brown Maid* another. Toke crouched to watch their play, and was offered wine, although the men were destitute enough. They had travelled together, they said, for many a year and to many a place. They had been with King Richard in Ireland in '94, and in France in '96, the year of the peace – but they were men of Lancaster, they had never been in Richard's infamous Corps of Archers. They giggled slyly at the thought of those men of Cheshire, scurrying around the countryside and hiding their hedgerows, tearing the badge of the White Hart from their jerkins.

The sergeant said: 'I am an archer of Lancashire, born and bred under a thorn, as the saying goes. But my father was with Pierre de Lusignan, the King of Cyprus.'

'When Alexandria was taken from the Mohammedans?' said Toke.

'Indeed,' said the sergeant, quite unamazed that a long-ago deed in a far-off land should be known of, here in the cold grey January in Oxfordshire.

Toke asked if they had news of the road ahead, but they were unconcerned by talk of robbers and gangs – they each carried a sword, and dagger, as well as their bows. They had been retainers of Sir John Bussy, poor dead Bussy. Toke asked why they had not enlisted with King Henry? They had a yearning, they said, for their own country, a yearning for the sound of the peewit on the moors, for a land where folk said swa for so, and bath for both, and where eyren were called eyren and not eggs.

Looking down from the fortress they could see a small hill covered in grass except for a patch of white earth. It was in the place, Toke told Flesshe, where St George had rescued the English maiden from the fiery Welsh dragon. The patch of bare earth was the place where the dragon's blood had spilled.

Was this dragon, Eleanor asked, a loathsome serpent, fierce and mottled, scorched by its own flames?

Toke dredged his memory for dragon stories.

'Why yes,' he said. 'It was indeed fierce and mottled. It measured fifty paces from head to tail. It soared at night through the air, then dived to its dark, cavernous lair beneath the earth.'

Did it guard gold goblets and silver vessels, asked Eleanor, and swords eaten through by rust from a thousand winters in the earth's embrace?

'It guarded the gold of men long dead,' Toke said, 'that lay under a curse of enchantment, and no man might enter, save the man whom God – the true giver of victories, the guardian of men – granted permission.'

The Lancashire archers nodded solemnly. God it was, that granted victories; God that guided *Killer* and *Wolf* and *Nut Brown Maid*.

'St George was a worthy knight,' said Eleanor.

Flesshe was not impressed. Patches of bare earth may or mayn't have been caused by dragon's blood. Such things were two a penny in Cheapside, where the gut of a dead saint or phial of the Virgin Mary's birth blood could be purchased for a silver groat. He wanted to see a unicorn. He wanted to see one *with his own eyes*.

Hanchache's eyes were on the bits of roast meat, following them with the intensity of a dog, from the spit to the archers' mouths. But the archers were hungry men. They ate calmly and deliberately, avoiding his gaze. Hanchache saw the last sliver of meat bolted, then turned his eyes back to the horizon, seeking out danger, seeking out Sir Robert de Rideware.

Danger came, but not until they had said farewell to the archers. They had left the old road west to Wayland's Smithy and turned north to seek a crossing over the River Ock. The ford at Barrowbush, when they found it, was swollen. They spent a fruitless hour seeking a dry crossing place. They returned to the ford, Toke in no good humour, and plunged their mounts into the cold water (Hanchache wading with the water up to his chest and crying piteously). They were across the river and a meadow and in sight of the great fields of Fernham when they saw smoke rising from the village.

Then Toke saw a group of men under the trees ahead of them.

Two knights, but with rusted plate, and leather jerkins instead of chain mail, standing by their mounts. The others – a dozen perhaps – were foot soldiers. In a second he absorbed the mixture of rags and fine clothes that they wore, the calculating expressions on their faces, their sudden stillness.

'Sir Robert . . .' stuttered Hanchache, and yes, Toke thought, or something worse.

'Back,' he said, turning his horse. 'Quickly!' he said, leaning over to grab the bridle of Eleanor's pony.

The trotted back across the meadow towards the Ock. A glance behind showed the two knights mounting their horses, and he knew they would be lucky to escape with a beating, their money taken, and Eleanor raped. They reached the river bank and plunged down into the water. He looked back and saw the two knights galloping towards them, the foot soldiers streaming across the meadow like greyhounds.

Their only hope was to meet the archers, the men of Lancashire. They struggled up out of the river, Hanchache wheezing and gasping, his lungs waterlogged. 'To the fort,' he shouted to Flesshe. 'Gallop, gallop!' They urged their mounts up the long sweep of the downs, up towards the great white horse carved in the turf over Uffingham. 'Gallop!' he shouted. 'Gallop!' Eleanor yelled at her pony, beating it with her switch, but gallop it would not, and Toke looked back and saw in despair that the knights were already across the river and were thundering behind them up the hillside, getting closer by the moment, while the men on foot stood on the far river bank screaming encouragement. It was hopeless. Hanchache was down; a lance swinging with a thud across his back. The first of the horsemen was almost upon them. He heard Flesshe cry out a warning. He looked ahead, at the distant fortress. It was deserted: the archers were long gone, there was no sign of smoke from their fire. He heard Eleanor shout something, and heard the shrill screech of the monkey. He pulled in his horse, meaning a last, desperate barter of money for their lives. He looked at the first knight, and his heart sank at the cold, vicious smile on his face.

Then the knight's smile was wiped out as an arrow pierced him, like King Harold, through the eye.

Ware, the sergeant, said, 'Threepence a day, for each man, to Hereford, with fourpence for myself as sergeant.'

Toke said, 'I could get Welsh spearmen for twopence, and grateful.'

'Davy's mother was a Welshwoman,' said Ware. 'We aren't prejudiced against the Welsh, are we, Davy? But archers cost threepence, my friend. And to go into Wales makes a long journey home.'

Toke nodded. They shook hands.

Eleanor said, 'My brother Thomas fought with Sir John Bussy.'

'Why then,' said Ware, impressed, 'we are almost your kin.'

She smiled at him.

Davy was recovering his arrow from the knight's eye, for arrows were of value. The English and Welsh arrow was three feet in length, and had a barbed iron point. The best arrows – he told an interested Flesshe – were always tipped with peacock feathers.

'Which way, my master?' asked Ware – his question a politeness, for with plague in the villages beyond Wayland's Smithy there was only one road, one track that they could take.

Two hours later, with the best of the day gone, they dropped from Buckland towards the place that Toke dreaded, the place he would have avoided if he could. Their progress had been slow for the archers would not run as Hanchache ran: as Hanchache formerly ran, for now he limped and howled. The sky was dirty yellow, and there was a smell of snow in the air. The girl was exhilarated, talking of knights and dragons, telling Flesshe stories from *The Knight of La Tour Landry*. There was a story – a true story, she said – of a maid who lost her intended husband by urging him to visit her. She lost him – said the story, the true story – because he was a serious knight, displeased by her pertness and light behaviour.

What, she wanted to know, did Flesshe the page think of that?

Flesshe thought the intended husband was no true knight.

They emerged from scrubby woodland. There was a meadow of reeds, a wooden bridge over a wide stream, and beyond that a further meadow and a stone bridge over a river. Eleanor, laughing at Flesshe, asked, 'Where is this place?' and Toke, who would have taken them to the ford at Bablockhythe had the Thames been not so swollen, said, 'The village beyond is Radcott,' and the girl stopped her pony, and stared over the watery marsh.

The Lancashire archers came up and also stopped, and leaned on their bows, and looked sombrely at the small stone bridge – built, it was said, by the Conqueror – that was so important in the minds of England's rulers.

The only bridge over the Thames west of Oxford.

The place through which all armies – whether led by adventurers or kings – had to come.

'Ah me,' said Eleanor softly.

It had been, what, twelve, thirteen years ago? De Vere, hurrying to London – desperate to get his small force south of the Thames – making a dash for Radcott, only to find the Earl of Derby ahead of him and the Earl of Gloucester at his rear. It had been December. It must have looked much as it looked now.

Eleanor said, in a voice that trembled, 'They were trapped, and there were so few of them. But they unfurled the standard, and they fought bravely. Yes, and they died bravely.'

Not de Vere, thought Toke. De Vere had abandoned his army and galloped downriver, to the ford at Bablockhythe and to safety.

The day was dying. The last gleam of yellow sun was extinguished. There was a wall of grey rolling down from the north.

'Snow,' said Ware, quietly.

She said, 'Sir, where did my father fall?'

Toke looked helplessly at the lie of the land. If the standard had indeed been raised, then it would have been on the reedy meadow beyond the stone bridge. The horse lines would have been behind a hawthorn hedge that was, even now, turning white as the first snow fell.

Blount would have fought on foot. When the archers and pikemen had scattered he, and the other knights, would have been left still in their heavy armour, turning this way and that, scarcely able to move. They would have been killed by common soldiers – tanners and ditchers and tallowmen – creeping behind them and slipping thin-bladed knives between breastplate and corslet. The knights would not have felt a thing until their boots filled with blood.

It was the modern way.

'Sir, where did my father fall?'

Toke pointed to the meadow where Richard's knights had fallen.

He wanted to tell her that her father had died in vain, for a king not worth dying for. That the Black Prince's son, Richard of Bordeaux, had been born with the worm of corruption in his heart.

But then, so much in Toke's lifetime had been consumed by maggots of corruption.

The boy, Flesshe, was crying.

Ware was looking at Eleanor, a strange expression on his face. He had realised now, thought Toke, who she was.

She said, in sudden doubt, 'Sir, when will my brother Thomas send to me from Ireland?'

He said, 'Your brother is dead.'

Her eyes closed and she slipped down from her pony. He leaned over to grab her and the monkey scratched at him viciously.

The snow blotted out the bridge, the river, the water meadows.

A cry, low and terrible in the darkness. Andrew jerked awake, his heart pounding, sweat springing from his forehead.

He put his hand, gently, on her shoulder. She was sobbing, long, heart-rending sobs. What time was it? He tried to look at his watch, but there was not enough light. The first grey of dawn came around three: they were still in the dead hours.

Her crying subsided. Her breathing quietened.

He lay back, staring up at the blackness of the rafters. He wondered if this was the first time the sound of human anguish had been heard in the night, in this church, in the six hundred years since the franklin was buried.

No. It would have been, on many occasions, a place of refuge. In times of civil war, of pestilence, of failure of the harvests. A place to crawl to in despair. A place for those seeking solace.

His bones ached. His sleeping bag was thin: advanced thermal fibres made for lightweight handling, but not for comfort on the tiled floor of a church.

There was the distant sound of a plane.

He put one hand out, lightly on Lizzie's hips, as she curled against the alabaster frieze.

'You must make reason sovereign,' Toke said, staring into the fire, 'over the foolishness of your flesh.'

Beside her, in a basket close to the embers, the monkey was curled asleep.

'Reason,' he continued, 'tells us that it is proper to hope and work for something that can be recovered, but it is a great folly to weep and languish for something irrecoverable. It is a displeasure to God to murmur against his will. It is a sin against nature, for grief will consume you to death.'

'I should like to die.'

'It is a sin to think it.'

They were again in a house of Franciscans, those monks who still burned the flame for King Richard. In another day they would be at Coln St Dennis, high in the sheep hills. Another day after that and they would reach Malvern; a day more, Hereford.

She stared also into the fire.

He thought of her life as a nun: for once at Dore she would be forced to become a nun. She would not be allowed to live as a guest – as her mother did at Ely – half in and half out of the real world. She would enter the gates of Dore and would take the veil. It was not the terrible fate it would have been a generation ago. She was of an aristocratic family, related through her mother to the Earls of Surrey. She would become, if fortune's wheel turned favourably, an abbess herself before she was thirty.

The nuns of England, in this dissolute age, had a merry enough time.

It came to him, in the night, in his cell, that perhaps she need not become a nun.

He was thirty, his wife dead, his only child dead of the putrid plague, of the boils that swelled and burst. *It is a displeasure to God to murmur against his will. It is a sin against nature, for grief will consume you to death.*

It was a lesson he had learned through experience.

He was thirty. He had ten, even fifteen years of life, God willing.

He thought of Eleanor.

There was talk that she had been betrothed to a young lord, Walter Manny. But it was her brother she grieved for. The brother who had gone to her at the palace at Sonning when the plot to kill King Henry had failed; who had promised to send to her from Ireland.

He thought of Eleanor riding before him, supple, weasel-thin.

Laughing; smiling at Flesshe.

He would marry her when his next shipment of alabaster was safe in Florence, when the money was lodged with the Flemish banker in London. He had bought his land. He was a possessor of three villages. Many a merchant's son had married the daughter of a knight before now.

He would write to Ely, to her mother at the abbey. Her dowry to the nuns of Dore would come to him (he reflected as he slipped into sleep) though the nuns might keep the monkey (it stung, still, where it had clawed his arm).

Next morning she said, defiantly, mounting her pony, 'My brother Thomas will send for me from Ireland.'

'Your brother is dead.'

'They lie who say so,' she smiled. 'Did you not know they always lie?'

He would not marry her. She was mad, or possessed. Demons were scattered like dust, everyone knew it, they rode like particles in the sunbeam, they came down like rain.

He urged his horse forward. In the distance he could see the Cotswolds. Beyond them would be the Malverns, and then Hereford, and beyond Hereford would be Dore. He would leave her, as he had promised. He would leave her to the nuns and return to his home in Staffordshire, to his three manors, to his own people.

She rode behind him. After a while he heard sobs. He turned and saw that tears coursed down her cheeks.

'He is dead,' she said, thickly, 'and I am alone.'

He was bending over her, kissing away her tears. 'Who? Who is dead?'

She couldn't think. It was still dark. The dead hour of the night. The hour of ghosts and ghouls.

'Oh Andrew.'

She took her cold, stiff hand away from the alabaster frieze, put her arms round him and held him tight.

17

Oxford

In Pope's study, the phone ringing. A voice, abruptly: 'Have you heard?'

A pale light at the mullioned windows, a star in the east, Venus shining brightly. It was four o'clock.

'Have I heard what?'

'Two planes have collided at Charles de Gaulle Airport. A Cathay Pacific Airbus with nearly three hundred passengers on board, and a Qantas 747 cargo plane. There are no survivors.'

Silence.

'You warned us,' she said, from far away. 'We can't say you didn't warn us.'

He took the phone and walked over to his desk. Mists lay over the Isis; trees were black along the water meadows.

'What's the link?'

'The Fox tracker satellite detected infiltration just after one-thirty a.m. your time. It's the first time it's picked anything up, but this was powerful stuff. It still didn't pick up the transmission source.'

'No,' said Pope, 'it would not be able to do that.'

'The guys at Electronic Security Command can't work it out. Sluder's going crazy.'

'What was the link to de Gaulle?'

'An air traffic controller was seen staring at his screen in what's described as a peculiar way. A colleague asked him if he was OK, and he said that yes, he was. The man wasn't satisfied and had a word with the supervisor. By the time they got back to him it was too late. The guy could have averted the crash but didn't. He said it was – I'm quoting now – "a great displeasure to God and a sin to murmur against his will".'

Pope had a brief remembrance of the grey-walled computer room at Utah, with Koenig slumped over his desk. A feeling –

overwhelming as he lifted Koenig's hand from the pad – of despair. Of uselessness in the face of events.

'A weariness. An emptiness' – words in a psychiatrist's report from Eagle, the last report sent by Miss Pagetti before she was moved to Berkeley. Both men at the HAARP site had reported severe depression.

'The French are linking all this to *Pasiphae*?'

'Not yet. All we've got is the flash report to the French Ministry of Civil Aviation, and that came through from the CIA less than thirty minutes ago,' she added, her voice faintly embarrassed. 'It was picked up by Magnum.'

The spy satellites. Ostensibly a joint British–US system, but GCHQ in Cheltenham suspected that the Americans were using it on England: at least on British units in NATO command. That Magnum was being used to monitor the French would be no surprise to anybody.

'The French will find the corruptions on the tape the moment they run an analysis,' she said, 'which will be in perhaps another five hours.'

'They might miss them. They don't know what to look for. Even if they do find them they won't understand.'

A pause. She said, 'You told us, you warned us. Nobody can hold you responsible.'

He said, 'I told them to close the system down.'

'I know that. I said that. Can you get back here?'

'We have to trace the carrier. Until we can trace the human interface there is nothing I can do in Utah.'

'You don't think, perhaps, it's Koenig who's the carrier?'

'I think he became a carrier when his brain became attuned to *Pasiphae*'s sub-molecular waves. The signal about Wilcox Airbase was picked up by Koenig, and was clearly not medieval in origin. The signal about Wilcox Airbase bothers me.'

'The Wilcox signal was from a war-games programme they ran at the base last fall. It was just something dredged up out of his memory.'

'I don't believe so, and if Koenig was conscious I'd want to run a test for false memory syndrome. I think he's a carrier but not the prime carrier. If he was the prime carrier it would mean his brain was still linked, now, to *Pasiphae*.'

136

'You mean his brain might still be being used to infiltrate the system?'

'Being used implies a deliberate act by somebody or something which is nonsense – and anyway, as I said, I don't believe he is the prime carrier.'

'I think I'll check with the hospital. See if there's been any abnormal brain activity in the last five hours.'

'Yes, OK.'

'You'll come over? There's some people who want to talk to you.'

He stared out over the water meadows, collecting his thoughts.

'Charles?'

'Somebody ought to go to Alaska. Talk to the HAARP security man, the guy who called the police. Talk to the operative who turned violent.'

Silence for a moment, then: 'You know, I'm getting real frightened?'

She was tired, he thought, and stressed.

'Try to keep things in proportion.'

'First Koenig, then a French air traffic controller, now you're telling me a monitoring technician in Eagle—'

'Can you get me a flight to Salt Lake City today?'

'I've booked you on the Phoenix direct flight. You'll be met by the chopper. There's a car picking you up in Oxford around ten.'

'Were any signals received at one-thirty a.m. this morning corrupted?'

'Oh boy, were they. I'm sending the stuff through to you now.'

'OK.'

He put the phone down. He sat and stared out of the window. The light from the east was spreading quickly. There was a lone jogger on the towpath. He went and made himself a mug of coffee, then returned to his desk. He felt weary, his mind clotted: he'd been awake till gone midnight, using the Internet to check medieval records at Cambridge, at the British Library, at the royal archive at Windsor.

A tiny bleep on his screen. The fax was coming through from Utah.

He read: *The Kyng our Sov'aign Lord willith chargeth and comaundith all and ev'ych of the naturall and true fubgetts of this his Realme to call the p'myffez to there mynds and like gode and true Englifhmen to endov' themfelfs with all there powers for the defence*

137

of them there wifs childeryn and godes and heriditaments ayenft the faid malicious p'pofes—

The signal broke up.

'Endovr', he knew, meant to furnish. It was six o'clock and the temperature was rising when he gave up trying to trace the origin of the signal. He had established that it was similar to a proclamation made by Richard III on the eve of Bosworth, but kings calling their subjects to arms was an oft-repeated event in the fifteenth century, and the scribes of the royal household would have juggled with a familiar formula – the words could easily have originated at the beginning of the century, the king could have been Richard II, calling his subjects to help him against the power of Lancaster.

He tried to assess what he had learned.

The other fragments, transcribed earlier, pointed to political events early in the year 1400. The language was similar to Langland's, rather than the English of Chaucer, all of which pointed to the West Midlands. There were ecclesiastical overtones – twice the reference to the hours of none and sext, to time being measured by the divine offices when most men were speaking of four or five of the clock, even though they may never have seen a clock. There was, in more than one fragment, a reference to D'or.

Buried gold, he thought, buried gold, somewhere in the West Midlands, somewhere, perhaps, near Langland's much-loved Malvern Hills.

He was studying maps of medieval Worcestershire and Herefordshire when the car arrived to take him to Heathrow Airport.

18

Dore

They sat outside the church in the early morning sun, by the stream that ran down from Vortipor's spring. The water, when they drank it, was surprisingly cold.

She told him everything she remembered.

'So you see,' she said, 'I'm the Lady Eleanor Blount. Not that you have to bow or anything, or call me my lady. You're not smiling. Do you not have a sense of humour, Andrew?'

He smiled faintly. 'OK. So you are the Lady Eleanor.'

'When I dream I live, somehow, in her body. Or she lives in mine – I don't know which.'

'Was there ever an Eleanor Blount?'

'Not that I can find out. And I've not been able to find out anything about my father who died at Radcott Bridge when de Vere marched south to save the king from the Appellant Lords. There's stuff about my brother, Thomas, though. He was one of the conspirators who planned to kill King Henry at Windsor just before the tournament for Epiphany in January 1400. We'd got a monk, a priest, who would impersonate King Richard until we could rescue him. A monk,' she added, as if anxious to convince him by her detailed knowledge, 'with auburn hair, called Maudelyn.'

'We?'

'I was with the queen. Queen Isabelle. We were at Sonning. We were all in the plot. It was terrible when it failed. The queen was in a panic about being implicated – she was only twelve or thirteen, you know. She sent us away. My mother went to Ely. I was sent with the franklin, sent here, to Dore. Thomas said he'd come for me.'

'What about the other bloke, the one who you thought you'd marry?'

'Bloke? *Bloke*? Ladies don't marry blokes. Walter Manny was a brave young lord; much more dashing than you, I might add.'

'Yeah, well, give me a horse and a suit of armour and we'll see. Did he exist? Was there a Walter Manny?'

'There was a Sir Walter Manny in Edward III's time. The king and the Black Prince discovered that Geoffrey de Chargny was planning to raid Calais for the French. So they slipped across the Channel, secretly, and when Geoffrey de Chargny turned up they sallied out into the frosty December morning crying out 'Manny to rescue! Manny to rescue!'

'Why?'

'Why, because Sir Walter Manny was the commander at Calais, and both the greatest king and the greatest prince in Christendom deemed it a courtesy to serve under him.'

'It all seems . . .' he sighed, 'I don't know. Very jolly.'

'No. Not really. By the time of Eleanor Blount there had been three, four visits by the plague – the "deadly pestilence" as they called it. Half the people in England had been killed by the Black Death, or by cholera or influenza or typhoid.'

'Yes. I know. It's been described as the golden age of bacteria. What were you dreaming earlier? When you cried out?'

'Did I cry out?'

'You woke me up. It was terrible.'

'I can't remember. The dreams go, almost straight away. Sometimes things come back to me later, at odd moments. I told you about the abjurer? The man being banished from the country for a felony? Another time there was a troubadour, I think, a sort of minstrel with tartan trousers, who didn't know any songs. He kept showing us his scrap of parchment, showing that he belonged to the guild of minstrels. There's a servant called Hanchache who has to run behind us, mile after mile, because he has no pony. Do you know what Jack o'Dover is?'

He shook his head.

'We ate Jack o'Dover pie, once, but there was none for Hanchache. There was a dead man at Radcott Bridge. I was looking at the field where the fighting was, where the river sort of divides – it's a meadow with the Thames running round both sides of it – and I was looking at the place where my father died, and I saw a dead man.'

'From the battle?'

140

'Oh no, this was years later, ten, thirteen years later – when was the battle of Radcott Bridge?'

He shook his head.

'This man had just lain down and died. He'd got to the bridge, and could get no further. And nobody cared. I can remember that. I can see it now.'

He looked at her. Her eyes were on him, but were vacant, misty: they were looking through him.

'You must promise,' he said firmly, 'not to sleep there again.'

She leaned over, cupped her hands, drank again from the stream.

'Lizzie?'

A car was coming slowly up the track.

'Lizzie?'

'Don't bully me.'

The car stopped under the trees. A woman came into the church-yard with flowers in her arms.

'I wondered who brought the lilies,' said Lizzie, conscious suddenly that she was wearing nothing but her long T-shirt, and that Andrew was wearing nothing but his trousers.

The woman stopped in surprise. 'Good morning,' she said.

They both said, 'It's lovely, isn't it?'

She went inside. Andrew stood up. He looked down at Lizzie. He said, 'I've been meaning to ask you for ages. Where did you get your personalised T-shirt from?'

'It is not,' she said, 'a personalised T-shirt.'

'Yes it is. ET standing for Enormous—'

'It stands, pig, for Extra Terrestrial.'

'Ah. I think I'll go and talk to the flower woman.'

'What for?'

But he was off, across the grass.

She sat in the sun, and wondered what time it was. Around seven, perhaps. At the camp they'd have finished breakfast and started work by now. Bill would be wondering where they'd got to. Perhaps every-body would assume they'd run away.

Andrew came back.

'Nobody knows the name of the franklin.'

'No, I know that.'

'Don't you think it odd that you yourself don't know his name? I

141

mean, if you're the Lady Eleanor Blount, and you're travelling with him to Dore?'

'I'm not interested in him. He's only a franklin. A rather ridiculous franklin, to be honest. A franklin who recites Langland's verse to impress people, a franklin with a page who stands behind him when he eats.'

'What a snob you are.'

'That's because I'm a lady.'

'The children from Newbridge primary school wrote a pamphlet about him once.'

'Yes, but it's disappeared.'

'They interviewed an old woman in Hay who remembered a story told to her by her grandmother.'

'But nobody remembers who she was, I've been through all this, and anyway she must be dead by now.'

'Her name was Mrs Gapper,' said Andrew, not without a note of self-satisfaction, 'and her husband was from Swansea, and her only daughter, who married a chap who worked for the district council, used to work in a cake shop. We'll check her out, and we'll track down the pamphlet.'

'The library's tried. They put an article in the local paper when the Oxford Medieval Society were trying to find out about the franklin. It was only a primary school end-of-term project, it was only a couple of pages.'

'You're a terrible defeatist.'

'Yes, well. I'm a Ricardian. We always lose. We lost at Radcott Bridge. We tried to rise for Richard of Bordeaux when he was already dead.'

'Richard wasn't much use, I have to say, when he was alive.'

'Ah, you Lancastrians,' said Lizzie. 'Doesn't the flower woman remember the story that was in the pamphlet?'

'She's never seen the pamphlet. She was a small child when it was written. Time passes.'

'Not really,' said Lizzie, as he pulled her to her feet, 'at least, not for all of us.'

Bill Hastings was giving one of his impromptu lectures. 'We're finding no pottery fragments at this level, because the people who first put up these defences did not have pottery skills. They relied, we can assume, on wood and leather . . .'

He saw them and glared. Sonia and Gareth, who thought of themselves as the expedition's romantic interest, looked disapproving. Everybody else grinned.

They went to the stove to make mugs of tea.

'What they did bring with them, however,' Bill went on, his voice heavy with disapproval, 'has been described as a revolution in town planning. Regularly spaced four-post houses, laid out like barracks. Small houses men lived in with their families, and passed to their sons, and to their sons' sons. Right, that's it. As soon as we've all had our breakfast we'll try to get an hour's work in before dinner-time.'

He hadn't any room to be pious, Andrew thought. Venetia looked shagged out and appearances were not deceptive.

At lunchtime they drove to Hay. They went to all the cake shops, and asked for Mrs Gapper's daughter, but nobody knew of her. They went to the church and searched unsuccessfully for Mrs Gapper's grave. They went in and out of bookshops. Andrew bought a copy of *The Fifteenth Century* by E. F. Jacob and a paperback book about dreams that had lurid sexual fantasies depicted on its cover. 'Why do they do that?' said Lizzie. 'Everybody doesn't dream about sex, why do they have to do that?' But it wasn't a question worth answering.

Late in the afternoon they had tea in a café. Andrew studied Jacob's book and said, 'It's all in here, you know. The plot at Epiphany. The flight of the king and the Prince of Wales from Windsor. The monk who was going to impersonate King Richard.'

'So you think I was making it up?'

'Not on purpose.'

'But making it all up all the same. Subconsciously, maybe, but still making it up.'

He drank his tea. 'I'll do a deal.'

'Deal? What do you mean, deal?'

'I'll help you find out about the franklin, if you stop sleeping in the church.'

'And just how, Mr Cleverclogs, can you help me find out about the franklin any better than I can do it myself?'

143

He said, 'I've got transport.'
She said, 'Transport?'
They both looked out of the window at his small, old, Morris Minor.
'That?' she said, incredulously. '*That*?'
He looked at it fondly.
'Andrew, it breaks down every ten miles.'
'It does not, actually, break down every ten miles.'
'Anyway, why do I need transport?'
'Bristol University library for a start. If there's nothing on the shelves we can use your student pass to plug into the Internet, check the Public Records Office, check Somerset House, check the big American academic libraries – for God's sake, PhD students over there have done incredibly detailed research on medieval England. Then we can check medieval church records, see if there's a terrier surviving for Dore—'
'A what?'
'A late-medieval record, generally a list of tithes – fancy you not knowing that. We can also check the tax returns of 1433 – he might have had a widow surviving until then. We're assuming he died about 1410, but if he married a young girl—'
'Young girl? What young girl?'
'Well, I'm guessing,' he said.
'Oh no. There is no way that I was going to marry a franklin.'
'I can't begin to tell you how this snobbiness disgusts me. Franklins did marry the daughters of knights, you know. They were up-and-coming, the New Men. Dick Whittington was a mercer but he was knighted and became Lord Mayor of London.'
'I know all about Dick Whittington.'
'So that's settled. We'll find out who the franklin was—'
'I've actually met Dick Whittington.'
'Yes, I remember you saying. And once we've found out who the franklin was you won't need to sleep in the church, OK? Good.'
He ate his shortbread.
She put her head in her hands.
After a moment: 'Lizzie?'
'You are trying to turn what's happening to me into a bit of fun research. You are trying to rationalise it all into a summer history project. You don't actually believe a thing I've said.'

She looked up.

'I'm not in a position to believe or disbelieve . . . but I think that when you go into the church, at night, you are open to all sorts of influences that could actually be dangerous – self-suggestion, hallucination—'

'What? What did you say?'

'Self-hypnosis even—'

'You know nothing, absolutely nothing, about it! Christ!'

She was trembling. 'And Richard Whittington was not the Lord Mayor,' she said, 'he was the mayor, just the mayor, right? And he was mayor twice, not three times, and as far as anyone knows he had no interest at all in cats.'

A girl behind the counter was watching them covertly round the hot-water urn.

Lizzie said, 'More tea?' and poured some for him, then, because the girl was still watching, she put her bit of carrot cake on his plate.

The girl still watched, undeceived by such signs of affection.

'I am utterly convinced,' Andrew said, 'that you should stop sleeping in the church.'

'You could sleep there with me.'

Why had she said that? Why did she just say things?

'I've thought of that,' he said, eating her cake. 'But I might turn out to be Hanchache, forever running behind your pony and not getting any pie.'

She laughed, a bit uncertainly. 'You just don't want to have to call me my lady.'

There was a pause.

'So,' he said. 'So who was this Malcolm then?'

'How do you know about Malcolm?'

'Venetia.'

'Malcolm was a nerd. What about this Lorna?'

It was Eloise who had told them all about Andrew's love life. Eloise knew all about everybody's love lives. What Eloise needed, Sonia said, smugly, was a love life of her own.

'Lorna was all right, actually.'

A woman, stout, middle-aged, was standing in the doorway, looking at them hesitantly. Andrew smiled across at her and said, 'Mrs Gapper's daughter?'

She came over. 'I thought it had to be you,' she said, 'from the description. I hear you've been looking all over for me.'

They sat her down and gave her tea. 'This takes me back,' she said. 'People used to come and interview my mum all the time in the Sixties.'

'I'm Andrew, and this is Lizzie,' said Andrew, politely. 'You would be Mrs . . .?'

'Newton.'

'And your mum was Mrs Gapper,' said Lizzie, 'who had an amazing store of stories.'

'And liked telling them.'

'Didn't you like your mother's stories?'

'Oh, they were all right. But dear me, how she used to rattle them out. She was a seer – a mystic, if you know what I mean. She could see into the past. I suppose you think we're all mad.'

'Not at all,' said Lizzie sincerely, darting a look of malice at Andrew.

'Apart from her mystic gifts,' he said, 'we understand she had stories of past events, passed down by oral tradition?'

'Welsh stories for the most part, told her by her grandmother.'

'Owain,' said Lizzie, 'of the Shining Helm?'

'I couldn't say.'

'Didn't she tell you them?'

'Oh yes. All the time when I was a young girl. My friend kept wanting me to go next door to her house and watch *Ready Steady Go* and *Six Five Special* on the telly, but I'd be sitting with my mum listening to her tales. We were a queer family. Then I left home, and Mum seemed to lose interest in her old stories – she said she'd forgotten it all, but Dad said it was more to do with Cliff Michelmore and nature programmes on the box. But then in her old age, when she was a widow, she seemed to remember them all again.'

'Did she live with you and your husband?'

'Yes, and my husband wasn't sympathetic. When he got home after working in the garage depot all day he didn't want her blethering on.'

'When she was telling her stories,' said Lizzie, 'did she ever mention the franklin of Dore?'

Mrs Newton looked thoughtful. 'Was he the one who slew the

White Dragon of Pennbluith, and sewed dragons' teeth into an ivory necklace for the Bride of Tintagel?'

'No,' said Andrew. 'That was Mort d'Arthur, or something like it.'

'I remember there was a story about a Saxon tyrant that marched into Chester. Twelve hundred monks won the crown of martyrdom and assured themselves a seat in heaven.'

'Did they?' asked Lizzie, her heart sinking.

'I used to try and picture it as a little girl. Blederic, the Duke of Cornwall, was our leader, and to me he was as wonderful as Bill Haley or Elvis.'

The tea shop was closing. The girl had got tired of earwigging and was noisily packing things away. They went across the road to a pub where Mrs Newton had a large gin and tonic. 'I do remember a chap called Malgo,' she said, anxious to please. 'He was a king who reigned fourth after Arthur. And he begat two sons, one of them called Ennianus and the other named Run.'

'Named what?' asked Lizzie.

'Run,' said Andrew, 'as in rabbit.'

'And Ennianus begat Belin, and Belin begat Iago. It's funny the things that come back to you. Where did you say you were from?'

'We're at an archaeological dig at Dore. We've become interested in the franklin in the church.'

'My mum,' said Mrs Newton, 'knew all about Vortipor's Fort. She could have told you a thing or two about Vortipor, and about Cadwallo, and his nephew Brian.'

'Brian?' said Lizzie.

'Brian,' said Andrew, 'as in Life of.'

'There was one story I remember,' said Mrs Newton. 'King Cadwallo was consumed with desire to eat a particular wild beast, and Brian went hunting. All over the island of Britain he went, looking for this particular wild beast, while King Cadwallo got hungrier and hungrier. In the end do you know what Brian did?'

They shook their heads.

'He cut open his own thigh, and sliced off a piece of flesh, and cooked it over a fire, and gave it to Cadwallo who gobbled it up and said how sweet it tasted. And in three days the king had got back his old cheery briskness and never ailed again.'

She laughed. She was on her second large gin.

'So you don't remember anything, anything at all,' said Lizzie, 'about the franklin?'

She didn't. But she knew that Vortipor had indulged in sexual excesses of a kind never before heard of in the island of Britain, and she advised them that she wouldn't, herself, sleep in the hill fort for a million pounds.

They drove back along the A438, the old Roman road. They ate in a pub in Staunton. They were silent, tense. She was going to sleep in the church; he was going to try to stop her. When they got back to the camp there was only Eloise, Jacob, and Badger sitting by the fire: Sonia and Gareth were at the pub in the village, as usual, and had taken Wolfgang with them. Venetia and Bill had gone for dinner somewhere.

Lizzie said, 'Dinner? Dinner as opposed to "Where's the grub then"?'

'Dinner,' said Eloise. She was labelling shards by the light of a gas lamp.

Badger was staring into the flames of the little fire, seeking, perhaps, some kind of mystic communion with other real-ale addicts. In three days' time he was going to North Wales in search of an ale given to him once by a little silver-bearded Welshman at a beer festival. The morning after the festival he had awakened in the knowledge that he had tasted the best beer in the world, but had forgotten its name.

'You probably dreamed it,' said Andrew, looking at Lizzie. 'It probably doesn't exist.'

But Badger knew that it existed. He would find the brewery somewhere in the misty valleys.

A party of students from Sheffield were supposed to arrive for the final week of the dig, but nobody seemed to know when they would turn up.

Eloise said, 'We're all running out of steam, aren't we?'

'It's the heat,' said Andrew.

'Still,' said Lizzie, trying to sound bright, 'we'll soon be in the mound.'

Eloise said, 'We broke into it this evening.'

'Did you?'

'Just after seven. There was only me and Jacob and Badger. The others had all gone.'

A silence.

'I think we're all losing interest,' said Eloise. 'Tomorrow we'll be digging into what might be the druids' ceremonial area, if this is anything like Croft Ambrey. We ought to be excited, but nobody's bothered any more.'

'No,' said Lizzie. What did it matter? Why did they so want to turn up a sightless skull, a bit of crumbling bone? To point a telescope into the past and adjust the focus. To add a footnote to the sum of knowledge about first century BC farming techniques, or the extent of intermarriage between Iron Age A and Iron Age B.

To stumble, perhaps, on untold treasures – Saxon gold, jewellery, the swords and shields of kings. Well, that was more like it. Lizzie smiled faintly. It debased the scientist in them, but it made them human. The fantasy that they might, one day, gently wipe a thumb along a blackened rim and feel metal – rub it slowly, so slowly, so delicately, and see the glint of gold, the flash of blue, red and amber stones.

Her experiences in the church. Was she just seeking another, different, way into the past?

Jacob played his guitar. They drank some cans of beer. Then Andrew put up his camp bed; and another, next to him, for Lizzie, then he put one up for Eloise who said, sadly, 'Thanks, Andrew, you're a gentleman.' There had been six men and four girls on the dig. 'She'll have a lad by now' her mum and dad would be saying to her cousins and aunts. But no, she, the romantic one, was yet again the only girl unattached.

'Sleep,' said Andrew, taking his shirt off. 'Tomorrow we find the hall of King Vortipor.'

'Listen,' said Jacob, stopping playing. 'There were no nations before Rome. It was Rome that brought the tribes together. Without Rome, Caradoc would just have been a petty chieftain ruling what his eye could see from his hill fort. Without the Saxons, Vortipor would have been a village elder somewhere, uncorrupted, a good man.'

'It's a twentieth-century view, Jacob,' said Andrew. 'But whenever, and wherever, there's always a guy who gets the upper hand and becomes *el Dictateur*, and always he wants *more*.'

'But the Iron Age wasn't like that,' said Lizzie. 'The hill forts were occupied by farmers and by craftsmen.'

'An age of innocence?' said Andrew. 'Before Eve took that apple?'

'That's the evidence,' said Lizzie. 'Those are the *facts*.'

A noise, a powerful, ominous roar, building fast, threatening: already Badger and Eloise had their hands over their ears. Lizzie turned and saw two red winking lights approaching at unbelievable speed.

Then the lights were overhead, and the roar was ear-shattering: a second later and the jets were gone, speeding up the long valley into Wales, and already they were wheeling, climbing, speeding towards the distant loom of the Black Mountains.

Every age corrupts, thought Lizzie. She said, 'Every age corrupts.'

'That is very true,' said Jacob solemnly.

'Every age is a little bit more vicious than the age before.'

'Yes,' said Eloise.

'How much have you had to drink?' said Andrew.

Did he love her or didn't he? If he loved her would he accuse her of making trite remarks?

'Not a lot,' she said coldly. 'You'd have been at home in the Stone Age, Jacob,' she added, getting up, 'playing your guitar, wearing animal skins. You,' she said to Andrew, 'should have been around in the year 1400.'

For it had, of course, been a trite remark. There was not an inevitable progression downwards. There was an arrow of time that said everything must collapse from order into chaos, but mankind built cathedrals and turned chaos into order. The end of the fourteenth century had seen cruelty, and corruption, and decay, that had never been seen in England since.

She picked up her sleeping bag and set off across the plateau. They watched her until she reached the rampart, silhouetted against the purple sky. Eloise said, 'She's going to sleep in the church again.'

Jacob said, 'Bill's right. A girl shouldn't sleep down there, not on her own.'

They were all looking at Andrew, lying back on his camp bed.

He sighed and got up.

She was waiting, on the path, at the place where it went down into the woodland. 'This hedge,' she said, 'is a particularly interesting hedge. I thought it was medieval, but actually it goes back to Saxon times. There's a charter covering the grant of an estate of five *cassati* or hides to the monastery of St Mary in Worcester, and the hedge is mentioned as the boundary.'

'What's that?' he interrupted, looking at distant red lights strung across the sky.

'Some sort of satellite station. SAS, I expect. Seeing what the world's up to, deciding who to beat up next. Don't you approve?'

'Lizzie—'

'This hedge dates back to Athelstan, to before Athelstan. No wonder it's incredibly rich in hedgerow species – lords and ladies, stinking iris. Goodness, wouldn't I like to be here in September—'

'Come back to the camp.'

'No.'

They stood in the darkness.

'Andrew, what if it is reincarnation? Five per cent of people, according to the hypnotist I visited, can remember their past lives. There's that woman who visits her sons and they're older than she is—'

'Drivel, absolute drivel—'

'What if I am the reincarnated soul – personality, whatever it is – of Eleanor Blount? Do you really expect me to just turn and walk away, and not use the best method I know to find out about myself, about what I once was?'

'We've been through this. We've agreed that we will research in the libraries—'

'We haven't agreed, you've agreed—'

'Come back to the camp.'

'No.'

He sighed. She could see that he was carrying his sleeping bag.

'OK,' he said. 'OK, let's go down there.'

The church was filled with the scent of lilies, the fresh flowers brought to the church that morning. They put down their sleeping bags, side by side. Andrew rolled up his shirt for a pillow and said, 'Christ, this floor is hard.'

Lizzie said, 'It's all right, there's nothing to be frightened of.'

He did not reply.

They lay together. She said, in the darkness, 'You have to put out your hand. You have to touch the tomb.'

'You're the one with a past life.'

'I don't actually think it is reincarnation. I think the franklin's tomb is somehow a conduit to the past.'

He said, quietly, 'Tomorrow, I vote we go to Bristol, get on the Internet.'

'Oh, Andrew . . .' Then she said, 'Can you smell anything?'

'Yes. Deathwatch beetle.'

'Not that . . . put your hand on the frieze, on the alabaster. Touch one of the flowers.'

'Tomorrow we start checking everything you remember, until we get a logical explanation. Then we go to France and pick grapes.'

No reply. He said, quietly, 'Lizzie?'

He reached for his small pocket torch.

Her eyes were closed. She was unconscious, breathing quietly.

He looked at her for a few moments. He wondered if it was some form of epilepsy.

He wondered what would happen if he took her hand away from the white alabaster rose.

After a few moments, he put his own hand on the alabaster.

Nothing.

He looked again at Lizzie.

Where was she? What was happening to her?

There was a faint smile on her face.

19

Hereford: The Feast of the Presentation, 1400

A man in the brown robe of a pardoner leaned towards her whispering that a silver groat bought a week less in purgatory, that his indulgences were better than any sold by grasping friar or gin-soaked monk. Bony, shaking hands held out thin scraps of parchment. He was desperate for a sale before the bishop's men found him and beat him for trading, unlicensed, in the cathedral.

'What will you give me,' asked Eleanor, 'for a small stone from Christ's sepulchre?'

The pardoner's smile turned into a sneering grin. He slipped away into the crowd.

'He is selling, not buying,' said Toke. 'And stones from Christ's sepulchre are the saddest relics in Christendom.'

'I had once,' said Flesshe, 'a stone from the bladder of the Emperor Diocletian.'

'Did you, page?' said Eleanor, politely impressed.

Why did she always call him page? He was a boy servant. That he stood behind Toke at dinner was a politeness. In Italy all merchants had servants to stand behind them when they ate.

She was looking up at the great west window. She wore her man's cloak wrapped tightly round her body. Whose cloak was it? Her brother's?

Her face was pale and pinched, her thick Blount lips colourless, her big Blount eyes swollen from weeping. It was an extravagance, thought Toke. An extravagance of emotion, a sin against God's will. She was fourteen. Death had been a commonplace since she first knew the world.

He said, awkward, abrupt, 'What would you look at first?'

She did not reply. She had slipped off again into a dream.

He said, knowing her mind, 'There is a knight who fell at Poitiers.'

She said, 'Ah, the flower of France fell at Poitiers!'

153

She was in her castle tower, in her garden of roses. Her mind was addled by the romantic fantasies of repressed French monks. No, he would not marry her.

Yet he lusted, he suffered. ('God gave man to lust,' said the old saw, soothingly, 'to encourage him to matrimony.') There was a black bile in his heart, for he had known, and scorned, merchants who married the daughters of noblemen: who delighted in hearing the daughter of a knight call them lord. Yet he lusted now for Eleanor. He lusted to hear her call him lord.

'When, sir, do we go to Dore?' she asked, as she had every day since they arrived at the city.

'When it is safe,' he replied, as he always replied.

But once delivered to Dore, she would pass beyond the veil: beyond his sight.

They saw the knight who fought at Poitiers, lying under his burnished helm with its vast spray of peacock feathers. They went to the Lady Chapel, to the shrine of St Thomas. It was January, not the season for pilgrims, and only a dozen or so visitors were gathered round the tomb of bright painted wood, honey-coloured stone, and snowy alabaster.

'Oh page!' said Eleanor. 'Oh, page!'

A vast, triple crown of candles sparkled over the tomb. A priest, dressed in white and purple robes, swung a golden orb of burning incense. Flames of coloured fire shot from the jewel-encrusted box that held St Thomas's bones: amethysts and rubies, and deep blue sapphires given in homage by a great king. Behind the screen the duty vicars choral sang:

> *Sancta Maria, ora pro nobis*
> *Ora pro nobis*
> *Sancta Virgo virginium*
> *Ora pro nobis.*

The bones of St Thomas earned the monks of Hereford a thousand pounds a year. Pilgrims were not disappointed (as pilgrims to Edward II's tomb at Gloucester were so grievously disappointed, the monks of Gloucester spending all their money building cloisters) but returned to their homes singing the marvels of Hereford: and the following year other pilgrims from their town or village, clubbing together in associations, chose Hereford for their summer visit.

Behind the leper rail a solitary shadowy figure crouched: deformed, blotched fingers reaching out to touch the saint's effigy. A priest passed between the pilgrims collecting alms. Commissioners from the Pope, he whispered, had vouched for two hundred and four cures at the shrine, including forty raisings from the dead. The boy Flesshe wanted to know when the next dead body would be brought in. He yearned, he said, to see a dead man stand up and walk. The priest looked at him coldly, and turned away. Toke said, 'This, boy, is the place where I will show you a unicorn.'

Out of the corner of his eye, he watched Eleanor.

'The last unicorn,' he went on, 'in all England.'

He smiled a secret smile under his capuchin.

Eleanor said, 'Be careful he doesn't try to sell it to you, page.'

They went out of the west door, carefully skirting the charnel pits and the three plague graves where swine grubbed around the shallow, illegal graves of the unbaptised. They walked through the Lady Arbour, through an empty building site; for the men working on the bishop's new cloisters had been sent to repair the city walls.

There was a new building before them, a ten-sided building, rose-red in colour.

'Is that where it is caged?' asked Flesshe.

'Aye, indeed,' said Toke, glancing slyly at Eleanor. She looked at him, half doubting, half believing.

'They say a lion,' said Flesshe, 'was caged once at the Tower.'

Toke said, 'It was in the days of King Edward III.'

Flesshe said, 'I wonder if they have trained the unicorn to dance and show its silver hooves?'

They went into the building. Cold January light flooded down through windows glazed with green translucent glass. A single column in the centre of the room fanned out in delicate ribs of stone, like the opening of a flower. Parchments hung from the new stone walls, or were rolled and stored in pipes. There was a smell of paper, and of ink, and of tallow. A priest, bobbing and smiling, beckoned them in.

'There, boy,' said Toke. 'There!'

Flesshe looked for the unicorn prancing on a sawdust floor.

155

'There, you see it?'

Flesshe looked around him.

The only map of the world that is in the world!'

It was not, truly, the only map of the world, but it was a great *mappa mundi* all the same. The priest, anxious for his silver penny, beckoned them towards the quilt of parchment hung from the wall. He described how it had been brought to Hereford from Lincoln – and oh what a tale there was to tell! – for the monks of Lincoln had wanted it back (Lincoln, they said, was on the map, Hereford was not) and they had sent emissaries to King Edward I asking for its return, and had petitioned Edward II, who had ordered the map to be returned to Lincoln, but the monks of Hereford had claimed it was too dangerous to move it, and Edward had been murdered at Berkeley, and Mortimer had been too loyal a Lord of the Marches to listen to the indignation of Lincoln's monks, and Queen Isabelle too besotted with Mortimer to listen to the babbling of monks anyway, and so Lincoln's claim to possession had faded, and after another fifty years of cunning and quiet the monks of Hereford were confident now of claiming it as their own.

'I was here with Langland,' said Toke, 'when a new name was added to the map. Now, attend to me. What name do you think that was?'

Eleanor was not listening. She was far away.

('Hereford' the travelling scribe had written, having found a little patch of space between two rivers, in a place that Trefnant the bishop had thought vaguely to be in the western world. The travelling scribe had written without confidence, in brown ink with a badger brush, then stared sadly at the ink as it dried.)

Toke took a candle from the priest, and held it up, and showed them where the city's name had been added. He showed them Jerusalem, France, and Rome. He showed them Babylon. 'See, see,' he said, 'the city of hanging gardens!'

Eleanor and the boy stared at the map in silence. It was not Babylon. It was a cloth of parchment.

'And here,' said Toke, pointing to the top corner, 'here is the unicorn.'

And there it was, a painted beast with its single horn.

'Oh page, page,' said Eleanor, 'your master has found a unicorn.'

The priest, anxious to please, was trying to show them other treasures, urging them away from the map – a dull enough thing with little colour about it – and holding his candle up to a vellum scroll on which the arms of England shone in red and gold.

Richard by the grace of God, king of England and France, and lord of Ireland, to all to whom these presents shall come, greeting. Know ye that by our special grace, and at the supplication of our chosen and faithful knight John de Burley, we grant from ourselves and our heirs to our favoured citizens of our city of Hereford ...

It was the city's charter.

'Alas for King Richard,' said Eleanor. 'Alas for Isabelle, Richard's wife!'

The priest was still suddenly, his smile fixed. Hereford was for Lancaster. Bishop Trefnant had been one of those who had pulled Richard down. In every tavern from the Sun to the Dragon (the Green Dragon of England, not the Red Dragon of Wales) men who worked in the cloth mills on the Wye, the tanneries and the barge buildings, the factory famous for making gloves, knew that Hereford was for Lancaster, and for hatred of the Welsh.

Eleanor said, suddenly, 'Sir Priest, is it safe to travel to Dore?'

The priest looked at her in astonishment, then said, 'As safe as it is to travel anywhere.'

'Sir, is the Lord Owain Glyn Dŵr raising an army?'

'The Welsh,' said the priest bitterly, 'are forever raising armies.'

'Sir,' said Eleanor, outside the cathedral. 'When do we go—'

'Be quiet—'

'I tell you I shall come to no harm from the Lord Glyn Dŵr!'

He seized her arm and dragged her back to their lodgings.

'Do you not know, madam, why you were sent from London? Do you think the king's ears do not reach this far?'

He was filled with a cold fury. He ordered her into her room and put Hanchache to guard the door. He sent in her food and swore that if she asked again about going to Dore he would beat her, or get the woman of the house to beat her.

He went again to the cathedral, and said to the priest, 'The nunnery at Dore. Tell me about it.'

'The nuns are void of conscience,' said the priest, 'drunken and unchaste.'

157

'Yes, yes.' Toke was impatient, for it was what priests said of every convent.

The priest looked at him, a franklin in a rich beaver coat. Toke said, 'I take a young girl to Dore. A girl nominated by the bishop of London, to be received by Dame Elizabeth and instructed by her in the regular disciplines.'

The priest silently passed to him a report by the abbot of Abbey Dore monastery, who had carried out an inspection of the nunnery on instruction of the Papal legate.

Item. Dame Alice Collis says that Dames Lettice Woodford, Margaret Moose, and Philippa Paget do not go to the dormitory immediately after compline, but wait longer. Anne Nores says the same.

Item. Dame Beatrice says the abbess is not impartial in her manner but shows greater affection to some nuns than to others, viz Dame Margaret Moose and Philippa Paget.

'At Dore nunnery,' said the priest, a shadowy, secret smile on his face, 'there is seemingly a firm understanding of the regular disciplines.'

What would you expect, thought Toke, reading the report, when you shut women up together?

He went back to their lodgings at the Green Dragon. She said, 'Sir, when do we go to Dore?'

He said, 'Ask that question again and I will have you beaten.'

She said, 'Sir, I would know when I go to Dore.'

He called two women of the house. He stood and watched as Eleanor was held over a chest and beaten.

Afterwards, her thin face white, her full lips bloodless, like ivory, she said, 'Sir, when do we go—'

He left her, locked in her room.

That night for supper he sent her only bread and water.

He also sent her a book: the ballad of Robyn Hode and the Earl of Chester.

A king's messenger came clattering over the Bye Street Gate, across the old Saxon ditch. France had closed the Somme at Abbeville. Bourbon was moving against the English city of Bordeaux. A fleet was assembled at Harfleur to descend on Wales, where Owain Glyn Dŵr had raised the dragon standard. All of northern Wales, valley after valley, was sending its men to fight for the heir of Llywelyn, who had sworn to burn down Hereford, the great capital city of English Wales, as his ancestors had burned it in the time of Edward the Confessor.

The city was in a ferment. A prison was made in the Boothall. Laws were passed against the Welsh – against their owning property, against their marrying English women. There was talk of traitors in high places, and aldermen were forbidden to walk alone outside the city gates, under penalty of a ten-shilling fine. From the castle battlements armed men stared out to the west, watching straggling groups of people streaming to the city from the Marches. From dawn to dusk gangs of men toiled to build defences round the tanneries and the cloth mills.

For the first time in a year the huge portcullis was lowered on the Wyegate.

'Tomorrow, sir,' said Ware, 'we go north.'

'I wish you would remain.'

But Ware was unwilling to remain. His men yearned for the moorlands, for home; they would not die defending Hereford against the Welsh, not for threepence a day.

Should Toke take Eleanor north to Staffordshire? Take her to his own manor? Should he write to her mother at Ely, and offer to marry her daughter?

He went to Eleanor's room. The door that should have been locked was open. He could hear her chattering to some girl of the inn. 'The queen had a tunic close-fitted, here . . .'

He stopped on the stairs. He imagined her, her hands running lightly down over her breasts, her waist . . .

'And on her head was a tiny crown. That was the only time I ever saw the usurper King Henry. He gave her a gold greyhound with a pearl hanging from its neck. But she liked Rutland best, though he gave her only a mirror shaped like a marguerite.'

Queen Isabelle had been eight when she had married Richard. The king, it was said, had pretended that she was a grown lady, and he her humble and adoring knight.

She saw him in the doorway.

She said, 'Sir, when do we go to Dore?'

That night Ware brought him a letter she had tried to send to Maud, kinswoman of Alice, daughter of Owain Glyn Dŵr, who was married to Sir John Scudamore of Kentchurch. She had given it to Hickey, one of the archers. (Hickey was the only man who had been able to make her smile after she learned of the death of her brother: he had pretended to be frightened of the monkey.)

The letter said, 'Well, Maud, it seems that the world is all quavering. It will rebound somewhere, so that I deem young men shall be cherished. Tell you this to Squire Manny. Tell him take his heart to him. Tell him I will be at Dore. Written upon St Valentine's Day, that is when every bird chuses a mate. God keep you. Your cousin's cousin.'

Toke would take her to Dore. He would have none of her.

The English coming to Hereford from the Marches became a trickle. The lands to the west, beyond the Wye, lay empty. Each morning men strained to see the flash of chain mail, the gleam of metal, but there was only the occasional glint of the pale sun on flooded lands.

Silence, except for the rushing of the Wye past the city walls.

The cloth mills started up again, though lookouts kept a constant watch to the west, particularly at dawn, and again as the sun went down.

Toke and Eleanor were on the castle battlements. Above them flew the red cross of St George. Below the wall celandines were in flower along the water's edge. Eleanor watched a heron.

'There is no law,' said Toke, 'beyond these city gates.'

Eleanor stared at the distant mountains, black on the western horizon.

'In Staffordshire I have a manor—'

She said, sharply, 'My mother commands me to go to the nuns at Dore.'

Toke felt the black bile, the black blood, thud in his heart.

'So be it.'

He would have none of her.

He said to Ware: 'If I provide mounts, will you go with us into Wales, for sixpence a day?'

Ware spoke to his archers. He said, 'We will travel with you for a week, sir. Then we will go north to our own country.'

The vast oak doors of the Friarsgate slowly opened. Beyond was the great ditch, crossed by a plank bridge, and beyond the bridge a few farmers waiting to bring produce into the city.

'You will return?' the mayor asked, greedy for the six archers, wondering if he dared forbid them to go.

'God willing,' said Toke.

'Glyn Dŵr willing,' said one of the labourers under his breath: he was a Welshman, sweating at having hauled on the gates.

They rode out. Toke ahead on his horse, as always; Eleanor holding her monkey; the boy, Flesshe; Hanchache on a pony at last, his long legs dangling to the ground. Ware and his five archers, now mounted, the last archer leading a packhorse.

The sun was behind them. The mountains of the west were a black gash on the horizon.

The guards on the battlements watched them ride into the empty lands.

20

Utah

Martha drove east across the moonscape, past the saguaro cacti and the tumbleweed. The sky was at once livid and dark, dying red streaked with blood. She flicked on her mobile.

She said, 'Update me.'

A voice in the military hospital: 'The EEG is still showing abnormal sleep-pattern brain activity although his eyes remain open. It's not just at night, when we turn the lights real low, and you'd expect him to be asleep and dreaming, and it follows no regular pattern.'

'What kind of waves are you getting?'

'Delta type for the most part, one to four cycles per second, characteristic of coma, but we're also getting intermittent spikes coming up, spike and wave patterns you'd expect with some kinds of epilepsy.'

'But it isn't epilepsy?'

'Nothing we recognise.'

Perhaps Pope was wrong. Perhaps Koenig was the prime carrier. Perhaps, from his hospital bed, from his state of unconsciousness, his brain was receiving, sending, processing, signals from *Pasiphae*.

Yes, perhaps Pope was wrong. Perhaps a tiny electrical flicker in Koenig's brain, a microscopic spasm in the fatty film of the neural network, really could bring an aircraft crashing down in France.

'The delta wave activity with the spikes,' she said, 'this was occurring around two-thirty yesterday?'

'Yes. Both the EEG and the geodesic sensor net picked up an abnormal pattern, similar to a mild epileptic charge, at two-twenty-one lasting for over sixteen minutes.'

She said, 'This sensor net. Is there any danger here?'

'The geodesic sensor net is like the EEG, it's totally non-invasive' – a defensive note – 'it's measuring, that's all, they use it on newborn babies, it's no different from positron emission topography or psychophysical investigation.'

'Right.'

'We want to move on to something else.'

'Yeah, I got the message from Sluder. You want to slice his skull open and fix electrodes directly to his brain.'

'It's nothing like as dramatic as it sounds.'

But for a man whose brain might now be an integral part of the world's most advanced communications network – for a man whose brain might be possessed of the power to wreak vast destruction . . .

'For a man recovering from a stroke,' she said, 'it might not be a good idea.'

The man at the hospital said, 'The EEG has severe limitations. It tells us the waves operating in the brain. It tells us alpha waves when the subject's relaxed, double-alpha, beta, when the subject opens his or her eyes. It tells us that he's dreaming, but not *what he's dreaming*. It's been described as like being in a room next to a cinema projector. You can hear the projector running, you know there's a film on the screen, but you can't see it. We need to know what's in Koenig's mind. I've been told that we *have to know this*. There's a guy from Washington, from the Pentagon, calling just about every hour. There's some professor in Oxford, England, who's been phoning the ward and claims to be working for Electronic Security Command . . .'

She closed her eyes briefly in despair. What did Pope think he was doing?

'The NSA is handling this, not the Pentagon or ESC, and you don't do anything without my say so.'

No reply.

A green glow appeared ahead of her, in the distance down the long, straight desert road. She passed a notice saying that she was entering the Uintah and Ouray Indian Reservation. A signpost pointed west across a dirt road to Bonanza. A sign came up advertising the Dinosaur Diner.

She said, 'Koenig's fiancée, is she still at the hospital?'

'No, she had to go home to keep her job.'

'You don't do anything till you get the OK from me. Is that clear?'

Reluctantly, 'You're the boss.'

And you'd better believe it, she thought grimly.

She ordered coffee and said, 'How's he doing?' and Mary Lou said, 'They found a blood clot in his legs and are fearful it will move to his lungs.'

'Oh Mary Lou, I'm sorry . . .' She looked concerned, though there was no real fear, she knew, about the blood clot: it was a devious cover for what might have to come if Sluder and his allies had their way.

'They may do a small operation.'

'Right.'

'They seem hopeful. They're talking about rehabilitation, which means getting his functions back, and health education, which means changing his diet mainly.'

'Has he spoken to you yet?' Martha said, feeling it was the right thing to ask.

Mary Lou shook her head. 'Not yet. But at least I know he's conscious in there. At least I know what he's thinking.'

She went to serve a trucker, who was sitting by the window looking out at the dark silhouette of the Colorado Mountains. Blues music playing now on the juke box: 'Sweet Home Chicago'. A notice said the Evening Special was spare rib steaks, but most of the truck drivers and commercial travellers were eating eggs-over-light and hash browns with crispy bacon, or bowls of chilli with cigarettes on the side: hunched and weary and thinking perhaps of home, or of that long, long winding road over the Wasatch Mountains to Salt Lake City. Mary Lou filled their cups with fresh coffee, tried to smile, but looked beaky and mournful. 'I left my heart in San Francisco' said the juke box. Her own heart was left a hundred and eight miles away, at a hospital near Hill Air Force Base. She came back to the counter. Martha said, 'You really know what he's thinking?'

Mary Lou nodded. She said, 'You know what he did Friday?'

Martha said, 'Tell me.'

Mary Lou leaned over the counter. She bit her lower lip. A tear came into her eye. She said, 'He squeezed my hand.'

'Oh, Mary Lou . . .'

'It might not sound much, but I went directly and told the nurse

165

and she came running in, and two other nurses, and they all wanted their hands squeezing just to prove it wasn't some sort of reflex reaction. "Squeeze my hand, Mr Koenig", they kept saying.'

'It sounds like a good sign.'

'Yeah, that's right. A real good sign. They said whatever moves in the first three months, well, that function is going to come back. That's why they do all they can to get some sort of response. They're very concerned to get his speech restored.'

'Yes,' said Martha.

'They got one guy's mouth muscles to work by putting cubes of frozen wine on his tongue, but I don't know that John ever drank much in the way of wine.'

Martha said, 'You said you know what John's thinking about.'

Mary Lou nodded.

'Is he thinking about you?'

Mary Lou said, 'Maybe.'

She was staring beakily at Martha; perhaps she wasn't so naive, wasn't so innocent, wasn't so trusting. She said, 'What I'd like to know is, what caused it?'

'Pardon?'

'What caused John's stroke?'

'Oh my, well, men of his age, Mary Lou. Age, lifestyle and maybe – just maybe – the job he does? Crouched over a computer screen all day long, no exercise, a deal of stress.'

A diet, she thought, that could kill at five hundred yards.

Mary Lou took her coffee cup from her and refilled it. She said, 'Do you know what he was working on, the night he got taken ill?'

'Whatever it was,' said Martha, 'I don't believe it has anything to do with his stroke.'

Mary Lou went to serve a commercial traveller with pie. She came back. 'Those new guys, those psychiatrists from government security. They keep wanting to know what he's thinking, what's going on in his mind. Every time I go there and sit with him they're waiting for me afterwards. They drove me to Provo once, to my sister's place, and all the time they were asking me questions about John, what I thought was going on in his mind, what I thought had been in his mind the day he had the stroke, did he ever talk about militia groups, anti-government militia groups, you know what I mean?'

'Yeah, I know.' Half of Martha's career with the NSA had been spent analysing right-wing militia groups.

'Well, anyway, once he's over this we're going to get married, and he's going to stop working at that place, and get away from that Sluder guy, and we'll open a Waffle House over in Colorado.'

She looked at Martha for approval. Martha thought of Koenig in a Waffle House, a mountain of cholesterol in a culinary killing field. She said, 'I think that's a great idea. But Mary Lou, you say you know what he's thinking—'

'I was talking to him about it, describing the sort of food we'd serve, the best fried chicken west of Tennessee, the best blueberry chiffon pie on God's earth, and it was then I felt him squeeze my hand. He'd been lying there, his eyes wide open, for days and days, and we didn't know if he was conscious or not, and those psychiatrist guys kept writing things on bits of card and holding them up, and messing with all this machinery and wires on his head, but when I said blueberry chiffon pie, well, that was when he squeezed my hand.'

'Did you tell the nurses how you got through to him? The things you were talking about?'

Mary Lou looked shifty.

'Don't you think you should have told them, Mary Lou?'

'After the way they lectured me on *rehabilitation*? After the way they practically said I'd poisoned him?'

Twenty minutes later, driving out on the track to the receiving station, turning towards the winking lights of the tall, slender radio mast, Martha called Salt Lake City again. 'I can tell you what's in Koenig's mind,' she said. 'John Koenig is dreaming of lemon meringues and blueberry chiffon pie. He's dreaming about a Waffle House in Aspen. If the Pentagon want something to report to the President, they can tell him that, OK?'

She parked and walked over to the reception centre. Sluder was leaning against the patio rail, in the place where cigarette smokers gathered to foul up the Utah atmosphere.

He said, 'Charlie Pope's back.'

'Yes. He flew into LA an hour ago.'

'Your doing?'

'Yes.'

'Jesus . . .' He shook his head, marvelling at the treachery of women.

'Larry, he's the physicist who worked closest with Hollbecker. Hollbecker's dead, if I could consult him I would. Are we going inside?'

There was dust blowing over the desert: grit stinging her eyes. Sluder said, 'John Koenig. There's still stuff going through his brain. Did they tell you?'

'They told me. Koenig's fiancée believes he's mulling over recipes, reliving great meals of the past, planning to open a restaurant.'

'There's *Pasiphae* stuff going through Koenig's brain,' Sluder went on, not listening. 'And logic says it has to be the same stuff – just going round and round. Maybe he did receive some kind of signal by direct transference.'

'That's the theory.'

'I'm not into all this morphic resonance, communing with the dead crap, but if somebody out there is hacking into *Pasiphae* they're using some very, very subtle means of entry, some way that's outside our disinfectant programs, some way that maybe is dangerous for human operatives to handle. An electronics genius of some kind, maybe, or a kid whose brain is precisely tuned to *Pasiphae* technology – a million-in-one chance – I'm thinking aloud here—'

'I appreciate that, Larry.'

'It may be that with Koenig some kind of synaptic modification took place. You know synapses? Connections between the nerve cells, maybe modified as electric pulses, nerve signals?'

'Picking up *Pasiphae*'s sub-molecular transmissions, yeah, Larry—'

'But only those transmissions corrupted by a hacker. Only the corruptions themselves. I'm not saying it happened. I just think we need to keep an open mind.'

For Sluder, thought Martha, this was a foreign language, this was awesome.

'Yeah, right.' She didn't say that this was where Charles Pope had been a week back; where Lucy Pagetti had been only hours after the first corruption was found.

'Maybe we need to do some different tests on Koenig. Maybe we need to open his skull and take a look inside, see what's cooking.'

She turned towards the door. Sluder said, 'You know Pope's found out about the guys in Eagle?'

'He hasn't found out. He's been told.'

'There's people in this state, Miss Crawfurd,' he said slowly, staring at her, 'out there, out in that good clean desert, who think the NSA and the CIA are part of a government conspiracy to corrupt and subvert the constitution of the United State of America. There are people out there who believe government agents such as yourself are secretly conspiring to put the Queen of England on the throne of the United States. I used to think such people were insane.'

'But not now, huh?'

'Let's just say that the old certainties have departed.'

'Larry, you are a respected scientist, a member of the international scientific community.'

'I am?' He looked surprised. 'I am?'

'None of this is easy for anyone.'

'I'm a respected scientist, honey, who's being asked to believe that some broad from AD 1400 is sending love poems to John Koenig. To *John Koenig*. And – no, wait, wait, and just tell me something – if I'm the respected international scientist, just what are you?'

She said, 'I've had a long journey, Larry. I'd like ten minutes to rest and freshen up before they get here.'

'You're a junior NSA security gopher. Right?'

'Yeah, right.'

'I moved an operative, a junior technical operative, back to Berkeley.'

'If you mean Miss Pagetti—'

'I mean what the hell, what the hell—'

'In the past nine days, Larry, more than forty signals sent through *Pasiphae* have been corrupted. We don't know why it's happening, or how it's happening, but the logic gates have been breached and the world's most advanced quantum communications system is compromised.'

Sluder's hand went instinctively to his chest: her words a silver bullet to his heart.

'It's corrupt to the core, Larry. It's dead. Pope's theory might be way out, but it's a theory, and it's a cohesive theory, and at this moment it's the only theory we've got, because, Larry, whatever you might think this is not the work of some weirdo in Kansas, or some mischievous teenager playing his dad's personal computer in South Carolina.'

She went inside. Sluder lit a cigarette. His hand was trembling. When he found that teenager, he thought, that super-intelligent, criminally minded freak, he would wash that teenager's pimply face and rounded, computer-hacker shoulders in tears of gratitude.

Ten minutes later two helicopters from Caltech came down in a cloud of dust.

Government was represented by the NSA and the director of the FBI's four computer extortion units. The military was represented by the Pentagon's assistant director of computer information strategy, and by a senior commander of Naval intelligence. Quasi-commercial interests including the New York Stock Exchange and Lloyds of London were represented through US-based international investigators Kroll Associates.

Pope said: 'I'm arguing, ladies and gentlemen, that there is a basic design flaw in *Pasiphae*.'

Silence. Already, Martha thought, they were working out who to blame, who to sue. But who was she kidding? They'd worked that out on the plane to California; on the chopper out to Utah.

The woman from Kroll Associates said, 'Can it be rectified?'

'In time.'

'In time? Jesus.'

'You all know where I'm standing on this,' said Sluder. 'Dr Pope's theory is wild and irresponsible. I think we'll get this sorted, and fast.'

'It's been two weeks, Larry,' said the Pentagon man, who was chairing the meeting, 'and you're nowhere. An anti-intruder tracker satellite has been sent up and has failed to establish either the method or source of infection. Dr Pope, continue.'

'The infection takes the form of textual fragments. These sucker themselves on to a genuine signal and have the ability to bury themselves deep in its sub-molecular structure. Sometimes these corruptions are easily detected, at other times only the disinfectant systems warn us that something is wrong. Secondly – and most importantly – there is evidence that these corruptions have the ability to pass directly from the machine and into the brain of the human processing operative. When this happens they appear to cause mood swings and personality changes.'

'These things can take people over? Take over people's minds?'

'It's an exaggerated way of putting it.'

They stared at him.

'Exaggerated, but not inaccurate?'

'You know as much as I do. It isn't happening all the time. To our knowledge it may only have happened once, perhaps twice. We're still in the dark, we're still on the outer edge of this thing. But you know what happened at Charles de Gaulle.'

'I'm not denying any of this,' said Sluder, quietly, stubbornly, wearily. 'The ability for information to pass directly from the machine into the brain of the operative is a consequence of the quantum nature of the system; it does not mean that the signals were not placed in the system, in the first place, by a straightforward, ordinary hacker.'

'No ordinary hacker could penetrate *Pasiphae*,' said Pope. 'And it is far more likely that a thought passing from the machine to a human brain also entered the system as a thought – as a mental process – and not as something tapped in on a computer.'

The man from the FBI anti-fraud unit said, 'Somebody's going to have to explain some of this.'

'At Worcester College,' said Pope, 'when we first had to explain to people who were not physicists the way *Pasiphae*'s quantum detectors worked, we found, slightly to our surprise, that the easiest way to describe *Pasiphae* was to compare it to the human brain. It's not as sophisticated as the human brain – the brain is a group of nerve cells containing on average ten billion neurons, *Pasiphae* is nothing like that complex. But the systems are broadly similar. The main difference, amusingly enough, between a human brain and *Pasiphae* is that *Pasiphae* does not have, or need, an olfactory cortex.'

'A what cortex?'

'It lets you smell things,' said the woman from Kroll Associates.

'Well, yes,' said Pope. 'Though in humans as opposed to primitive animals, the olfactory cortex has been modified to include such things as emotion and sexual behaviour.'

'*Pasiphae*,' said Sluder, 'can't smell, can't cry, and can't screw.'

'Dr Pope, continue,' said the man from the Pentagon, wearily.

Pope spoke of the human brain's nerve impulses, and of the cellular composition of neurons, and the insulation provided by myelin, and its peculiar ability to maintain the ionic charges over long distances. He explained how the passage of information from one neuron to another was mediated by chemical neurotransmitter molecules diffused across narrow intercellular gaps known as synapses. He spoke of Hardy, the Oxford professor of zoology in the fifties, who had worked on the feasibility of individual organisms being in psychical connection across space.

'To sum up, we may now have to accept that thoughts originating in a human brain have the ability to attach themselves – without needing the medium of a computer or even a conscious decision – to *Pasiphae*'s quantum signals.'

The Navy man: 'You truly believe that charged ions in the electrojet, millions of ions all fifty miles up in the higher atmosphere, are interrelating with the nerve functions of an individual human brain?'

'I'm saying that a charged ion is a charged ion. Chemical processes are of the same family, even if they are on a totally different scale.'

'Charlie,' said Sluder, 'you are aware that the brain sends electrical charges at fourteen hertz, whilst a normal communications satellite uses frequency bands of over six thousand megahertz?'

Pope paused. He was tired and thirsty and conscious that he was not putting his case well. It had been a long flight and he had not slept, but had worked constantly, and he wanted to go on working now, fearful lest the ideas in his head dissipated.

'I am aware that *Pasiphae* operates in the quantum world and may now be allowing human brainwaves to communicate over very long distances.'

Not only distances of space, thought Martha, but of time. She waited, in dread, for him to say it. He was looking round, hesitating . . .

The man from the Pentagon said, 'Let's break for coffee.'

The man from the FBI: 'OK. *Pasiphae* is supposed to have freed the

US, at incredible cost, from the threat of cybercriminals and logic bombs. You are telling us that it has done neither of these things, that, on the contrary, criminals can now invade computer networks just by closing their eyes and *thinking*.'

'That may lie in the future.'

'What about now? What do you think is happening now?'

'I believe that somewhere in the world there is a human brain operating as a carrier – a transmitter if you like – of the invasive texts.'

'Why? Why the extra complication? Why do you believe that the thoughts are not those of the person linked now to *Pasiphae*?'

'Because I believe that they originate in the early fifteenth century.'

He'd said it. Martha closed her eyes.

Silence.

The woman from Kroll Associates: 'I was told something of this on the plane. I thought it was some kinda joke.'

'Air strike Wilcox,' said the Navy man. 'These words do not exactly have a medieval ring to them.'

Martha opened her eyes. She said, 'Air strike Wilcox was not detected on an incoming signal but written on a pad by an operator here in Utah who worked last year on a war-games exercise and who was in the process of suffering a severe stroke.'

'Everything about this,' said Sluder, 'apart from the Wilcox signal, bears the hallmark of a computer hacker. This is so typical of what a computer freak would do, so typical of a computer freak's warped sense of humour. These guys are clever. They may be socially inadequate, but boy, are they clever.'

'If you believe *Pasiphae* is being deliberately hacked into,' said Pope, 'why can't you trace the source of the signals, and find out how they are doing it?'

'Christ, Charlie, just because we don't know how something is being done does not mean that the most likely, sane, logical answer is the wrong answer.'

'I agree,' said the man from the FBI. 'Yes sir, I agree.'

Pope said: 'I had all this two weeks ago. You were wrong then, and you're wrong now. If nothing's changed will somebody please tell me what I'm doing here?'

A pause.

'No, no, I'm not buying it,' said the woman from Kroll Associates. 'I do not believe that we have spent so much time, and so much money, devising a system foolproof against infiltration, only to be told that it is receiving messages from the spirit world.'

The chairman said: 'What do you want us to do, Dr Pope?'

'Close *Pasiphae* down.'

'For how long?'

'For as long as it takes to find the carrier.'

'How close are you?'

'I've spent the last three weeks subjecting all known corrupted tapes to analysis. The language is English of the late fourteenth century. There's a reference to gold. We'd be unlucky to find that the interface between medieval England and *Pasiphae* was a Mongolian yak herdsman.'

The fraud expert from the FBI: 'Messages from five hundred years ago telling us where the treasure is? Jokes about Mongolians? What is this, a kiddies' movie?'

The meeting was with him. They didn't like Pope, they didn't trust him.

But *Pasiphae* was being infiltrated.

And he was the physicist who had led the *Pasiphae* technology team after Hollbecker's death.

And three hundred people killed at Charles de Gaulle Airport might be only the prelude to a logic bomb exploding in the Pentagon computer complex.

'OK,' said the chairman. 'We shut *Pasiphae* down for seven days. During that time Dr Pope is given every facility to try to find the carrier, if carrier there is. The FBI looks for hackers, and we devise an electronic shield to combat the infiltrations. OK, Larry?'

Sluder nodded.

The man from the Pentagon looked at his watch. It was nine o'clock. 'This meeting is closed.'

It took sixteen minutes to program the shutdown: to send the series of signals that, one by one, closed down *Pasiphae*'s neural network subsystems, and disabled her whisper antennae.

21

Dore

She leaned over him and touched his lips gently. He opened his eyes. She said, 'Let me in. I'm cold.'

He opened his sleeping bag and she slipped in with him, lithe as an eel.

He said, 'Isn't this blasphemy or something?'

'What?'

'Well, you know, in a church?'

'What I want,' she said, snuggling against him, 'is a cuddle.'

Her fine, gold hair was against his face. She was breathing softly in his ear. 'Well?' he said.

She lay still. She sighed. 'It's gone.'

'What's gone?'

'I don't know. Everything.'

'Did you not dream?'

'Oh yes. But it's all different somehow.'

She lay breathing gently.

'What happened?'

After a moment she said, 'We were in Hereford. He wants to marry me. The franklin wants to marry me. But I'm desperate to get to Dore, so that I can be rescued by Walter Manny.'

'It's all very Freudian.'

'Why? Why Freudian?'

'A young girl in the power of a lustful middle-aged man.'

'Oh, God, that's so obvious and so predictable and it's just what Venetia thought. Who said the franklin was middle-aged?'

'Wasn't he?'

'Middle-aged for then, maybe. Not much over thirty. He had me beaten.'

'What?'

'With a whip. For disobedience.'

'Dear God.'

'It was common enough in those days. It didn't have to be sexual—'

'Oh come on, of all the girlish fantasies—'

'You know all about girlish fantasies, do you?'

They lay together.

She said, 'I didn't mind. I wasn't resentful.'

She wriggled round. The franklin was above them but his face was hidden. She put out her hand, touched the alabaster frieze.

She said, softly, 'Dead bones.'

'Listen. I think we should pack in the dig.'

'What? How can we?'

'There's only a week left. I think we should go to France. To the grape harvest.'

'Yes, Andrew, you said, but there isn't going to be a grape harvest, they haven't had rain in Bordeaux for eight months.'

'They'll be harvesting in Provence. Up in the mountains, under the melting glaciers. The fields will be blue with lavender. We'll live in a tent and eat goat's cheese.'

'And I'll forget about the franklin?'

'You don't need a middle-aged bloke lusting after you – not one that's five hundred years old, at any rate.'

'Christ, men. All I want is a cup of tea. No, Andrew, I will not do it here.'

'Outside then.'

'No. No. Here.'

She closed her eyes. She expected to see the franklin's face against the retina of her mind; but there was nothing.

Andrew said, 'Shit.'

He rolled off her.

The church door had opened.

It was the flower woman.

She stood by the table, by the vase of lilies, and stared at them.

'I couldn't sleep,' she said.

They lay in a pool of light pouring down through the east window, as still, in their sleeping bag, as the medieval man and woman under the coverlet of stars.

176

'We are supposed to have water on Mondays, Wednesdays and Fridays, but there is nothing coming out of the tap. A six o'clock in the morning there is nothing coming out of the tap. I think something terrible is happening.'

Lizzie turned her face away. She looked up at the east window. She thought: *The fourteenth day of the fifteen days of the destruction of the world. The day when all men died.*

The woman went and sat in a boxed pew and bowed her head.

Andrew said, quietly, 'Come on.'

They wriggled out of the sleeping bag. They tiptoed quietly down the aisle.

'Goodbye,' the woman said, in a muffled voice.

'Goodbye,' they said politely.

Outside, the sun was throwing dappled light down through the circle of oaks. 'I want to go to Hereford,' said Lizzie. 'To the cathedral.'

'Come with me to France.'

'The cathedral. Please, Andrew.'

She stood, the moving light rearranging patterns on her face, her hair, her body, her gold-brown legs.

'Is that where you were? Is that where you were in your dream?'

She nodded.

He turned and went to the spring and dashed water over his face, and drank from his cupped hands. He said, 'Come and drink, you're dehydrated.'

'I want to go to the cathedral.'

He drank again. 'You said it was different. You said everything had changed.'

'I know. It isn't what you think. I'm not trying to bring things back. I'm not trying to cling on.'

They passed the satellite station with its red lights that winked through the night. They crossed the Wye Bridge and the sun was a ball of fire. 'Another scorcher,' said BBC Radio Hereford. 'Remember that standpipes are in operation today west of the Wye and if you live in parts of the city that do have mains water, please, please use it sparingly.'

Andrew parked on double-yellow lines in Broad Street. 'This is just being stupid,' Lizzie said, but he was already getting out of the car. 'There's time for a cup of tea, I didn't say we didn't have time for a cup of tea—' but he was striding away, over the parched earth towards the cathedral church of St Mary the Virgin and St Ethelbert the King.

The interior was cool, filled with a dim light.

He said, curtly, 'What now?'

His voice echoed in the emptiness.

'All these pews,' she said, bemused.

'Lizzie?'

She led him to the tomb of Sir Richard Pembroke, the knight of Poitiers.

His tomb was mutilated. His hands had been chopped off.

'Oh, Andrew,' she said. 'He was so beautiful. He had his helm and shield hung over him. There were peacock feathers and painted leopards, and a sign that said, "Here lies the flower of English chivalry".'

'OK, what now?'

'Please, Andrew, please.'

'What are we doing here? What do you want to see?'

She felt close to tears. She said, 'The shrine of St Thomas.'

The fourteenth-century shrine had been destroyed in the Reformation. She led the way to the old shrine, the stone coffin in which Hereford's saint had first been laid to rest, in the time before his fame, in the time before he had started to cure diseased flesh, to raise bodies from the dead.

There were no vicars choral; no blaze of candles; no burning of incense.

Instead, above the shrine, a bright rectangle of metal floated, appearing to defy gravity.

It sparkled with blue, silver, and mauve lights.

They both stood and stared.

'I never could work out the difference,' said Lizzie quietly, 'between a saint's nimbus and his halo.'

Footsteps in the silence. A man wearing a long blue cloak came down the dark side aisle. He saw them and stopped.

'If you've come for matins and communion,' he said, 'it's in the Lady Chapel.'

'Thank you,' said Andrew.

The priest smiled and went.

Lizzie stared at the shrine of St Thomas, at the floating rectangle of light.

Andrew walked over to the wall, to a notice. He read out, 'The effect of floating is achieved by simple wires, and by lights shining up from the shrine itself. The colours are caused by controlled voltages running through anodised titanium.'

He turned to her. 'The satellite station at the end of the valley.'

'What?'

'You don't think it could be causing a local electrical disturbance? You don't think there could be a microwave leakage of some kind?'

'I don't know what you're talking about.'

He looked at the nimbus, the shimmering band of colours over the shrine.

'No, I don't either. Are we going to matins?'

In the Lady Chapel they knelt with three other worshippers. When Lizzie looked up she saw that one of them was Mrs Ifor-Williams.

The service started. The familiar words, the comfortable responses, said every day in this place since the time of Cranmer.

'O God, make speed to save us.'

'O Lord, make haste to help us.'

And before Cranmer? What words were spoken daily here in the eighth century, wondered Lizzie, when the first cathedral was built of wattle and daub, and Putta was the first bishop? Or in the eleventh when Robert de Losinga built his cathedral of Norman stone? Or in the fourteenth century when the plague victims were piled in the charnel pits beyond the great west door, and the citizens prayed that Owain Glyn Dŵr and his Welshmen would not sack the city?

Lizzie heard a voice, an echo.

Sancta Virgo Virginum.

Holy Mother of Virgins.

Ne reminiscaris, Domine . . .

'Remember not, O Lord, our offences,' she said to herself, her eyes closed, 'nor those of our parents: neither take retribution on our sins.'

Matins ended. There was silence. Lizzie remained kneeling, her head bowed, Andrew beside her. After a while two or three other people came in: people on their way to work, a man with a briefcase, a woman with shopping bags. The communion service started.

'Let us remember the victims of cholera in Bangladesh,' said the priest, 'and all those who have died or have lost their homes in the floods in Queensland, and in Florida. Let us remember the farmers who have seen their crops wither in the drought. The cattle farmers, here in Herefordshire, who are facing such difficulty in keeping their animals alive. O God, the Creator and Preserver of all mankind, we humbly beseech thee . . .'

In due course Lizzie knelt at the rail and took the bread.

The body of our Lord Jesus Christ, which was given for thee, preserve thy body and soul unto everlasting life.

Andrew watched her and thought: this is why we are here. It is an exorcism.

Lizzie drank the wine.

Drink this in remembrance that Christ's blood was shed for thee.

'The peace of God, which passeth all understanding,' said the priest, at the end of the service, 'be with you, and remain with you always.'

Lizzie sighed. The tension drained from her body.

'They're very upper class, the cathedral vicars, aren't they?' said Mrs Ifor-Williams admiringly, as they stood in the North Porch. 'So very posh, so very English?'

The two priests had, yes, been a bit upper class, thought Andrew, or perhaps it was just the effect of their dashing blue cloaks.

'And this is your young man?'

She was smiling at him.

'Could be,' said Lizzie. 'Andrew, this is Mrs Ifor-Williams.'

'Miss Whitburn told me what a nice lad you were.'

'The lady with the flowers?' said Andrew, intuitively.

'She's a friend of mine. Well, more of a colleague you might say.'

'What,' said Lizzie, 'from the library?'

'Goodness no. They can only put up with one of us in the library. So did you find your franklin then?'

'No,' said Lizzie. 'But perhaps it doesn't matter.'

Mrs Ifor-Williams, beady and Welsh, looked at her.

'That's a shame,' she said. 'Miss Whitburn and I both thought that you had the gift.'

'Ah, the gift.'

'If you know what I mean.'

'If I had it, Mrs Ifor-Williams, it has gone.'

One of the priests came out. Mrs Ifor-Williams looked at him uneasily and said to Lizzie, 'Come and see me before you leave Vortipor's Fort, won't you?'

She flitted across the close towards the museum and library. The priest watched her thoughtfully. He said, 'You know Mrs Ifor-Williams?'

'Yes,' said Lizzie. 'I was a bit surprised to see her here actually.'

The priest smiled faintly. 'Yes,' he said, 'even in these ecumenical times. Well, so long as she doesn't expect us to return the compliment.'

He laughed and went off across the close himself, his blue cloak shimmering like a heron, thought Lizzie, a memory stirring. Where had she seen a heron, soaring up in the morning sun? Where had she seen celandines by the water's edge?

'Andrew,' she said, 'I have got to have a cup of tea.'

They went to the Green Dragon and ordered breakfast.

'What was all that about Mrs Ifor-Williams?'

'Ah, well,' said Lizzie, drinking tea and eating buttered toast, 'I only found out myself when I phoned Dr Dyson-Jones to ask about Herefordshire's Anglo-Saxon charters. He's dropped a lot of dark hints about Mrs Ifor-Williams, and it turns out that he's a strong Welsh Methodist, and so was Mr Ifor-Williams, the Co-op assistant manager of the hardware department in Pontypridd. Elva on the other hand—'

'Who?'

'Elva. Mrs Ifor-Williams. It's a name she acquired in sixty-seven. You've heard of Woodstock?'

'Woodstock wasn't in sixty-seven.'

'It doesn't matter, Andrew, it doesn't matter. Elva Ifor-Williams is a druid. A druidess. Oh wonderful . . .'

Eggs and bacon and grilled tomatoes came.

'She's the Arch-Druidess for Herefordshire, and Miss Whitburn is a sort of sub-druidess. I didn't know you'd ordered sausages.'

'Yes,' said Andrew, not giving her one. 'A sub-druidess, eh?' he mused.

It accounted, he thought, for her lack of surprise when she found virgins and hornèd beasts before the altar, going at it like knives.

They were back at the dig by ten and got some hard looks from Bill Hastings. Venetia, looking shattered, said, 'Take no notice, he's got nothing to complain about.' Eloise smiled in sympathy. Bill Hastings, it was assumed, was a vigorous and demanding lover.

They worked through the day, without a break, edging the two trenches delicately into the post-Roman mound. In the evening they all went down to the pub at Newbridge. It was Badger's last night. He was off on his mission through North Wales, seeking out the perfect ale given to him once by a whiskery Welsh merlin. 'You're like a knight of the Round Table, Badger,' said Sonia. 'A knight on a quest.'

'Yes, yes, but I can't understand how you can go *now*, Badger,' said Eloise. 'Not when we're so close to the centre of mound.'

Badger said, 'It'll only turn out to be a couple of firepits and a few pigs' skulls.'

They all played darts. Andrew said, 'Bill, can I have a word?' and they went to the bar to get some more drinks. Lizzie thought, 'Here goes.' When they came back they were both smiling.

'These two,' said Bill, 'are off to France to the flaming grape harvest.' There were cries of dismay. 'But on the other hand,' Bill went on, 'Venetia's staying.'

'Am I?' said Venetia. 'I don't remember saying anything about staying. I thought I said I'd booked a flight to Geneva for Saturday.'

Bill said firmly, 'You're staying.'

Venetia said, 'Oh well.'

She looked peaky but plucky.

'But Lizzie, you surely won't go till we've broken into the mound?' cried Eloise, wondering if she was the only person in the world with any natural curiosity. 'It'll only be a couple of days now, won't it, Bill?'

'Depends on how many major finds we stumble across, how many hoards of Celtic silver our trowels turn up, ha, ha.'

He gave Venetia a kiss. He was in fine fettle, a man winning on all fronts.

Lizzie looked at Andrew. 'If Lizzie wants to,' he said, 'we'll stay another two days.'

She smiled.

It was midnight. They went out into the darkness and piled into the Land Rover. Eloise drove, back up the narrow winding road, up to the ridge. There was a slight breeze tonight, warm, carrying the scent of wild thyme.

Andrew put up a camp bed, as usual, for Eloise. As usual she said, 'Oh Andrew, you're a gentleman.'

He put beds up for himself and for Lizzie.

He said, 'OK?'

She nodded.

'You're not going to go sliding off?'

She shook her head. She kissed him.

'It's gone,' she said. 'I told you.'

They lay, side by side, looking up at the sky.

There were occasional flickers of light across it; spasms of white tinged with green, but nobody said anything: for days newspapers had carried reports about the aurora borealis, the convulsions of ionised particles in the outer atmosphere, being seen in Britain's southern skies. It was all down to freak weather conditions, said the papers.

She listened for the distant sound of a flute, but heard nothing. She wondered if Eleanor had ever become a nun. She wondered if Eleanor had ever existed.

Why did babies dream for ten hours every day? Were they really being programmed with memories of the past? Programmed from the ancestral memory of humankind?

Perhaps she'd picked up somebody's individual memory: perhaps it all went back to her early childhood.

Either way, it was over.

With one hand resting lightly on Andrew's arm, and with curtains of light sweeping across the northern sky, she slept.

22

Utah

'Sluder's spending his time with the FBI anti-fraud units,' said Martha. 'They all agree that you're a foreign freak who should never have been allowed into the US of A. They're working through a list of known female hackers.'

'Why female?'

'They're trying to narrow the field. The fake-medieval poem – their words not mine – was written by a woman, so the hacker's presumed to be a woman. Three days ago they flew to Maryland to check out some fifteen-year-old high-school kid known as Wonderweb Woman. They've got this Wonderweb Woman kid under some sort of home arrest. They've got psychologists trying to make her write poems. Her lawyers are threatening to sue for cruel and unnatural punishment.'

'I'm gratified,' said Pope, 'that you can still find things funny.'

'You think it's a joke? You want me to show you the newspaper from Riviera Beach, Baltimore?'

'Christ.'

He spoke sourly: he resented having been summoned from Oxford.

'Anyway, are you OK?' Martha looked round the room. 'You really like this place?'

Pope was in a motel. It was a motel with a pool, ten miles south of Highway 40, along the road to Bonanza. He had two computers, one linked to Imperial College, London, and the UK academic web; the other directly to Berkeley and Pasadena.

'This place is fine.'

She picked up a book and read out the title. '*Taxatio Ecclesiastica Angliae et Walliae auctoritate Papae Nicholia.*'

'*Ecclesiastical taxation of England—*'

'*And Wales, by authority of Pope Nicholas.* I did receive an education, Charles, it does happen occasionally in the States.'

'Well, that's more than I can say for England.'

'What's the relevance to *Pasiphae*?'

'There's a mention of a church in one of the corruptions. The *Taxation of Pope Nicholas* is one of the very few medieval church sources in print and available to me in America, and even so it had to be flown in from San Francisco.'

'You couldn't get a copy in Bonanza public library?'

'No.'

His face was pallid, there were owl-like smudges under his eyes.

'You need to rest.'

'I have to find the carrier.'

She looked out of the window. There was a patio and a pool, and beyond it the red rocks of Utah. She said, 'They've almost got the protection shield figured out. They've got the National Laboratory on the job, Option Red with IBM's RS/6000 computers in parallel processing. They're reconfiguring the databands. Do you think it'll work?'

'Maybe.'

His eyes were on his screen.

She said, 'I'll leave you to it, then, OK?'

He looked at her.

'Obviously,' he said, with a sigh, 'obviously, it's possible to reconfigure *Pasiphae*'s quantum systems so that they do not pick up a particular human carrier. But that isn't to say they'll be any better off. They might find they're suddenly tuning in to a thousand – a hundred thousand – human brains. They might find they're picking up shopping lists from housewives in Madrid, or credit documents from vacuum-cleaner salesmen in Paraguay.'

She said, 'Charles, are you progressing at all?

He leaned back in his chair. He closed his eyes. After a moment he said, 'Play me f27c.'

She sat at the second computer. She clicked a mouse. On screen appeared: *Item Thomas Carrog hys hed was yeft'daye fett uppon London brydge lokyng into Kent warde and men feye yt hys brother ys efcaped to Sanctyary to Beverley fo yow tell ye nunns of D'or. Sr John Creveker efcaped owt of Wales wt can C fperys as men feye and is in Bristol, tho yong Manny is ded tel ye nunns.*

He said, 'Can you read it?'

'Item. Thomas Carrog his head was yesterday set upon London Bridge, looking into Kent ward and men say that his brother is escaped to sanctuary to Beverley so you tell the nuns of D'or – is that nuns of gold? A nunnery called the golden nunnery perhaps? – Sir John Creveker escaped out of Wales with a hundred spears as men say, and is in Bristol, though young Manny is dead tell the nuns.'

'We can date that fairly precisely to March 1402. Now look at f19d.'

She clicked the mouse: *by Blacberd or Whyteberd that ys to fey by God or the Devyll get yow D'or*.

She said, 'By Blackbeard or Whitebeard that is to say by God or the Devil, get you gold. I just love these old English phrases. There's a richness still in the language I guess we've kind of lost over here. You're telling me that the words "gold" or "of gold", in French, are repeated.'

He said, 'Now f30d.'

As it appeared he said: 'This is the latest corruption. It was in a signal sent via *Pasiphae* just before the satellite was closed down.'

I wolde ffayne have the mesur wher he lythe both the thykneffe and compafe off the peler at hys hed and ffrom that the fpace to ye Alter and how many Taylors Yards it is. And I wolle have albastar f^r ye tomb D'or.

'I would fain have the measure where he lies,' said Martha, 'both the thickness and compass of the pillar at his head, and from that the space to the altar, and how many Taylor's Yards it is.'

'And I will have alabaster,' said Pope, softly, 'for the tomb of gold.'

She looked at him.

'Three mentions,' she said. 'But don't you find it strange that in all three fragments the words "of gold" are written in French, and the rest in English?'

'It's odd, yes. But up until the middle of the fourteenth century French was the official language in England. It was the language of the law, of the nobility.'

'What's a Taylor's Yard?'

'I have no idea.'

'That's sad, Charles. You should take care you don't let these good old phrases fall out of use.'

187

'Dear God, there's nobody in England under thirty who knows what a yard is, never mind a Taylor's Yard. Do you think we go round saying "Hey marry marry, by Blackbeard or Whitebeard I'll give thee a Taylor's Yard the nonce"?'

'But of course you do,' she said, clicking her way into a dictionary. 'Not while people like me are listening, of course, but when you're on your own. Where did this last fragment come from?'

'A signal concerning European Union timber product tariffs. It took five decoders the best part of a day to winkle it out. The corruptions are going deeper, finding new hiding places. This one was found nestling in a neural processor – very *very* elegant.'

She looked at him. 'You know you're scary when you talk like that? As though they are living, thinking organisms?'

'I'm just saying that when the transfer of information involves the simultaneous passage of signals among many alternative paths, you will find the reinforcement of favoured routes, and you will find that those routes will penetrate deeper, and will be more difficult to spot.'

'Taylor's Yard,' she said, peering at her screen. 'I'm getting nothing. But yard, as a unit of measurement, was Old English. In the mid-fifteenth century it was also a rod used for punishment. Perhaps we're talking about a stick used for beating tailors. When did you eat?'

'Eat?' He looked at her vaguely.

She sighed. The room was in terrible squalor: plates of half-eaten food, breakfast food – muffins and bacon mainly – were on the bed. 'Don't they ever want to get in here and clean the place up?'

'I don't let them.'

She picked up the phone and asked for housekeeping, and said, 'Dr Pope will be going out for a couple of hours. I guess he's been a real pain, but perhaps you could get his room cleaned up?'

Pope said, 'I'm not going anywhere.'

'Come and look at the Native Americans. Let's go and buy some Native American beads and stuff. Come on now,' she coaxed, 'you know you like Native Americans.'

'Native Americans? Are you talking about Red Indians?' he said as he was led out into the inn's green courtyard, past its aquamarine pool.

'Now don't be provocative. Just because you're almost a senior citizen does not entitle you to be provocative.'

They bought him a pair of soft leather snake boots, and a video about the Ouray Native Americans. They walked under the pines by the Green River as it flowed towards Desolation Canyon.

'I'm getting a picture of the medieval sender,' he told her. 'Although I should say senders, because there are actually two of them.'

'How do you know that?'

'It's a feeling. An intuition.'

'You be careful about the amount of time you spend staring at that screen. Think of John Koenig.'

'I'm analysing tapes. Koenig received a direct, emotional shock. So did the air traffic controller in Paris. And I suspect – though Sluder won't confirm it – that something similar happened to the computer operative in Alaska.'

'The security report says he got in a fight over a woman.'

'A directly transmitted emotion. Fear. Anger. Acute depression.'

He stared over the river, not listening. 'The fragments, of course, are different. With the fragments we are receiving thoughts that have been *formally composed* into language by a human brain. This, of course, is what strengthens Sluder's argument about a hacker.'

'But you said it can't be a hacker! Oh Christ, Charles . . .'

She wondered how she would face Sluder if Wonderweb Woman of Maryland turned out to be a medieval English language freak.

'Of course it isn't a hacker. It's actually impossible to conceive of anyone outside a couple of dozen universities, or government communications centres, creating a machine that could infiltrate *Pasiphae*. OK, in theory, a big telecommunications company could do it. OK, a couple of big national government agencies outside the US could do it – GCHQ could do it, for that matter, at Cheltenham.'

'GCHQ?' said Martha on a note of false surprise. GCHQ was Sluder's suspect number one after the kid from Maryland. That morning he had called her and said: 'OK, Miss Crawfurd. Name me one world-class communications centre that might also contain a rogue scientist with a sophisticated knowledge of both English medieval history and dialect peculiar to the English West Midlands?'

GCHQ's guilt had almost screamed out. It was the successor to

Bletchley Park where Hitler's codes had been broken, where the world's first computer, *Colossus*, had been built. It was full of humorous coves.

'You recently spent six months at Cheltenham, Miss Crawfurd?' Sluder had said, his voice heavy with meaning. 'You recently spent six months at GCHQ?'

'Larry, are you telling me I've been turned by MI5?'

'I'm not saying anything,' said Sluder.

In the London Embassy, she thought the CIA would be building an identikit of Sluder's possible rogue hacker: an English computer buff in his late forties, wearing maroon socks, and sandals, and reading the *Guardian*.

They went into Vernal. Pope wanted to eat pie in the Last Chance Café, but Martha steered him firmly into the La Cabana restaurant in the Sage Hotel and ordered guacamole and enchiladas. 'What I'd really like to see,' said Pope, reading from a leaflet, 'is the Utah Shakespeare Festival. Where's Cedar City?'

'South Utah. A long way.'

'They have Shakespearian costumed jugglers and a Renaissance Feaste with two es that you eat without utensils, and actors go round all day speaking, it says here, careful Olde with an e English.'

'Are you genuinely a sneery English bastard, or are you just pissed off?'

'I'm pissed off,' he said, not wanting to confess the awful truth.

She drove him back to the motel. She said, 'They'll start *Pasiphae* up again once they've got the shield in place.'

'I know.'

'You've got two days, at most.'

He turned on his computers. He sat, hunched, before them. He seemed to slip, gratefully, into a different world.

She watched his face.

'Listen, I'm genuinely worried about you spending so much time on that machine. Whatever you say, I'm worried about the quantum physical link between the *Pasiphae* signals and your brain.'

He turned to her. 'What do you want me to do? Save the world or stop exposing myself to personal danger?'

'Both,' she said.

'A typical woman's answer.'

'Oh boy, oh boy.' She shook her head from side to side. 'He talks about Red Indians. He sneers at Utah folk appreciating Shakespeare. And he's sexist.'

She left him. He had food sent to his room, and worked till gone midnight.

Next morning he was back at the computers when Sluder arrived. Sluder seemed nervous. He looked weary. He said, 'How are you doing?'

'The fragments are not all by women. Why did you think they were?'

'Our textual analyst guys came up with the theory. It was intuitive, they said. They couldn't account for it. You know you can get a feel for these things?'

'The fragments originate in the mind of either a young girl, a girl of education, or a knight of the shire.'

'A knight, yeah? Sir Lancelot stuff?'

Sluder was being polite; he didn't believe a word of it.

'No, not a knight proper. A knight of the shire would be a member of the country gentry, a tax assessor perhaps, a man who held his own court, a member of parliament. He might be a merchant of some kind. He could have been quite well off – a franklin, perhaps. In *The Canterbury Tales* Chaucer describes a franklin as "a householder, and that great was he; St Julian he was in his country".'

'Hey, that's good. I must write that down.'

'And Chaucer said that in the franklin's house "it snowed of food and drinks".'

Sluder had had enough of poetry. He said abruptly, 'OK, so why is he sending us little notes?'

He sounded drained. He kicked off his shoes and lay down on the bed, pushing aside a plate of dried-up, curling burger.

Pope said, 'Did you want something in particular?'

Sluder said, 'Your Miss Pagetti. She keeps shooting her mouth off about morphogenetic fields. She says she and her pet dog can talk to each other. She says she and her spaniel hold conversations.'

There was a theory, Pope knew, that dogs could mentally tune in to the thought processes of their owners. It was an extension of ESP research, it was a theory supported, as were so many theories previously considered fantastic, by quantum mechanics.

Sluder said, 'Have you got a minibar in here by any chance?'

Pope decided he wasn't in the mood for a beer and a chat about the paranormal. 'I'm trying to trace the carrier, Larry. I'm nearly there, I need to get on.'

Sluder sat up. 'Listen, is there any way a girl in high school – a kid in, well, let's say Maryland – could know all that stuff about knights and franklins? Could she have read about it? These kids spend hours on their computers and there are some freaky, way-out sites on the Web. You're sure your knight of the shire hasn't gotten himself a page on the Internet?'

A dry rasping noise, like a disturbed rattlesnake. Sluder was laughing.

The phone went. Sluder said quickly: 'The guy at Eagle – the monitoring technician who got into a fight. The new security officer found him downloading a pile of stuff, strictly *verboten* stuff, to his own computer.'

Pope stared at him. 'Why the hell didn't you tell me?'

'When he was discovered, he hit the security guy over the head and bust his skull.'

Pope picked up the phone. 'Yes?'

'Has Sluder seen you?'

'He's here now. The stuff the Alaskan computer operative was copying, was it—'

'*Pasiphae* signals, yes,' Martha said.

'You realise this man might be the carrier?'

'I realise.'

'Where is he now?'

Sluder said, 'He made off into the forest. He'll be going through hell. Those mosquitoes, in Eagle, are the size of your fist.'

Pope said, into the phone, 'We have to find him, talk to him.'

'There's a chopper on its way.'

'Am I the only person in the organisation who still worries about "Missile strike Wilcox"?' said Sluder. 'Who thinks that such a message did not originate, perhaps, with a knight of the shire, forsooth?'

Pope closed down his computers and went. Sluder slept awhile, until a boy came to clean up the room. He wandered out into the green courtyard, and sat by a pool that was the colour of molten copper, its surface disturbed by a fretful, gusty wind. A couple drinking vodka gunslingers gazed up at black clouds stacked against the sky, and then called up their tour operator and cancelled their boat through Desolation Canyon, and reflected that maybe they ought to have vacationed in October.

Sluder sat and thought about John Koenig. Something had passed from the computer to his brain, and somehow, despite his stroke, despite his apparent lack of consciousness, his brain was still working, was still *doing things*.

Eventually he phoned the military hospital. Could they test for false memory syndrome on a subject who was to all intents and purposes unconscious?

What sort of permissions did they need to open up Koenig's skull, and try electrical stimulation on the grey matter within?

23

Alaska

The Air Force plane tossed in a sea of turbulence. It rose up vast waves with its engines labouring, then slipped over the ridge and plunged down, down, down, its jets screaming as they sucked at the vacuum.

Down it fell, into the trough.

Martha answered her mobile and then said: 'The security guy's dead.'

Pope stared out of the window, through the swirling clouds, at the lightning that forked down over the gunmetal blue of the north Pacific.

'Did he manage to say what happened?'

'It seems the computer operative had been behaving oddly. He claimed he was hearing voices.'

'What kind of voices?'

'Who knows? The security guy found him late last night, working the decode at the HAARP, with a downlink to his place in the woods – he lives in a cabin with a super pentium 3000 processor and two San Francisco Whole-Earth freaks, both girls. Don't ask me what the social arrangements were.'

'The what?'

'The arrangements vis-à-vis sex, Charles, vis-à-vis who slept with whom,' she said, rolling her eyes, spelling it out for a man who was nearly a senior citizen.

'Is he still hiding in the forest?'

'I guess so. It's a murder rap now. They'll be sending cops up from Anchorage.'

Pope closed his eyes and tried to sleep. It was useless. He opened his eyes. She was looking at him with that Californian earnestness he so dreaded. 'Charles,' she said, 'do you have any views about the existence, after death, of the human soul?'

'I am sure,' he said, 'that the storm is less threatening than it seems.'

'No, listen. Do you believe there is actually such a thing as the human soul?'

They might soon, thought Pope, find out the answer. The plane was rising like a bird, then crashing down, then rising and crashing all over again, like a stone skimming across the surface of a pond. They were the only passengers. He peered down the long, dim aisle past the rows of empty seats. He had the curious feeling that not only was the cabin empty, but also the flight deck: that they were on a ghost plane piloted by ghostly, sub-molecular forces.

'I mean, what can we be talking about here?' she said. 'A few chemical reactions? A few electrical charges, running round the brain? When we die and electrical activity in our brain ceases does—'

The plane rose more violently than ever before then thudded down on the invisible surface, jarring Pope's neck, and making Martha clutch the seat back in front of her.

'Christ,' she said.

'Does Christ what?'

'Does everything die with it? Die with the brain? You know they've tried to prove the existence of a soul by measuring the loss of body weight when a person dies? They carried out a controlled experiment in Massachusetts, and established a body weight loss of about an ounce the moment that the person ceased to draw breath.'

'It means nothing. The body loses weight through sweating.'

'Yeah. So a guy in Los Angeles tried the experiment in two ways: one with bodies dying in the open air and then with bodies dying when they were sealed in a tube.'

Pope looked at her, startled.

'Mice,' she said. 'He used mice, not humans.'

'Do we have to talk about dying?' said Pope. 'Do we have to talk about it right now?'

'Sorry,' she said.

An Air Force officer was coming slowly down the cabin, holding on to the seats on either side of the aisle. He said, 'You guys want anything to eat?'

Pope shook his head. Martha said, 'What have you got?'

The officer went away. Martha said, 'This guy in LA found that mice in the open air lost weight when they died, but the mice sealed in the tube did not lose weight. Therefore, the soul is not part of the physical world, it does not have a chemical existence.'

'Perhaps all he proved was that mice do not have souls,' said Pope, looking out of the window through a momentary break in the clouds, peering down through a vast, deep chasm and seeing the Alaskan coastline. 'What's your point, anyway, why are you telling me all this?'

'If you're right – if *Pasiphae* is being infiltrated by the thoughts of persons who lived in medieval England – are we actually talking about their souls? The part of them that left their body, and yet which still exists?'

After a few moments Pope said, 'The word "soul" is too emotive. Scientists already have the technology to make a microchip that can be connected to your neuronal system. This chip will record your life as it happens – what you see, what you hear, what you smell, what you feel, more importantly *what you think and what you believe*. This chip can be taken from your body at death.'

'So the human soul is just a memory chip?'

'Maybe.'

'It makes you feel better, does it, Charles, to talk about a memory chip than about a human soul?'

'Yes,' said Pope, not prepared to argue religion and metaphysics, but feeling close to his Maker.

The Air Force officer came back down the cabin. One hand moved jerkily from one seat back to the next. The other held a regulation Air Force-issue meal tray. He said, 'Please watch the fruit salad doesn't hit the roof.' His eyes flickered upwards. Perhaps he would be the guy who would have to clean it off.

Pope said, 'What's that out there?'

Below them now were vast, spiralling banks of deep purple.

'Novarupta,' said the Air Force officer, 'biggest blow-out since 1912.'

'What?' said Martha. 'What did you say?'

'Volcanic dust,' said Pope. 'When do we land?'

'We're due at Eielson in one hour forty minutes. You ought to be taking photographs,' he added, nodding out of the window before staggering back through the empty cabin to the flight deck.

197

Some time later Martha said, 'Ghosts are electrical patterns, aren't they, Charles?'

'Ghosts?'

'Tracks of energy left behind like the wake of a ship?'

'Ghosts, human souls – listen, you are trying to find comfort in familiar concepts, and OK, it doesn't actually matter what you call them – souls, ghosts, *deus ex machina* – as long as you don't try to attach a lot of quasi-religious baggage to what can be explained in a logical scientific way.'

After a while he dozed and then, as the plane steadied, slept. Martha ate her way through the meal tray, then dozed herself as they passed over the Wrangell Mountains. They began their descent towards Fairbanks. It was nine o'clock at night, but there was no sign of darkness: in August, Fairbanks had over twenty hours a day of direct sunlight.

Pope woke up as they came in to land. He said, 'I'm betting on the computer operative being the prime carrier.'

'A man in Alaska, linked to the souls of two people who died five hundred years ago in medieval England?'

'You keep using that word soul,' he said, irritated. 'But why shouldn't it be a man in Alaska? Most Canadians are of English descent. Countless Americans have English forefathers.'

'Or Scottish,' said Martha Crawfurd. 'But not many of them are called Barrendov, which is the name of the computer guy at Eagle.'

They stepped out of the plane into massive heat, but this was nothing, said the mess sergeant, the temperature had broken through a hundred in the shade at Fort Yukon. Somebody in Utah had been funny and booked them into a motel at North Pole. They arrived at midnight, with marmots whistling in the stunted pines and a big sign saying WELCOME TO SANTA CLAUS HOUSE. The girl on reception told them the story as she brought them sandwiches and beer. A guy called Miller had set up a house in the wilderness and called it North Pole and one year, on December 25th, he went around in a Father Christmas outfit, and in the course of time he had a daughter and she was christened Merry Christmas Miller. 'It all happened in the old pioneer days,' said the girl. 'In the days when you could build yourself a house, build yourself a town even, and call it what you wanted and nobody interfered.'

'When was this?' asked Martha.

'Oh, back in the Fifties,' said the girl, vaguely, 'or maybe 1960.'

On the television news were pictures of volcanic glass, ash, and sulphur fumes spewing out from Novarupta. Nobody was that excited. A newsreader commented that there had been eighty notable earthquakes in Alaska in the twentieth century. There was no mention of the murder of a security man at the Eagle HAARP site.

Next morning Pope sent a card to England postmarked 'North Pole'. The chopper came for them from Eielson, and landed in front of the pole itself.

The pilot was tense. 'You know there's electrical storms forecast?'

Martha said, 'Yes, they said.'

'I told them to make it clear.'

'They made it clear.'

'I have no objection to taking you, so long as you know what you're heading into.'

'We understand. You know where the site is?'

'Of course I know where it is. I brought the guy out, the guy who died.'

The helicopter rose over the spruce pines. Soon the forest started to give way to taiga, the Russian land of twigs. The pilot told them they were passing Sourdough Camp: he was detouring north to keep on a line with the Steese Highway. After an hour they were in a dust cloud and the pilot was flying by satellite navigator, a green dot pulsing on the chart in front of him. 'Ash from Novarupta,' he said through his microphone, waving an arm at the swirling brown mist. Martha nodded. No longer able to look out for grizzly bears she rummaged in her bag for *Hello!* magazine, brought for her from England by Pope. A few minutes later her mobile went. It was for Pope. It was a query, she told him, from Oxford. Something to do with him not paying for his hogsheads of burgundy wine, and his share of the stuffed boars' heads consumed nightly at high table.

He took the phone. It was Worcester College: a demand for a Senior Common Room subscription he had failed to pay when he rushed to America. Also the Atmospheric Physics Lab at Oxford Brookes University wanted a prestigious guest speaker at the Digby

Elliot centennial dinner: had he any influence, they wondered, with Dr Sluder?

'I'll try,' he said. 'E-mail me the details.'

'Are you still at the Bonanza Inn?'

'Sometimes,' he said.

'What a life,' said the girl at the other end. She was one of the departmental secretaries, the chatty one from Cowley.

The pilot said, cutting into the call, killing the mobile, 'I don't trust the navigator, I'll be going down as soon as I find a clearing or a road.'

Pope imagined the crash, the wreckage strewn through the spruces, the rotors slicing their tops and chopping off a dozen little Christmas trees. He imagined the chatty secretary from Cowley: 'I said to him "What a life" and in seconds, literally in *seconds* he was dead.' It would be the talk of the department for a week.

They peered out into the brown, gritty cloud. Occasionally they saw the tops of trees. For a moment there was swirling water: a river. The pilot, referring to his chart, said, 'Shit', then swung the craft round and followed the water downstream.

One thing about a river, Pope realised, was that it couldn't turn itself into a mountain with a sheer rock face for them to smash into.

The pilot said, 'We had warning of all this.'

Tension and stress ran like liquid through the earphones.

'The met boys told us this was going to happen. I said I'd do it, do the job, but by Christ, lady, it had better be as goddamn fucking important as they said, you getting up to Eagle.'

'Yeah, it's important.'

Time passed. The river was quite wide and slow-moving. There were occasional rocks, pools of swirling white water.

Martha said, calmly, 'Do you know where we are?'

The pilot didn't reply at first. 'That down there,' he said eventually, 'is the Yukon River. Our satellite navigator is wiped out – maybe there's too many charged particles in this electric soup. It's telling me we're west of Eagle, coming through the Yukon-Charley National Preserve. According to the navigator we should be looking down on Woodchopper Creek, but I'm telling you that down there is the Yukon River.'

'That's OK. Eagle's on the Yukon,' said Martha. 'We just follow it down.'

He didn't reply.

A few moments later he said, 'Did you see a cabin? Did you see that?' and the helicopter wheeled gently. The brown clouds were clearing. They could make out a stretch of river bank: a cabin with a pole, flying a flag, a dirt track, but no open space large enough for a helicopter to land.

They resumed their cautious journey downriver. Pope said, 'I presume that was the border.'

The pilot said, 'Yeah, I presume that too. There's a Canadian Air Force base at Dawson. We'll fuel up and maybe I'll try again.' He sounded more relaxed. He pressed a switch and talked to his base.

'If that's the Yukon and we're over the Canadian border,' Martha said, quietly, 'we must have flown over Eagle in the last ten minutes. We didn't see a thing. It doesn't make sense.'

The brown fog was thickening again. Pope could smell sulphur. A light on the instrument panel was flashing. The pilot was talking more urgently now: he was through to a Canadian air traffic controller. Then he switched on the intercom. 'The filters can't cope. If we had the version of this chopper equipped for Saudi we'd be able to cope, but nobody expected a sandstorm in Alaska.'

It was ash, and shards of pumice, and needlepoint fragments of volcanic glass that were clogging the air intake.

The pilot would put the craft down, he said, in the water. They'd have ten seconds, maximum, to get out of the cabin: it didn't sound much, he said, but it was plenty. He seemed more worried about the chopper, but thought they'd salvage it at no great cost, providing it wasn't caught up in rapids, providing it sunk quietly to the river bed.

He said: 'The moment I yell out, you release your lapstraps and *move*, you understand?'

They understood.

In the event, as he brought them down over the foaming brown waters, a small open space appeared on the bank, and he cruised into it like a hangar.

There was a sudden, massive jolt as a rotor arm hit a tree. Pope felt himself flung forward, a pain searing through his shoulders and neck – so agonising, so severe, that for a second he lost conscious-ness. He could hear Martha shouting. Then she was pulling him back in his seat, leaning over him, trying to reach the door switch. His nostrils filled with the thick stench of aviation fuel and hot oil. He released his own seat belt. She pushed him, out of the door. He fell a few feet to the ground.

The helicopter had landed on a hidden stack of long cut logs. It was leaning over at an angle, slewed round with its rotors embedded in a tree. Looking up they could see the pilot still hunched in his seat. For a dazed moment Pope thought he was leaning forward over the phone – was busy, perhaps, reporting their position.

Martha said crisply, 'OK, let's get him out.'

They clambered back inside. The pilot was semi-conscious and breathing heavily. He had released his safety harness when he thought they were about to hit the water, and his head had slammed into the instrument panel. They half lifted, half helped him out of the helicopter, carried him away from it, and laid him down on the carpet of dead pine needles. He had a cut on his forehead: already there was swelling and contusions. He murmured something about the rescue beacon, then drifted into unconsciousness. A cloud of insects swarmed over his face, attracted by the blood oozing from his forehead.

They made a tent over his head using Pope's shirt, but it was useless at keeping the flies out. They tried to dab his face, where it was free from blood, with anti-mosquito cream from the first-aid box.

'The chopper,' said Pope. 'Is it going to catch fire?'

'Not now,' said Martha.

Pope climbed back into the helicopter and tried to work out if the directional rescue beacon was on. Martha sat by the river, which was nowhere near wide enough to be the Yukon, and used her mobile to call Utah.

The line was constantly breaking up. It took twenty minutes to link her to the Royal Canadian Mounted Police at Dawson. She had no way of giving them their position. 'The pilot thought he was following the Yukon, but I don't believe he could have been.'

They asked her questions about landmarks, river tributaries. She told them about the wooden shack with the Canadian flag. 'I'd say it was about ten miles upriver from where we are.'

She told them the pilot was gravely injured.

By the time the link finally broke up the pilot was dying. She knelt down and gently held his hand, shocked to think they knew nothing about him, would not have known his name, even, had it not been sewn, military-style, on his shirt.

'Oh Christ,' she said, 'he's going. It must be internal bleeding inside his skull.'

He was gone. Pope also knelt by him as his life ceased, and his soul, as Martha believed, departed his body.

'Oh God,' said Martha. 'Oh dear God look at that.'

She was staring upriver. Over the tops of the pine spruces a vast wall of blackness was rolling towards them: a tidal wave of darkness, moving seemingly slowly, but in fact phenomenally fast: rolling over pine trees and river bank as they watched.

Pope looked quickly round.

He said, 'Do we have anything to hold water?'

'Empty Coke cans.'

Pope ran the few yards to the helicopter. They filled the four empty Coke cans with water from the river. They got back to the helicopter cabin seconds before the wall of darkness swallowed them.

24

Salt Lake City

Koenig was lying unchanged, though he looked less fat than on Sluder's last visit: the silky vitamin sheen had gone from his facial skin, which was now grey and fell in folds, making him look like a jowly, unhappy bloodhound. An intravenous drip ran up from his arm to a bottle of colourless liquid. His eyes were open but, as far as Sluder could tell, unseeing.

Koenig's fiancée believed he could hear, see and understand. Sluder put down the flowers he had brought, and smiled at Koenig warmly, just in case this was all true. He said, gently: 'Well, John, old pardner,' and waited for the tear to fall from Koenig's eye.

Nothing.

Sluder sat down by the bed. It was quiet in here. Restful. No phone calls, no e-mails, no faxes. No relentless demands for information, for *progress*. There was not even the ticking of a clock. He could smell the flowers, and that was somehow restful too.

He sat for a while, wondering if the computer guy at Eagle would turn out to be the hacker, the Captain Crunch of the Arctic. The girl from Baltimore, Wonderweb Woman, had been cleared: she was one super phreaker, that child, but 'The cat sat on the mat' was her limit as a poet, and she thought Merrie England was a burger bar in Disneyworld.

'Well, John,' he sighed, 'I don't know how long we can afford to wait around like this.'

According to his fiancée, Koenig had communicated with her by squeezing her hand. The nurses were sceptical: they had not been able to get any response.

He took Koenig's hand, soft and flabby and curiously cold, in a firm, Western grip.

'You hear me, John?'

Nothing.

205

Or was there a movement in the eyes, a glint of recognition, of intelligence?

'Well maybe you're the wise old monkey, just lying there, not saying nothing. There's all hell let loose back at the station. There's some hacker managed to find a way into the whisper technology, broken through the logic gates. The guy from England, Pope, says it can't be done. You ever heard those words before, John? Do you remember the phreaker who used a main lab computer in Berkeley to raid half the systems in California?'

And the East Coast university student who released a worm into the electronic wild – a worm that replicated itself again, and again, until it infested six thousand major systems and closed down a tenth of the Internet. And the guys at Hamburg's Chaos Computer Club, who hacked their way into NASA and the nuclear arms lab at Los Alamos.

'Nobody believed any of it was possible. Nobody believed a couple of guys on a personal computer in Hamburg could break into NASA, nobody believed a Cornell student could send a worm into every UNIX-based computer in the USA. But it happened then, and it's happening now. Can you hear me, John? If you hear me, can you squeeze my hand?'

He thought about the unexpected nature of life. What he'd have said, had he known two weeks ago that he would ever ask John Koenig to squeeze his hand.

He gave a low laugh, the quiet wheeze of a rattlesnake.

Jesus, he was tired.

He looked at Koenig, the man who had worked on Telstar in the early Sixties, who'd been a senior technician when Intelsat I opened up two hundred and forty telephone circuits across the North Atlantic.

'We've given our lives to this game,' he said emotionally.

Koenig had two broken marriages. Sluder hadn't been home in a week. He'd telephoned once, and his daughter had answered. Mom was out at bridge, she said. She herself was busy baking cookies for the elderly as part of her effort to earn her civics badge at high school. Yeah, her boyfriend was helping her make the cookies. 'Love you, baby,' Sluder had said sadly. After a lifetime in advanced telecommunications he knew the acoustic of the bedroom phone extension when he heard it.

206

'Our lives, our hopes, our dreams. Listen, John. This phreaker, this hacker, did she send the signal about Wilcox Base as well as the Olde English stuff? It was direct transference, OK, we're having to get our heads round that and it isn't easy, you're the only guy it works with, the rest of us just plod along waiting till the deciphers come through. But you're a wise old bird, John, you wouldn't pick up a corruption without having an instinctive idea of the type of person who sent it. Are we talking Chaos Computer Club, here, John? Are we talking organised crime, or just some kid in Arkansas?'

The door opened. The NSA agent guarding Koenig came in. Behind him was the neurosurgeon flown in from Washington Army hospital, and the fiancée, Mary Lou, who was looking frightened.

The neurosurgeon said, 'I thought you might like to explain.'

Sluder said, 'Mary Lou, I'm deeply grateful to you for coming here.'

'That's OK.'

She hadn't wanted to come. She had no means to get the two hundred miles to Salt Lake City and the boss of the Dinosaur Diner had threatened to sack her if she missed any more shifts. Sluder had phoned the Dinosaur Diner and said, 'Mister, this is a matter of national importance we're talking about,' and the motel owner had said, 'No, mister, this is Mary Lou Copeck we're talking about and tonight's Bluegrass Night and she's the Nightingale of Vernal County, and she sings here tonight or she never damn well sings here again— No, no, you listen, the first I knew she was engaged to this guy in Salt Lake City was the day she walked out of my restaurant in mid-shift with a dental equipment salesman from Kansas . . .'

Sluder had listened for a while. He was untouched. The whole world was crying out its woes, and the troubles of a Utah motel owner were less than a sigh in the wind. He said, 'We need her. We're sending a helicopter.'

'A helicopter for Mary Lou Copeck?'

'Get yourself another bluegrass singer, and send us the tab.'

He said, now, 'We need your help, Mary Lou.'

She looked at him distrustfully.

'Is it possible that you can ask John here some questions? Hold his hand, and find out if he can in any way respond?'

They sat her down. She took Koenig's hand.

'Ask him,' said Sluder, 'if he remembers the night at the receiving station, the night he was seeking out the corruptions in the tapes.'

He glanced up at the man from National Security. The man looked to be in pain.

Mary Lou asked the question. Koenig's eyes stared up at the ceiling.

They waited.

Mary Lou shook her head.

The neurosurgeon called in a nurse. She pressed a switch. There was the faint hum of an electric motor. Koenig's head and shoulders rose. His eyes now looked at the far wall, which had on it a photograph of vacationers on the Wasatch ski slopes. The nurse carefully adjusted Koenig's pillows. She left.

'Ask him,' said Sluder, 'where the words "*Crimen lesæ majestatis*" came from.'

'The words what?'

'Just say it.'

Nothing.

Sluder said: 'Try Missile strike Wil—'

'No.'

It was the NSA agent.

Sluder looked sadly, regretfully, at Koenig. He shook his head slowly. He stood up and went outside. The security man and the neurosurgeon followed him.

Mary Lou sat holding Koenig's hand. She looked at the wire net over his head, new since her last visit. It was like an old-fashioned hairnet, but covered in bright metallic buttons. She wondered what it was for. She wondered if they'd take her back to Bonanza in the helicopter, or just leave her here in Salt Lake City. She thought of her sister, living on the trailer park near Provo, who was convinced that Koenig would wake up and say incredulously, 'I asked you to marry me, Mary Lou? Are you nuts or sumpn'?'

The men came back.

Sluder said, 'Mary Lou, you know John here's a divorced man, divorced twice, with no children?'

She knew.

'Well, it seems his parents are dead, and his only brother also died, a couple of years back . . .'

He was an orphan in the world. She hadn't realised. She was all he'd got.

'The point being that if you are, as you say, his fiancée, that could according to the state of Utah make you his next of kin.'

What did he mean *as you say*? She looked at them, frightened.

'Depending of course on any documentation there might be.'

They were looking at her expectantly.

She said, 'There's no documentation.'

'And how long had you been engaged, Mary Lou, when this happened?'

'About five hours.'

The security man was smiling.

'And was anyone a witness,' said Sluder, 'to this engagement?'

'Yep, I guess so.'

The smile disappeared.

'There was a salesman, a guy who peddled air-conditioning.'

And yes, they'd be able to find him. He was visiting a firm in Roosevelt, he was hoping to sell air-conditioning for a whole new development of luxury cabins at Cedar View and Bluebell. The people at Roosevelt would know who he was.

The neurosurgeon said, 'I think we assume that Mary Lou's status is established. Mary Lou, we may have to operate on John here. We may need you to sign a form.'

The responsibility was terrible.

She said, 'I guess if you feel you need to . . .'

'We need to treat the aneurysm, to allow oedema and vasospasm to subside. While we're in there, it may be that we could do an experimental programme . . .'

Sluder shook his head gently. The word experimental had been a mistake.

'By which I mean attach electrodes to different parts of his brain, and apply very mild stimulus. This is not as dramatic as it sounds, the brain has no nerves, it cannot feel pain.'

'Is all this necessary? Is it needed to make him well?'

A pause.

'It may assist in bringing him out of coma. The main purpose, however, is to test electrical activity in the hippocampus, which is the area of the brain where memory is generally believed to be stored.'

'You said experimental programme. Is this being done to help John's condition?'

Another pause.

'No, I can't say that.'

Shit.

Sluder's phone bleeped. He went outside. It was Miss Pagetti. She said, 'You need to know, Miss Crawfurd's helicopter is missing. It never reached Eagle.'

'How long overdue is it?'

'Three hours. It ran out of fuel an hour ago. They can't get search aircraft into the area because of volcanic debris.'

The door opened behind him. It was Mary Lou, tears streaming down her face.

'Last word from the pilot,' said Miss Pagetti, 'was that his navigational equipment was malfunctioning. There's a report from the Canadians of a helicopter crash but we have no details.'

'OK.'

She said, 'That's it? OK? That's all you have to say?'

'Make sure I'm kept in touch.'

He watched Mary Lou disappear down the stairs. The phone was still held to his ear. He heard Miss Pagetti say 'Jesus, what an asshole' before cutting the link.

He called his office. There was an urgent signal from the CIA. The French had analysed the tapes from Charles de Gaulle Airport. They were warning the world's intelligence agencies of a new type of electronic intruder: a new kind of hacker.

They didn't yet suspect a friendly power, they didn't yet link the intrusions to *Pasiphae*.

They didn't know, thought Sluder, that a new kind of worm was now in the electronic wild, insinuating its way into systems it encountered, coiling into corners and replicating itself.

He had a moment of panic; a moment when his stomach muscles contracted. Then he got a grip. They'd come clean with the French once they'd traced the hacker, eliminated the fault, put the disinfectant tools in place. The French would be able to sue for compensation for the next twenty years.

The neurosurgeon and NSA agent came out of Koenig's room. The neurosurgeon said heatedly, 'You all seem to forget that I have taken an oath.'

'Shit, we've all taken an oath,' said Sluder.

'Not a government oath. Dear God . . .'

The man from the NSA said, 'It doesn't matter. Agent Crawfurd wasn't playing ball anyway.'

Mary Lou looked out over the Great Salt Lake, over Antelope Island. A group of students came by rattling cans, raising money for the 2002 Winter Olympics, but left her alone when they saw the tears rolling down her face. She checked her purse, to see if she had money for the coach fare to Vernal. Then she decided she couldn't leave John, not now. She'd go to her sister on the trailer park near Provo.

She wondered what her boss at the Dinosaur Diner would say, and guessed that he'd sack her. She set off in search of a phone to call her sister. She didn't honestly expect that John would ever recover, ever come back to her. They'd done something to his brain out at the government station in the desert: something they were frightened to tell her about.

But she wasn't going to leave him. Not while he still breathed. As she walked under the subway the words of Faron Young's 'I Miss You Already' were running through her head, so that the tears fell faster than ever down her cheeks.

25

Yukon

The torture of insect stings: red blotches covering the soft flesh of her arms, neck and back. She was afraid of blood poisoning, of fever; but Pope was worse. His face had puffed up almost beyond recognition, his eyes were black slits that streamed with everlasting tears.

'Any luck?' she called out.

He was messing with the helicopter's radio. He'd been messing about with it for seven or eight hours. If he could get the radio working they wouldn't be dependent on a mobile with weak batteries.

'This stuff,' he said, frustrated, 'this transceiver stuff, is just so . . .'

'Simple?'

'Obsolescent.'

She wondered if she could allow herself another dip in the river. Every so often she submerged herself, holding her breath until the swarm of insects dispersed from their living meal. But it didn't do any real good. Five seconds after she emerged the insects were back, hungry and vicious. The two tubes of insect repellent cream were almost used up, and she couldn't, in all conscience, keep washing it away in the water.

'Oh God,' she said, quietly, closing her streaming, itching eyes. 'Oh dear God.'

But it was better than it had been. It was much better than it had been. For twelve hours they had huddled in darkness inside the helicopter cabin, breathing a mix of aviation fuel and sulphur fumes. When she slept she dreamed that volcanic ash was falling like snow, and she was drawing it into her lungs and drowning in a sea of glass and pumice shards.

She didn't dare sleep after that. She dosed herself on aspirin and anti-malaria pills and sat in a haze, her ears buzzing gently. Beside her Pope worked away at his laptop, patiently putting the last of

Pasiphae's corrupt signals through the sort of analysis that Option Red, with its 2.5 thousand billion bytes of memory, would have managed in 0.1 seconds.

But it was the program that mattered, not the machine. She'd once spent two days at Oak Ridge National Lab working the Intel Paragon XP/S 150 and at the end of the session the technician assigned to her team had grinned and said: 'It's easy to come up with the answer. The difficult part is in coming up with the question.'

Somebody had said scornfully, 'That is just such a cliché.' But clichés, she reflected, were clichés only because they came up so often.

Slowly, the intense darkness had lifted. Hour by hour they had watched, until the spruce pines acquired a deeper blackness against the charcoal sky; until the treetops were individually silhouetted. They didn't say much. Once Martha spoke about the Alaskan earthquake of 1964. 'It caused waves on the canals of Venice. There was a picture, in the geography book at my high school, of Venice with a gondolier. A boy called Samuel K. Grosvenor said that one day he'd take me there. I was greatly impressed.'

'Where was all this?'

'Cincinnati. It was before we moved to LA. Not a lot of people from Cincinnati get to go to Venice. Cincinnati is not as cosmopolitan as you might think.'

'I don't recall,' said Pope, 'I've ever had cause to think anything about Cincinnati.'

'Snooty, snooty. Listen, I remember reading that parts of Alaska were in pitch darkness for several days after the 1964 eruptions.'

'Quite likely.'

'If we can rig a line so we don't get lost, one of us can get down to the river. The water should be drinkable even though there's all this stuff in it. There's water purification tablets in the medical kit.'

'We don't need water yet.'

She badly wanted to move. To do something, however pointless. 'Just before we touched down,' she said, 'did everything seem blurry to you? I was looking through the side window and everything went suddenly out of focus.'

'Yes, I noticed it.'

'You reckon that was the volcano causing an earthquake?'

'For the debris to drift down this far the eruption must have happened soon after we took off from North Pole. There may have been small earth tremors later.'

Time passed.

She said, 'I wonder why they don't call us.'

'There's nothing they can do until they can get a fix on the beacon.'

'You're sure it's working?'

'It's got its own power pack.'

She reached for her mobile. 'I'm going to find out what's happening.'

'It takes five times the power to call out than to take a call coming in.'

They sat in silence. She wondered how he got to be so damned smug. When the chopper had come down she had been the one acting coolly and decisively, her NSA training proving its worth, while Pope had stumbled around in confusion. Somehow, in the hours that followed, he had acquired a moral superiority. His intellect told him to sit still and do nothing; easier advice for an Oxford don to take, she told herself wryly, than Action Girl.

She dozed.

Her phone bleeped.

'Yes?'

It was the Royal Canadian Mounted Police, who were co-ordinating emergency services in Dawson City. They said, 'We don't reckon you're on the Yukon.'

'No.'

'More likely the Porcupine.'

'Where's that?'

'About a hundred and fifty miles north of Eagle.'

'Christ.'

'You got enough to eat?'

'Yes. There's enough survival packs to last another week.'

'We're in touch with your folks in Utah. They've a computer model running in the Weather Center in Washington. It says they ought to pick up your satellite signal in twelve hours.'

'Twelve hours?'

'Approximately.'

'Thanks.'

They dozed. Pope woke to find her opening the side door of the helicopter.

'Where are you going? We don't need water yet.'

'I'm going to the john.'

'What?'

'The ladies, Charles. The lavatory. Jesus . . .'

When she'd climbed back she said, 'I can see the fir tops.'

Five hours later there was enough light to see the river bank. And they could see, again, the pilot's body, and they could understand, now, the sickly, putrid smell that they had secretly been blaming on each other.

Pope crawled out from under the fuselage. 'The connection to the aerial is severed. I'm wasting my time. I thought a corpse took days and days to get in that state.'

'Not in this humidity,' said Martha. 'Ought we to bury him?'

'I don't know that we can bury him. We've nothing to dig with.'

The insects were a cloud over the pilot's body. It was that that was attracting them. They were feeding on him, and then, for a change, they were feeding on her and Pope; happy to take their meals on the hoof.

'I hope it doesn't attract grizzlies,' said Pope. 'Although I suppose it would solve the problem if it did.'

'A grizzly's diet is eighty per cent vegetation.'

She'd learned that on an NSA survival course.

'What about the other twenty per cent?'

'Fi fie fo fum,' she said, 'I smell the blood of an Englishman.'

He turned back to the helicopter's radio. She slipped down again into the river, letting the coolness soothe her itching, inflamed skin, holding her head under water. Whatever Washington's Weather Center predicted, she guessed it could be a week before the atmosphere cleared enough for the satellites to pick up their distress beacon. They'd survive a week, she thought, as far as food and water was concerned.

But she didn't think she could survive the insects.

'Either we move from here, or we move the body,' she said, later, close to tears.

216

'The Canadians told us to stay put.'

'Oh Christ, look at that,' she said.

The darkness was returning: waves of black smoke rolling down through the pines. They filled their Coke cans with water from the river and retreated once again to the helicopter. She dosed herself on aspirins and anti-malaria tablets, and some kind of antihistamine pills she found. She drifted into a haze. She prayed for unconsciousness.

Hours passed.

'Her father and brother are dead,' said Pope, softly.

'What?'

The screen of his laptop glowed green.

She said, 'I thought your battery was exhausted.'

'I've linked it up to your mobile.'

'Oh Jesus. Oh no. Now listen—'

'Look.'

She read: *As for ye Yong Jentylwomān whos ffader and broder be dede I gwv xij^{li} fyggs and viij^{li} reyfons w^{t} potts off oyle for Lente.*

'As for the young gentlewoman whose father and brother be dead I give 12lb of figs and 8lb of raisins with two pots of oil for Lent. Now look at this.'

He rapidly pressed the keys. On screen appeared: *Pray for and all hir kynne as longe as the nunnery D'or ftantt.*

'Pray for and all her kin as long as the nunnery of gold standeth. I don't know that we shouldn't be looking in France. We're in the middle of the Hundred Years War, this church could be in Aquitaine.'

'Charles,' she said. 'Charles, why are you using up my fucking battery?'

But he wasn't listening.

She slept. Again he woke her. It was still black outside; she was still in a living hell. Why had he woken her, she raged, feeling hot anger then tears of self-pity, why had he woken her? He was holding up the laptop.

'No . . .'

But her eyes went to the screen.

Mekely befechyth you, in the reu'ence of allmygty god to render helpe and focour me in myne grete neceffite.

He said: 'Meekly beseeching you, in the reverence of Almighty God to render help and succour me in my great necessity. The girl's

217

in the nunnery. She's in trouble. She's appealing to him, to the franklin.'

'Charles,' she said, 'how do you know this?' She looked at his face in the green light. 'There's nothing about a franklin, nothing about a girl and a franklin.'

The green light vanished.

In the darkness he said, 'She's at the nunnery, and she's asking him for help.'

They were both asleep when the mobile bleeped faintly. It was Utah. The satellite had picked up their distress signal. They were not on the Porcupine, they were on a tributary of the Yukon, east of Forty Mile. Soldiers from the Ontario Regiment were training in the mountains west of Coffee Creek and would be with them in approximately seven hours.

'Another seven hours, oh Christ,' said Martha.

Miss Pagetti in Utah said, 'It's a big country you're in. It's called The Last Front—'

'Yeah, yeah – listen, these soldiers. Will they bring a body bag for the pilot?'

Miss Pagetti didn't know.

Pope said, 'Find out what's happened at the HAARP site.'

'The cops haven't been able to get there from Anchorage,' said Miss Pagetti. 'I think I ought to close down now to conserve your battery.'

Already the mobile was too weak to call out.

Martha took more of the antihistamine pills and slept. She woke suddenly. He was leaning over her, shaking her gently.

'Leave me be,' she snapped, subconsciously aware that in all the books she'd ever read where a man and a woman were lost in jungle-like conditions the moment came when, despite extremes of exhaustion, danger, hunger and thirst, one or both of them demanded sex.

He pointed. A Canadian soldier was standing on the edge of the clearing, a great grin on his sweat-streaked, dust-coated face.

They gave Martha and Pope tea from their flasks. They helped them smear their faces with insect repellent cream. They put the pilot's body in a temporary grave, covered with logs. There were ten of them, and they had two Jeeps back in the forest. An hour later Martha's face was being soothed by a flow of cold air-conditioning and she was through to Utah where Sluder said, 'We thought you were dead, honey.'

'Just eaten alive. What's happening?'

'We're ready to reactivate *Pasiphae*.'

'We were given a week, Larry.'

'The shield's in place. We've got clients screaming.'

'Has John Koenig regained consciousness?'

'I guess John Koenig was a red herring. I guess it was just a stroke through overeating.'

'The guy in Eagle?'

'Everybody goes crazy in Alaska.'

'Larry . . .' she started, but realised she was wasting her time. She asked for a chopper and was told the volcanic eruption was the third largest since 1964 and that Alaskan emergency services were stretched to breaking point, and that there would be no air traffic north of Anchorage for at least forty-eight hours. 'I understand it'll take the soldier boys around twelve hours to get you back to civilisation,' said Sluder cheerfully. 'Look on it as a holiday. How's Charlie Pope? He never did strike me as the outdoor, camping type.'

'Bye, Larry.'

She was patched through to NSA in Chicago. She spoke briefly, then passed the phone to the Canadian lieutenant. She went to the second Jeep where Pope was sitting with his laptop linked to the satellite fax. Pope said: 'I'm getting Miss Pagetti to search through lists of medieval nunneries in England and France.'

The Canadian lieutenant came over. 'We're being asked to take you to Eagle. It's still being cleared with the Ministry of Defence in Ottawa and with the Alaskan State authorities, but nobody sees any reason why it shouldn't happen, so let's get moving. We're to take you to a HAARP. What the hell is a HAARP?'

'Ask Charles,' she said, 'he's the technical guy.'

A HAARP, Pope told him, as they jolted in convoy along the forest track, was a High Frequency Active Aural Research Programme. It was an ionospheric heater, an antenna high in the upper atmosphere created out of charged electrons and ions and plasma. 'An Anglo-

Norwegian team made the first HAARP back in the Eighties. They heated a patch of the ionosphere until it vibrated exactly in tune with musical chords. Then they beamed up Wagner's 'Ride of the Valkyries'. I've heard the tape. It's phenomenal – Wagner in a vast auditorium, fifty miles up in the sky.'

'You're musicians, then?' asked the lieutenant, disingenuously.

'You've got it,' said Martha.

'But you haven't any instruments.'

'We threw them out of the helicopter to lighten the load. Charles sacrificed his grand piano to save our lives, didn't you, Charles?'

She felt light-headed. A couple of hours previously she'd have sworn that she would never joke about anything ever again.

A voice on the intercom: 'We're over the border, sir. Two k east of Millers Camp and Crooked Creek.'

They were on a forest track. There was nothing to mark the Canadian side that they were leaving, but after twenty yards they came to a crude, hand-painted sign: WELCOME TO ALASKA nailed to a tree. The voice on the intercom told them they were entering the Yukon-Charley National Preserve.

An hour later they reached a cluster of cabins in the woods. Ahead of them fifty or sixty huge steel masts criss-crossed with power lines and bristling with antennae, towered over the firs. They pulled up on the edge of the clearing, and sat looking up at the Pentagon's ionospheric heater. Its compound was surrounded by a fire fence, some ten feet high, covered in netting to keep out animals. A soldier went and tried the metal gates: they were locked. There was a wind blowing now, a high, hot wind with a smell of sulphur.

There was a humming noise. A faint drumming in the air.

Martha got out of the Jeep. She felt her energy, buoyed on chocolate and coffee, drain from her body. Pope was standing looking through the wire at the concrete blockhouse. He seemed old and weary, she thought, his face deeply etched with volcanic dust.

The lieutenant said: 'I'm not sure about breaking in.'

He too sounded tired, exhausted.

'We have not come all this way,' she said, 'to be stopped by a rabbit fence.'

The lieutenant told his radio operator to raise base. The soldiers started brewing tea on a stove. The radio operator called, 'Sir . . .'

The lieutenant went and spoke on the phone. He came back and said, 'They're talking to the Pentagon.'

They sat and waited. They drank mugs of sugary tea. The wind hummed through the antennae. Fifty miles above them, up through the maelstrom of volcanic dust and electrical storms, the charged electrons of the ionosphere were being bombarded by high-frequency radio energy beams. Controlled by scientists in Maine, experiments were taking place into methods of reducing the number of particles in the radiation of the Van Allen belts; into increasing the life expectancy of satellites; into locating underground water, oil, and mineral deposits.

She stared at the low, concrete blockhouse. Its green-painted door – a token gesture to environmental values – was closed. Its windows were shuttered with steel. So this, she thought, was where the ELF-like, sub-molecular, quantum-world signals from *Pasiphae* came to earth.

The lieutenant was called to the radio. He came back and said, 'OK, we're going to cut through the locks. Can I have a word?'

He led Martha and Pope to one side.

He said, 'What about radiation?'

Pope said, 'The site uses ordinary electricity brought in by over-head cable from Eagle.'

'Radiation does not have to be nuclear in origin.'

'There should be no danger to health.'

'Should be no danger – it's that word "should" that bothers me. I had an elder brother in the Gulf, in the West Mercian Regiment, and they told him there was no such thing as Gulf Sickness.'

'We will go into the compound on our own,' said Pope. 'We won't need you once we're through the wire.'

'Right, OK.'

A soldier said, 'These wire cutters are fucking hopeless, sir. We'll have to use the saw.'

Martha was passed another plastic mug of tea, thick with sugar and condensed milk. The soldiers sawed at the steel lock. It seemed that nothing stirred in the scrubby spruce trees around the site, but after some ten minutes a soldier said, quietly, 'There's two guys with rifles watching us.'

Martha spotted them. They were wearing dirty tartan hunting

221

jackets and peering out from some scrubby ferns. There was something sinister about their faces, but that, thought Martha, might just be prejudice: they clearly hadn't shaved for several days. Their guns were held loose but their fingers were on the triggers: it would take about two seconds for them to be raised into a firing position.

After a moment the lieutenant said, 'Armscote and Cannon stand to, but inside the Jeep, nothing visible.'

Two soldiers looked startled, then disappeared under the canvas back of a vehicle.

Martha said, 'The Canadian Army must not open fire on American citizens in the state of Alaska.'

'Those are automatic rifles they've got,' said the lieutenant. 'If they open fire on us we do not just lie down here and die.'

He turned to his radio operator and said, 'Get me HQ.'

'I'll go and talk to them,' said Pope.

'No,' said Martha. 'An English voice will not be helpful.' She walked across the clearing. The two men watched, impassive, as she approached.

'Hi, my name's Martha Crawfurd, National Security Agency,' she said, showing them her pass. 'Do you know anything about Mr Barrendov, the technician here?'

They looked at her, her streaky, blotched face, her matted hair, her weeping eyes. Then they looked beyond her to the Jeeps, each of which had a small Canadian flag painted on its side and a Canadian Army pennant flying from its aerial.

'The Canadians have brought us through from near Dawson,' she said. 'It seems there'll be nothing flying from Fairbanks for another twenty-four hours.'

She wondered how much they knew about Barrendov. 'We're here because of an alleged assault on the security guard . . . do you know where Mr Barrendov might be? Has he come out of the woods yet?'

'They took him to Eagle.'

'Took him? Who took him?'

'Medics.'

'Was he unwell?'

The younger one giggled.

Barrendov, he said, had hanged himself.

'Yeah, right,' she said wearily. She reflected that she could have stayed in Utah and heard this information. 'You can do nothing in Alaska, honey,' Sluder had said, 'except get eaten alive.' Sluder had been so right. Why did she never listen to Sluder?

'I suppose it was because of the security guard?'

No, they said. He'd hanged himself because of his guilt at having operated the Pentagon's devilish machine.

'At having operated *what*?'

'He killed himself because that thing in there,' said the older one, 'has brought the worst electric storms to Alaska of any summer in living memory.'

Martha said, 'Listen, listen, you guys need to know it would take a million HAARPs and all the energy from the world's electricity for a whole year to have any effect on one single, solitary thunderstorm.'

They looked at her cunningly. The older one winked fatly. So why, he said, had Barrendov come creeping out of the forest – where the police from Anchorage would never have found him in a million years – and gone to his cabin, and hanged himself?

'And why,' said the younger hunter, scoring a shrewd point, 'have the Canadians come over the border to blow the whole damn shooting match to blazes?'

'I told you why the Canadians are in Alaska. It's an emergency. Can you take me to Barrendov's cabin? Are the two girls he lived with still here?'

The two whores, they said, grinning, were back in Fairbanks.

The lieutenant shouted that they were through the wire. She turned and saw that Pope was already walking into the compound. 'Thanks for your help,' she said hastily.

She ran back across the clearing, and in through the open gates. After a moment's hesitation, the Canadian lieutenant and two of his men went in after her.

They crossed gravel covered in dry, dead weeds. Above them a myriad wires hummed: first low, then loud, making them glance up uneasily. Pope was waiting for them at the blockhouse door. It was locked. A soldier went for an automatic rifle. They stood and waited. The two hunters had come out of the undergrowth, and were standing at the gates by the Jeeps. The younger one called out, 'You don't need a rifle, you need dynamite.' The older one shouted, 'You shoot at a metal door, you damn fool, and you'll have bullets ricocheting everywhere.'

They took cover. The lieutenant lay down on the gravel. He fired a sustained burst at the lock. At the third attempt the door swung open.

Inside were two bleak bedrooms, each equipped with institutional Army beds. There was a shower room and lavatory. There was a mess room with a low table covered in shooting magazines. There was a kitchen with nothing in the fridge other than tins of beans and bacon, and packets of potato flakes and pasta.

Pope and Martha found the control room. It was surprisingly small: rows of neat equipment terminals, a modest bank of three monitors. Two screens were switched on. They were being run by remote control from Maine. The third screen was blank. Martha said: 'It's dedicated to *Pasiphae*.'

She tapped in a message: it was acknowledged.

Pope entered the passwords. He said, 'I'd appreciate some coffee.'

She said, conversationally, 'Yeah, so would I.'

A pause.

'I wonder,' she mused, 'if anybody'll make us some?'

He was staring at the screen. She sighed, went to the kitchen and made coffee. It was ten p.m., though still light outside, the sky a sulphurous yellow. She wondered about food, though she had no appetite. Perhaps the Canadian soldiers would have a cook among them.

When she came back he said, 'How many corrupt messages has Utah processed?'

'Fifty-three,' she said.

'There's a log here that says fifty-nine.'

Barrendov, it seemed, had been working on corrupted files since before the first alarm had been raised by the Navy. He had been way ahead of Utah: way ahead of Koenig.

He had kept them to himself – tiring, perhaps, of Dungeons and Dragons books. Perhaps he enjoyed a challenge. Perhaps he thought it was a new sort of computer game.

Pope felt overwhelmingly tired.

She said, 'Do we patch them through to Chicago for analysis? Do we ask for time on Option Red?'

He said, 'Give me a couple of hours.'

She looked at him and hesitated.

'Listen,' she said, 'we know this stuff is capable of direct trans-ference, right?'

'I'm nearly there, Martha.'

'Direct transference to human brains, like Barrendov's brain and Koenig's brain – brains that have been conditioned by delving too deep for too long—'

'I know what I'm doing.'

'Oh Jesus,' she said. 'Oh Jesus what a stupid thing to say.'

He was already calling up the hidden signals.

She sighed. 'OK. Two hours.'

He looked strained and old: but of this world, she thought.

He knew that Option Red would find the corruptions, would find where they nestled in the quantum-neuron cells, in the DNA-type clusters of subatomic particles that formed the *Pasiphae* trans-missions, in that bizarre and ambiguous quantum world where single particles could go through two holes at the same time, and matter could exist simultaneously in several states, and where pairs of electrons could influence each other even though they were a light year apart.

It would find them, and would delicately extract them.

But it wouldn't *feel* them. Option Red would never be suffused by the despair and melancholy of the High Medieval Age. It would never suffer a stroke. It would never bring an airliner crashing in flames. It would never be driven to commit suicide.

It would never, at the end of the day, find the answer.

She came into the control room. She said, 'Lucy Pagetti's cracked it. She's found the place. It's a valley on the Welsh border. It was called Dŵr by the Celts, D'or by the Normans and now it's called the Golden Valley.'

'And does the Golden Valley have a franklin,' said Pope, hunched over the console, staring at the screen, 'buried in a church?'

'God knows, but Lucy Pagetti's been on to some archive in Lincoln and they say it had a nunnery at the end of the fourteenth century.'

'Ricardians,' said Pope. 'The Franciscan conspiracy.'

'Yeah, right, and there's a lead to the carrier—'

A light flashed. She picked up a phone. 'Crawfurd. OK. The pad's due north of the compound. We'll be ready. Thirty minutes from now.'

Pope said, 'The carrier? She's found the carrier?'

'A British government satellite station near the Golden Valley is used for *Pasiphae* commercial transmissions. Two days ago they had a phone call from an archaeology student, asking if possible microwave leakage could cause someone to have symptoms of epilepsy.'

Pope said, 'Epilepsy?'

'He'd been reading up on hallucinations in a computer medical encyclopaedia. It seems his girlfriend's been having visions of the past.'

'Christ,' he said, and reached for the other phone.

'What are you doing?'

'Getting somebody there from Oxford. How do we get out of here?'

'The Canadians are sending an Air Force helicopter from Dawson. I'm going to Chicago, but I'll come over to England as soon as I can. Sluder's already on his way over there. He still reckons she'll turn out to be some teenager phreaker.'

The red light flashed again. Martha picked up the phone.

After a moment she said, 'They'll be reactivating *Pasiphae* in some thirty seconds. They're entering the protection codes now. Any comment?'

'Tell them not to do it.'

Martha said into the phone, 'Listen, we believe this to be premature and dangerous.'

'Tell them anybody who thinks infiltration can be stopped by a new configuration of protection codes is crazy. Tell them the carrier is already showing symptoms of epilepsy – say we could have another Koenig on our hands—'

The *Pasiphae* screen came alive.

'Tell them to turn it off – here, give me the phone—'

The jumble of codes running down the *Pasiphae* screen changed to a slim, bright blue vertical line.

The quantum program was running.

Pasiphae was enabled.

Mary Lou sat stroking Koenig's hand. She looked at his face, his open, seemingly unseeing eyes. Her sister said she ought to go back to Bonanza, forget about him. 'He's gonna be a vegetable for the rest of his life. How soon's it going to be before they start coming on to you for his hospitalization fees? Lots of guys say "Let's get married". Maybe he wanted to screw you.'

Her brother-in-law had laughed at that one.

'But he's not going to be doing any more screwing or marrying, and you're a sucker, Mary Lou, you always were . . .'

Her sister was a bitter, angry woman, she reflected, turned coarse by years trapped in low-class trailer parks.

She said, 'Honey?'

A shadow, an unfamiliar look, crossed his face, although as far as she could tell his facial muscles had not moved.

She held his hand.

'Honey, if you can hear me, can you give me some indication? Honey, do you want me here? Do you want me to stay here? Honey, John, do you remember proposing that we get married?'

The words sounded sad, she thought. They sounded pathetic.

'Can you hear me, John?'

A tear fell on the back of his grey hand.

A nurse was on the other side of the door, looking through the glass.

They all wanted her to go. Her sister at Provo, the hospital staff. Every day the people from the receiving station offered to fly her back to Vernal.

She wouldn't go. He had squeezed her hand once, gently, affectionately: she knew this had happened, even though the nurses had been unable to feel any pressure.

'It's OK, John,' she said. 'It's OK, you don't have to worry about a thing.'

A sudden spasm.

The machine in the corner of the room started to bleep.

The door opened and the nurse came quickly in.

227

26

Dore

The two trenches had met, four metres into the mound. By lunch-time they had found evidence of a raised platform, almost certainly built after the Romans had taken the fort and killed or enslaved its inhabitants. They took a short break then worked on, through the heat. In mid-afternoon they found what might have been fire-pits. By early evening they were turning up fragments of charred bone.

'It's druidic,' said Bill, delighted. 'It's definitely druidic.'

'Firepits and pigs' skulls,' said Jacob. 'Badger was not wrong.'

'There might be human skulls in a bit,' said Sonia. 'You don't know what we're going to find in a bit.'

When the light failed they stopped work, except for Lizzie, who was digging away, with her trowel, on the far side of one of the excavated trenches, following a small vein of burned-red clay.

'OK, pack it in,' said Bill Hastings.

Venetia poured glasses of red wine and passed them round. Bill stood silhouetted against the setting sun, talking into his mobile.

'The level,' he said loudly, 'is not just one or two generations into the pacification, as at Croft Ambrey, this is AD 500 we are talking about. Undefiled Late Iron Age ritual. Bone fragments – goat, cattle – broken pottery. No, we have not yet found evidence of headhunters, or druidic human sacrifices, but we still have almost a week to go. What? Well, yes, you can call it Camelot if you want to, there's nobody from AD 500 around to argue – yes, we *might* have unearthed the bits of plate used by Arthur and Guinevere. *Might* have done, right?'

Wolfgang said, 'I don't know that this rubbish is morally OK. Sponsorship by British Gas to excavate Troy is one thing, but a motor parts distributor from Munich coming up with a few thousand euros, we should not be prostituting ourselves.'

Eloise said, 'Drink your wine up, Wolfgang.'

Gareth and Sonia started to spoon spaghetti and garlicky meat out of the pot. Andrew called, 'Lizzie! Supper!'

It was almost dark. They could see her, in the excavations, a will-o'-the-wisp scraping away by the light of a torch.

'I'll get her,' said Eloise.

Andrew said, 'No, I'll go.'

'Honestly,' said Sonia. 'Young love.'

Andrew walked along the line of the trench.

'Bill says to leave it till morning. Come on. Supper's ready.'

She was scraping at the soil, at a vein of clay that was red in the daylight, black by the torchlight.

'Lizzie?'

She stopped. She sighed.

'Why is it that everything I do is wrong?'

She looked up at him.

'Anyway,' he said, 'there's no point in digging any more. We're off to France in the morning.'

The students from Sheffield ought to have arrived but hadn't. Venetia left a big sign outside the mess tent, saying where they were, then they all piled into the Land Rover and went down to the pub at Newbridge. Eloise was sad: she was always sad when she had to say goodbye. 'But it's been a good dig this year, hasn't it?' she said, a bit tearful after her third half-pint of cider. 'We'll all get together again next year, won't we?'

She always exchanged addresses, and always sent Christmas cards. She kissed Andrew several times, and then kissed Bill Hastings. 'We've nearly another week yet,' said Bill. 'I'm not going anywhere. You don't want to kiss me.'

'Yes, you kiss him,' said Venetia. 'You have him for a bit. Give a girl a rest.'

'Honestly,' said Sonia.

'Give me a kiss, Wolfgang,' said Eloise, enjoying her sorrows.

They came out of the pub at midnight, and were following Bill Hastings's torch, which should have been guiding them to the car park but instead was somehow wandering its way across the road.

Venetia said, 'Where's he going?'

'Oh God, he's taking us swimming,' said Sonia. 'He said he would, and he is.'

Bill's voice called from ahead. 'Come on, come on, you dozy lot!' His torch flashed back across the Hay-on-Wye road, making the cat's-eyes gleam.

They went down a path overhung with elder, heavy with blossom. Venetia called out: 'Oi, somebody take that torch off him. He's not to have the torch if I'm swimming in the nude.'

Gareth shouted, 'Can I have it, Bill?' and Sonia said, 'Oh yes, and what do you want it for then?' and called out: 'I'll have it! I'll have it! Bill! Give me the torch!'

Venetia said, 'Oh, the children, the children.'

Eloise – sobering up fast – said in a whisper: 'I'm not taking my knickers off, are you taking off yours?'

Venetia, thoughtfully, 'Do you know, I think I might.'

'In Germany everybody swims nude,' said Wolfgang. 'But a sudden temperature change after alcohol is not a good idea.'

The perfume of elder, and now an even more overpowering scent: honeysuckle. Somebody was close behind Lizzie: Andrew, of course. A hand on her arm, gently stopping her. A hand on the back of her neck. She let him kiss her, but when his hand moved up to her breast she pulled away.

'No . . .'

'Yes.'

'Swim,' she said. 'We're having a swim.' She kissed him. She could taste salt on his lips.

'I love you,' he said.

'Yes,' she said. 'Yes, I know.'

She pulled away and ran after Wolfgang, out into the meadow by the Wye. It was a place where people stopped during the day to picnic: one of the few places left where the water was still deep enough to swim. She quickly took off her clothes. Sonia had the torch and was waving it about excitedly. Its beam caught Bill's bottom, white, beefy and surprisingly hairy, disappearing into the water.

A scream, a cheer.

'But if Sonia's in the river,' cried out Venetia in a puzzled voice, 'who's got the torch?' It was a remark for which she would never, by Sonia, be forgiven.

A car with its headlights on came down the Hay-on-Wye road. Venetia was revealed, for a split second, naked and lovely. Jacob was also caught in the light, equally naked, and illustrating (thought Lizzie) that four pints of Hogsarse triple-strength ale was less disabling than might have been supposed.

And who, come to that, was he getting excited about?

A cry of shock from Eloise, exposed in her knickers by the car's lights.

Lizzie slithered quickly down the river bank.

Where was Andrew?

I love you.

She loved him. Why hadn't she said so? Why was she always so frightened of exposing her feelings?

The water was cold. There was mud between her toes, a sudden pain as her foot struck a stone. She waded out towards Bill, who was splashing and roaring like a grampus. Suddenly she was caught in the torch's glare: Sonia – sufficiently well endowed herself to be generous – doing the boys a favour.

The boys roared.

'Dirty old men!' Lizzie cried, embarrassed. She fell forward. Suddenly she was swimming. The water was cool and delicious. Why hadn't they done this before? Why hadn't they done this every night? She felt, as she had in the cathedral, an enormous sense of release; she felt as if she were waking from a long dreamlike state. She was herself, Lizzie Draude – she was not a reincarnation of Eleanor Blount, or if she were it did not matter, for she was living here, now, and the past was gone, and as for trying to escape into it – well, 'this way madness lies'. By tomorrow night she would be in France, a parched and desolate France, but another land, another place.

Already she could hardly believe that she had slept, night after night, in a medieval chapel, and tried to commune with dead bones.

She called out: 'Andrew, Andrew!' in case he was upset, sulking.

Bill and Venetia were throwing water at each other, chasing each other, both seemingly intent on being caught.

'Andrew!' she called.

'Andrew, Andrew!' called Wolfgang and Jacob.

She smiled and rolled over on to her back. The sky above was blue velvet. Even here, out in the river, she could smell the sweet scent of honeysuckle. Honeysuckle and roses. Her heart suddenly began to pound, and she turned rapidly on to her front, and began to swim back to the shore.

But the shore had gone. And the cars on the Hay-on-Wye road had gone. She again tried to cry out 'Andrew' and the page yelled in alarm, and the monkey shrieked and sunk its claws deep into her shoulder.

27

Letton

The rope had slipped through the nerveless fingers of the ferryman and the boat was swinging out into the crashing torrent. Ware and Hickey plunged into the water and grabbed it, but they could not haul it back against the current. They shouted out to the other archers, but it was Toke who stumbled down the bank and into the freezing Wye, and seized her (the monkey again clawing for his eyes) and half dragged, half carried her to the bank. The boat, a coracle, vanished into the mists. The ferryman stared after it in shock until Ware gave him a blow that sent blood spurting from his head.

He staggered off downstream, disappearing into the mists himself.

They stood in the drizzling rain, staring at the ghostly willows overhanging the far shore. Then they turned northwards, up the river bank, in sodden clothes and with only an hour of daylight left.

They had intended to cross the Wye at Moccas, but had found the bridge swept away, or destroyed. They had followed the river, looking for another crossing place. The country here was a desolation. It was poisoned land, a fever-ridden valley, much of its land untilled since the last great plague thirty-five years ago; the span of a man's lifetime.

They crossed the great field of a derelict manor. Under a withy hedge was a wooden bowl, and in it an infant wrapped in rags, guarded by a small child that put up a cry when it saw them approach across the cold steaming clay. Beyond the hedge they found a peasant and his wife, with four heifers so thin that Toke could count their ribs.

The infant was crying now; a thin, tired wail.

The man called, 'Children be still.'

His clout hood was full of holes, his hose hung in rags over his gaiters. His wife had wrapped a winnowing sheet round her body to keep out the cold. Her feet were bare on the wet soil. From one of them blood flowed.

'Does the bridge stand at Letton?' said Ware.

The man did not know. He had never, in all his life, been more than two villages away from his manor; he had never had permission of his lord.

He and his wife stared up at Toke's horse, at Eleanor with the tiny, black, hairy-faced child at her bosom; at the archers in their leather jerkins black with rain.

'Where is the manor?'

The man mumbled, in a tongue half English, half foreign, *Welsh*.

The manor was derelict. Lordship had passed to the Bishop of Worcester.

'Can you guide us to Letton?'

He stared at them, amazed.

They moved on. Behind them the child and the infant cried out for food. Again, they heard the man call out, in a voice filled with weariness and despair, 'Children be still.'

The light began to go. To the east, perhaps no more than a mile, was a Roman road. They had already crossed it once – at the old Roman town of Kentchester, where a dozen derelict villas still stood above ground, shadowy outlines in the rain of the February afternoon.

Perhaps they should try to find the road once more. It would take them to Hay, where there would be an inn, and they could cross the river by the bridge.

Ware said, 'We must find shelter.'

Yes, they must find shelter. Toke's head ached. He was shivering uncontrollably.

They reached a riverside village, a huddle of broken-down cottages, roofless and abandoned. There was a mill that had collapsed and been despoiled of its cut stone. Dark shapes flitted between the buildings.

'Outlaws,' said Ware.

Hanchache stuttered, 'Sir Robert de Rideware.'

Ware laughed. Sir Robert would not squat himself down in a leaking hovel. He was famous for forcing himself on abbots, claiming to be travelling on the king's service and leaving no fee when he left.

They found a cottage with three of its walls still standing. They tried to mend the roof but most of the branches came crashing down, the earth sods with them. They built a small shelter of a kind, and Eleanor and the monkey crouched inside it. They brought in the horse and the ponies. The hearth was filled with sodden black ash. There was no hope of finding dry wood.

'Is it yet none?' Eleanor asked.

Her eyes gleamed from under her furs.

It must be four o' the clock, Toke guessed, although he had not seen a clock since leaving Wantage. It was an hour, at least, past none.

Mists rolled down the river. The day died. They crouched and ate curds, and bread that was made from rye and beans. Eleanor had a good appetite, Toke thought, for one so thin. He himself was ravenous. He had a fever: he had felt it before they left Hereford. His plunge into the icy river had brought it on to sweat with alarming speed. His head pounded. He thought with intense longing of his home in Staffordshire, of the manor he had bought when the Genoan bark yielded such high profit. His mind drifted to talk of spice islands in the seas beyond Ireland. Dick Whittington had been tempted to invest in a planned voyage from Bristol, but in the end had not done so. For all his dealings, Whittington was a cautious man. 'If there are spice islands to the west,' he asked, 'why do no merchants come to us from them?' In Hereford, Toke had looked again at the *mappa mundi*. To the east were lands and rivers, gryphons and unicorns and elephants and lions. These things truly existed – the voyage of the Genoan bark and a hundred other similar vessels a year to London River proved it to be so. But on the Hereford *mappa mundi* there was a great emptiness to the west. And from the western seas no vessels ever came. Whittington was a wise man. Toke would not venture his capital on a fool's errand.

There were flickering lights on the walls of a cottage nearby. The sound of a pipe. A carol – plaintive and melancholy against the distant roar of the Wye. Eleanor sang quietly.

> He said 'Ba-bay'
> She said 'Lullay'
> Be virgin fresh as rose in May . . .

The archer Hickey joined her, singing in a deep voice.

> Her lips were brachet sweet . . .
> They say.

Eleanor was smiling. Yes, her lips were sweet as brachet, as honey, thought Toke. He said to Hickey: 'Be quiet.'

A shape, a shadow, flitting across the dirt tracks between the cottages. A voice offered them a place at the fireside, offered food – then, after a pause, wheedling and cunning, offering brandy.

'Soldiers,' said Ware quietly. 'Lads back from France.'

'And the rest,' said Davey.

Outlaws. Broken men. Peasants who had fled their villages, where they were *ascripti glebae* – bound to the soil, bound to grind their corn at the lord's mill, unable to give their children in marriage without their lord's consent. Driven to the greenwood, and calling themselves, as often as not, bold Robyn Hode.

The man was offering brandy again. Brandy, and a seat at the fireside.

Toke said he would buy fire and dry wood for a silver groat. The man argued. In this season, on this night, in this place, the gift of fire was worth the very crown of Navarre. Toke said: 'A silver groat for the gift of fire, and two groats for dry wood.'

Flaming brands were brought spitting through the rain. The fire blazed up, the horse and ponies shied and had to be taken out of the hovel. Hickey sang:

> Now all that I may swank or sweat
> My wife she will both eat and drink . . .

Eleanor laughed. She sat in her bour of dripping branches, her hands held out to the flames.

The fire in the other cottage died down.

The last note of the pipe trailed away.

The night might yet pass in peace. *Ne reminiscaris. Domine* . . . said Toke to himself, his head buzzing with fever. Remember not, O Lord, our offences: neither take retribution on our sins.

'*Kyrie eleison*,' he said, suddenly.

'Lord have mercy on us,' said the boy, wide-eyed, troubled.

Eleanor was looking at him curiously.

There was a sound from outside the hovel. A stone being disturbed. Ware said, 'Boy,' and handed Flesshe a short dagger. Toke withdrew his own dagger from its sheath, his thumb testing the edge.

Again, the scrape of a stone.

Toke said, 'Can you use your bows?'

Ware shook his head. In this rain he did not dare take his bow from its oiled cloth.

Hanchache held his thin Italian knife. He was trembling in every limb, a greyhound waiting to be unleashed.

A sound from above. They were on the crumbling walls, on the remnant of the roof.

A clod of earth hit the fire and sent sparks shooting. Black shapes fell down among them. Hanchache gave a scream that turned into a gurgle – the sound of a man whose throat was being cut. There was a sharp intake of breath and cry of pain from one of the attackers as Ware thrust with his knife. Flesshe screamed. The fire blazed. Toke saw a face with a sign on its forehead: F for falsity, a runaway serf caught and branded for working for wages higher than the law allowed. He had Flesshe's head pulled back, his eyes were on the boy's neck seeking the place for a perfect cut. A moment later Hickey's knife went into the man's stomach.

Christe, eleison.

It went in to the hilt, and Hickey turned it slowly as the man died.

Eleanor watched, her eyes gleaming in the firelight. In her arms the monkey barked, a shrill angry noise.

Three men were dead: Hanchache, and two of the attackers. The others had disappeared into the darkness.

Christe, eleison. Christ have mercy on us.

Hanchache had been with him for five years. He wished for a moment that it had been the boy Flesshe who had been killed: but no, the boy's father would be a trouble, nobody would make trouble over Hanchache. He looked down at the body of his servant and blamed Eleanor Blount. He said, 'I pray you, put him outside.'

To grieve, sigh, languish, weep and groan over an irrecoverable thing is a great folly and displeasure to God.

Ware and his archers would take turns to stand guard, but nobody expected the outlaws, the broken men, to come back. The horse and ponies had not been stolen, which was a small mercy.

Toke drifted into a feverish sleep. He should have gone to Staffordshire, he should never have agreed to take the girl to Dore. The Blounts were finished. Of all the family there was only an old woman praying on her knees at Ely; an old woman and this girl.

He woke suddenly. It was still night. His forehead burned, yet his body was shivering with cold. He sat up, his head swimming. He reached for a handful of wood, and threw it on the fire. A half-burned branch was disturbed and fell. Sparks flew upwards and a bright yellow flame spurted briefly, showing figures curled up asleep – and the boy Flesshe curled in a ball but with wide-awake, staring eyes.

Who was standing guard?

Where was Hickey?

There was a movement in the girl's bour, under her cloak, her man's cloak.

In Toke's head, the mocking song:

> He said 'Ba-bay'
> She said 'Lullay'
> Be virgin fresh as rose in May . . .

He drew out his dagger.

His mind filled with an unbelievable rage against the demons that danced in every mote of dust, in every drop of falling rain.

28

Dore

She was Toke, not Eleanor. She was the franklin of Dore. When she touched his tomb she breathed life into his desiccated lungs and sent blood spurting through his shrivelled veins and through his dry, corrupted heart. When she touched his tomb he lived, and his passions lived, and his dry bones stirred, and he lusted again after Eleanor. She was the franklin of St Michael and All Saints. She was possessed.

She sobbed as she scrambled up the hillside through the English lime trees and the oak and the holly.

She was possessed.

A movement ahead: eyes in the thicket. Grunting, scuffling – a black boar scrabbling to get away, and the realisation hit her: a truth half suspected, half concealed, so terrible that she had been shutting it out from her consciousness.

Her body, as well as her mind, had now been taken back in time.

She was in AD 1400. It was just after the Feast of the Presentation. She felt the bitter cold knifing into her naked flesh. She felt the stinging snow.

The franklin had wanted her, and now he had her.

She fell to the ground and closed her eyes, closed them tight, screwed them up, sobbing, her hands clawing slowly at the earth.

There was a drumming noise in her brain. Slowly she brought her hands up to her head, and tried to stuff her ears with soil and leaves.

The helicopter came down over the ramparts, over the woods, then moved out over the river. It passed over the pub at Newbridge, its searchlight showing a group of young people sitting round tables in the beer garden, a police car, and a minibus with SHEFFIELD HALLAM UNIVERSITY on its side. The helicopter wheeled gently, and began to climb back along the ridge in the direction of Hay.

An Army Land Rover pulled into the car park. A police inspector strode towards it shouting, 'Who authorised that helicopter? Do you realise she may be mentally disturbed? Do you *want* her to run out in front of a car and get killed?'

A young Army officer said, 'I think the idea is to keep her pinned down to the woods.'

Four more Army Land Rovers were turning into the car park. The inspector looked at them in amazement. 'But who called the Army out?' he asked. 'What the hell's going on?'

'From what I've been told, which isn't much,' said the lieutenant, 'we're doing the Yanks a favour.'

'Yanks? What Yanks?'

But the lieutenant was striding off shouting orders.

The soldiers were from 21 SAS. They had eager, smug expressions. They had been told that a naked lovely was on the loose, and some of them even believed it. They jollied themselves into two platoons, compared maps, and disappeared into the woods waving torches. Only the drivers were left, sitting smoking and looking fed up at being left behind, and two civilians, middle-aged and tired-looking. One of them was talking to the lieutenant, the other came striding over.

'Is there anybody here,' he said loudly, 'who has any account of what Miss Draude might have said during the recent period of time? Anything that might have been cause for concern vis-à-vis her mental state, during the past few days?'

The inspector, who was talking on his mobile phone, stared at him. 'And exactly who might you be?'

'My name's Sluder, Dr Larry Sluder.'

'You're the Yank – the American – who called the Army out? Is the girl American?'

'Not to my knowledge.'

A girl said, 'Excuse me, can I please speak to whoever's in charge?'

'Sure,' said Sluder. 'What is it, honey?'

'Dear God,' said the inspector.

Pope came over. 'It's all right, Larry. I'll handle this. We're acting under the aegis of the Home Office Scientific Investigation Unit. We need to talk to anyone who was with Miss Draude recently.'

'OK. Right, you talk to this young lady and I'll try and find out what's going on. There are people here from the Home Office Scientific Investigation Unit,' the inspector said, into his phone, turning away. 'No, love, I've never heard of it either.'

'And you are?' said Pope.

'Venetia Peel.'

'All right, Venetia, let's go and sit down. You were her friend?'

'Yes.'

They found an empty table in the beer garden. Sluder followed them. Strings of fairy lights suddenly came on; the landlord responding hopefully to the arrival of the thirsty SAS.

'We know she's disappeared into the woods,' said Pope. 'Tell me what happened before that.'

'We were swimming. We'd been here in the pub, and then we decided to go for a swim.'

'Without costumes?' asked Sluder.

'Well yes, actually.'

'Skinny-dipping. That's legal here?'

'Why shouldn't it be legal? – Venetia, surprised.

Sluder was lost, thought Pope. His theories were in tatters. He was trying to cling on to the things that he could understand.

'Go on,' he said to Venetia.

'OK, so we were all in the water. There were eight of us – no, nine. Lizzie suddenly gave a cry. It was lucky we heard her – we were all, well, larking about a bit, you know.'

Sluder said, 'No, honey.'

'She gave a cry,' said Pope. 'Then what?'

'Andrew swam towards her. Bill called out for the torch, but Sonia had it. She'd been waving it about, trying to shine it on the girls.'

'The girls?' asked Sluder. 'Why the girls?'

'I don't know, I suppose because the boys were telling her to, we were all a bit pissed. What time is it?'

'Nearly four a.m.'

'Christ, she's been lost for four hours.'

Pope said, 'What happened after Lizzie cried out?'

'Sonia was hysterical, and it took a minute to get the torch. She thought Bill was chasing after her – I expect she hoped he was. Andrew could hear Lizzie crying, sobbing – we could all hear her when Sonia stopped screaming. He saw her reach the shore and sort of collapse on the bank. But by the time he got there she was gone.'

'This Andrew, is he her boyfriend?'

'Yes. That is, there's a bloke in Norwich, but she's given him the push. She was going to France with Andrew.'

The inspector was coming across the garden towards them.

'Did Andrew go after her?'

'He went up through the trees as far as the road. He couldn't see where she'd gone. A car came past and he tried to flag it down, but it wouldn't stop.'

The inspector said, 'He was stark naked. It was an old couple. An old farmer and his wife. They phoned the police from Eardisley.'

'So what did Andrew do?'

'He came back and found his clothes.'

'Can I speak to him?'

'He went searching for her. So did Bill – Bill Hastings, he's the dig leader – and Jacob, and Wolfgang. Gareth and Sonia are at the camp, and so's Eloise. She'll drive down here and tell us if Lizzie turns up.'

'Have they got phones?'

'I've got a mobile, and so has Bill.'

'Do you know where they're searching?'

'They were working their way along the ridge. They'd got a shirt for her, jeans and stuff.'

The inspector said, 'There's a report of an incident near Middle-wood. A chap who breeds wild boars. He says something frightened them. They're sensitive things, wild boars, much more shy than you'd expect.'

'You'd be shy,' said Venetia acidly, 'if you'd been hunted to sodding extinction.'

The lieutenant came over from his Land Rover. He had a map, which he spread on the table. 'You've heard about the pig farmer at Middlewood? We've also got a report of a chap who was in the woods over that way and heard a woman crying.'

His map was covered in clear plastic. He drew a circle with red chalk. Sluder said, 'What was he doing out in the wood, this *chap*?'

'Badger-watching, he says.'

244

The inspector said, 'Black magic, wouldn't surprise me. They're all at it in these parts, eh, John?'

The landlord was handing round mugs of tea. He nodded his head. 'Women of fifty or sixty,' he said, 'running round the forest glades with flappy arms and sagging tits.'

Venetia was looking at the map. She said, 'Oh, but that can't be right. Why, that's over two miles away. She ran that far? With bare feet? Oh Christ, I feel sick.'

The inspector and the lieutenant went to the police car to work out where to post men and vehicles along the roads. Soon the Army Land Rovers left, the drivers grinning, hoping that fortune would smile, and that they would be the one who ended up cuddling the naked lovely to keep her warm. 'Drive very, very carefully,' the lieutenant said to each vehicle as it turned out of the pub car park.

Pope said, 'Venetia, when this was first reported to the police, somebody said that Lizzie was mentally disturbed.'

Venetia nodded.

'Was that you?'

She nodded again.

Sluder said, 'She didn't have a kind of obsession with the Internet, by any chance?'

'Please leave this to me, Larry, OK?' said Pope. 'In what way was Lizzie abnormal?'

The helicopter was back. It was high over the battlements of Montdore, its spotlight a round moon in the blackness. The lieutenant ran to his Land Rover and spoke into a phone. A moment later the helicopter moved west, along the ridge towards Merbach.

Venetia was looking hesitant. 'Listen,' she said. 'Who exactly are you? You say you're Home Office, but what's this all about? Why should people come rushing from London in the middle of the night just because Lizzie's been, well, taken ill?'

'Honey,' said Sluder, 'to find this lady I have come all the way from Utah.'

She looked at him with disbelief.

Pope said, 'I know it's difficult for you to understand. But there was already somebody here from Oxford, making enquiries with the police, looking for Lizzie, when this happened. And we ourselves were on our way across the Atlantic.'

'You look terrible,' said Venetia. 'Are you all right?'

'It's just mosquito bites.'

'From Utah?'

'Alaska. Please tell me what you know about Lizzie's state of mind.'

She paused for a moment then said, 'I think she believed she was a reincarnation of a girl who was somehow connected with a man buried in the church.'

'A franklin?'

'Yes.'

She was staring at him. 'How do you know that?'

The helicopter's drone faded. She said again, 'How do you know that? She told me about it once, but I didn't take much notice. She had this dream – regression – in which she was being brought here, to a nunnery at Dore. Then she found out that there actually was a nunnery here. Now will you please tell me who you are, and what's going on, and what's the matter with Lizzie?'

'I can tell you that she isn't experiencing a reincarnation,' said Pope. 'At least, if she is it's nothing to do with what's been happening here at Dore. And I can tell you that she isn't mad.'

At least she hadn't been mad, he thought, looking up at the long ridge, at the woodlands stretching away into the darkness; not until now.

'You're scientists, right?'

He nodded.

She said, after a moment, 'I suppose it's that fucking satellite dish on the Hereford road.'

Pope said, because it was the easiest explanation, 'Yes.'

'That was what Andrew thought. He knew it was affecting her mind. Christ, somebody'll pay for this.'

'It was nobody's fault,' said Sluder.

'Oh dear me,' said Venetia, 'don't you go thinking that for one minute. Did you say you were the bloke in charge?'

'Now lady . . .' said Sluder, a mirthless smile on his face.

The inspector was back. 'There are more soldiers coming at dawn, that's in just over an hour. We've got a WPC at the camp, in case she turns up there. I need to know what to say to our public affairs officer.'

'To your what?'

'Press officer. She'll have to deal with the papers.'

'How will they know about it?' asked Pope.

'You think,' the inspector said, 'you can do all this, and nobody'll notice? You think one of those squaddies isn't going to call the *Sun*?'

A vehicle was approaching: a car that drove past, carefully not exceeding the speed limit, four young men inside it, pale, worried faces that looked at the brightly lit pub, the cars in the car park, but did not stop. The inspector spoke into his personal phone, gave the car's number and listened to the result with grim satisfaction. He dialled again and gave some orders.

'I hope you're not diverting your police cars to pick up passing burglars?' said Venetia.

'I'm doing my job, if it's all right with you, miss.'

'But it isn't all right, I've just told you it isn't all right.'

She was crabby; she'd been up all night.

The inspector moved away.

Sluder said, awed, 'You talk to the cops like that in England?'

'How do you want me to talk to them? God, I must have some aspirins.'

She went to find some. Pope sat gratefully drinking tea, smelling flower blossom on the night air, grateful not to be in Alaska. Venetia came back and dissolved her aspirins in a glass of water. The students piled into their minibus and drove away up the narrow road to the fort. 'They're from Sheffield,' Venetia said. 'Poor sods. First they broke down for six hours at Trowell Services on the M1, which is an experience that would scar you for life, then they found all this going on.'

Another vehicle drove up, an ambulance.

The inspector said, 'They wanted to send a psychiatrist, but I told them we'd already got two psychiatrists.'

'Physicists,' said Sluder.

'What?'

'We're physicists, not psychiatrists.'

'There's things happening here,' said the inspector, 'that I'm not being told about.'

The lieutenant came over. 'Is one of you Dr Pope? There's a message from a Miss Crawfurd to say that she's landed at RAF South

Cerney. She ought to be here in about three hours. I'm also told that I'm to liaise with you.'

'OK,' said Pope. 'Let's get moving. Let's find this Andrew.'

'I'll call up the chopper.'

Andrew was at Arthur's Stone. He was leaning against the capstone that had been raised some five thousand years ago. He was more weary than he would have thought possible. It was almost dawn. From along the lane that ran along the ridge of the hill there came a distant shout, but a weary shout, not a shout of triumph, or discovery. Bill or Jacob trying to make contact.

Arthur's Stone was the rendezvous, the place they'd agreed to meet up.

He ought to move, to keep searching – to double back down into the woods. But where should he look? In a barn? A haystack? There were no haystacks these days, and they had looked in every barn, in every farmhouse doorway. They had been walking or running for three hours.

Wolfgang came trudging slowly up the road.

'Anything?'

Andrew shook his head.

'Perhaps she's back at camp.'

'They'd have come for us.'

Wolfgang sighed and lay down, stretched on the turf, his head against the capstone that had been split into two pieces, so legend had it (tales told down the generations by old ladies in Hay), when King Arthur fought a giant, and the giant was slain and fell to his knees on the stones.

'I'm going to check the church again,' said Andrew, suddenly.

'What's the point?'

'It existed in the fifteenth century, it exists now.'

'Wait for somebody to come, wait for Venetia.'

But Andrew was gone, limping across the lane and over a stile.

Wolfgang sat while the sky grew less dim. Dawn showed thunder-clouds rolling in from the west, from the Black Mountains across the valley: a flash of lightning, a gust of warm, rain-filled wind. It was the first rain over Western Europe in two months, and he waited for it eagerly: but the clouds passed to the north, towards Old Radnor and Knighton. After a while he lay back against the capstone and dozed. He woke when the helicopter came down, in the field next to the monument: he had been spotted from the air, a tiny human figure laid out as if for sacrifice.

It was five o'clock when Pope quietly opened the door of the church. He saw the lilies on the small, polished oak table. He saw the box pews, and behind them the massive, painted arms of England. He saw the altar, and beyond it the east window with its stained-glass corpses under a starry coverlet, its grinning skeleton.

He saw the franklin's tomb.

A young man wearing trousers but no shirt was sitting defensively over a body that was itself curled in the foetal position, one hand outstretched, touching the tomb's alabaster base.

Pope spoke briefly into his mobile.

He walked quietly up the aisle. He went down on one knee, and looked into Lizzie's unconscious face.

Andrew said, 'I thought it might be dangerous to wake her.'

He had put hassocks round her body, and put his shirt over her, covering her as best he could.

Pope touched her arm, which was bruised and scratched. He looked at her feet, covered in dried blood, scored with dirt-filled cuts.

Andrew said quietly, 'You're a doctor?'

'No, but one will be here very soon.'

Pope looked at the tomb and the massive pillar behind it. At the frieze of alabaster. In his head were the words *I would fain have the measure where he lies both the thickness and compass of the pillar at his head and from that the space to the altar . . . and I will have alabaster for the tomb.*

He looked at the dark shadow of the franklin's face. The face he had seen, in his mind, in the sunless forests of the Yukon; in the green glow of the computer room at Eagle, Alaska.

His mobile bleeped.

It was Martha. 'Is she OK?'

'I don't know.'

'It's happened again. A corruption in a *Pasiphae* signal has jumped the barrier.'

A pause.

'And?'

'It penetrated the brain of a Japanese guy. A market maker in Tokyo.'

'Market maker?'

'On the stock exchange. We can't confirm the link with *Pasiphae* until the tapes are decontaminated, but a major technical sell was triggered on an exchange main computer. They've got the guy in protective custody. He's quoting a primitive version of the *Malleus Maleficarum*, if you know what that is.'

'*The Hammer of Witchcraft.*'

'Yeah?'

'Perhaps the most poisonous book ever written.'

The codifying of terror. The authorisation of extermination, printed almost a hundred years after the franklin had lived, but embodying the corruption of centuries.

Pope looked at the franklin's tomb, at the stone effigy, the wisps of stone wool curling from the pillow, the ironic look on the franklin's face.

He said, 'When did it happen?'

'Just after midnight British Summer Time.'

Pope looked down at Lizzie's calm, sleeping face.

Midnight was when they had left the pub, gone down to the river.

Martha said: 'Hello? Charles?'

'Yes,' he said. 'I'm still here.'

'There are fears of massive falls in London when it opens in two hours, and New York later today.'

'I don't care a shit.'

'Charles, do you understand the consequences in human life, in poverty, in starvation, in war, in the spread of disease, if the world's financial system collapses in the space of ten hours?'

There was the sound of a vehicle outside. It would be the ambulance.

'There's no malice in this,' he said wearily. 'There's no direct intelligence targeting airliners and stock markets.'

'I'm not convinced about that. It seems to me there may be things that even you can't understand about all this.'

Again he looked at the stone effigy of the franklin.

He said, 'Where are you?'

'Just driving into Hereford.'

'Is *Pasiphae* closed down?'

'Christ, yes.'

'Who was it called the Army out?'

'The Pentagon got on to the MoD. It might even have been that the White House got involved. This is high-priority stuff now, Charles. Are you OK?'

'Yes.'

'I'll talk to you soon.'

The paramedics were in the doorway.

Pope said, 'Blankets round her but she mustn't be moved, her hand must not be taken from the alabaster, until the doctor has seen her.'

He did not know whether she was in a sleep of exhaustion, or whether her brain had crashed the way a computer might crash during overload.

Or was her brain even now running programs elsewhere?

Was her warm, breathing body now a permanent transponder – linking a satellite over the Atlantic to the medieval world?

29

Hereford

It was evening now. The heat still lay like a blanket over the town, over the castle gardens, over the Bishop's Meadow on the west bank of the Wye. The river itself had a strange colour – at one moment gunmetal grey, at another rippled with a brassy sheen. The flower-beds along the city walls, that should have been bright slashes of asters, and pansies, and geraniums, were plantations of perfect dried flowers, having died so quickly and so intensely in this most remarkable year.

Outside the *mappa mundi* building workmen had put up a new, large sign, a warning against drinking Wye water. The queue of tourists had been replaced by people carrying the two-litre plastic jerrycans issued to each household by the city council. It was peaceful enough here: two girls were playing violins under the leafless trees of the cathedral close; there was an ice-cream van. In France there had been riots when standpipes had failed, criminals having ingeniously tapped into the water mains and syphoned water off into tankers, the way criminals in ancient Rome syphoned water from the great viaducts.

The heatwave seemed unending. Every night the television weathermen showed the same map, with the same, extraordinary zones of high pressure. They tried to give comfort by reporting on horrors elsewhere.

But there were changes, Pope thought, staring out to the west. The air was fractionally cooler, now, in the evening, than it had been a week ago when he flew to Utah.

There had been a rainstorm over the border, over Offa's Dyke.

Lizzie had been given a CAT scan during the day, doctors searching for evidence of dead brain cells, looking for the yellow stain on the screen that would indicate a tumour. Her brainwaves had been measured on an EEG machine. The CAT scan did not indicate anything abnormal. The EEG showed her to be in a state of constant D sleep, which suggested that she was probably dreaming.

'Dreaming? Dreaming of what?' Sluder asked.

'It may be that the mind is repairing itself,' a doctor had told him, seemingly unworried.

'I'll be told the moment she recovers consciousness?'

'Her parents and fiancé will be told the moment she recovers consciousness.'

The fiancé was her boyfriend, Andrew. He had quietly formalised his relationship to Lizzie so that he would have uninterrupted access to her bedside.

In the afternoon Sluder had installed himself in the Green Dragon Hotel, and busied himself setting up a computer link to Berkeley and to Utah. Martha had hired cars for herself and for Pope. She had disappeared to Bristol, investigating Lizzie Draude's background.

Pope had spent the afternoon at Dore, looking at the dig.

He had walked down the pathway from the ramparts, down through the medieval woodland of oak, and English lime, and wild service trees. He had sat, for an hour, alone in the church, watching the afternoon sun move slowly along the alabaster frieze of the franklin's tomb; watching the motes of dust dance in the shafts of light.

In the early evening he heard that Lizzie had recovered consciousness, and had been moved out of the intensive care unit, although nobody was allowed to see her except for her close family.

He waited until nine o'clock, then walked slowly through the cathedral close and up to the gardens of the Castle Green. Under the turf, the lines of the old walls were palely visible – skeleton bones of the Norman castle, revealed by the dry weather. He sat for a while by the Nelson monument, erected, he guessed, in the place where the old keep had once stood. There were people on the bowling green; white shapes in the gloaming. There was the soft click of balls. It must have been very unsatisfactory, he thought, bowling over grass as dry as copra matting. The gardener must be broken-hearted over the state of his lawns.

The light faded. The bowlers called it a day and left. He saw a heron come gliding down over the shallow, sluggish stream that was the Wye. The evening star was bright over the distant Black Mountains. He walked down the hill to the hospital and said to reception: 'I'm here to see Miss Elizabeth Draude,' and they sent him up to the ward. The night nurse was attending a patient behind a screen, and he found his way to Lizzie's small, private room without being challenged.

Lizzie lay in a bed with a blue counterpane. She did not stir, nor did Andrew, who was curled up asleep on the floor, his body against the cold radiator, his head on a rolled-up jumper.

Pope sat down and in time also drifted into a sort of sleep. He jerked awake when an auxiliary nurse rattled past with a trolley. She poked her head in and gave him a cup of milky tea, already sugared. She looked at Andrew, shook her head in official disapproval, then smiled, all the world loving a lover.

Pope drank his tea slowly. His eyes were still puffy and swollen, his skin still inflamed with insect bites and stings. An indignant nurse, earlier in the day, had told him to have some sense and go to Outpatients, but he had not done so. He was deadly tired.

A distant bell: Hereford cathedral. Midnight. The beginning of the old night office. Soon, he thought, it would be time for lauds, 'the morning praises'.

Lizzie stirred. She sighed. Her hand moved slightly, the fingers curling.

There were occasional distant noises: a nurse speaking loudly but patiently to an old man who had awakened from a nightmare. Telling him he was all right. 'Everything's all right . . . *all right.*'

Ah! Pope smiled ruefully.

A sister looked in, assumed that Pope was Lizzie's father, and went away. In a little while she returned with another cup of tea, and gave it to him without speaking. Pope stood, stretched himself, and looked out of the open window. There were playing fields beyond the river. They were bleached white in the moonlight. There was a faint breeze, a faint coolness.

Another bell from the cathedral.

Something flew across the moon: an owl, silently hunting. There were bats, too: round the ivy that covered part of the hospital wall he saw the flickering shadows of the pipistrelle.

Lizzie moved uneasily.

Pope looked towards the distant smudge of the hills of Wales. The hills around Dore. The breeze was from the west. It carried with it, for the first time, the scent of autumn.

Lizzie sighed again. Her breathing, which had been low but audible, was now silent.

Pope said, quietly, 'Can you tell me about the franklin?'

She did not reply. Andrew, curled in the shadows, was sleeping the sleep of exhaustion, the deep sleep of the young.

'Can you tell me about the franklin of Dore?'

Nothing.

'Can you tell me his name?'

She said, 'His name is Toke.'

A pause.

He said, softly, 'Toke . . .'

She said, 'I'm frightened.'

'You needn't be.'

He went back to the bed and sat down. He finished drinking his tea, quietly letting her collect her thoughts.

Her eyes were travelling round the room: the curtain track running round the ceiling over the bed, the plastic curtains, the metal locker with its dim night light, the EEG machine, the sign saying that her consultant was Dr Budgen, and that her specific nurse was Nurse Fairbairn.

'Do you know anything else about the franklin?'

She said, after a moment, 'Alabaster.'

'Alabaster?'

'Very fine, very beautiful alabaster.'

'Ah yes,' he said, remembering. 'The frieze round his tomb.'

'No.'

'No?'

'More than that. Can I have a drink?'

He poured a drink of water and gave it to her.

'Are you a doctor?'

'No. I'm a scientist.'

She stared at him for a moment, then drank thirstily.

He said, 'Your mother has been phoning all day.'

A startled look. 'What?'

'Your mother, from Singapore.'

'Oh, Christ.'

'Shall I get hold of her for you?'

'No.'

A pause.

'Tell me,' she said, 'why I shouldn't be frightened.'

He told her about himself. Told her about *Pasiphae*. At one point she said, 'Where's Andrew?' and he realised that she was not really listening.

He said, 'Down there.'

She looked down at the boy, curled against the cold radiator. She seemed comforted.

'Shall I go on?'

She said, 'Yes, I'm all right. Go on.'

She was half distracted. Some part of her was still in the Other-world. He guessed that she was trying to recall and restore her dreams, her experiences, to turn them into memories.

'It is believed that you have been fantasising,' he said. 'It is thought that you have read somewhere about a franklin in love with an aristocratic young girl. It needn't have been a franklin in the Middle Ages at all, for that matter – it could have been a modern story – the essentials being a worthy man of humble origins in love with a girl of high breeding. Or vice versa. Love without hope. There have been many such stories since the dawn of time.'

She smiled faintly.

'You did history A level. You know perfectly well about the abdication of Richard II and his death in Pontefract. You are an archaeology student taking part in a dig, here in Herefordshire. You have taken to sleeping at nights in the church of St Michael, next to the tomb of a franklin. As a result it is believed that your unconscious mind has woven a fantastic story of a franklin bringing an aristocratic girl to Dore in 1400. A story which you are now recalling in dreams.'

'No other dreams in the world were ever like these dreams.'

'No other dreams have existed on the same quantum level of communication as is used by *Pasiphae*. Your subconscious mind – the psychiatrists in America are already telling us – is creating

257

fantasies and then passing them on. They are thus stronger – this is the theory and I cannot fault it – stronger and more vivid, in the way that a running river is stronger and more, more *alive* than a stagnant pool. Unlike the rest of us you have an outlet for your dreams, and that outlet is *Pasiphae*. But *Pasiphae* doesn't know what to do with them, and either at random or through some logic of its own, it adds them to other signals that are passing through the transceiver. When defensive protocols are put in place it learns how to evade them. It is receiving signals, and its basic biological urge – not really biological, of course, although many of the neurosystems simulate a biological situation – its basic urge is to pass those signals on. When scientists in Utah and Virginia set up new disinfectants it buries its illicit signals deep, and in some ways it changes their form, making them polymorphic so that the disinfectants do not recognise them.'

She said something in a whisper.

'I'm sorry?'

She said, irritably, 'Why me?'

'The issue of why you, and as far as we know you alone, are equipped to transmit your dreams, your experiences, is of intense interest to every physicist connected with the *Pasiphae* programme and every agency that relies on its security. But it isn't something that you need worry over. Every brain is different. Your own happens, in some way, to match exactly the . . . *wave settings* – I'm trying not to be technical, I'm sorry – upon which *Pasiphae* operates. We are in the realms of quantum mechanics. The idea of a human brain sending a signal directly to a satellite would be insane using ordinary radio-wave signals. A telecommunications satellite, a new generation sat with spot beams might operate at thirty, even forty gigahertz for its uplink – the smallest satellite uses over six thousand megahertz while a human brainwave is around ten hertz. But the quantum world is different. In the quantum world the idea that individual organisms can be in psychical connection across vast distances is quite old hat, as a theory. Not that we understand it. The unity of physics, the perfect understanding, was supposed to have come by the millennium, but it hasn't.'

She was not listening. He was explaining things badly: he was explaining things that did not need to be explained. She was still exhausted. He hadn't slept himself, properly, for days out of mind.

Basically, she was not interested in the unity of physics.

He said, '*Pasiphae* will have to be redesigned. It will have to operate in a world even more shadowy than at present, a world in which it cannot possibly interact with the human brain, or indeed the brain of any mammal, for I do not know what the Pentagon, let alone Lloyds of London, would say if they started picking up the night-time fantasies of dolphins. I will leave you now, though if you don't object I should like to talk to you tomorrow, when my brain is a bit less stupid.'

She said, 'So I was making it all up?'

'It's the theory.'

It was the theory that had been put forward by NSA and Pentagon psychiatrists, with increased confidence, during the course of the afternoon.

'It would seem to fit the facts as we know them. It's logical. It's rational.'

'But you don't believe it.'

He hesitated. He said, 'Before I met you, before I knew about you, I had convinced myself that *Pasiphae* was picking up memories, thoughts, that had been on the plasma web, the world line web as it's been called, for six hundred years.'

She smiled; a faint, ironic smile.

'But it may be that I was wrong.'

'No,' she said.

'No?'

'There are things in my dreams that I could never have known. There is a reality in my head that my imagination could never have created. But I am not picking up thoughts. I am living them.'

She closed her eyes.

He waited a moment. Then he stood up, stiffly, feeling his old bones.

She said, more loudly, 'In the hour of my distress, when all terrors me oppress, and when I my fault confess, sweet spirit comfort me.'

Andrew stirred. He sat up.

Pope put a finger to his lips and shook his head gently.

Lizzie slept, a sleep in which no dreams, or nightmares, or quantum signals would disturb her.

But for how long? Her mind, her brain, had adapted itself to the weird, incredible world of quantum communications. Whether she was being pulled back into the past, or creating monsters in the dark, hidden recesses of her own brain, made no difference as far as her sanity was concerned. *Pasiphae* had altered the state of her mind. The channels were open. The routings had become established, familiarised with use.

Also a lover of Herrick, he said softly:

> When the fears and hellish cries
> Daunt mine ears and fright mine eyes
> And all terrors me surprise
> Sweet spirit comfort me.

He left them. He walked down the long corridor, past the nurse sitting with her face illuminated by a green-shaded light, went down in the lift and out into the false dawn.

30

Hereford

He woke from a deep sleep. The faded, orange curtains, drawn against the daylight, were moving in a faint breeze. There was the clatter of pots from the hotel kitchen, the savour of roasting meat. The phone by his bed was ringing. Martha said, 'Hi, sleepyhead, Martha Crawfurd here,' as if there were dozens of Marthas who might have been ringing him up. 'Do you want to come to a conference? I'm in the bar.'

She was sitting next to an open window, looking out at the street through a mass of scarlet geraniums. She said, 'Did you know pilgrims have used this inn since AD 1100? I wonder how many of them sat here watching the world go by. I've got you a pint of best bitter. Did you know that Elizabeth Draude had had a very upsetting love affair, that ended only a month ago, just before she came to the dig?'

'No.'

He sat down.

'The guys she shares a flat with in Bristol told me. Lizzie was crazy about a middle-aged man, a schoolteacher from Norwich she met on holiday. She'd been going with him for two years. She thought he was going to get a divorce. Men, eh?'

'You don't know what he was going through.'

'I don't care what he was going through.'

'If you cut us, do we not bleed?'

'No, you don't, you bastards. Anyway, the evidence about Lizzie's mental state is stacking up. She had a subconscious desire to escape, emotionally, into a relationship that was clear-cut and easy to handle.'

'Easy to handle? A girl of fourteen and a strange man who must have been in his thirties?'

'Dreams are the expression of repressed desires. You dream you're playing a piano but you're really dreaming of some kind of sexual intercourse. Listen, I've had an amazing day. I've seen a certain Dr

261

Dyson-Jones, and I've taken tea with a real live druidess.'

'That is not as extraordinary,' said Pope, 'as somebody from Cincinnati might think.'

'No? Not even when she's a little lady in the public library called Mrs Ifor-Williams? She's an ex-hippy, Mrs Ifor-Williams, she was never at Woodstock but she's got the video. She was married to a department store manager in Pontypridd, which is in Wales. He played 'Lay Lady Lay' most beautifully on his guitar, but she ran away from him and has become notorious, according to Dr Dyson-Jones, because of her druidical activities. She lives in a cottage near Eywas Harold and makes elderberry wine and casts spells. If you see somebody in a white sheet it won't be the head of the Ku Klux Klan, as you might imagine, it'll be Mrs Ifor-Williams or her assistant Miss Whitburn.'

'Did you get my message?' asked Pope. 'Saying that the franklin's name was Toke? That he may have been a merchant dealing in alabaster?'

'Yeah, I got your message.'

She looked away; out of the window, through the geraniums.

'Well?'

'It's not a lot to go on. Lucy Pagetti's running a search but there are perhaps records of five per cent of the population of England in 1400, and by no means all of those are on computer.'

'He was a franklin. A landowner. He would have left a will – but it's no use looking at Somerset House, they only set up the probate registry in the mid-nineteenth century. I don't know if the medieval prerogative courts are on the academic web. She may be able to find out more about the church at Dore by running through the Medieval Calendar of Papal Registers.'

'Yeah, right. The problem is, Charles, that I'm getting queries from the NSA over misuse of computer time.'

'You're a top agent.'

'No,' said Martha. 'I was put on to this case because I majored in English medieval history.' She sighed. 'Oh shit, Charles, we've found the carrier . . .'

'And like Sluder,' said Pope, gently, 'you're assuming that all *Pasiphae* did was pick up the dreams, fantasies, that were running through her brain.'

'It's mind-blowing enough for God's sake, a human brain communicating on a quantum level.'

'But it's manageable. I can see that it's manageable. There's nothing new in a scientific sense, it's just an example of quantum mechanics in practice, it keeps us well away from ideas about human thoughts transcending time.'

'Charles,' she said, 'there's no need for you to go out on a limb over this.'

'I'm already out on a limb. Will you keep looking for a franklin called Toke?'

'But what's it going to prove? If I can find written proof that a guy called Toke existed, then so could Lizzie have done – but OK, I promise. I'll bring the data analysts in Chicago on board, I'll cheat more time on the Pentagon computers. But try and get me something else to work on, please? Something helpful, like "The King's treasure is buried four Taylor's Yards from Athelstan's blasted oak where the old sheep sits i' the forenoon" – and we'll drive out and find the oak, and the sheep, and when the sheep's gone we'll go back and dig and find a hoard of silver.'

There was a roar of laughter from the bar, where estate agents and land surveyors, hot and thirsty in their tweedy jackets and brogues, were meeting for their Friday-evening drink. It was all so simple, thought Pope, looking at them enviously. Minor public school, perhaps a year at Cirencester, then the routine of provincial city life. The rise and fall of land prices, roast beef dinners at the Rotary club, pints of ale in the Green Dragon.

'I'm going to do some telephoning to the States,' said Martha. 'Sluder wants us to meet him for dinner, at nine. He's found a Thai as in Thailand restaurant. He can't get over this city being so cosmopolitan. Last time he was in England, towns this size had a Berni Inn serving very small steaks and that was it. Do you want to dine with Sluder?'

Pope nodded. Sluder was being humble and apologetic. He had twice said 'I guess we were both wrong about this one' meaning that Lizzie Draude wasn't a Maryland high-school phreaker, and neither was she in psychic communication with the Middle Ages.

'You look shagged out,' said Martha.

'*Pasiphae*,' he said, 'must not be reactivated.'

'Not till they know what's the matter with Lizzie, no,' she said carefully.

'Sluder has got Berkeley working on new transmission protocols. He's worked out that the HAARP can pick up signals using frequencies lower than any used by the human brain, and he's acting accordingly. He hasn't worked out that his new plan might well put *Pasiphae* in contact with the night-time fantasies of the common earthworm, or perhaps the more stupid kind of Newfoundland dog.'

'Let me stick my neck out,' said Martha. '*Pasiphae* will not be reactivated until the medics say Lizzie Draude cannot be harmed.'

'The Pentagon's ten-billion-dollar worldwide communications network, indefinitely suspended because a girl in England thinks she's been possessed by a fifteenth-century franklin?'

The estate agents at the bar roared and brayed. One of them had just told a joke, and they liked a good joke to round off the week.

As he went through the cathedral close the bells were ringing for evensong. He went inside and stood quietly for a few moments, listening to the service which was being held in a part of the building he could not see. *Lighten our darkness, we beseech thee, O Lord; and by thy great mercy defend us from all perils and dangers of this night* . . . He was not, himself, of a spiritual nature. Most physical things, he felt, could be explained by science; most religions by man's ego requiring an afterlife. He wandered up the dim north transept. He came to the shrine of St Thomas with its glowing nimbus of titanium wires. He read the notice that explained it, and another notice which invited him to pray, and to seek strength and blessing from God.

Self-consciously, feeling himself something of a poseur, a clutcher at straws even, he did so.

There was a doctor standing by the ward reception desk, looking like a man who'd forgotten he had a home to go to. He said, 'You're Pope, the Oxford physicist? I'd like a word if you've got a minute.'

They went into the ward patients' common room. It was small and narrow, with some armchairs and a television set. A nurse was sitting eating a pasty she'd microwaved. The doctor hesitated. She said, 'It's all right. I'm just going,' and left them.

They sat down. He said, 'I'm Dr Budgen. Did you know Lizzie's being moved to a private hospital?'

Sluder had told him about it, on the phone.

'She's given her permission. She's twenty-two years old, she can go where she likes. It's difficult for me to justify letting her have the bed; she's physically well enough to be discharged. The electrical activity in her brain is abnormal and there is evidence that she suffered an epileptic fit focally in the temporal lobe, but we would expect to treat the condition with drugs. She doesn't need to be in hospital, it's not life-threatening.'

He looked at Pope hesitantly. Then he said, 'I have had two conversations with Lizzie. When I speak to her I seem to be talking to two people – two personalities.'

Pope said nothing.

'I've been trying to bone up on clinical neurophysiology. Psychiatrists at Southampton University have done some interesting work on decision-making and quantum physics. Do you know about it?'

'Only vaguely.'

'You'd expect brainwaves to be located strictly within the brain, and communicated only through the normal five senses. But there's a growing body of evidence that this is not so. There's a theory that the brain might be able to communicate in terms of quantum mechanics, with all that that implies. You agree?'

Pope said, 'Yes.'

'There's a theory that microtubules in the brain are not merely scaffolding for cells, but can activate quantum activity. Your satellite, *Pasiphae*, operates on theories of quantum physics?'

'There are few things in modern physics that don't, either in theory or practice. A transistor radio only functions because of the application of quantum theory. But yes, essentially, *Pasiphae* uses quantum fields to relay information. And when you say quantum mechanics and all that that implies, the most significant implication is that quantum theory is not hostile to action at a distance. To observe something can change it.'

'Don't,' said the doctor, with a wry smile, 'start on about Schrödinger's cat.'

'Someone thinks something, someone emotionally close to them instantly starts to think the same thing. Someone looks at a playing card in one room, and somebody in another room knows which card they're looking at. All the damning data, as somebody has said, from parapsychology suddenly has a home. Premonitions of danger – precognition – cease to be just lumped in with the baggage of the "paranormal" and become part of accepted scientific rational theory.'

He paused. At the back of his mind he was aware of something significant, something important, that had eluded him.

'And because action at a distance is part of quantum mechanics,' said Dr Budgen, 'a human brain can achieve what would normally be absurd, and communicate with a satellite thousands of miles away?'

'In quantum mechanics,' said Pope, 'a human brain could communicate, directly and instantly, with a similar source in the Andromeda galaxy.'

The doctor stood up. It had been, his look implied, a long day. He looked at Pope: 'Her fiancé, her boyfriend. He says that Lizzie believes she is picking up signals, messages, from the past. That she is in touch somehow with people who are dead.'

Pope nodded.

Budgen stared at him.

'A quantum theory that allowed precognition,' said Pope, 'would hardly disallow retrocognition.'

Again, a feeling that something important was eluding him.

Dr Budgen said, 'Do you think she is possessed?'

'It's an emotive word. But yes. Perhaps she is. For three weeks, now, I've been trying to do the maths.'

He went down the corridor. Before he reached her room his nose picked up a faint sweet scent, recognised but unidentified. He looked into her room and saw a vase of white lilies on the bedside cabinet. He said, 'Can I come in for a few minutes?'

She nodded.

'Weren't the flowers like that in the church at Dore?'

'Miss Whitburn.'

He sat down. 'There can't be many churches that have active pagans on their flower rota.'

'The church hasn't always been there. Anyway, she's only half pagan. In the springtime she and Mrs Ifor-Williams bless the apple trees for the farmers.'

'How are you feeling?'

'I have a constant headache. They tell me it's natural.'

Andrew appeared in the doorway. He went round the bed and sat down, and took her hand. Pope opened his laptop. 'I'd be grateful if you could try to answer some questions for me.'

'And perhaps,' said Andrew, 'you could answer some for us. In the first place, was there microwave leakage from the satellite station?'

'Oh Andrew, please . . .'

She put her hand over his.

'I promise you that I will explain everything,' said Pope. 'When I understand everything myself. Lizzie, when you last regressed into the past, did anything particularly distressful happen? Anything that might have made you feel great pain?'

A pause.

She said, sounding slightly surprised, 'I killed a man.'

Silence.

'Why?'

'He was sleeping with Eleanor.' A pause, then: 'He was making love to her. Andrew, I don't know if I want you here.'

'I'm staying.'

Pope said, 'But aren't you Eleanor?'

'Not always.'

'If you are not always Eleanor then who are you?'

A pause.

'I'm the franklin.'

'Can you tell me about him?'

A pause. She shook her head.

'Where he lived? Do you know where he lived?'

Again she shook her head.

He looked down at his laptop, stared at the silvery-green screen, as he had done for so long in the darkness of the crashed helicopter. 'Imagine you are the franklin,' he said. 'Imagine you are now the franklin of Dore.'

He looked up.

A faint smile . . .

'He beat her,' said Andrew. 'He whipped her.'

She said, 'Shhh, Andrew.'

'Did he? Did he beat you when you were Eleanor?'

'It isn't important.'

'Have you heard this before:

> *For when I count and make a reckoning,*
> *Between my life, my death, and my desire,*
> *My life alas, it serves for nothing,*
> *Since with your parting departed my pleasure.*
> *Wishing your presence setteth me on fire:*
> *But then your absence makes my heart so cold,*
> *That for the pain I know not where to hold.*

Did Eleanor write that to the franklin?'

'No.'

'But you've heard it before. Are you sure Eleanor did not write it?'

'Eleanor could not have written that to save her life! The franklin gave it to her – it was an example of proper womanhood, of loyalty and devotion, written by the Lady Essex, as it happens—'

'Has it ever been published?'

'Of course it hasn't been published – but what does it matter? I've been living a past life – somebody's past life – but everybody tells me it came out of my imagination, out of the stuff I've read, out of my subconscious sexual fantasies and feelings of aggression. I've had two doctors telling me that it's all OK, that I've simply experienced a temporal lobe aura, that it's stuff they get to deal with all the time, that these feelings of single overwhelming emotion are just typical characteristics of a partial seizure. You all think it's because of Malcolm, you think I'm trying to get my own back or something—'

'No,' said Pope. 'No, I don't believe that, or anything like that.'

He sat quietly for a few moments. Then he said, 'Is there anything, Lizzie, that you feel you can talk about? Anything at all about the franklin, about Toke?'

After a while she began to talk about Eleanor.

He was aware of the scent of the lilies.

They were opening in the evening, and would perfume the night.

*   *   *

'Lizzie's parents are divorced and both living abroad,' said Martha, dipping her spoon into perfumed, transparent soup. 'She's an only child. Her mother's remarried and lives in Singapore – she phones Lizzie all the time, according to her flatmates in Bristol. Her father's something to do with oil exploration and works in Venezuela. She hasn't seen him for two years. Her friends think this Malcolm guy was some kind of substitute father figure.'

'I guess she's using fantasy,' said Sluder the counsellor, 'to work out the problems in life. But that doesn't mean' – he glanced anxiously at Pope – 'it isn't fascinating stuff. I mean, what an imagination!'

He was trying to be conciliatory. The decision to turn on *Pasiphae*, three days ago, had been his. At some point, as sure as night followed day, there would be a multimillion-dollar bill for damages. He wanted Pope on his side.

Pope ate his food. Martha looked at him. She sighed. She said, 'OK, Charles. Tell us what you've found out.'

'Eleanor Blount was one of Queen Isabelle's entourage. She was at the meeting in Kingston upon Thames when the monk Maudelyn, an actor manqué, was chosen to impersonate King Richard. When the plot to kill Henry failed she was sent for safety to Dore.'

'Safety from whom?' asked Sluder, showing a polite interest. 'King Henry?'

'No, from the conspirators who had not been exposed, and who had not been killed by the mob, or hanged at Oxford. Her mother was afraid for her. That was why she was sent quietly from London, in the company of a franklin.'

'Are you telling me,' said Sluder, 'they'd have murdered a girl of fourteen?'

'You would have to look to Italy to find a world more coldly corrupt than England at the end of the fourteenth century. The Black Death had wiped out a third of the population. There were villages where children of five or six found themselves alone in a world where everyone else was dead and where the corpses of the last adults to die lay rotting in the street. There were scores of poor knights, their prosperity destroyed because there was no one to till the fields. There was anticlericalism, and there was superstition. Nobody believed in anything. It might be a sin to garrotte a fourteen-year-old girl, but no

269

sin to lock her in a cell and let her starve to death. It was a time of darkness, of despair, of terrible weariness of the spirit.'

There was a pause. Sluder said, 'It sounds like Washington DC. What are these?'

Martha said, 'Singapore noodles.'

'This is all taking us right back to Freud,' said Sluder. 'One minute she's the franklin, then she's the girl. This is classic repressed bi-sexuality. But it doesn't matter a monkey's. We have to find out how these memories, call them what you like, are being triggered. We have to find out where in her brain they are coming from. We have to find out how they are finding their way to a satellite twenty-two thousand miles over the equator. We have,' his tone became faintly religious, 'to do all that we can to check that there is no damage, no permanent damage, to this young lady's brain. Tomorrow she gets moved to a hospital used by the British Army, by the SAS. We've got a top neurosurgeon coming from London. We're flying in one of the best neurophysiologists in the world, from Phoenix. The idea is that we try to provoke one of these fits she's been having—'

'Not by switching on *Pasiphae*?'

'Well . . .'

'No. No way.'

'OK, fine. I just wanted your opinion.'

'Listen, every time synaptic modification takes place it becomes more and more likely that signals from the same source will pass through again. The mind is lazy. The mind likes to do what it did before, the way it did it before. Descartes more than three hundred years ago conceived of memories being stored as fluid flowing through pores. Each time Lizzie slips back, the process of slipping back becomes easier. Pour hot water on to a membrane of wax and eventually the water will find a tiny pinprick hole and will drip through. Pour hot water on again, and the hole will get bigger. Pour more hot water on—'

'OK,' said Martha, 'we're with you.'

'When *Pasiphae* was reactivated it triggered her even though she was away from the church, swimming in a river and fully conscious. She is becoming more susceptible to some process of morphic resonance. If we don't find out what it is, and quickly, it might reach a point when the normal protections don't apply. When her brain can be taken over, at whim, by the past, and she can do nothing about it.'

'OK, OK,' said Sluder wearily. 'So how do we help her?'

'Find the franklin. Find him in history. Find out what we're up against.'

'Oh Christ, Charlie . . .'

Andrew said, 'Gareth said today, "Only those who attempt to go too far, truly know how far they can go", and Bill said, "What's that, Gareth? That's jolly good", and wrote it down in his notebook. He says he's compiling a collection of Garethisms. How are your feet?'

'Painful.'

'They're amazing things, feet. Did you realise they have more bones in them than in the rest of the human body put together? Do you want me to go away?'

'No.'

'I love you, you know.'

'Yes, Andrew.'

'They'll move you to the other hospital tomorrow. Do the tests. Sort you out.'

'Yes.'

He settled in the small, uncomfortable chair and fell asleep. She stared up at the ceiling. She said, 'I'm sorry,' but he did not hear her. Soon her mind had left her body – it was there, down below on the bed, with Andrew slumped beside it – why didn't he lie down in the corner, curl up? – then the hospital had vanished, and she was back in the church in Dore, in her usual place, on the tiles by the alabaster frieze, by the old, dull oak of the pews with their musty, wormwoody smell that reminded her of her childhood. The light of the day was almost gone: a dull deep red glow against the west window beyond the font. Down the nave she could just make out the vase of white lilies.

The silence of the hours. The Norman font fading into blackness. She lay, her heart slowly quietening, her fingers gently touching the carved white alabaster rose.

She said again, 'I'm sorry,' and in his uncomfortable chair, Andrew stirred.

He got up and looked down at her.

'Lizzie?' he said, softly.

271

She did not hear him. The smell of roses came, sweet and sudden, and the stench of blood.

Then a voice, saying: 'Eat, sir! You must eat!'

31

Clyro

There were Carmelites at Ludlow, Cistercians at Grace Dieu and at Tintern. He heard the names spoken, argued over, and prayed to God they would not try to reach Grace Dieu. Ware could find his way to Christ's Sepulchre in Jerusalem better than to Monmouth: the girl had thought Hereford a day's ride from St Paul's. He said, 'Aston,' and they gathered round him, faces peering down, eyes inquisitive and, he thought, kindly. He wondered if they were still in the hovel. He tried to say 'Aston' again, but his mind drifted into a mist. He swam back to consciousness only when Ware tried to feed him. Ware and his archers should have been long gone on the road to Lancashire, he thought worriedly, as Ware opened his mouth and forced in some sort of pap with his fingers.

> *Little man, little man, where were you born?*
> *Far off in Lancashire under a thorn,*
> *Where they drink buttermilk from a cow's horn . . .*

He remembered that archers were notorious wizards and spat the food out.

'Eat, sir! You must eat!'

There was a wizard in the Rhineland who had shot three arrows in the image of Jesus, and thus denied the Holy Trinity, and from that day forward he could shoot three arrows a day, and those arrows killed any man he chose should die, wherever that man hid himself.

'Eat, sir, eat!'

But he spat out the pap and summoned sacred words to save himself: IESUS † NAZARENUS † REX † IUDAEORUM, and with the grey porridge dribbling from the side of his mouth shouted: 'The Word was made Flesh!' which was the best protection against wizards he knew (though it was said in Tobias that 'the devil has power against

273

those who are subject to their lusts' and he had lusted, God knew, after the girl).

'Amen, but eat, eat!'

It was her. It was the girl, the witch. Her slim fingers were stuffing the pap into his mouth. He silently said: *I adjure thee, thou ancient serpent, by the Judge of the living and the dead . . .*

'Eat!'

Now her hands were holding water she must have carried up from the river: they had no pitcher, no cup. He turned his head away and the water spilled over his face. She was shouting to Flesshe to hold his master.

Drive out O Lord the power of the devil. Banish his artifices and frauds. Let the wicked tempter be routed.

'What is he doing? What, sir, are you doing?'

There were witches who collected male members, who collected pricks. They kept them shut up in a box, where they moved themselves like living members, and ate oats and corn. It was a matter of common report in Bavaria that a man of Ratisbon had gone to a witch and asked her to restore his prick to him, and she had taken him to a bird's nest where several pricks were stored. And when he tried to take a big one, she had said he could not have it, because it belonged to the parish priest.

His hands clutched feebly between his legs.

'Hold him. Hold open his mouth.'

Other authorities in Germany and Italy said that witches could not really steal a man's living member, his *harness* as the common folk called it. Certainly, after they cast their spell the body seemed smooth to the sight, but a priest in Padua had explained: *It is an illusion, it is a glamour, it is done by drawing out an inner image from the repository of the memory, and impressing it on the imagination. But it is nonetheless true that the devil can inflame a man towards one woman and render him impotent towards another. He can prevent the flow of the semen by closing the seminal duct so that it does not descend to the genital vessels, or does not ascend from them again, or cannot come forth, or is spent vainly . . .*

'Eat, sir, eat . . .'

His head was held back. Her fingers, imperious, were in his mouth. He ate.

In a moment of lucidity he saw that it was snowing. He heard Ware saying that they must move. He heard her shouting at Ware, telling him to go then, if he must. He fell back into furry blackness, into the pulsating warmth.

He woke at night. The roof had been mended. There was a fire. She sat with her man's cloak round her shoulders, staring into the glowing embers. The archers and Flesshe were under sheepskins, curled and deep in sleep. They had crept together for warmth, for the preservation of the spark of life. She saw that he was awake. She came over to him, knelt by him.

She was shivering uncontrollably.

He said, 'Hickey?'

'You killed him.'

She leaned over, close to his face. When she spoke he felt her warm breath on his cheek. 'He lay by me to give me comfort, and you killed him.'

Ah . . .

She said, 'I have no fat. The cold eats me.'

Yes, she had no fat. She was thin as a weasel.

'You killed him because he kept me warm.'

He said, 'Be my wife.'

'You are mad.'

'I will write to your mother.'

'You say I am a witch.'

'You cannot be a nun.'

'You know that I cannot be otherwise.'

He said, 'No silver pins for your head, no silk gowns. No rings on your fingers but the ring of your profession. You were not made for that life.'

'You think nuns do not couple?'

They were a crude lot at court, he thought. As crude as peasants. But the whole world was filled with tales of the wantonness of nuns.

'Be my wife.'

She said, 'I'll tell you what. I won't sleep with another nun.'

Did she laugh?

Silence, though he heard her shivering, her teeth chatter.

'Come here with me,' he said, trying to lift the furs that covered him, 'and I will keep you warm.'

Would she give less to him than she had given to Hickey?

Would she creep under his furs?

'You are mad.'

She went back to the fire, to the embers. She threw on a few scraps of twigs. She sat and held her shaking hands to the tiny flames.

He watched her. In time he slept.

She shook him awake. She said, 'The snow has stopped. You must ride, or we must tie you to your saddle.'

He said, 'Aston. I will go to my manor.'

She did not reply. Ware and Davey lifted him on to his horse, tied his feet in the stirrups. His head slumped forward, down on the horse's neck. From the corner of his eye he could see Flesshe staring at him in dismay. Flesshe looked hungry. He had been a plump lad when they left the Jerusalem. Toke remembered how he had given morsels of cheese to a tavern girl.

They were all watching him. He struggled to sit upright. He said, 'We go to my manor at Aston.' His head fell forward again. They tied his arms round his horse's neck. They set off, and as his horse's head moved, so his horizon moved; one moment he was looking down at the hooves of Flesshe's pony, the next at the river and the white, thick wooded slopes beyond it, then he was looking up at the sky still pregnant with snow. Soon his head span and he felt the sweat break out, the fever returning.

They would kill him. He would die.

He heard Flesshe, shouting in alarm.

A crisp voice. 'We cannot stop.'

Eleanor. But it was her brother's voice. She was a Blount. She had the eyes, moon-like and staring, the full mouth, sensuous and arrogant. There was more than a touch of madness about the Blounts.

Ware was arguing.

'Sir, sir!'

It was her again. She was shaking his shoulder. He raised his head.

They were in a waterlogged meadow of dead reeds. A track ran to the west, towards the mountains. Another track, deemed no doubt a road in these parts, ran north into scrubby trees.

'Sir, tell them we must go to Dore!'

The track north would be to Weobley, he guessed. There would be an inn of sorts leeched against the castle walls. If not, the castle itself would provide hospitality of a sort. Two days' further travelling and they would be with the Carmelites at Ludlow. Two days more and he would be in his manor house, with its black and white walls, its polished tiled floor, its glazed windows.

'Sir, you have vowed to take me to Dore!'

He was a franklin, not a knight.

His face slumped gently forward. Suddenly her face was close to his. She was bending over, staring up at him. Her moon-like eyes were filled with tears of frustration.

'Sir, you have made a vow . . .'

Her face was filthy, her skin grey, her hair – sprouting now in tufts from her high forehead – was matted with grease, the scalp pricked with dried blood from the bites of lice.

'Sir!'

Indignation. He smiled, remembering her cry: *Worts. Worts a day old!* He looked at her full lips, still as sweet as brachet.

She said, 'He's gone. He's senseless.'

But he was not senseless. He raised his head. He looked at Ware. He nodded his head, almost imperceptibly.

He dreamed, as they rode, of his manor at Aston. He had last seen it at Martinmas, when the acorn-fed pigs from the forest had been killed and salted. He had watched as hams coated in treacle had been hung along the beams in the kitchen.

The wooden bridge at Whitney was down, the ford at Calhalva impassable. The mountains that had once been a line of bruised blue beyond the river fields now towered above them. They were back on the Roman road to the west; their horses' hooves thudding on the old metalled highway of the legions. They were entering the kingdom of Brutus and of Utherpendragon, the last stronghold of Cadwallader. In late afternoon they came to a great earth wall that crossed the river and ran northwards, up into the mountains. They stopped to rest their horses. Toke, all his energy concentrated on staying upright in the saddle, heard Eleanor tell Flesshe that the wall had been built by Ambrosius Merlin, to protect the last realm of King Arthur.

'It was built, page, in a single night.'

'What, all of it?'

'All of it.'

277

Toke reflected, as his head fell to his horse's neck, and an archer gently stopped him from keeling over, that the boy would believe anything.

A freezing night. Wind swept down from the mountains and threw up eddies of stinging snow. Without the road they would be finished, they would perish. But the straight, white road led them onwards, up into the mountains. This was the road, he thought, taken by Gracianus and Maximanus, the last Roman kings of Britain. *To Agicius, three times consul, come the groans of the Britons! The sea drives us into the hands of the barbarians, and the barbarians drive us into the sea*, they wrote to Rome. Then they brought the tattered remnants of the British legions west, into the fastness, and threw up a wall behind them.

They came to a hovel, then another. One of the archers banged on a door. The peasant replied that he had no food, no means of making a light – though this was a lie, for he had the embers of a fire, they could smell woodsmoke. Eleanor would have knocked his door down, but one of the archers spotted a castle, a square keep in the Norman style, on a grassy rise through the trees.

Soon Toke was lying on straw. He was wrapped in dry furs. He was warm and comfortable until his horse pissed on him. He cried out, and Flesshe came, but could not move the horse because the stable was so small. In the night his horse lay down, and he moved cautiously to its side, and huddled against its back.

At daylight Flesshe brought him a hunk of bread stuffed with slivers of meat. He lay on straw in the stable door and watched a gang of smiths and masons at work refortifying the great gate and portcullis. The archers had made a fire and were drinking spiced ale they must have begged or stolen from the kitchen. He ate his bread and meat. Flesshe brought him ale in a wooden cup that was greasy and soft with age, discarded by the high table and handed down to the servants. Flesshe presented the cup as he had been taught, bending his knee in courtly fashion.

Toke looked round for Eleanor. He said, 'Where is she?'

'She is with the lady of the castle.'

Toke stared malevolently at him.

'Walking in the pleasance.'

Flesshe crouched nervously while Toke drank, then took the cup and went. Ware came and squatted by him. Toke said, 'Your man, Hickey—' but Ware said, 'He was no man of mine.'

Toke said, 'He was . . .'

He could not find the words. The lady Eleanor, he thought, would have had no trouble.

Ware nodded.

'With her consent?'

'Who knows?'

'I am weary unto death.'

Ware nodded again.

He knew, they all knew, that he was besotted with the girl.

Ware told him that the castle's owner was John de Triplowe, kin to Lord Mortimer. De Triplowe's wife was kin to Roger Monnington of Sarnesfield, who was married to Margaret, daughter of Owain Glyn Dŵr.

A fine mix of loyalties, thought Toke. But Mortimer was a Marcher baron, he would not throw in his lot with a Welsh petty lord. The castle was being refortified by command of the king. He winced each time the blacksmith's hammer rose and fell, but enjoyed the clean air, fresh with the smell of burning charcoal and of red-hot iron. He realised that he had never before been in a castle keep where the air did not smell of excrement.

He was watching them forge the massive cross-bar of the new portcullis when she came: Eleanor, who had been walking in the Ladies' Pleasance.

She came stepping through the half-frozen mud, her bright sanguine gown showing beneath her brother's cloak. Graceful, weasel-thin, jumping easily over a small lake of water and horse dung. The archers were sitting round the fire telling stories with a Welsh magician. She greeted them all warmly and kissed Flesshe on the mouth – she had been pretending that he was a page, a young nobleman squire, for so long, thought Toke, that she thought it was true. She was awkward, self-conscious. She was avoiding his eye. She laughed with Ware, and looked at the coney he was skinning for the pot. Suddenly she turned from the fire, and sat by Toke, on the straw. She said, chattily, 'Did you hear of my lady's magpie? She has a magpie that talks, though it would not talk to your page. Do you think that magpies can truly talk? In the book of *The Knight of La*

Tour Landry there's a story of a magpie that saw its master's wife eat an eel – a special, fat eel, that he was saving for a great feast – so it flew back to its master and told him what his wife had done.'

Toke said nothing.

'Your page said to me, "Why does this magpie not speak?" And I said, "Because, master page, you are not its master." '

Silence.

She said, stiffly now, 'I am sorry there is not an apartment where you might sleep. I am myself with the lady Cecily.'

She would be in the family room above the Great Hall. They were a century behind the times, here in Wales. If the castle boasted even one tapestry-hung bedchamber with private shitting-hole it would be a sophisticated place. He thought of Richard's palace at King's Langley, with its panes of coloured glass, its bath chamber with hot water from a copper pipe.

Richard's corpse had been taken to King's Langley, he had learned in Hereford. His coffin had been followed by thirty torch-bearers dressed in white, and a hundred dressed in black. His queen, the child Isabelle, was refusing to marry Prince Hal. The talk was that she would have to be sent home to France, and her dowry paid back to the French king.

'Her lord returns today. She will ask him if you may sleep in the Hall tonight.'

'With my lord's servants?'

She sighed, her look saying how difficult it all was.

He owned half a Genoese bark. He was lord of three manors, with a mill and sixty peasant families in demesne – and this in Stafford-shire, where the land was fruitful, not in a land of bogs and starvation. He could very likely have bought de Triplowe three times over.

She said, 'Are you well now, sir?'

He said, 'You are foolish.'

She looked away. After a moment she said, 'Ah yes, indeed. Which is why, as we know, I must make reason the head of my council and my chief governor.'

'Listen to me. You think you will not be long left in the nunnery at Dore. You think a knight will come to rescue you – some handsome lad on a steed caparisoned with gold, a silver lance in his hand and a flamenco-plume on his helm. You think to be carried off to a castle in the mountains, sung poems in a pleasance by your knightly lover. You dream, I dare say, of being ravished.'

She gasped. 'What?'

'You dream of being fucked' – he used, now, the Saxon word understood even in places where they called eggs eyren – 'by some Sir Gawain o' the Green.'

Her wide eyes had become enormous. Not that she was shocked by the word, which was used often enough at court, particularly by Queen Isabelle in her English lessons.

Ware and the archers, who could hear every word, were staring thoughtfully into the fire.

'Is it Sir Galahad, or Sir Gawain, or a Frenchman in your mind?'

'I am to be, sir,' she stuttered, 'a bride of Christ.'

'A bride of Christ,' he said, 'my arse.'

One of the archers grinned, then looked solemn again. Ware passed him the skinned coney and he slipped it into the pot.

She looked at him. There was a spot of bright red in each of her cheeks.

'Perhaps,' she said, 'there is a knight who will come for me. A chivalrous young knight. If so it is no concern of yours.'

Toke thought of the young knights at Richard's court. Their ornate turbans, their pouched jackets, their tight multicoloured leggings, their long, pointed shoes with gold buckles, their mincing ways.

'Chivalry?' he said. 'Chivalry died in England when Jack Straw stormed the Tower, and invaded the queen's bedchamber. It died when Jack Straw stood and mocked her, madam, and pinched the nipples of her breasts – and the queen's knights, those glorious chivalrous knights who had kept vigil and sworn to save so many maidens from so many dragons of a certain size—'

Ware and his archers were smirking.

'Stood petrified, madam, with smiles on their faces and sweat, the sweat of bloody fear, my lady, coursing down their cheeks. By the living Christ, it is knights who are the biggest thieves and villains in England. When Adam delved and Eve span, who then was the gentleman? Well?'

The lady of the castle, the kin to Glyn Dŵr's daughter, was calling, waving her arm. Men were running from the battlements, jumping in excitement down the wooden stairs. A trumpet sounded, dogs yelped. Sir John de Triplowe rode into his castle of Clyro, his squire and page and six men-at-arms behind him. They rode through the fresh white wood-shavings, in from the misty wet track, into the muddy court of the keep.

De Triplowe's eyes passed without interest over the franklin, and the archers, and over the other passing travellers who had taken shelter in the stables – a tinker, two farmers with a small flock of fat sheep (that Ware and his archers had been quietly eyeing), the travelling Welsh scribe and seer who had last night prophesied that a worm would give birth to seven lions with goats' heads, and the lion-goats would, with the fetid breath from their nostrils, corrupt married women into common prostitutes, so that fathers would not know their own sons. The lion-goats – he had told a goggling Flesshe – would then be slain by the Dragon of Worcester in alliance with the great Boar of Totnes.

De Triplowe's page and two servants helped him to dismount. He was a heavy man, immense in his mail hauberk, his basinet with pendant camail. He looked like a knight from a past age, thought Toke: in southern England the camail had been abandoned for the past year or more, replaced by a light steel gorget over neck and shoulders and steel taces over the groin. This knight was so heavily clad he would need two pages to support him in battle otherwise he would fall over.

Toke watched him clump his way up the stone stairs and waddle into the Great Hall. Eleanor said abruptly, 'I am to go to Dore. Your escort is no longer needed.'

His escort no longer needed . . .

The blood was rising behind his eyes.

'But I thank you, sir . . .'

A man-at-arms, a young knight, came out of the Great Hall and called out to her in French.

'I thank you for your company,' she said, stiffly, formally, 'and your protection. I thank you on behalf of my mother, and of Dame Elizabeth at Dore.'

She stood up. She looked down at him.

He pulled himself to his feet. He bowed. As he rose he looked into her eyes, and saw a questioning look. Fear? Uncertainty?

The knight called again, in languid French.

Eleanor . . .

She hesitated.

Eleanor . . .

She suddenly moved one pace forward, put her hands up, lightly on his shoulders, and kissed his cheek.

The blacksmith hammered, and the sparks flew upwards.

She ran back across the court. Flesshe, his boy, his page, said in a tearful voice: 'It is the young Walter Manny. Manny is the chivalrous knight.'

But he knew that; he had known that since Hereford.

He left the following morning. His head was clear. The horses were fresh. They clattered at speed away from the castle at Clyro: the franklin in front, his beaver gown flying in the wind, his five mounted archers and the packhorse behind; the boy Flesshe trotting furiously on his pony. None of them looked back to see if they were being watched from the walls, or from the windows of the great keep. They turned the bend on the river, and were gone.

She said, 'Ah me.'

'Do you know the name of his manor?'

'Ah me,' she sighed.

'Where is the franklin going to? Where is his manor?'

She opened her eyes.

Pope looked down into a great sorrow.

In a second it turned into an emptiness, into a vacancy.

As he went down the stairs Sluder was coming in through the swing doors, into main reception. His hair was unbrushed, and stuck up in wisps. His face was jowly and pale. His placatory smile was gone. He'd been humble for long enough. He said, 'I have had ESC calling me three times before two a.m. Then I have this. OK, Charlie. We need to talk.'

Martha came in behind him. She said, 'What happened?'

'She regressed. She went back on her own. Andrew called me.'

They went down a corridor, and found a rest area by a drinks vending machine. Martha said, 'What do the doctors say?'

'They've given her a different drug. A barbiturate. She's out cold. If she wasn't going to Bryn Llandoth, they'd want to move her to the Frenchay Hospital at Bristol.'

Sluder pulled out his mobile phone. Martha said, 'Not here.'

'Shit—'

'It's not allowed. You saw the notice.'

He stuffed it back into his pocket. He said, 'ESC wants *Pasiphae* back in commission.'

Pope said, 'No. Don't even think about it.'

'If I tell them we're doing something – tell them we've got the best neurosurgeon in England on the job, that we've flown in a neurophysiologist from Phoenix – well, OK, they'll maybe give me another twenty-four hours.'

'Are we any closer,' said Pope, 'to finding the franklin?'

'Jesus,' said Sluder, 'if I hear one more time about the fucking franklin—'

Martha said, 'We are no closer, there is no record of him in history.'

'Listen, Charlie,' Sluder pleaded, 'you were right about the signals reaching *Pasiphae* directly from a human brain. You were right, I was wrong. I'm big enough to say that I was wrong. I was looking for a phreaker who'd cracked the system, and I was wrong. Am I, or am I not, big enough to say that?'

Martha said, 'Yeah, you're big enough, Larry.'

'Be big enough to say that you are also wrong, Charlie. Be big enough to admit it's all in her memory, it's stuff she's read in history books all mixed up with dreams about a mystery guy buried in a church – Jesus, all that stuff about the plot to kill King Henry, all that about the monk Maudelyn is *known*, it's there on the Internet, I checked it out when I got back to the hotel, all she did was put herself in the plot with lots of detail that nobody can possibly prove or disprove – we're playing games here, we're acting like we're in some *Mysteries of the Paranormal* TV show or something.'

'Have you ever thought, Larry, how strange it is that nobody knows where, in the brain, memories are stored? Has it never seemed strange to you that if memory traces exist in the brain, nobody can find them?'

'Maybe they have, maybe you're behind on the research. It doesn't matter. What are you talking about memory for? You want a debate on morphic resonance at three a.m?'

Sluder sat down. He put his head in his hands.

Martha said, 'She's regressing on her own. If she's going to regress, why not do it under controlled conditions, why not try and learn something?'

Sluder looked up. 'A test for false memory syndrome? Yes? We get the entire team over from Phoenix?'

'I was thinking,' said Martha, 'of regression under hypnosis.'

'Shit – regression under hypnosis is poncing around, those guys in Washington want action, they want to see her skull opened up.'

Martha said, 'Well this is fucking England, Larry, perhaps we need to remember that.'

'OK, OK, she's nothing to do with us, we reset the parameters and *Pasiphae* goes back on-line, and maybe in ten years the US government has to pay out on some medical insurance claim but by then I will be long, long retired, honey.'

Andrew came down the corridor.

They stood silent. Guilty.

Andrew went to the drinks machine.

Pope said quietly, 'We have got to find out what the franklin wants.'

'What he wants?' said Sluder. 'We have to find out what the franklin guy *wants*?'

'Has anybody heard from Lucy Pagetti? Has anybody heard how she's getting on with the Worcester diocese archives?'

'Charlie, Charlie . . .' Sluder sighed, shaking his head. 'I don't seem to be getting through to you, somehow. Listen. The doctors believe that Lizzie may have experienced an aura. Do you know the symptoms people have when they experience an aura? They hallucinate. They suffer memory disturbance. They suffer from déjà vu – they think they're experiencing something that happened to them before. They suffer from *jamais vu* – they have feelings of unfamiliarity, of being disconnected with the real world—'

'OK, Larry,' said Martha, 'keep it quiet, we hear what you're saying—'

'Charlie, they suffer depersonalisation, flashbacks, motor disturbance during clouding of consciousness – "ambulatory automatism" is what the medics call it, but to you and me it's a girl going wandering off up a mountain after a midnight swim.'

Martha said, 'Just shut up, OK?'

Andrew had got himself a can of Coke. He joined them. He said, 'In there, with Lizzie . . . you asked where the franklin was going to, where was his manor. But she hadn't said anything about the franklin or about a manor.'

They all looked at Pope. Andrew puzzled, Martha concerned, Sluder shaking his head and smiling a warm, false smile.

Charlie, his smile said, had well and truly toppled over the edge.

32

Bryn Llandoth Hospital

'It's no use. She's not responding.'

Martha said, quietly, 'Do you know why?'

'No,' said Caroline. 'There's some sort of barrier. It was the same when I tried to regress her before. That time there was something in her recent past – her boyfriend.'

The room had French windows that looked out on lawns, rhododendrons, and a backdrop of mountains. The hospital claimed to be one of the most advanced in the UK and also one of the most luxurious. It had five stars for its clinical diagnostic centre and five stars and a rosette for its cuisine. It had a wing controlled and paid for discreetly by the British government.

Pope was staring down at Lizzie. Her suntan was fading, her skin seemed smudged; dirty. There was a blue bruise under her eyes that made them look large, moon-like. Her fine gold hair was spread over the pillow – a nimbus round her electronically wired skull. 'Do you believe she is back there?' asked Pope. 'Back in the fifteenth century?'

'I can't say. She's shut me out.'

'You're certain it is Lizzie who has shut you out?'

'Who else?'

'Somebody else she may have had an emotional relationship with, perhaps?'

'In the fifteenth century? It could be. People often have inhibitions about things that happened in their past lives. But we are trying to go too far too fast. If I could counsel Lizzie over a period of time, take things more slowly...'

The dry sound of a rattlesnake: Sluder, in the corner of the room, laughing.

At the EEG machine Mitch Lean said: 'The deltas with spikes have subsided. We're getting alphas. She's now in normal sleep.'

He had arrived from Phoenix in the early hours of the morning. He had gold-rimmed spectacles, tiny gold hairs on the back of his clean, pink-scrubbed hands, a gold bracelet. He reminded Martha of a dentist she had known in her childhood.

Sluder: 'Isn't there a drug you can give her to induce a regression?'

'Yeah, metrazol, if you can get it authorised.'

'Forget it,' said Sluder gloomily.

'I've now got blocking of the alphas,' said Lean, his eyes on the EEG machine. 'I'm losing the alphas.'

Silence.

Caroline said, in a matter-of-fact voice, 'Lizzie?'

Lizzie's eyes opened. She stared up at the ceiling. She slowly moistened her lips.

'You've had a little sleep. Do you want a drink?'

She nodded her head. Caroline poured her a glass of water.

The French windows were open to let in the faint breeze. Wood pigeons could be heard, cooing softly.

Lizzie drank thirstily. She said, 'I always have a headache.'

Mitch Lean said, in a friendly voice, 'It's natural. Don't worry.'

Lizzie's hand went up to her head: her fingers ran slowly across the electrodes. 'Where's Andrew?'

'He'll be here soon,' said Martha.

Lizzie looked puzzled.

'He phoned from Eywas Harold to say his car had broken down.'

She smiled. 'Poor Andrew.'

Then she closed her eyes.

Sluder and Pope and Martha went out into an ante-room and spoke in low voices.

Lizzie lay and wondered what they were saying.

Sluder was saying: 'Half our commercial customers are cancelling their contracts and defying us to take them to court. That Japanese guy, that options trader in Tokyo, he was spouting medieval stuff even as he fell on his sword, and a dozen people heard him. That English reporter, the guy who wrote about the Army chasing naked girls? Well he's now asking questions about scientists sent crazy by paranormal force-waves. The word is out. The problem is no longer contained. There's guys in New York who are frightened of looking at their screens.'

Martha said, 'Can we go and talk this through over coffee somewhere?'

'Outside,' said Sluder. 'The Brits say this place is secure. I say nowhere is secure outside Vernal County, Utah.'

He walked out.

Martha said, 'Oh Christ . . .'

'Go and talk to him,' said Pope.

'You realise what he's going to say?'

'Yes.'

'And there's nothing I can do that will make any difference?'

Pope said, 'I can't afford to spend any more time or energy worrying about Sluder. If he turns *Pasiphae* back on, and Lizzie's brain is destroyed as a result, then I will destroy him. Tell him that.'

He went back into Lizzie's room.

'Oh Christ . . .' said Martha again.

She went outside and followed Sluder down a path through a mass of dark shiny rhododendrons. On the roof of the building men were fixing satellite dishes, running cables down to an Army mobile communications vehicle. There were clouds over the mountains, over the summit of Bryn Llandoth. Hikers were coming down a path through the trees from Offa's Dyke. They were laughing, joking about waterproofs.

'Rain,' said Martha. 'Everybody is praying for rain.'

'I am not praying for rain. I am praying that we get this girl sorted fast—'

'OK, Larry,' she snapped, 'we know.'

'Charlie's gone off with the fairies. He's in some kind of psychic relationship with Lizzie Draude himself, or thinks he is. They're both in fantasy land.'

'What if he isn't in fantasy land? What if he's right? What if *Pasiphae* has opened up a conduit to the past, have you thought about that, Larry? What if that girl in there is actively interfacing with the Middle Ages? Are you going to fuck it up?'

'I'm past caring. Even if it's true, which it isn't, some other bastard'd get the Nobel Prize.'

The soldiers on the roof were calling to each other as they angled the satellite dishes. Sluder said, 'Do you know the price we're paying for all this? Do you know how much time on Magnum the British are demanding in return for the minimal assistance they're providing here?'

'They've given you half a battalion of the SAS,' Martha said, 'What more do you want?'

'It's the pleasure they take in our discomfiture,' said Sluder, 'that gets my goat. Honey, this is crunch time. By tonight we'll have a satellite link to the University Hospital at Berkeley and Good Samaritans in Phoenix. We'll have infrascan and Option Red standing by. We'll have the best neurosurgeon in London ready to carry out an investigative operation. We either go for it, or tomorrow we just walk away from this.'

'Give me one more day to check on the stuff she's coming up with.'

'What stuff? The hey-nonny-no some boy said to some girl in a palace at Sonning five hundred years ago? You're wasting your time. The press office in Washington has prepared a statement. It will admit there's been a complex technical fault – due to the fact that *Pasiphae* is operating on the very frontiers of science – but that everything is now fine. And as far as I'm concerned everything is fine. The perimeters are now such that it is impossible for direct thought transference to a human brain, and yeah, I've heard Charlie's jokes about earthworms and amoebas exchanging philosophical ideas from opposite sides of the world but frankly if it happens it's something we can live with.'

'Larry—'

'OK, I can see her.'

A nurse was waving to them, urgently, from the open French windows.

The green line on the EEG was dissolved into a series of jagged peaks.

Mitch Lean said, 'We've got spikes again, twenty emsecs in duration. It's not caused by lesion or the cortex or there'd have been a background of slow waves. This is due to abnormal influences from a distant source.'

Lizzie was moving: her limbs were moving. Her hands moved—

'Stop her,' said Lean. The nurse gently took Lizzie's hands away from the electrodes on her skull.

Sluder and Martha came in through the French windows. Caroline said: 'She's in hypnosis. Shall I try to speak to her?'

'Yes,' said Pope. 'Yes, try now.'

'Lizzie?' said Caroline quietly.

Nothing.

'Lizzie?' said Caroline. 'Lizzie, can you hear me?'

Lizzie laughed.

There was a long pause.

Pope said, 'Try again.'

'Lizzie? Lizzie? Can you say yes if you can hear me?'

Lizzie laughed again.

'She's distracted,' said Caroline.

'Ask her where she is.'

'Lizzie? Lizzie, where are you?'

Nothing.

Caroline said, 'Something's happening to distract her.'

A long silence.

'Well something's going on,' said Mitch Lean. 'I'm getting spike and wave activity in all leads.'

Martha watched the second hand go twice round the face of her watch.

'Lizzie?' said Caroline. 'Lizzie, can you hear me? Lizzie—'

Lizzie: 'They've chased him.'

A pause.

'Chased who? Who have they chased?'

Silence, then: 'She's thrown the bull at him. The abbess has thrown the bull at him!'

Lizzie laughed again.

Sluder said quietly, 'Thrown the bull? The *abbess has thrown a bull*? Who was this abbess, the great abbess giant of Hereford or what?'

'Please be quiet,' said Caroline. 'Lizzie, why has she thrown the bull?'

Silence.

Martha went quietly over to Pope's laptop computer and turned it on.

'She's at Dore,' said Pope. 'But it could be years later. She could be an old woman, an old nun.'

Martha said, 'No. The valley was razed by the Welsh in 1402. The nunnery was burned down.'

'Why has she thrown the bull, Lizzie?' said Caroline again.

'Because of the monkey.'

Sluder: 'Monkey? Did she say—'

'Tell us about it,' said Caroline. 'Tell us about the monkey.'

Silence.

Mitch Lean said, 'We are now seeing brain activity in the region of the left hippocampus. This is a known location for the activation of conscious memory.'

Sluder: 'Memory. You got that, Charlie?'

Caroline said, 'For heaven's sake will you be quiet!'

Martha's fingers rattled at Pope's laptop. She said, 'It may be she's talking about a papal bull issued against the keeping of pets in nunneries. There was a craze, it says here, all over Europe, in the late fourteenth century, for nuns to keep pets, particularly dogs and apes. There were some nasty rumours about the nuns.'

Sluder said, 'What kind of rumours?'

'Sodomy,' said Pope.

'Jesus.'

'They were only officially allowed to keep cats,' said Martha. 'Even then, even in AD 1400, the cat was becoming recognised as the companion for women who lived by themselves.'

'This is known? I mean, she could have read this?'

'About the cats?'

'The bull!'

He was very stressed.

Caroline said, 'Will you please stop talking? Will you?'

Lizzie, half amused, sly: 'It is always Agnes Poney the abbess chooses, and always Dame Margaret who beats her.'

A pause.

Caroline said, 'Who is Agnes Poney? Is Agnes Poney your friend?'

Nothing.

'Lizzie? Can you tell me what is happening to you?'

Lizzie laughed again.

*   *   *

She had watched from a window as the abbess threw the wooden-boxed parchment with such deadly aim at the abbot's summoner.

It had made her laugh for the first time in months.

Her smile faded. She turned to gaze, as she so often gazed, at the track that wound its way up the valley towards Hay. Welsh flowers were a splash of yellow in the woods. She remembered how she had sat at this window two years ago, watching the daffodils bloom, sitting learning her rules.

Novices must be diligent, humble in bearing, conversation, and devotion.

'Ah me,' she sighed.

A nun came in. Dame Alice, mad and cunning but not unkind. She was daughter to an ap Tudor of Clorach, cousin to an ap Tudor of Erddreiniog. 'You have heard,' she said breathily, her eyes darting about, 'the news of Glyn Dŵr?'

'I have heard nothing,' said Eleanor, 'for so long a time.'

'He has captured Mortimer. He has with him his brother Gryffyn and the great Philip Hanmer.'

Glyn Dŵr was said to have a curious banner, painted over with pictures of maidens with red hands. If she were ever to meet him she would ask about the maidens with red hands.

'The friars of Llanfaes say the people of Glamorgan will rise. They say the Maelienydd and the Mortimer lordships and Blaenllyfni on the Usk will fall before the leaves fall from the trees.'

The nuns, thought Eleanor, were such schemers.

Dame Alice wandered out.

Eleanor sighed and looked down at her book. It was *The House-holder of Paris*. Queen Isabelle had given it to her. 'Little ever came out of Paris,' the franklin had said, 'that was not lewd.'

She smiled faintly and looked out at the daffodils.

She wondered why she thought so often of the franklin.

She could hear the nuns at their harps. They sang dreadfully. Ballads about Ednyfed Fychan, senechal of Llywelyn the Great (Dame Blod was of the bloodline of Ednyfed Fychan, of the ap Tudors) and of Arthur, the Welsh king (the abbess, when she was not lamenting the death of her bastard girl-child, hinted at descent from Gwenivere).

There was a new song, that had passed like quicksilver from out of the misty valleys and all over the kingdom; a song that had summoned the Welsh home from all over England.

Owain was an eagle, with a bright, shining helm . . . *Eryr digrif afrifed, Owain, helm gain, hael am gêd.*

'Christ,' said Sluder, 'she's speaking with tongues.'

Caroline said, 'I think you'll find that it's Welsh.'

'Where do we find somebody who speaks Welsh? Doesn't Arizona State have a Welsh-language department? Isn't it part of their Ethnic Languages School, out near Bluff Canyon?'

'I don't think we need go quite to Arizona,' said Martha. 'And please be quiet. And please stop acting more stupid than you actually are.'

'You don't know how stupid I am,' said Sluder pityingly, 'or how stressed.'

Caroline said, 'Lizzie? Can you tell me what you are doing?'

'Koenig had a stroke,' Sluder whispered to Pope. 'I've got a premonition I might be heading that way myself. At least they've got a good cardiac team in this place. I checked it out.'

'Lizzie?' said Caroline. 'Lizzie, can you hear me?'

In *The Householder of Paris* she read a recipe for boiled chicken. You first took almonds and pounded them and mixed them with wine. Then you added figs and ground ginger, cloves and cinnamon. This you heated over the fire with honey. Then you poured it over the chicken.

Perhaps the franklin would be eating boiled chicken in his manor of Aston, with Flesshe serving it up in courtly fashion.

Chew liquorice, she read (turning to a page of hints to the young wife in the bridal chamber with her old goat) to sweeten breath before love, before *l'amour*. But would a young English knight care for liquorice as much as a fat old Paris merchant?

She was almost sixteen. Soon the summer of her life would be gone.

Each nun shall have one dish of meat or fish, appropriate to the season, each Monday, Wednesday, and Saturday each dish worth a penny.

Each nun to have five measures of superior ale every week.

No secular or any man of religion shall be allowed to enter the cloistral precinct unless he is a great and noble personage and this for a very good, obvious, proper, and significant purpose.

She could picture the franklin now, saying to his page: 'I will show you the last unicorn in all England.' She could picture him standing in a valley on the High Malverns, on a day when hazel catkins were yellow on the bough, and fair maids of February – that peasant children called snowdrops – were in flower. Standing in the pale sunshine reciting the terrible songs of Langland, telling him a poem about dew on daisies dunked full fair . . .

A week after she had arrived at Dore he had sent her a present – figs and raisins and a pot of Italian oil. The abbess had kept it for herself.

Last year, after the sacking of Ruthin, when the valley was alive with rumour of Shrewsbury having fallen to Glyn Dŵr, and the Prince of Wales having been killed, there had been a caller at the nunnery – an archer. An archer from Aston, said Dame Blod. But had not the archers gone back to Lancashire, to their own land where the peewit called? The abbess said the archer was on a mission into Wales for his master, a mission to do with the carving of alabaster for a knight's tomb in Carmarthen, in a church by the shining sea.

He had called to enquire as to the abbess's health, which was gracious (said the abbess) of a franklin.

And had he enquired about Eleanor?

Not at all.

She lied. She was diseased in the mind. She slept in her private chamber when by monastic law she should have slept in the dormitory. Sometimes she slept with Margaret Moose, her new favourite, sometimes with Richard Huyes, her domestic chaplain. She had given Huyes a feather bed with a bolster, and two sheets, part of the dowry of Dame Katherine. She had had a girl-child by him, and cared for it in the nunnery for three years, until it died. It was the death of her child that had diseased her mind.

Eleanor had seen the letter written by the franklin. Agnes Poney, the nun who was no longer summoned to the abbess's bed, the nun whose hands were tied and beaten nightly by Dame Moose during games of Hot Cockles, had found it and stolen it. 'Tell the nuns of Our Lady of Dore,' the franklin had written, 'that Sir John Creveker is escaped out of Wales with a hundred spears as men say, and is in Bristol, though Young Manny is dead . . .'

Young Manny is dead.

It had been Isabelle, the child-queen, who had married her to young Walter Manny.

'Take her!' the queen had cried, and Manny, an awkward lad (who had been forced to confess his love for Eleanor after the queen saw him give her three violets and a pear), had taken her hand.

'Now say it!'

Here I take you, Eleanor, to my wife, to have and to hold until the end of my life, and to this I plight you my troth . . .

'Now you, now you say it!'

Here I take you, Walter, to my husband, to have and to hold . . .

'Release her hands. Now you must kiss . . .'

And the cooks made a feast, and there was a mazelin, a loving cup.

She sang, now, softly,

> They set him first the sweet wine
> And made in a mazelin
> A royal spicery.
> With gingerbread that was full fine,
> With liquorice and cumin . . .

'You are my husband,' Eleanor had said, drinking the sweet spiced wine. 'You are my wife,' Walter had replied uneasily. And the queen, who was eleven years old, had insisted that they go naked to bed.

Eleanor remembered it now. And she remembered the only other man she had known naked, Hickey, the archer, who had lain on her to stop her shivering from the cold.

She remembered his blood, running hot through her blue, mottled fingers.

Walter Manny was dead, and Hickey the archer was dead. She had not known either for more than a month.

She sat at a desk. She wrote: *Come to me.*

She felt her heart pound.

There was a Welsh merchant from the vale of Towy, who was staying the night in the house of guests. The English had seized his goods in recompense for English goods burned in the sacking of

Ruthin, and he was going to Shrewsbury to appeal in person to the Prince of Wales. She would see him, somehow, speak to him, ask him to carry her letter.

If you could be content with my poor person, she wrote quickly, hurriedly, but, she trusted, truly, *I would be the merriest maiden on ground.*

But what if he had found himself another wife in Staffordshire? Tears formed in her eyes. *But good, true and loving Valentine*, she wrote, crying at her own nobility. *If you think yourself not so satisfied with my poor person, then let it pass, and let me never more be spoken of, though I shall still be ever your true bedeswoman and pray for you during my life.*

Next morning she went early out of the chapel and found the merchant. He sighed at the naughtiness of nuns, but took her letter and promised to take it to Shrewsbury, though how it would be got from Shrewsbury to Aston he could not tell. 'If you take it yourself,' Eleanor told him, 'the lord of Aston will give you a silver crown.'

She reckoned ten days. She watched the road from Hay; watched for an archer, for the sight of a beaver coat flying in the wind. One day she saw a pony being ridden at speed down the track. It was a servant of some Marcher lord, Eleanor decided, bearing more tales of rebellion for the nuns of Dore and for the monks of Abbey Dore. Soon the man was shouting to the workers building the granary, and pointing up to the hills. Eleanor craned her head out of the window, and saw smoke, thick and black, rising over the ridge.

Only Pope and a nurse were left at Lizzie's bedside. He sat and watched her face as the sunlight, falling through the trees outside the window, played over it. She did not have that shadowy look of irony today, he thought: she seemed younger, her features less formed. She was no longer the franklin, but Eleanor.

Yes, she was now Eleanor Blount. He wondered if she would ever again be Lizzie Draude.

She was sleeping calmly. The EEG screen showed long sinuous curves.

He went outside. Martha was sitting against the wall, in the shade. She said to him, bluntly: 'The neurosurgeon's here. It may be best that they operate.'

Operate to seek out the franklin – find him, wherever he lay secreted. If they could not curb him with drugs, they would dig for him with a knife. They would search for a cluster of molecules – of particles even, perhaps a chain of photons – with a bright, gleaming scalpel.

Pope laughed silently at the stupidity of it. He thought of the corruptions in *Pasiphae*'s signals: how adept they had become at coiling and secreting themselves; how skilled at finding new hiding places, at evading the disinfectant programs. The franklin, he thought, would not be exorcised that easily.

'You ought to take a rest,' she said. 'You ought to have a break.'

'I'm going to the church at Dore. Do you want to come?'

She looked up at him, sadly, and shook her head.

33

Dore

There were autumn flowers, now, in the vase on the little table: Michaelmas daisies, blue gentian, dahlias. Bats flitted round the ceiling of the nave – a window had been opened, possibly opened deliberately in order to let them in. Bats ate up deathwatch beetles and did not, whatever old wives said, get stuck in ladies' hair.

A great stillness.

A great peace.

He walked down the aisle. He looked up at the east window, with its allegory of the fourteenth day of the fifteen days in which the world would be destroyed. A doomwatch clock, frozen for six centuries.

Was the clock ticking again?

He turned to look at the franklin's tomb. The plaster effigy. The thin, ascetic face with its look of irony – but did it really capture the face of the man who lay buried beneath? It would not have been drawn from life, the sculptor would not have personally known the franklin. It must have been described to him. Who by? Eleanor Blount?

I will have alabaster for the tomb . . .

He crouched down on the Victorian tiles and put his hand on the alabaster frieze, lightly tracing the outline of flowers, his hands a few inches from the calcified bones, the mortal remains.

The mortal remains were nothing. They were dust. They were atoms. But could a thought – an emotion – ever cease to exist? Was there perhaps something of the franklin – something other than bones, other than solid corrupting matter – still here? Something haunting his mortal remains?

He took his hand, slowly, away from the alabaster.

He went outside. He climbed slowly up the path to the fort, through the limes and the wild service trees. In the undergrowth was the vivid orange of stinking iris, the blue of woundwort. At one point he stopped and looked down into the valley of Dore. He could see the distant white disc of the satellite relay station. It was used by the SAS at Hereford – the only British regiment that had been able to communicate directly with its battle headquarters during the Falklands War. It was also used by *Pasiphae*.

He thought of Lizzie, hurrying down this path, night after night. Believing herself summoned. Going into the empty, silent church. Lying down by the imprisoned atoms, molecules, of the franklin's long-corrupted flesh.

The thin girl in flappy shorts, Eloise, was working on a trench together with the bearded boy with a sly grin. They stopped work, gratefully, and sat down. The boy got out a stone flagon of cider and they asked how Lizzie was. Eloise was not so much hostile as reproachful. 'Now see what you've done,' her look seemed to be saying, 'with your scientific experiments.'

The others were in Hereford, showing the students from Sheffield round the museum and cathedral, taking them to see the *mappa mundi*. The dig would end in three days' time.

'Have you found anything of major significance?'

'We've established that the mound was a ceremonial religious site,' said Eloise, 'used by druids in the first two centuries after the Roman conquest.'

'No hoards of buried gold?' he asked, thinking of Martha.

Sensational finds, they told him, were not what archaeology was all about. Skull drinking cups inset with precious stones and human heads embalmed in cedar oil might come the way of some archaeologists, but it really didn't matter. 'Each dig, whatever it produces,' Eloise said nobly and severely, 'adds to the sum of knowledge.'

He was shown a teat from a Roman baby's bottle.

He said, 'Why is it called Vortipor's Fort?'

'Because it's believed to be the place where he raped his daughters,' said the boy. 'And the stream is called Vortipor's stream—'

'No Jacob, please, Jacob—' said Eloise.

'Because it ran red with their menstrual blood.'

'Jacob, you are gross!'

'But the details were bowdlerised in Victorian times,' added Jacob, 'as you'd expect.'

'Have you found any evidence of occupation in the early fifteenth century?'

They hadn't. Pope didn't know why he'd asked the question.

'Nobody would have occupied the fort in the late medieval period,' said Jacob. 'The Marcher castles were all built by then. Anyway they'd have been afraid of goblins and elves.'

'Except that Lizzie told me that this is where the nuns were raped,' said Eloise.

'What nuns?' – Jacob, surprised.

'I don't know.'

'Where was that?' asked Pope. 'Where did she say the nuns had been raped?'

'The mound. "They raped them here", she said.'

'You girls,' said Jacob, quaffing his cider, grinning slyly.

'Shut up, Jacob,' said Eloise, looking worried that she might be adding to evidence of Lizzie's mental instability.

'When was this?'

'The evening before she had her attack. She went on working after the rest of us stopped – you remember, Jacob, she kept scraping away until Andrew made her come and have supper.'

A king raping his own daughters in the Dark Ages . . . nuns raped in the Middle Ages. Pope wondered if the incidents were one and the same. A tradition of a shocking incident – shocking even by the standards of such times – passed down through the generations. Or was this just a place that had seen many shocking things?

'Can you show me?'

They walked across the grassy centre of the fort, across the two trenches that had revealed the Iron Age town.

'The nuns were raped here on the mound?'

'That was what she said.'

'Presumably nobody in the fifteenth century would have known that this was a place where druids made sacrifices to their gods?'

'Who knows?' said Eloise. 'The druids have survived. Their traditions are maintained.'

Jacob said, 'Bollocks.'

'Yes, all right, Jacob.'

'They just dress up in sheets and bless the apple trees.'

'Now they do, Jacob, you don't know what they did in the fifteenth century.'

'Are we going down the pub then? Where's Bill?'

'Shagging Venetia, isn't he?' said Eloise tartly, showing she too could be one of the lads.

They were going to Newbridge for something to eat. Pope said he'd join them. They walked down the path to the church and he gave them a lift to the pub in his car. He bought them drinks and they told him about the dig, and about Venetia and Bill (primitive, primeval passion), and Sonia and Gareth ('Some girls,' said Eloise, knowing it to be true, 'have to take what they can get') and Jacob looked more sly than ever when Eloise, who had had three gins, said, 'The love-fairy hasn't sprinkled you with stardust, has she, Jacob?'

Slowly they relaxed and talked about Lizzie, and the beginning of her strangeness, and when they had first noticed it, and what a brick Andrew had been. They ate outside, in the garden. Moths, huge and velvety, fluttered round the strings of coloured lights. They were poor students who normally had cottage pie and chips. Pope said, 'I'm on expenses, don't worry.' Jacob ordered steak and Eloise ordered Wye salmon and hollandaise sauce. They chuckled happily: they longed with a deep and passionate longing to be one day on expenses themselves. Pope offered Jacob cider or a pint of real ale, but on this occasion Jacob didn't have any objection to sharing a bottle of claret.

They asked, eventually, about Lizzie's illness.

'Bill says she has to stay in hospital for tests . . .'

'Yes. Also, her feet were badly cut.'

'Does she still think she's . . . well . . .' Eloise looked embarrassed.

'A reincarnation,' said Jacob bluntly.

'No,' said Pope. 'No, I don't think so.'

'What was it all about then?'

'It seems to be a form of epilepsy,' said Pope. 'Localised epileptic focus in the temporal lobe, to be technical.'

They told him there'd been a reporter from the *Sun* out at the dig earlier, showing an interest in their Iron Age remains, quite fascinated by the similarities to the excavations at Croft Ambrey, and only casually asking if anyone had a photograph of Lizzie, preferably sunbathing in the nude.

Later, he drove them back to the camp: up the narrow road to the stile and the sign saying ANCIENT MONUMENT. He watched them trek over a large field, through the clumps of gorse and hawthorn, towards the ramparts.

The sky was black and thick, though occasionally there were flickering white lights to the far north, like the end of the reel of an old movie. The aurora borealis: far earlier in the year than usual – far further south than usual – something else for the newspapers to get excited about.

For a split second a ripple of white luminescence lit Eloise and Jacob, two tiny figures climbing over the southern rampart of the fort.

He tried to use his mobile phone, to check on Lizzie at the hospital, but couldn't get through – the high-energy atomic particles in the sky, fanned by the solar wind, were affecting terrestrial magnetism and interfering with radio transmissions. He drove down to the Hay-on-Wye road, meaning to turn right towards Hereford, back to the Green Dragon Hotel, but on impulse, without conscious thought, found himself driving back towards Newbridge, and turning up the track to the Church of St Michael.

The track ended. He pulled up and sat in his car, looking at the dark shape of the church, the trees.

Was the soil here acidic, as it was over much of the fort? Did everything here dissolve, perish? Was everything in the centre of the sacred circle, beneath the church's foundations, crumbled to dust? Or did the tokens still remain – the red clay to symbolise blood, the ox-head insignia, the skull drinking cups inset with precious stones, the human heads embalmed in cedar oil?

Did they lie here, still, in this sacred ground? Here in the place of the Magi, those intermediaries between this world and the next? Those guardians of the Underworld?

He left the car. A curtain of white light fell from the sky, over the glade, then was gone.

Deep darkness inside the church. He felt his way towards the east window. The franklin's tomb was a dim paleness by the altar. He spread his coat on the Victorian tiles, cool to the touch, and lay down, and put his hand on the frieze of alabaster flowers.

303

Quantum mechanical theory allows not only retrocognition, of the past, but precognition, of the future.

Why was this suddenly bothering him so, eating away at the back of his mind?

What was he doing here? *Pasiphae* was shut down, there was no conduit to be opened. If he dreamed of the franklin that would be all that it would be: a dream.

There was a scent – a sweet scent overlaying the must of age. It was the lilies, he thought – but the lilies were no longer in the church. It was curious: his mind, his brain, was associating the scent of lilies with this place.

There was another smell.

It was elusive; strange but familiar.

Roses.

Another scent.

He took his hand from the alabaster and sat up, sweat pouring down his face, overcome by an overwhelming feeling of nausea.

His phone was bleeping. He flicked it open.

Martha said, 'I've been trying to raise you for an hour. She went into epileptic coma at nine forty-five. Grand mal but without the usual convulsions. Naseby's going to operate. He's got infrascan on line from Berkeley.'

A pause.

'Can you hear me, Charles? He's going to operate. He's going to pump some kind of quinal barbitone sodium and then operate.'

Next to Pope was the dim white of alabaster: above him the painted plaster face of the franklin was lost in darkness.

They were going to use a knife to exorcise a ghost.

'Charles?'

'Yes.'

The smell again, sudden, strong and nauseating.

'Charles, are you OK?'

Roses and something else – something that smothered his consciousness, his power to think, to reason.

The stench of blood.

'Charles, listen carefully, I want you to tell me exactly where you are . . .'

Blood and roses. They were the twin themes of the Middle Ages.

Blood and roses, violence and romance, disputations between hope and despair, cruelty and chivalry. *La Belle Dame Sans Merci*, a woman who should have been full of pity but who was pitiless, had held fifteenth-century knights in thrall.

The franklin had been buried like a knight.

He looked up, up into the darkness.

Charles, tell me where you are!

From somewhere a bell, tolling the hour.

Sweat ran down into his eyes.

'Kidwelly and Llanbadarn stand firm,' said a voice, 'and there is a franklin who would rescue the nuns of Dore.'

Pasiphae was enabled. He knew it, knew it for a certainty. *Pasiphae* was running and the channels to the past were open and stronger than they had ever been.

'My Lord Bishop has sent to them that they should go to the nuns at Hereford but they would not go . . .'

His mobile fell from his fingers.

Black tendrils were licking round the edges of his brain, tendrils that whipped back only to come again, and again. He dug his hand into the alabaster flowers and felt blood spurt over the white roses.

Pasiphae was enabled. Programs were running. Lizzie Draude's mind was now the critical part of the chain, the DNA of her brain genes moulded and shaped, the synapses between her nerve cells modified, the complex molecules of ribonucleic acid adapted. The logic gates were breached. *Pasiphae* was enabled and the black tendrils of past thoughts were powerful enough to overcome a living, conscious brain.

Quantum mechanical theory allows not only retrocognition, of the past . . .

Yes, of course! Of course! Now he understood why Lizzie Draude had been summoned, night after night, to the franklin's tomb.

. . . but precognition, of the future.

Now he knew the purpose.

'My lord, there is a franklin,' said the voice again, this time stronger, echoing round his skull, 'who would rescue the nuns of Dore.'

34

Shrewsbury

He was in a great hall where torches lit a canopy emblazoned with the royal arms, and the air was filled with the smell of burning sandalwood and the sweat of unwashed monks. Voices echoed and tumbled around him – cries for help: from Beaumaris to Bala, from Pembroke in the far west (outside the principality, but that would not stop the rebels) to Ruthin in the north – poor sad Ruthin, half burned to the ground only two years ago.

'At least the castles of the English lordship stand firm!'

'Harlech is under siege. The French are landed . . .'

Prince Hal was a lad for the wenches, they said – a lad who liked to spend his evenings with drunken knights that nobody had heard of. But he sat now in the Great Hall of Shrewsbury Castle as sweating riders brought in news of French landings, of settlements burned, of Glyn Dŵr – Glyn Dŵr, the lawyer squire who had famously pranced his way up to the Scottish campaign with a scarlet flamingo feather in his helm! Glyn Dŵr the miserable petty lord of a dozen poor estates! Glyn Dŵr who was now proclaimed Prince of Wales!

Another rider – one of the king's messengers who sped across the principality on fast horses, without escort, relying on their speed and wit to outflank trouble.

Mortimer was defeated.

There was a silence in the hall when that news was whispered.

Mortimer, the great Marcher lord, with an army of eight thousand men, had been defeated by Glyn Dŵr and Rhys-ap-Gethin in the valley of the Lugg.

'All Herefordshire,' said an adviser calmly, 'is now open to the rebels.'

Another said, 'The false Welsh nation should be utterly destroyed.'

'To business,' said the prince, the boy of fourteen, sharply. 'What is next?'

The monks sat in long rows, wearily copying orders while the prince's intelligence staff tried to point out the Valley of Dovey's distance from Llanbadarn to soldiers who could not write their names. And the torches burned into the night. And royal messengers sped south to Ludlow and Hereford, east to York and to London.

Three armies would be raised. They would attack Wales from Chester, from Shrewsbury, from Hereford.

The monks toiled at copying their orders.

'My lord, what's next . . .'

'Sir, there is a franklin who would rescue the nuns of Dore.'

Toke moved forward towards the dais.

'You have made a vow?' said the prince abruptly.

Toke nodded.

The men round the dais stared at him thoughtfully. Many great kings, in their time, had made vows – generally to recover Jerusalem – and the country had paid dearly for them. But a vow was a great matter. Once taken, a man might not rest until it was fulfilled. Men were commonly to be seen hobbling along the great roads of the kingdom – Watling Street, Iknield, Fosse – men who had perhaps vowed to visit the hundred shrines of the most holy relics. A man might make a vow one drunken night in a warm tavern and find himself a beggar on the cold wet roads for ten years.

'Aye,' said the drunk knight, 'a vow to strip the nuns all naked.'

No one laughed. Men who had made vows had their own compact with God. The knight, one of the prince's tavern companions, looked uneasy.

'I have vowed,' said Toke, 'that I will save them.'

A voice: 'Glyn Dŵr will not harm nuns.'

Another voice: 'He burned the abbey at Cwmhir.'

'Anyway, it's not Glyn Dŵr, it is Rhys the Black's rabble' – a weary spy, forty-eight hours without sleep – 'French pirates, Yorkshiremen sent by Bugger Scrope, none of them paid for twelve months.'

Toke said, 'I have twenty mounted archers, my lord, in my service, but would hire twenty more from the commissariat.'

'If we send twenty mounted archers,' said the voice of the commissariat, startled, 'to every house of women in danger of being raped by Frenchmen there'll not be a solider nor nag left in Shrewsbury.'

'Get the nuns of Dore to Hereford. Move swiftly,' said the prince in a firm clear voice. His own father was haunted by guilt for the death of King Richard, and had vowed a crusade of atonement if God would grant peace in his kingdom. 'Twenty archers of my guard, but I say that by Blackbeard or Whitebeard you will bring them back within the week or pay a price. You are?'

'William Toke.'

'Master Toke. God go with you.'

The franklin bowed.

Outside, the commissariat made him pay dearly for his archers: a rate of a shilling a day, and he was to provide their food, shelter and mounts. Another gave him a proclamation, wet still with ink, the fiftieth or sixtieth turned out that night by the monks.

Owinus de Glendordy with others diverse, his rebels and traitors, disabled and attainted by the authority of the High court of Parilaiment, of whom many be known for open murders, advowterers, and extortioners . . .

It was almost midnight. He arranged for mounts and food, for arrows from the arsenal – eight hundred arrows, tipped with peacock, Ware had insisted. Each arrow cost a mark, which was scandalous, and each archer could shoot twelve in a minute, which meant he was taking less than two minutes' supply. He assigned the freehold of his manors at Kingsland and Aston to cover the cost of the arrows and the archers' equipment: their iron caps and swords and daggers, their mounts – two for each man. A treasury official was pressing a drink into his hands, talking smoothly as the commission was made out.

'What's your income, man? Forty? Fifty? There's many a knight with less than forty pounds a year . . .' He was shrewd; he guessed Toke's income at more than fifty pounds a year; he had heard, perhaps, of the Genoese bark.

'It would greatly please the king were men of substance such as yourself to take up their responsibility . . . Sir William Toke, say, for four hundred marks?'

Toke knew he could be a knight for two hundred marks, if he so chose. The king was desperate for money.

It was nearly one in the morning. The monks were filing out of the castle, off to say their prayers. In the outer keep horsemen were eating from a cook's stall; a young officer and his troop, prepared to escort a train of wagons to Hereford. Flesshe was with them, drinking wine from a vintner's tent.

Toke called to him. They left the castle. A gaggle of the ladies of the prince's court, who should have been asleep in their chambers, watched them from the chapel windows. They pointed admiringly at the franklin who would go rescue the nuns of Dore.

They were out of Shrewsbury an hour before dawn. They went down the Roman road, through Stretton, past the great abandoned fortress of Caradoc. Twenty of Toke's own retainers and hired men, and twenty mounted archers of Prince Hal.

The manor of Minton was packed with folk from the countryside, their cows herded inside the yard, penned against the wall. At Stokesay they rested for ten minutes and changed a horse that had gone lame. Then they were again on the road, the Roman road that was now no more than a track by Clungunford to Leintwardine. They reached Wigmore and found the drawbridge up and the bailey a wailing, arguing mass of tenantry. Mortimer's steward fell on them with relief. 'Ten thousand men are marching through the hills from Pilleth,' he said, thinking they had come to aid him. 'They're burning every village, every house.'

'Are they south of here? Are they at Dore?'

The steward knew nothing of Dore. The rebels had taken the great Mortimer, the Lord of Wigmore, and the world was turned upside down.

They watered their horses sparingly and left by the sally port.

Dawn.

As they went towards Kington they watched for men on the hills; when they forded the Lugg they looked for dead bodies of Mortimer's men in the fast-flowing river. At Pentre Jack they saw blue smoke in the sky over Hay.

They crossed the Wye near Stowe. The bitter cold water was up to their chests, their horses half walking, half swimming, the archers holding their bows over their heads. Further up the river herons dived, then soared with fish in their beaks, droplets of water dropping like diamonds in the sun. It was a bright May morning, the hillsides creamy with hawthorn blossom, the air scented with the first cuts of grass.

They rode on, south towards the valley of Dore.

A shout: there were men ahead of them, on the hills.

Toke shaded his eyes. He saw a long spur of a hill ridge and the ramparts of an ancient fortress.

As he watched there was the flash of swords, perhaps of armour.

An archer, a captain of the prince's guard, said, 'Too late.'

Too late, too late.

He was outside the church, out in the grove. Someone was pulling him, helping him, telling him to fight the dark powers that overwhelmed him.

But it was far, far too late.

A woman's voice: *I adjure thee, thou ancient serpent, by the Judge of the living and the dead* . . .

The sky was filled with streamers of white light – with curtains, fans, and consuming flames. A wind swayed the oak trees so that tendrils of mistletoe trailed back and forth, and it seemed to Pope that thoughts, ideas, emotions were abroad that went back far beyond the time of the franklin.

Yes, retrocognition and precognition were two sides to the quantum coin. Why had he not realised what it meant?

O God Creator and Defender of the human race. Who has formed man in thine image . . .

He knelt at the stream and dashed water on his face and tasted blood, and lifted a handful of water and saw his fingers stained black with blood as the thick liquid ran through them.

Look down with pity upon this thy servant . . .

His head was borne down with heaviness. There was a terrible weight on his shoulders. He was being pulled back into the church.

For the ancient adversary, the arch-enemy of the earth, enshrouds him in shuddering fear . . .

The wind blew in a sudden gust: white banners of light swooped over the tall oaks.

A man's voice, speaking loudly and urgently: *The majesty of Christ commands thee, God the Father commands thee, the Holy Spirit commands thee, the mystery of the Cross commands thee.*

He said, 'Whoever you are, you must take me, now, to Bryn Llandoth,' but his voice was not heard, and the rustling trees around him faded away as black tendrils coiled round his mind, and pulled him gently back, back to the church, back to the franklin's tomb.

35

Bryn Llandoth Hospital

Sluder came out and said, 'Where's Charlie?'

'I don't know. His phone keeps breaking up.'

Sluder was nervous and excited. 'Charlie ought to be here.'

'If he was he'd probably kill you.'

He said, 'Shit, he's a physicist not a medic,' and went back into the observation gallery.

Martha stood and hesitated. She had been able to hear Pope's breathing: heavy, laboured – oh Christ, this had been coming, she told herself, looking out of the window at branches tossing in the hot wind, at the sky rippling with white light. Like Koenig in Utah, like the air traffic controller in Paris, like the computer operative in Alaska, the market maker in Tokyo. Pope had spent too many hours gazing into the crystal ball; he'd finally been trapped by the necromancer.

Sluder's head poked out of the gallery: 'They're getting ready to take a piece out of her skull.'

'Jesus, Sluder, do you have to be so fucking crude?'

She could hear a high-pitched whine like a dentist's drill, smell the burning bone – but she knew her senses played her false: she could hear and smell nothing from beyond the thick rubber doors of the theatre.

'He'll kill you, Larry. He'll kill you when he knows.'

'She signed the consent forms. Honey, this guy is the best neurosurgeon in England.'

'When he finds out that *Pasiphae* is back on, he will tear you to bits.'

His face creased in disgust. He went back into the gallery.

Martha punched Pope's number into her phone.

The number you have dialled is unobtainable.

She could smell something sweet, cloying. A vase of lilies stood by her, incongruously, on a window ledge. Lizzie had wanted them in the operating theatre and had held them tight as the nurse injected her with Pentothal. They had taken them from her nerveless hands as the trolley was wheeled along the shining corridors.

The number you have dialled is—

She turned and went into the gallery.

It had three monitors, a computer terminal, and several phones. Sluder was on one phone, talking either to Berkeley or Option Red in Iowa. Through the tinted glass she could see the operating table. Lizzie lay on it, covered in white shrouds. Two surgeons stood on either side of her, their faces masked.

'Why is her head covered?'

'Sterile sheets,' said Sluder, putting the phone down. 'She's cocooned in sterile sheets. They just have a small opening to work through.'

'Can she breathe?'

'Well of course she can breathe. See the tube, the endotracheal tube? That's delivering anaesthetic up her nose. I got them to give me copies of the consent forms,' he whispered, showing her. 'And that guy in there, Naseby, is the best neurosurgeon there is.'

'Fuck off.'

'Will you stop saying that? Will you please stop saying that?'

A tube was being connected to Lizzie's arm from a bottle of clear liquid.

'Why the drip?'

'It's going to take several hours. She'll lose a lot of fluid. Bones bleed.'

'Bones do what?'

'They bleed, honey. So do blood vessels on the surface of the brain.'

He'd been at his laptop again, reading his medical encyclopaedia.

A voice said: 'Is the camera on?'

In front of her a television monitor came alive. The camera was pointing to a corner of the theatre. It slowly swivelled, picked up in sudden focus a nurse's eyes: their intensity. It moved quickly away. It came down over the operating table: over the small neat opening in the white sheet.

Naseby said, 'Good morning, Berkeley.'

In one hand he held a slim, shining knife. A wire trailed from it, to a power point over the operating table. 'For laymen watching, I intend to make a scalp flap by cutting away the skin . . .'

Martha stared at the monitor, fascinated, as the knife sliced gently and skin was peeled back.

'It's called a diathermy knife,' whispered Sluder. 'It's real neat.'

Bone was cut and bent. Martha would have sworn that bone could not bend, but when three sides of the opening had been cut, and a fracture made along the crease, she saw with her own eyes the bone bent back. It revealed soft pink flesh covered by a glistening membrane.

A voice, soft, intimate: Mitch Lean the neurophysiologist. 'We are now ready to attach the first of the sensors.'

Naseby's assistant was using forceps to pick up a tiny silver disc. A thin wire glinted in the bright light.

'At half past nine tonight,' said Naseby, 'we saw a sudden increase in brain activity followed by excessive and synchronous nerve-cell discharges compatible with grand-mal epilepsy. There was the loss of consciousness that goes with it.'

His voice was matter-of-fact, relaxed. 'In view of the negative CAT scan and the failure of drugs like Epilim to control the fits, a decision was made to operate. The EEG indicated the localised epileptic focus to be in the right temporal lobe.'

Martha said suddenly, 'Perhaps it's going to be all right.'

'Sure it's going to be OK, honey,' said Sluder comfortingly. 'Everything's going to be just fine.'

Naseby said, 'The CAT scan, by the way, shows Lizzie's head to be of normal size, with a two-inch thickness of brain tissue between the ventricles and the cortical surface.'

'Scanners in place,' said a quiet voice, not from the operating theatre but from across the Atlantic.

Naseby and his assistant were putting the silvery sensors, one by one, on Lizzie's exposed brain.

'A positron emission tomography scan was carried out on the patient earlier this evening,' said Naseby. 'Again, for those listening and watching who are laymen, positron emission tomography measures blood flow to brain cells, and is normally used as simply a measure of brain activity. However, research at the Good Samaritans

Regional Medical Center in Phoenix suggests that certain brain cells become active when they retrieve memories. The theory is that true memory will involve more activity as it calls up sensory perceptions like smell and touch. Lizzie's brain was scanned and at the same time she was asked about supposed-memories previously recalled during hypnotic regression. The indication was that stored memories were not – I repeat not – being retrieved. In other words that the things she described were fantasies of her mind, perceptual illusions common in partial epilepsy with complex symptoms.'

'You hear that?' said Sluder. 'You hear what the guy said? Jesus, I wish Charlie was here now.'

'Alternatively,' Naseby went on, 'it could indicate that the patient's supposed-memories were coming from an external source. Those of you who have an interest in theories connected with morphic fields will no doubt draw your own conclusions.'

The camera zoomed gently down over Lizzie's opened skull.

'For my part,' Naseby said drily, 'I would not like to say where in the brain memory is stored. If anybody finds it, please let me know.'

On the television monitor: Lizzie's brain. Blood running like dye through the protective fluid.

Sluder said, 'It feels nothing. You can take slices out of it, while the patient's still conscious, and they don't feel a thing. Nobody understands the brain. There was a guy with an IQ of around a hundred and thirty, but when they did a scan they found his brain was the size of a peanut.'

Surgical instruments delicately placed electrodes on the pink flesh.

'The quantum computer is on line,' said an American voice through the speaker, slightly metallic. 'Option Red is now running.'

'This is it,' said Sluder, with repressed excitement. 'This is crunch time.'

A jagged line across the computer screen. A monitor flashed to life. A turbo flickered on the computer.

Naseby: 'Those who are not convinced by theories involving morphic resonance or interference to the brain on a quantum level will note that Lizzie has shown the following classic symptoms associated with temporal-lobe simple partial seizure. She has described epigastric sensations, hallucinations of smell, taste, and vision, and distortions of perception, in particular feelings of déjà vu. She has described sexual sensations. She has experienced severe automatism in which she ran into a wood while responding to a hallucination. During this attack she suffered a massive emotional seizure, the predominant feelings being of fear and panic. Esoteric explanations are more interesting, of course, and not to be dismissed, but the more mundane explanation may prove adequate at the end of the day. We are now using the sensors to localise the focus of electrical activity. Having done so we will remove the electrodes, and surgically excise the area of the focus.'

'What he means,' said Sluder, 'is that he'll cut it out.'

Martha said, 'I'm going to see if I can raise Charles.'

'Yeah, you do that,' said Sluder absently: Pope was yesterday's problem.

A voice from Iowa: 'OK, we have the pictures. We have direct feed into Option Red.'

Martha stared as computer-enhanced brain images appeared on the third screen: information beamed across the Atlantic and then fed back in different forms.

Dark red spots, spreading then contracting.

'This is the way to do it,' said Sluder. 'This is common sense. We can analyse half a million sub-molecular actions every second on Option Red. I thought you were going to phone Charlie?'

The camera was descending gently, going in close. The electrodes sat, spring-loaded, on Lizzie's brain. Blood welled up and ran in rivulets down the side of her shaved skull. Glancing away, looking through the glass, Martha could see a nurse quietly replace the blood-soaked wadding.

'I said,' said Sluder, 'aren't you going to—'

'OK, OK, I'm going.'

His phone rang out but he did not answer. She called the camp, and spoke to Bill Hastings. She said, 'Is Andrew there?' and was suddenly aware that Andrew ought to have been at Bryn Llandoth, ought to have been told that the operation was going ahead.

Bill Hastings said tensely, 'Is there a problem?'

'No, nothing to alarm him.'

'Thank Christ . . .'

'I'm at the hospital, at Bryn Llandoth. Can you tell him they're operating, now, on Lizzie? Tell him there's nothing to worry about, but he ought to know. And can somebody go down and look in the church?'

'What?'

'Dr Pope was going there earlier. I've been trying to get hold of him but his mobile's not answering and he isn't at his hotel.'

There was muttering on the other end of the line.

Bill Hastings said, 'Do you know what time it is?'

'Yeah, it's exactly twenty-two minutes past one' – Jesus, where did this boy come from, Kansas? – 'I think he might have had an accident of some kind.'

The door to the gallery opened.

Sluder said, 'Something's happening.'

Back inside the gallery a voice from Option Red in Iowa could be heard from the speaker: 'What is this we are getting? Please tell me what we are now getting.'

Mitch Lean, suddenly tense: 'There's a change. There is a change to deltas with edges. We now have ten-fourteen hertz spike activity in all leads.'

Naseby looked up, his eyes startled over his mask.

She was climbing up through the holly, the thick friendly holly, while one of the four knights of Llanddy shouted at her to climb faster. 'Quickly, quickly!' screamed the fat knight who had sworn a sacred oath (sworn it a week ago when Glyn Dŵr was thought to be many miles away beyond the northern mountains) to preserve the lives and honour of the nuns of Dore.

'Faster! Faster!'

She remembered the franklin telling her of knights who had sworn to protect King Richard's mother, and had stood smiling as Jack Straw's men pinched her royal breasts. Would the four knights of Llanddy stand and smile as Glyn Dŵr's soldiers pinched the breasts of the nuns of Dore? And would Dame Moose, sweet Margaret Moose (who hated men but went so obediently to bed with the abbess) also have her breasts pinched?

They struggled up the hillside. The servants who should have helped them had fled – all but the gardener who had got Agnes

Poney with child. They were higher now. She could see fires burning in the night – from Hay and Clyro in the west, to Eardisley in the north. Dame Alice was whimpering – she who was an ap Tudor of Clorach, cousin to an ap Tudor of Erddreiniog, who sang the songs of Owain – *the ever-conquering son of Gruffydd Vychan, the brave bulwark, the graceful and liberal possessor of the vale of Dyfrdwy, which was a great and rapid stream* – but she was whimpering with fear now that the conquering Welshmen were close.

Why was that? Why did she fear the man she had sung about for so long?

The Abbess Elizabeth was ahead of them, on the track, arguing with one of the knights of Llanddy. This knight was mounted and was shouting that they should have flown to Hereford, to the safety of the city walls. It was strange to see a knight sit his horse and shout. The abbess said proudly, 'The Lord Owain will not harm the hair on a nun's head' – but perhaps, thought Eleanor, the knight was not thinking about the nuns' heads.

'To Hereford!' he was shouting, pointing with his arm, his mail rattling on his breastplate like pebbles: but they all knew that it was too late.

Too late, too late. The sky was red over Hay. A ribbon of red ran down the valley. They were beacons of fire now between Dore and Hereford.

The knight was looking for a reason to desert them: to gallop round the fires and carry the news to Hereford's city walls. 'I will fetch help,' he cried, 'I will go to my Lord Scudamore at Grosmont—'

His voice was drowned in cries of fear and anger.

From below, in the valley, tongues of flame leaped from the mill, from the new granary. The nunnery roof was ablaze.

The knight spurred his mount upwards, through the trees towards the fortress.

Upwards they went. There was rustling in the trees, in the darkness. One of the foot knights screamed, and then was gone – plucked from the path by black shadows, by demons. Then they were hurrying through the ancient gates of the fort: through the blackened stumps that had been there since time out of mind, past the sheep hurdles. Villagers were here from a dozen English enclaves: Westbrook and

319

Middlewood and Bonny Lands – confused Welsh and English from Mynydd-brith and Pen-henllan, who had watched the burning of Hay. In the centre of the camp women and children protected the livestock. The men and boys were on the ramparts. They were armed only with staves and daggers. But even so the rebels, it was thought, would leave them be.

The Welsh attacked before dawn.

It had been a mistake to have brought the cattle, the hens and ducks, the sheep. The remaining three knights of Llanddy had wanted to drive out the beasts – to give them as peace offerings to the rebels – but the villagers had refused.

Now, in the darkness before first light, the Welsh attacked. In King Arthur's time a thousand warriors would have lined the wooden palisades: now the palisades were gone. There were sixty village men at most, and three knights of Llanddy.

The attack petered out. Their lives, cried out a voice, amused, for five pounds. Another voice said ten pounds. Ten pounds, and the cattle and sheep. The Abbess Elizabeth called out that she was the Abbess of Dore, a good friend of Glyn Dŵr, of the Lord Owain. The voice replied that in such case she should pay twenty pounds and – said another voice – five naked nuns.

'What was that?' cried Sister Moose, that slender, blue-eyed child. 'What was that he said?'

Dame Alice whimpered. Agnes Poney, in child to the gardener, clutched openly at her lover. Dame Blod looked stoic.

A French voice called out.

A knight of Llanddy said: 'It is the pirate, Jean d'Espagne.'

Eleanor sat in the darkness and thought how she would have swooned, once, over a French pirate. But the French were a strange people. Queen Isabelle ate her dinner at nine o'clock in the morning. The obedient housewife of Paris was taught: *Lever à cinq, diner à neuf, souper à cinq, coucher à neuf.* Perhaps she should recite it to the pirate. But did pirates care anything for the rules that governed a young wife of Paris? To be a pirate was to defy dinnertimes.

She laughed.

Margaret Moose, trembling, said, 'What is it?'

'Nothing.'

'The Mother of Christ protect us.'

320

She was looking hither and thither for the abbess, but the abbess was with the men.

Dawn. The nuns looked south, to the morning light over the plain of Hereford. Eleanor looked out to the north, to the distant Wye, to the Shropshire hills.

A child screamed.

Men were on the western ramparts, grey figures in the half-light.

The villagers rushed to fight them off.

A knight of Llanddy stood by Eleanor, his ashen face sweating in the cold. If he did not fight – Eleanor knew he was thinking – the Welsh might only beat him and steal his armour. If he raised his sword they would surely kill him.

Eleanor looked down over the eastern battlement. Men were coming slowly up through the trees, through a vast haze of bluebells. Twenty, thirty men, perhaps. She looked again to the north, to the track from Ludlow. The crisp dawn air was spiced with the scent of hawthorn blossom.

At her side the knight of Llanddy prayed out loud.

Then he was there no longer.

She looked down at the men climbing towards her through the bluebells, through the fresh greenwood. She ventured a smile as they came jumping over the ramparts.

The Abbess Elizabeth cried out, once, horribly, as her gown was thrust back over her head (to hide her ugly mug, said a soldier). Dame Alice was still singing the ode to Owain of the Shining Helm as she was raped. Her song suddenly ceased, which was a blessing.

The knight of Llanddy – the one on horseback who would have flown to Hereford or to Grosmont – was lying with his throat cut. His horse was dead beside him. Men were carefully unlacing its armour while others sliced into its steaming meat. A boy held up its surcoat, embroidered with the knight's heraldic arms. He danced round with it, then threw it down. It was the chain mail, the enamelled stirrups, that were of value.

Other soldiers were staggering, drunk, through the gap in the ramparts. They were looking round for something to steal, for bodies to be picked clean. Others were carefully examining the rampart walls, seeking pockets of new-dug earth where the villagers might have buried their silver.

A man was playing a flute, stolen from the nunnery.

A fire had been lit, blue smoke rising in the still, sweet May morning.

Anne Nores was moaning, a high-pitched moan that would get her throat cut if she wasn't careful, thought Eleanor, who was crouched with three of the oldest nuns, keeping her head down in prayer, keeping as still as she could.

Why wasn't Anne Nores quiet?

Why would she attract attention?

Ah . . . a man turned, saw Eleanor with the corner of his eyes (why had she not kept her head down?), dropped the meat he was eating, and came towards her.

Behind him came another man: a boy really.

Although she had vowed to make no noise, she screamed.

But it was little different, in the event, from Young Manny under a French quilt at Sonning, with the child-queen urging him on; little different from the archer whose name she had now forgotten, who had promised to keep her warm on a cold February night.

Later, as she lay against the grass rampart, her eyes again fixed on the track from the north, she saw horsemen moving rapidly towards the village – too rapidly for men in armour. As they galloped closer, through the fields by the Dore River, she saw that there were perhaps forty of them.

'It is the Lord Owain come to save us, to save us from the French,' said Dame Alice, daughter of Gwilyn ap Tudor of Clorach, blood congealed on her lips.

But it was, thought Eleanor, tears in her eyes – for she had seen his beaver coat – a greater lord than Owain. She rested her head on the cold green grass. When she looked again the riders were through the village and moving up the hillside. Men below the rampart were peering down through the trees, shouting to each other. She could see an archer crouched in the sprouting bracken, his bow pulled taut. As the riders came up through the trees he shot his arrow, but before he could take up another a horseman was on him, leaning down and stabbing him through the chest.

'That was Davey,' thought Eleanor to herself, proudly.

The riders disappeared round the side of the ramparts, searching for the entrance to the fort.

She had crawled under a sack, though the men had seen the place to which she had crawled, had idly watched and thought she was as well under the sack as anywhere until they had eaten and drunk and wanted her again. Twice they had been over and kicked her to make sure she was still there.

She was under the sack on the cold grass, her head throbbing, her body burning.

Agnes Poney was dead. God only knew what of. Shame perhaps. Or perhaps her heart had just stopped beating. No more games of Hot Cockles for Dame Agnes, thought Eleanor, shivering violently; no more tied hands, no more little slaps to make her fingers burn.

She had wriggled, with her sack, to the edge of the rampart. Soon she would be saved.

A pain shot through her back.

Two men. One of them had kicked her. The other leaned down to grab her by the hair. She tried to wriggle away but she had no strength. A raised arm, black against the grey morning. It came down.

A nurse cried out in shock.

It was heard through the plate glass as well as through the speakers.

'Christ,' said Sluder. 'Oh Christ, look at that.'

Blood was seeping up through the sterile white sheets.

Naseby looked up at the theatre sister. She moved forward and with a gloved hand raised a sheet.

On the television screen, Lizzie's naked body. Her arm, suffused with blood.

Naseby and the assistant surgeon, motionless, staring down.

Martha said, quietly, 'It's stigmata.'

'What?' – Sluder.

'Stigmata of the mind. Something has happened to her, something so terrible that it has had a physical manifestation.'

The sheet dropped.

Naseby: 'Remove the electrodes.'

A voice from Berkeley: 'If you take off the electrodes you will kill the programme.'

'Option Red is active,' said the voice from Iowa, cutting in. 'Option Red is getting something.'

323

'Her blood pressure is rising,' said the anaesthetist. 'She is regaining consciousness. She is now beginning to feel pain.'

Naseby said crisply, 'We are removing the electrodes. We are closing up and coming out.'

Blood trickled down the rampart, down through the daisies. She opened her eyes and blinked for a few moments, smiled faintly, and said, 'Page.'

In two years how he had grown! His face was covered in angry spots from eating sweet pastry and goosefat, a boy's besetting sin.

She said, 'Oh, page!'

He stared down at her in horror.

She said, 'Help me.'

He knelt by her. A moment later, above her, was the franklin. The same look of deep melancholy on his face, the same eyes under the beaver hat. She tried to smile.

He said: 'Who did this?'

Eleanor tried, but could not speak.

Flesshe was sobbing.

Again the franklin said, 'Who did this?'

But it was a rhetorical question. Murder, ravishment, robbery. In Langland's verse the Petition of Peace had cried out against the rapacity of king's officers who broke into farms, raped the women, took wheat from the granary and left in payment a tally on the king's exchequer.

He took off his fur coat and knelt and wrapped it round her.

Like Flesshe, he was crying.

Ware came running over. He said, 'There's a hundred or more of the bastards coming up the hill.'

Toke said, 'Do we hold any of them alive?'

Ware said, 'A score maybe.'

They were huddled by the remains of the fire, either wounded or too drunk to run away.

Toke said, 'Kill them.'

A while later, again opening her eyes, Eleanor said, 'Beware of Wales, Christ Jesus must us keep, that it make not our child's child to weep!'

And later again, 'Sir, will you be content with my poor person?'

Toke, sitting holding her, said, 'Aye.'

'Then I am the merriest maiden on ground.'

Then she laughed and cried.

Ware said, 'Sir . . .'

Toke gently laid her down. Two of the nuns, Margaret Moose and Dame Katherine, were brought to her. The Abbess Elizabeth was dead. She had killed herself, said Margaret Moose. Dame Alice had gone mad: but Dame Alice had always been mad.

All on a fine May morning, Eleanor thought, staring up at the blue, blue sky.

'We are still getting something, England. The signal is very powerful. Is the geoscanner still in place?'

On the screen, on the link from Iowa, a green fuzz.

Pixels forming, dissolving, reforming.

'I repeat, is the geoscanner still in place, England? Are the electrodes still in place?'

'The electrodes are removed.'

'Then what the hell am I getting here?'

Naseby and his assistant were working at speed, bending back the bone, covering the flesh of the brain. The anaesthetist quickly removed the endotracheal tube.

Lizzie's arm moved.

'Hold her!'

Her eyelids fluttered.

The anaesthetist said, 'She's coming round. I'll try to control it.'

Mitch Lean: 'I have deltas again, deltas with spikes. I don't understand this—'

'The screen—' a nurse.

The green fuzz forming and reforming.

Two eyes stared out: ironic, inquisitive, cold.

The English archers did not draw back the arrow, as the French did, but held their right hand at rest upon the nerve, and pressed the whole weight of their bodies into the horns of the bow. Their farthest range, to penetrate cloth but not armour, and to kill, was twelve-score paces. The Welsh and French were seventy paces away when Ware said: 'Bend your bow.'

325

When they were fifty paces away he looked at Toke.
Toke held up his arm.
At forty paces he brought it down.

The pixels dissolved. The eyes were gone.

I have seen the past, thought Martha. I have seen the past brought to life. I have seen the dead brought to life. Behind her the door opened. She heard Sluder say, mechanically, 'Charlie, you made it.'

She turned. He stood in the doorway, swaying, his face grey. Behind him, holding him upright, were Andrew and Bill Hastings.

'Retrocognition and precognition,' he said. 'OK? Do you understand me, Martha? If one holds good so does the other. Koenig wasn't just picking up signals from the past. He was picking up things that hadn't yet happened. What this means is . . . what it can only mean is . . .'

But Martha was already on the phone.

Above the Atlantic a ripple ran through *Pasiphae*'s whisper antennae.

36

Key West, Florida

A passenger on the cruise liner *Sun Princess* first caught the missile on video a second after its yellow fireball broke the skin of the ocean. For another second she tracked it upwards, but then its small external jets came into play and she lost it as it snaked down again to within a few metres of sea level, at the same time turning and disappearing in a blur of speed towards Louisiana.

Fifteen seconds later, while the captain of the *Sun Princess* was radioing a furious complaint to the US Coastguard Service, computers in Air Force Combat Command, Virginia were warning that a submarine-launched missile was entering New Orleans air space. The computer also threw up the name of the launch vessel: it was the Russian Odessa-class nuclear submarine *Petersburg* that had been observed leaving Poljarnyi on the Kola Peninsula three weeks previously, and picked up again two days ago cruising down the Virginia coastline.

Another thirty seconds and Moscow was being asked: 'Is the missile armed? What is the target?'

Moscow refused to admit that the *Petersburg* was even in the Atlantic.

The missile had disappeared from radar screens, but was predicted to be somewhere over Baton Rouge, heading into the American heartland. It was profiled as a DM Mark II device similar to the Boeing AGM-86: sophisticated enough to dodge under civilian and most military radar.

Renewed pressure was put on the now panicking and aggressive general on duty at the Frunzenskaja Embankment, the Russian Pentagon.

Was the missile armed? What was the target?

These were the only questions asked, the only questions that mattered.

'The *Petersburg* is in Murmansk . . .' said the Russian.

'The *Petersburg* is not in Murmansk. We know that this is a mistake. We know that your ICBM silos are not active. Tell us the target. Tell us if the missile is armed.'

An Air Force intelligence officer, loudly: 'OK, we have the target. We have the target.'

On his screen was a security flash from the National Security Agency in Chicago.

It warned of a possible missile attack on Wilcox Base, at Fort Huachuca in Arizona.

A clock – known as the Armageddon clock – started to tick over the banked computer terminals of the Combat Command crisis centre.

Assessing the missile's speed and characteristics it showed Impact −17 minutes.

'Is the missile armed? Is the target Arizona? Is the missile armed?'

The Russian general on the Frunzenskaja Embankment was denying that the *Petersburg* existed.

More than half of Arizona's hundred and fifty radio and television stations refused to put out a public warning, fearing that the message was a hoax, and that they would be liable for massive damages resulting from traumas, suicides and road accidents. It was NBC that put out the first public alert, nationwide, at Impact −9 minutes.

In Washington the President was told that detonation of the DM Mark II's single nuclear warhead over Fort Huachuca could be expected to kill some 1,000 military personnel at the base itself (70 senior personnel were expected to survive in the command bunker) and perhaps a further 10,000 in an eleven-mile radius: much depended on how many people took cover from the initial burn-flash, the extent of cloud cover, and how quickly rescue services were able to enter the contaminated zone.

Second-degree burns from the flash would extend to a radius of twenty miles. Radiation and fallout would affect El Paso and Ciudad Juarez within thirty minutes – but unless the wind changed direction, Phoenix and California would not be affected. In answer to the question 'Can't we bring it down?' the President was told that continental US surface-to-air batteries no longer existed (there had been forty squadrons in 1964, now there were none) and the United States had no active anti-ballistic missile system in operation. The President asked about the Safeguard ABM site at Grand Forks, North Dakota, and was told that it had been closed down following the perceived decline in the Soviet threat.

'What about Interceptor Force Command?' asked a presidential aide. He was told that Interceptor command nowadays relied on tactical air units as available.

In Virginia, computers threw up two possible ways to stop the missile. One was a Midox surface-to-air battery being prepared in New Mexico for transfer to Kurdistan: but by Impact −8 it was known that it would take three hours for its missiles to be armed.

The second possibility was to shoot the missile down from the air. There were more than a dozen fighter squadrons along the Russian missile's path: but none of them, Combat Command itself confirmed, were capable of getting armed planes airborne in less than twelve minutes.

There was a query over a training base in South Colorado.

The Armageddon clock said Impact −7.30.

The Colorado training base asked for details of the missile's course and speed and current location and was told that it had been briefly picked up on radar by a Dallas USAF site, at the very periphery of the base's range. At that point it had been heading across the border into New Mexico, using its internal terrain contour navigation system to dodge low beneath commercial radar nets.

At Impact −6 a solitary F16 was ready for take-off from the Colorado base. The pilot had just brought his plane down from an exercise. His F16 was still armed with two live missiles. In the confusion orders were given to refuel the plane − which was down to ten minutes of flying time − then it was realised that there was no need, no point.

At Impact −5 the plane was airborne, the pilot still trying to remember details of the inertial guidance systems of the Russian DM Mark II.

329

With Impact –4 showing on the Armageddon clock, Army Command passed from Maryland HQ to California HQ.

Warnings were now being broadcast on all of Arizona's radio and television stations. In Wilcox Base authorised personnel were hurrying into the command bunker and other personnel were taking cover in the concrete blockhouses and barracks. Many men – most perhaps – still believed they were taking part in an exercise. Only in the last moments, before the command bunker closed, did a small group try to force their way to safety, arguing that as the base's ICBMs were not to be launched there was no reason for named personnel – senior officers, launch crew, and computer technicians – to be given priority. The sentries fired their automatic weapons, killing two men, before themselves retreating into the command centre, pulling the bunker's five-inch-thick steel doors closed behind them.

The pilot of the F16 was reporting 'No contact. No contact.'

From Phoenix's four main hospitals, columns of ambulances, led by police cars, headed eastwards towards the desert, towards the twenty-mile sanitary cordon thrown round Fort Huachuca.

Impact –2.

The Russian missile was coming in, low across the desert east of Albuquerque. Its sensing devices detected its target. Its internal gyroscopes and accelerometers corrected its pitch and velocity; vanes and deflectors carried out the necessary adjustment. It was flying according to plan; it was working smoothly; it was a missile to be proud of.
    At Impact –1.45 it crossed the small town of Duncan and began to climb ready for its detonation at optimum height.
    It was picked up instantly by the F16's radar.

The F16 curled in the sky.
    The two objects – plane and missile – came together at right angles. The pilot activated his aircraft's computerised fire sequence. Its Walleye X missiles were each equipped with an infra-red homing

device and miniature television homing system – but air-to-air combat was, perhaps, the only area of air or sea warfare left where personal human fighting skills still mattered: where only the skill of the operator could place the launching platform so that its missiles killed the target.

This pilot was twenty-one years old, and was still training.

At Impact −1 he fired his first missile. The Russian DM Mark II dodged it with ease. The pilot had no time to reposition himself. Through the clear, pure, Arizona air he could see the Russian nuclear missile's external jets flicker, its nose tilt down.

He fired his remaining Walleye X interceptor.

His eyes flickered to his radar screen. His eyes registered that the Walleye had missed its target.

The Russian DM Mark II had disappeared.

He banked sharply over the Salt River, and looked down for the mushroom cloud.

37

Dore – Utah

The Bishop of Shrewsbury came in January, a cold, cruel month for making visitations, but it had been urged on him as a matter of great piety by John of Thornton, the abbot of Abbey Dore. It was a business that concerned one of the nuns who was living still, after two years, in the ruins of the Dore granary.

His eyes looked over the landscape bleakly. The great field was still abandoned, covered in dry thistles. The hovels burned down by the Welsh and French had not been rebuilt. Half a century of plague, of the Black Death, had ravaged this land as it had ravaged all Europe. But here there was a particular curse. Eadric the Saxon, killed so shockingly by the Normans in 1067, still walked, it was said, through the old woodlands. Poisoned water – said the villeins – ran down the hill from King Arthur's Fort. And here, two years ago, the nuns of Dore had been raped.

When the Welsh rebels had been driven back from Hereford's city walls, the lord who held Dore had moved his peasants to his manor of Newbridge. The village had been deserted. Since then folk claimed to have heard wolves howl in Dore, a cry not heard in a generation, but recognised by every listener.

Last night, in the guest chamber at the abbey, the bishop had stood by the stone casement and listened for the cry of the wolf. A cold air had swept down from Dore, from the blackness of the high valley, but he had heard only the rush of the river, the bark of the dog fox, and the answering scream of the vixen.

The villagers were romancing, as they always did.

But there had been talk of a more dangerous kind. Two women from Eywas Harold had deposed to the abbot that nuns had come to them at night and killed their baby children, and had feasted on their children's flesh or else made unguents from their limbs to anoint broomsticks on which they flew invisibly . . . and the abbot, a wise man, had sent to Dore, and told the three nuns who still lived in the granary ruins (innocently eating mice and berries and wild oats) that they must leave.

Now, up the valley, came the bishop. His cortège passed through the deserted fields, and wound up the track to the parish church. There were a few horses tethered: the lord and his lady of Hardwick; a pony bearing the livery of the lord of Grosmont – not, presumably, the earl himself, but a representative. Villagers from old Dore had come on foot, over the hill from their new dwellings by the Wye. It was the Epiphany of Christ, and the porch was decorated with the glowing red hips of the dog rose, and with bright, brilliant beech leaves. There was mistletoe in the tiny Norman window of the porch: the bishop reflected that in these valleys the old religion survived, and crossed himself.

She knelt by the altar. She was very slender. He looked down on her head and felt a great pity. How old was she? Nineteen? Twenty? He feared that what she intended would drive her mad.

Dame Alice was clearly mad, and sat gibbering in a pen. The third nun, Dame Katherine, stood with a bowed head. The abbess of the convent at Shrewsbury had agreed to take in both these nuns, the mad and the sane, without dowry.

He said to the figure kneeling before him, 'You understand the dangers to the mind and spirit of what you propose?'

'I do.'

The bishop remembered the tales told of the nuns of Dore. Tales of the Abbess Elizabeth, who had kept her bastard girl-child for three years until it died, who strode like a man and swore like a man, and meddled in affairs of state. 'Do you say that King Richard is alive?' the infuriated abbot of Abbey Dore monastery had asked her once, at the time of his famous visitation, and she had replied: 'I do not say that he is alive, but I do say that if he is alive he is the true King of England.'

Oh for a few more men like the Abbess of Dore! Unlike his brother at Hereford, the Bishop of Shrewsbury still nurtured deep unease at the usurpation of the crown. And was Richard, indeed, dead? There were rumours, even now, that he was escaped to Scotland – a former minstrel at his court had found him, it was said, sitting weeping in the kitchen of Donald, Lord of the Isles.

The Abbess Elizabeth was certainly dead. She would sin no more
– and oh, what a sinner she had been! On his visitation the abbott
had found the nuns sleeping two to a bed, the abbess eating alone
with her favourites, and nobody awake to keep the night office. 'The
abbot commands the abbess that she eat at all times in the refectory
and she never to have anyone in bed with her,' the abbot had
thundered after his visit. 'Two scrutineers, without exception senior
nuns, shall be appointed to observe night and day whether all the
nuns come to mass' – but to the Bishop of Shrewsbury he had written
that his command would not be obeyed; that Dore nunnery was a
sink of lasciviousness and treason.

'You will be content,' said the bishop now, 'never again to speak
with the world?'

'I will be content.'

It was this child, according to rumour, that the abbess had taken to
her own bed, in the last days, even when Glyn Dŵr was stealing east
through the valleys from Radnor. He looked down on her slender
shoulders, her hair the colour of ash bark.

'Child?'

She looked up. He saw that her eyes were blue, which was the
colour of consistency. 'You will be content to leave your companions,
to speak to them never again?'

'I will be content.'

She had built a house of wattle, under the oaks. It was guilt,
perhaps. It was remorse. The rape of the nuns, after all, had been a
punishment for their sins.

He hurried through the mass and the remainder of the
examination. A bright January light flooded in through the casements
– illuminating the bright paint on the tomb by the altar, filling the
church with beams of sunshine – but the days were short and it was
a long ride to Leominster. When it was over, and he had found her in
no way hesitant or wavering, but wanting unfailingly the life of an
anchoress, he absolved her, and caused her to be released from the
yoke of obedience.

And speaking clearly she made a new profession before the high
altar.

And after the assent of the common people had been given, she
paused for a second to stare at the new tomb effigy – executed the

335

previous summer by an artist sent from London by command of the king – the plaster face so real, the eyes so vivid, it seemed the dead man only slept.

Then she turned away and was led to the house built on the north side of the church.

There was a young woman of the congregation, a girl richly dressed in a green velvet pelisse lined with fur, who cried out as the anchoress went inside her house of wattle.

But the anchoress did not look back.

'And the door was fastened with locks, and with bars, and with keys. And she was left, as is believed by many, in joy of the Saviour, in peace and quiet of spirit.'

'This is not,' said Pope, looking out over the Green River, over the falling red leaves of autumn, 'a happy ending.'

'Who said you can always have happy endings?'

'I seem to want them more as I grow old. What did she live on?'

'The charity of the common people. And bequests. That was how Lucy Pagetti first got on the trail. A woman in the parish of Middlewood who left two shillings to Dame Margaret Moose, anchoress in the house by the church of St Michael and All Saints.'

'But what of Eleanor?'

'She married a guy called Flesshe.'

'Flesshe?'

'Yeah, and she made the best apple pie in England and they had ten children and lived as happy as can be.'

'Eleanor married a man called Flesshe?'

'Listen. You ready?'

She read: 'In the name of God, amen. Twentieth June in the year of the Lord 1431. I Eleanor de Flesshe, late wife of Thomas son of John Flesshe, with a whole mind make my testament. I bequeath my soul to Almighty God and to our Lady St Mary, and my body to be buried by my lord in the church of Aston. And I bequeath to the mother church of Shrewsbury two shillings, and also I give and bequeath to the high altar of Dore a new towel of four ells.'

He looked down at the tamarisks by the river. 'He died for her,' he said. 'He died for love of her. And she gave him a towel of four ells.'

'Yeah, well, a lot of the world's great love stories end in

anticlimax. At the time the franklin died he was buried with great honour as a true knight. Lucy Pagetti thinks the king and the Prince of Wales might have gotten involved. You know about the Prince of Wales, Prince Hal?'

'I know about Prince Hal.'

'Yeah, but did you know he was only fourteen years old when he was wenching and drinking with Sir John Falstaff and waging war against Owain Glyn Dŵr? They really matured early in those days. Anyway, Lucy came across something in the Shrewsbury archive about Prince Hal paying for the burial, with full honour, of a merchant knight who did great service against the Welsh. That was what the children at Newbridge found, back in 1968 when their teacher took them on a trip to Shrewsbury records office. Somebody told them the merchant knight was believed to be the franklin buried at Dore, and that was what they wrote in their pamphlet.'

'Have you traced a copy?'

'Lucy put an appeal out on the Web, and a former pupil called her back. The woman didn't have a copy, but she remembered it. Then Lucy went looking round the academic nets for Toke's will, as you suggested, couldn't find it, but came across the will of Eleanor de Flesshe. She'd have got there sooner only Aston was part of Shrewsbury diocese at that time, not Lichfield, and she was looking in the Prerogative Court of York instead of the Prerogative Court of Canterbury. Stupid mistake, eh? She's over there now in person, prowling around, and she says she is truly mortified.'

'Eleanor de Flesshe . . .'

'Lucy Pagetti says it was common gentrification of Piggsflesshe,' sand Martha helpfully, 'and indicated a Saxon family moving up in the world.'

'The will doesn't say anything,' he said, 'about ten children and apple pie.'

'You just have to use your imagination.'

A row of helicopters passed over the mesas, over Dinosaur and the Gates of Lodore, heading south down the Arizona state line. They were searching for the Russian missile that had disappeared from the F16's radar. Many Arizonians, according to the tabloid press, believed that it had been 'taken out' by flying saucers; that friendly aliens had saved the world – or at least saved this small, but to its residents important, part of it. The official belief was that the Russian missile's control system must have been affected by the F16's second Walleye X interceptor, causing it to spin off course. It was believed that it could have flown upwards of five hundred miles before crashing somewhere in the desert or mountains.

It was known, now, that it had not been armed with a nuclear warhead. Had it been (the Russians assured their American counterparts on the high-level commission of investigation) it would never have been possible for one crazy weapons engineering officer to authenticate the firing sequence.

They went back to the desert receiving station. Sluder was excited. The Pentagon had given the go-ahead for a *Pasiphae* satellite over the Pacific. There was talk of a HAARP in north-eastern Siberia and he was being tipped as project coordinator. He said, 'You found him then?'

'Yeah, I found him,' Martha said.

'Who'd have thought you'd be a Wild West freak, Charlie, you an Oxford man? We've got a staff steak 'n' beans barbecue in a week's time, and you're cordially welcome.'

But Pope was flying out of Salt Lake City late that night.

They drove along the dirt track to Route 40. The Dinosaur Diner's green brontosaurus glowed ahead of them across the desert. They pulled into the car park and could see Mary Lou peering out of the dusty windows. She was a little bird, all skin and bone, in her cowboy shirt and chef's hat. When they went inside she was busy serving a commercial traveller, saying to him, as she said mechanically to them all, 'Why don't you rest up awhile here? Get your head down for the night, this is surely the best and most reasonable-priced motel in the state of Utah . . .'

Few travellers, looking up at Mary Lou's beaky, anxious face, thought that they were being propositioned.

'I sacked her after she went to Salt Lake City the second time, and no way was I going to take her back,' said the motel owner, confidentially, serving Martha and Pope with coffee. 'To be honest with you, she may once have been the Nightingale of Vernal County, but this cowboy-outfit stuff is way out of date for country singers. It's all tight satin and high-heeled boots these days, even in Utah, and there's a gal at Best Western Dinosaur Inn the guys are just flocking to see . . .' He sighed and shook his head. 'No, I'm a real fool to myself, but when she turned up here one evening last week, looking so miserable . . .'

'How are you, Mary Lou?' asked Martha, when she came over.

She gulped and smiled. 'You just never have to give in, right?'

'Right,' said Martha, though Pope wondered why not.

'I guess I'll be OK. I guess I'll *have* to be OK.'

Her smile was like glass.

The day before his second, fatal aneurysm, Koenig had recovered consciousness, and had recognised her. 'Do you still want to marry me, John?' she had said, bravely, and he had smiled and nodded, and the nurses had cried it was so moving.

The next thing she knew was a telephone call to her sister's trailer, telling her he was dead.

She pulled a letter out of her jeans pocket. It was an offer of fifty thousand dollars compensation – for distress, said an obscure department of government which recognised, without prejudice or admittance of any kind of liability, her status as John Koenig's fiancée.

'It seems so strange. Four weeks ago John was just one of my regular customers, a fat guy who liked a big dab of butter on his hash browns. Suddenly he was my fiancé, my only true love. And now he's gone.'

Pope would have liked to hear her sing, but it was three hours still to Bluegrass Night, and Martha, anyway, couldn't have borne it without sobbing herself to bits.

They drove into Vernal. He bought some Utah-made glass teardrops in the Trailway Art Shop, a present for his secretary in Oxford and a sad reminder, he said, of Mary Lou.

'That is sick,' said Martha.

'No,' he said. 'It's poignant.'

They drove to the airfield where he was due to catch the shuttle to Salt Lake City. 'I suppose you know,' he said, 'they're being evasive about the *Pasiphae* design team.'

'Yeah?'

'They've dropped the consultancy.'

'Maybe they reckon you're a busy man.'

He looked at her reproachfully.

'Yeah, OK, maybe they reckon you're trouble. Did anybody ever call you trouble?'

'No.'

'Well that's what they're calling you now.'

They were actually calling him unstable. 'There is too much parapsychological baggage muddying the waters where this man is concerned,' a report on Pope had said. 'At the end of the day the quantum-psychic connection is still no more than entertaining speculation.'

They watched the small plane come in to land. She said, 'Well, I guess that's it,' and looked embarrassed.

He said, 'You'll be able to get over for the Digby Elliot centennial dinner?'

'I'll be there. Tell them to start fattening the swans.'

'It's usually wild boar.'

'They're cheating you. Those so-called wild boars we saw in Herefordshire were just nervous and skittish.'

'All right, it's usually nervous, skittish boar.'

'I'd like to see Lizzie again. I'd like to know she's OK.'

And you as well, she thought, giving him a glance: to know that you're OK. For he had been in a terrible state when Miss Whitburn had found him in the churchyard at Dore and had called the astonished, excited vicar of Dore to exorcise his devils. And since then, when they were in England, she had more than once seen what she could only describe as an ironic shadow cross his face: a look of the Otherworld.

But that had been in England.

It all seemed different in Utah.

A group of teenagers, off back to Salt Lake City after a week kayaking down Desolation Canyon, came into the small terminal building.

She said, 'See you then, trouble,' and kissed him.

The teenagers were wearing dinosaur T-shirts and baseball caps. She had bought Pope an Indian headdress, to go with the cowboy hat she'd bought him at Phoenix.

Dore in the rain. Reporters wearing Barbours and wellingtons. Two policemen under yellow capes. Blue and white plastic ribbon stretched on metal wands round the excavated mound. Bill Hastings and Venetia Peel – he in waterproof leggings, she wearing shorts.

'The first discovery was here – no, here, if you look, *here*.'

The *Sun* photographer was more interested in Venetia's long brown legs, with rainwater trickling down them, than in nobbles of grey bone sticking out from the flinty turf.

'Approximately fifteen skeletons have been so far revealed. The Home Office has granted an exhumation order, and the bones will be reinterred in the churchyard. Other skeletons, undoubtedly, will remain, and the site will hopefully be the subject of a further archaeological excavation.'

'Can you date the bones?'

'Not with any precision.'

'So they could be from King Arthur's time?'

'Why, please tell me why,' said Bill Hastings, 'has it always got to be King Arthur?'

'Yeah, I know, but is it at least conceivable that this might be Camelot? Could this have been the last battle with Mordred?'

'No it couldn't. At a guess I'd say these bones are from the thirteenth or fourteenth century.'

'Not Vortipor?' – the *Sun* reporter. 'There's a biddy down in the village says King Vortipor raped his daughters up here.'

'Vortipor was sixth-century, and there was only one daughter, and even if he did rape her – and you shouldn't rely on Gildas, you know – it was said to have been a willing rape, she being a shameless daughter and his wife being recently dead.'

'Bloody hell,' said the *Sun* reporter. 'So this Kinky King Vort—'

'And there is no reason to suppose he killed her, and anyway these skeletal remains are all males.'

A girl reporter: 'They'd been in a battle?'

'Very likely. The evidence is that they were all killed.'

'In the Wars of the Roses, then?'

'Possibly.'

'Richard III,' said the *Sun* man, who did not like to be thought of as ignorant, 'and the Princes in the Tower?'

'No,' said Bill Hastings drearily, 'these are not the bones of the Princes in the Tower. There were only two princes, not fifteen.'

'It was a joke.'

'One body,' said Bill Hastings, not laughing, 'still has the metal tip of an arrowhead lodged in its spine. There are indications that others may also have died from arrow wounds. Some of them may have been executed with swords. They were buried, we can assume, close to where they fell. The true importance of this find is that it represents a snapshot in time of a group of young males – all mid to late teenagers – who died suddenly and unnaturally.'

The reporters were looking bored. They were on a yellow hill covered in dead, sodden grass and brown cowpats. All they could see was misty rain and gorse. They wanted a lake and a gleaming sword. They wanted a gold bowl with the legend KING ARTHUR HAD ME MADE engraved on it. They wanted a silver ring with the letters G for Guinevere and L for Lancelot entwined in a love knot. At the very least they wanted skulls used as drinking cups by druidical cannibals.

The *Sun* photographer said to Venetia, 'Can you hold up a piece of bone for me, love? Can you hold a piece of bone up?'

'No,' said Bill, 'no she can't.'

'Well never mind the bone then, just look this way. Look towards me, love.'

The rain had soaked her hair, her shirt, her shorts. She was exulting in the wet; letting it pour over her, revive her.

'For Christ's sake, Venetia . . .'

'Pull your shoulders back and breathe in.'

'Venetia, do you actually want your tits all over Page Three?'

'I suppose,' said the man from the *Financial Times*, 'you will be hoping to attract funds for a more specialist archaeological analysis next year? Perhaps looking to collate social information – dental decay, the extent of arthritis in the bone joints, for example?'

'Lovely. Now try it without smiling. This time just look a bit arrogant . . .'

'Yes,' said Bill, 'I am hoping to come back next year.'

Venetia said, 'We're all hoping to come back next year.'

'You can't just undo your top button?'

Bill Hastings said, 'Next year, with a bit of luck, things will go according to plan, because this year, I don't mind telling you, things have been a bit bloody peculiar.'

'No, love, the button of your shorts, not your shirt . . .'

* * *

Lizzie stared at the rain trickling down the windscreen. She said, 'You remember giving me the ballad of Robyn Hode? It were great shame, said Robyn,

> A knight alone to ride,
> Without squire, yeoman, or page,
> To walk by his side.

I mocked you for having a page. Don't you remember that?'

'No.'

'I was mocking Thomas, as well. Don't you remember anything?'

'Nothing.'

'I always got on well with Thomas. We had to hide it sometimes – take care not to let you see.'

She glanced at him, smiling faintly.

'Shall we walk over,' said Pope, 'and see what they're doing?'

Lizzie looked out through the misted-up window, beyond the yellow-flowering gorse, the pale blue harebells, at the distant figures standing round the place where the Welsh boys had been killed.

'My poor head would get cold,' she said. 'Anyway, I don't want to see any reporters. That's where I was raped – where Venetia is now, having her photo taken. The archers had stakes of wood. I remember thinking they were to tether the horses, but the archers hammered the stakes into the ground in front of them.'

'They were to stop cavalry, to stop the knights. They did it at Agincourt.'

'Yes, but I didn't know that. I was a girl of sixteen, and this was year and years before Agincourt.'

'Tell me what happened.'

'Don't you remember *anything*?'

'How could I?'

'Because it was you. Because you were there.'

'If I was there, it has gone.'

'Yes, well, that was what I kept telling people, but they still went on asking me questions.'

'The franklin was in charge?'

'Yes. You'd been to Italy. You'd been to the Holy Land, you'd watched the fighting against the Turks.'

'Go on.'

'I was only just conscious. I'd lost a lot of blood and I was thirsty. I'd tried to drink the dew from the grass. You picked me up, and held me. I wanted a drink, but didn't dare ask. Then the Welsh and French attacked. They had some archers of their own. You were killed.'

She moved in her seat, uncomfortably.

'The franklin was killed before his archers shot their arrows?'

'Yes. Just as he was about to give the order.'

So that was it. A bolt of rage, of pure, terrible energy, caught in the microtubules of the franklin's brain, suspended in time for six hundred years until *Pasiphae* came on line, provoking a quantum level collapse into an actual physical state.

Rage, anger, frustration.

And a passion that had lasted for six centuries.

'How did you come to marry Flesshe?'

'He was the franklin's heir. His own children were dead. It was quite common in those days for a man to adopt a boy from another merchant family.'

'I see.'

'We were lucky, Thomas and I. Not many people in the fifteenth century married for love. Don't you think we were lucky?'

'Had he lived,' he said, 'would you have married the franklin?'

'Well, yes.'

'Yes?'

'People married where they were told to marry, or took what they could get. You know that.'

'Did you not love him? Did you not love him at all?'

She glanced at him, then quickly looked away.

'Did you not love the franklin? He loved you more than the world.'

She stared out of the window.

'There was nobody in the whole world,' she said after a moment, 'that I trusted more.'

He turned to look at her. The silk scarf round her shaved skull was like a nun's white coif. Her high forehead was as it had been when he first saw her in the Jerusalem tavern. In his nostrils came the acrid smell of burning charcoal, the sharp clean wind blowing down from the Welsh mountains. He saw her as he had last seen her, in the castle of Clyro, looking up at him for reassurance, for safety.

'No,' she said, staring out over the hilltop. 'No, I never loved him.'
She turned and looked into his eyes.

'Sorry,' she said.

Andrew was coming towards them across the field from the ramparts, bowed down under the weight of his rucksack. He put it into the boot and clambered wetly into the back of the car. Lizzie said, 'Well what's wrong with it now, then?'

'The battery's flat.'

'The battery's flat, right.'

Pope started the car. They moved off. Andrew said, 'This morning, when I phoned the hospital to check when you were coming out, I had a long talk with Mr Naseby the neurosurgeon.'

'It sounds like Mr Bun the Baker,' said Lizzie.

'He explained what happened to you. He was telling me how the brain creates fantasies, particularly with this type of temporal-lobe epilepsy. The important thing he stressed was that now the drugs are controlling it, you should put the entire experience behind you.'

'Yes, I know,' said Lizzie. 'And that's all right, isn't it, because in three weeks we're going to France for the grape harvest.'

At the bottom of the lane they turned towards Hereford. After a short time they went past the track that led to the church of Dore.

'But listen,' said Lizzie, not giving the church a glance, 'what's all this about us being engaged?'

'I had to say that,' said Andrew, 'to make them let me into the hospital.'

'Oh you did, did you?'

But she didn't sound upset.

Perhaps Eleanor de Flesshe really had had ten children, thought Pope. And perhaps she really had made the best apple pie in Staffordshire, and been as happy as could be.

He drove them into Hereford, through the pouring rain.